S0-BBJ-337

DISCARD

scrap of history *into* a story of cou-
'o meet the challenges of nature—
ote about a group of pioneers in
˙nia Sierra, Kirkpatrick weaves
˙ˍn, and a few men too) who fight
˙ˍo save those they love."

Sandra Dallas, *New York Times* bestselling author

˙ˍat an incredible journey this novel is! Without ever trivial-
izing or sentimentalizing the harshness of the circumstances,
Kirkpatrick centers her novel on the bonds of community, family,
and friendship that sustained these strong, complicated women
through a harrowing winter trapped in the Sierra Nevadas. There's
not a false note in this book. It's moving and beautifully told, and
I absolutely loved it."

Molly Gloss, award-winning author of *The Jump-Off Creek*
and *The Hearts of Horses*

"I can wholeheartedly recommend this book. Jane gets the facts
as right as they can be got out of the stories of the various participants in the experience of the winter of 1844–45 in the Sierra
Nevada of California. Anyone can tell you what it was like—dirty
and hungry and cold and lonely. Jane puts the heart-pounding,
breath-taking, adrenaline-soaked feelings into the thoughts and
the mouths of the people who lived the experience as real-time
commentary on the events. The thoughts and words may not be
exactly what those folks were thinking and feeling, but I believe
in my heart they could be."

Stafford Hazelett, editor of *Wagons to the Willamette*

"Award-winning western writer Jane Kirkpatrick tells the remarkable story of survival of the Murphy-Stephens-Townsend Overland Party of 1845, the first to bring wagons through the Sierra
Nevada into California. Unlike the great loss of life suffered by

the tragic Donner Party the following year, all fifty
the party survived, despite harrowing ordeals in mount.
often with nothing to eat but tree bark. As with so many (
books, she tells the story of the women who are so often ig
in western histories—giving birth along the trail; enduring t
own illnesses to comfort near-starving children; taking charge
emergencies, such as helping rescue a drowning man or a stranded
horse; and resisting men who try to shout them down when they
insist on being heard. And don't overlook Jane's acknowledgments
at the end where she says she hopes this story 'might celebrate the
honor of self-sacrifice, the wisdom of working together, and the
power of persevering through community and faith.' This wonderful new book accomplishes this, and more."

R. Gregory Nokes, author and former editor for the *Oregonian*

ONE MORE
RIVER

TO

CROSS

Also by Jane Kirkpatrick

ONE MORE RIVER TO CROSS

JANE KIRKPATRICK

Revell

a division of Baker Publishing Group
Grand Rapids, Michigan

© 2019 by Jane Kirkpatrick Inc.

Published by Revell
a division of Baker Publishing Group
PO Box 6287, Grand Rapids, MI 49516-6287
www.revellbooks.com

Printed in the United States of America

All rights reserved. No part of this publication may be reproduced, stored in a retrieval system, or transmitted in any form or by any means—for example, electronic, photocopy, recording—without the prior written permission of the publisher. The only exception is brief quotations in printed reviews.

Library of Congress Cataloging-in-Publication Data
Names: Kirkpatrick, Jane, 1946-, author.
Title: One more river to cross / Jane Kirkpatrick.
Description: Grand Rapids, MI : Revell, [2019]
Identifiers: LCCN 2019006997 | ISBN 9780800727024 (pbk.)
Subjects: LCSH: Survival—Fiction.
Classification: LCC PS3561.I712 O54 2019 | DDC 813/.54—dc23
LC record available at https://lccn.loc.gov/2019006997

ISBN 978-0-8007-3706-1 (casebound)

Scripture used in this book, whether quoted or paraphrased by the characters, is taken from the King James Version of the Bible.

This book is a work of historical fiction based closely on real people and events. Details that cannot be historically verified are purely products of the author's imagination.

Published in association with Joyce Hart of the Hartline Literary Agency, LLC.

19 20 21 22 23 24 25   7 6 5 4 3 2 1

Dedicated to Jerry
For showing me how to cross rivers
and keep going

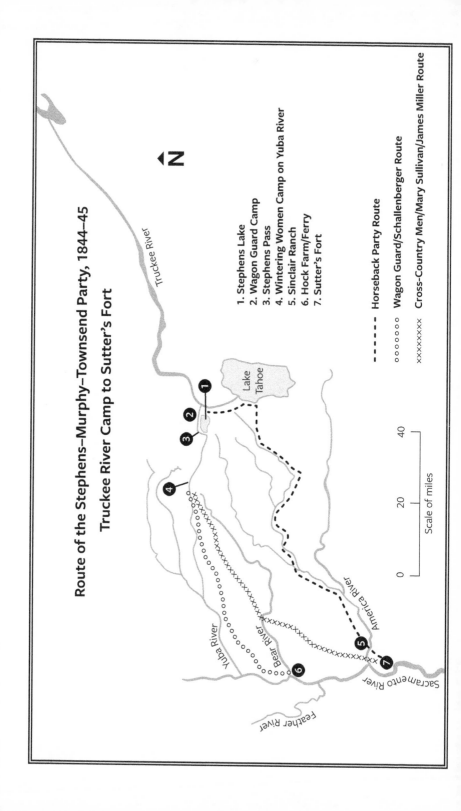

Route of the Stephens–Murphy–Townsend Party, 1844–45
Truckee River Camp to Sutter's Fort

1. Stephens Lake
2. Wagon Guard Camp
3. Stephens Pass
4. Wintering Women Camp on Yuba River
5. Sinclair Ranch
6. Hock Farm/Ferry
7. Sutter's Fort

- – – – Horseback Party Route
- ooooooo Wagon Guard/Schallenberger Route
- xxxxxxx Cross-Country Men/Mary Sullivan/James Miller Route

N

Truckee River

Lake Tahoe

Scale of miles

0   20   40

Yuba River

Bear River

Feather River

Sacramento River

American River

Courage doesn't always roar. Sometimes courage is that little voice that at the end of the day says "I'll try again tomorrow."

Mary Anne Radmacher, poet and artist

And not by eastern windows only,
When daylight comes, comes in the light;
In front the sun climbs slow, how slowly!
But westward, look, the land is bright!

Arthur Hugh Clough,
"Say Not the Struggle Naught Availeth"

The Stephens-Murphy-Townsend Overland Party

1844–45

Ellen Murphy (Townsend)—spirited beauty; daughter of Martin Murphy Sr.

Elizabeth "Beth" Townsend—asthmatic, wife of Dr. John Townsend, Ellen's sister-in-law

Daniel Murphy—hunter, struggling brother of Ellen

John Murphy—hunter, trained as Irish slinger, brother of Ellen and Daniel

François Deland—chef and French-Canadian servant

Oliver Manet—oxman and French-Canadian servant

───────── **Wagon Guards** ─────────

Moses Schallenberger—hunter, 17 years old, brother of Elizabeth Townsend

Joe Foster—hunter, aid to Captain Stephens

Allen Montgomery—gunsmith, confident husband of Sarah Montgomery

———— The Wintering Women ————

Mary Sullivan—wears Aran wool sweaters, rounded braids at her ears, is Irish-Canadian—sister of John Sullivan and two younger brothers Michael and Robert

Maolisa (mail-issa) Bulger Murphy—housekeeper extraordinaire; mother of Elizabeth Yuba, BD, Mimi, and two others; wife of Martin Murphy Jr. ("Junior")

Ailbe (all-bay) Murphy Miller—wife of James Miller, mother of Ellen Independence and four others, daughter of Martin Sr. Has premonitions.

Sarah Armstrong Montgomery—quilter and knitter, wife of Allen

Isabella Patterson—widow; hoping to transform her life; daughter of Isaac Hitchcock; mother of four, including Lydia

Ann Jane Martin Murphy—"round as a rutabaga," wife of James Murphy, mother of Kate and Ide (ee-day)

Margaret Murphy—one of the two single Murphy aunts; sister of Johanna, Ellen, and Ailbe Miller and Murphy brothers

Johanna Murphy—the other single Murphy aunt; sister of Margaret, Ellen, and Ailbe Miller and Murphy brothers

———— Also at the Wintering Cabin ————

James Miller—hunter; husband of Ailbe; father of William and four others, including Ellen Independence

Patrick Martin Sr. ("Old Man Martin")—weak left arm; father of Dennis, Patrick Jr., and Ann Jane

Seventeen children total including BD, scampish son of Maolisa Murphy; infants Ellen Independence and Elizabeth Yuba; Lydia Patterson; the Sullivan "little boys"

Cross-Country Men

Captain "Capt" Elisha Stephens—hawkish nose, elected leader of party, blacksmith, trapper

Martin Murphy Sr.—widower, praying leader of party, Irish/Canadian/Missourian

Dr. John Townsend—physician, entrepreneur, husband of Beth

Martin Murphy Jr. ("Junior")—husband of Maolisa Bulger and father of Elizabeth Yuba

John Sullivan—assumes role of parent, Irish-Canadian, brother of Mary Sullivan

Bernard Murphy—son of Martin Sr.

James Murphy—husband of Ann Jane, father of Ide

Dennis Martin—has a lisp, rescuer, son of Patrick Sr.

Patrick Martin Jr.—son of Patrick Sr.

Old Caleb Greenwood—guide and trapper, pilot for the party

Britain Greenwood—buckskin-clad mixed-blood son of Caleb

John Greenwood—tobacco-chewing mixed-blood son of Caleb

Isaac Hitchcock—father of Isabella Patterson, grandfather and mountain man

Also four ox drivers

Prologue

Mary Sullivan stood outside the circle of men, watched through the triangle of elbows as they nodded and commented about the markings the Paiute drew in the dirt. Dust, the color of ash-laden snow, shrouded their brogans and britches as they stared at the desert lines indicating rivers, mountains, and lakes. Based on the scratching of a stranger, the men would decide their next course.

A dog barked. A child cried and was comforted.

One day, Mary vowed, she'd make her own choices, be clear about what mattered in her life, and hope to have the courage to act on that.

PART I

1

Sanctuary

October 1844

For a second day, the company that seventeen-year-old Mary Sullivan traveled with found sanctuary beside a river edged with willows and rocks in the shadow of distant mountains. Their green-painted Schuttler wagon had passed through a long desert onto this place of promise, where the sunset of pinks and yellows colored the rush of water. An Irish whistle rang a tune in competition with the bodhran likely pounded by Old Man Martin. The music gave respite in the midst of their slow journey toward the Sierra Nevada.

Mary scrubbed at the washboard. She wore her dark hair braided in rounds at her ears—just as her mother had—and she scoured her brother's pants like her mother had too, hundreds of times. It was what women did. *Such stains.* The boys ground dirt into cloth the way dogs rolled in mud: they saw it as a lark. She sat back on her heels. And why shouldn't they have fun? They were young. Mary licked the blood from her knuckles. Perhaps their boisterousness served as a bridge from sadness to acceptance.

The breeze cooled her face, and she returned to pound the stiff cloth harder. Her back ached. The other women chattered to each other at the river's edge. She could join them—they'd welcome her—but she wasn't kin. What she wanted to do was tear off her poke bonnet and stand on her hands, maybe. Wouldn't that raise Irish eyebrows? She smiled. In Quebec when she was alone on the family's farm, she'd done such a thing, her linen skirts falling around her face like a waterfall. Her head buzzed, and she remembered laughing out loud, feeling strong as she saw the world upside down and made up poems like *Skirts and boots dance in the air, while tongues and eyes birth laughter.* But here, next to this river heading toward the mountains, she must express decorum or risk her brother's wrath.

"Did our mother neglect to teach you properly that your knuckles still bleed?" Mary's brother John stood over her now, accusing. He'd come upon her, silent as sunset.

She wondered if he still grieved.

She squinted up at him, shaded her eyes with her hand, her bonnet having slipped behind her, resting on her back. "How about you finish these trousers to show the little boys how it's done and that a man can do it as well as a woman."

He grunted. "A good effort, sister. You're behind on your duties and we have animals to tend to. I expect your help. Finish up."

She stood, twisted the pants to remove the water, then rubbed damp hands on her skirt. "See? All ready." She loved working with the oxen, scratching their big heads, feeling their velvety ears, and was happy indeed to give up scrubbing for that even when her brother demanded it.

"Take the clothes up to the wagon and meet me at the corral. You can hold the lead while I scrape out their hooves."

She made her retort a tease. "Maybe you'll take the rope and 'tis meself who'll clean their feet." She bundled the duds into her arms. "I'm closer to the ground than you."

He grunted. "Put your bonnet back on."

She was tempted to counter him, but instead she stayed silent and followed. Standing on her hands would have to wait for another day.

20

Sarah Armstrong Montgomery imagined the wispy clouds above her to be threads ready to be sewn into a quilt-backing as blue as bachelor buttons. If they found this balmy weather in Alta California, Sarah would stay there for life, contented as a honeybee, queen of its hive. Sarah had made a nest leaning back against the wagon tongue, a quilt rolled up behind her as a back-rest. She'd removed her bonnet as she sat in the shade, brushed strands of blonde hair away from her eyes. She'd need to stitch up a loose portion of her faded green wrapper, but she could do that tomorrow. Laughter drew her eyes to her husband standing beside lovely Ellen Murphy. Allen Montgomery was a fine-looking man even if he did spend more time grooming his mustache than Sarah thought necessary. But today she had no complaints. Like the rest of the Stephens-Murphy-Townsend party comprised mostly of Irish Catholics, optimism perfumed the scene around her and Sarah felt relieved—relieved of the worry she'd carried with her from Missouri when she'd feared that they were heading toward trial and trouble and perhaps their deaths. She envied the Irish Catholics they traveled with. Their faith buoyed them like sticks on a stream flowing ever toward their destination, weathering bumps and bruises while praying over beads. And the truth of it was that nothing had gone terribly wrong these past five months.

Best of all, earlier that day, the men had met a lone Indian, and the elders—as she thought of them, old men of experience leading this company—had used sign language and drawings in the dirt to communicate. The Paiute, whom they'd named Truckee, gave them directions, advising them to follow this river they'd camped beside until they arrived at a fork with a smaller river heading west and another flowing south. There was some confusion about which way wagons would travel most easily. Earlier parties—the Bidwell-Bartleson train for one—had abandoned their wagons in 1841, so avoiding their aborted trail was optimal. It was this

Stephens-Murphy-Townsend party's goal to take wagons all the way to Alta California—a foreign land south of the vast Oregon Country and far north of the province's Mexican capital. Which stream they'd follow to get there Sarah wasn't certain, but either supposedly would end near Sutter's Fort. The men would decide once they arrived at the river's fork. But for now—they had a plan: travel until the decision place. A plan always comforted Sarah.

She looked at her fingernails. Still strong. Another good sign they'd carried with them the right foods and portions. Murphy wives and sisters snapped wet petticoats and sheets they'd rinsed at the shoreline. Children scampered with hoops or played "catch me" in the heavy dust. Her own clothesline, strung earlier, sagged with the laundry she'd washed that morning. She heard aprons and wrappers flap in the late afternoon breeze. Time to take them down. She watched as dark-haired Mary Sullivan followed her brother toward the corrals, head down. Mary was a quiet soul, a loner, carrying her brother's duds. *Duds.* Such a spritely word for mundane things like worn clothes or cloaks.

Sarah ran her palm over her stringy blonde hair. It needed a good wash. Tomorrow. Captain Stephens said they'd remain another day, then start out on the last leg. *Last leg.* What did that really mean? Only one leg left to stand on? Or the last table leg to attach for a finished product? Words were entertaining. She could amuse herself for hours with words. If only she could read them.

Ellen Murphy retied the ribbon around her hair and lifted the auburn mass of curls from her neck, bending as she did to cup a palmful of river water she flicked at Allen Montgomery. He skipped backward. "Is this your way of suggesting I bathe, Miss Murphy?"

"Not in the least, Mr. Montgomery. 'Tis my way of helping cool a man's effort to help a woman on so warm a day." She curtsied and smiled.

Allen had offered to help, a kind gesture Ellen's brothers would never think of. He was a handsome man, gentle with his wife from what Ellen had seen on their journey west. He hoisted the laundry basket onto his shoulder and the two walked side by side. Some married men were gentle, Ellen decided. Were they that way to begin with or did marriage rub off harsh edges, love bring out their goodness? She enjoyed the company of men. Some men. And it was her limited experience—she was only twenty years old—that married men were safest to engage with. Married men were committed, and most respected their marital boundaries, none more than Allen Montgomery. Ellen relied on that restraint, which allowed her to enjoy an occasional tease and toss of her hair while in the company of men.

"All tidied up," Ellen said as Sarah Montgomery approached them. "Your husband's a good wringer, he is."

Sarah laughed. "I get him to help with laundry whenever I can. Good strong hands, that one."

"And shoulders."

Ellen noticed how Sarah subtly brought her husband closer to her hips, letting Ellen walk as though alone, as they headed toward the wagons paralleling the river. Allen's face carried a tint of pink, broken by his mustache, the ends braided on either side of his smile.

The aroma of cooking meat caused Allen to inhale. "Smells good, darlin'." Sarah walked backward in front of him.

"I hope you like it. You're welcome to stay for stew too, Ellen."

"'Tis laundry-hanging that calls me name," Ellen said. "Another time, certain."

Allen pointed with his chin to activity behind his wife. "You'd better get Chica out of the way or she'll have our supper first."

"What? She's back?" Sarah turned and sprang forward while the dog circled the hanging cast-iron pot. Smoke from the small fire spiraled upward. Fortunately, the stew was too high for the dog to topple, but not for lack of effort. Chica bounced around, barking, and Sarah shooed her off.

"The pup has a way of finagling food," Ellen said. "I'll walk her home. Come along, you little chancer. 'Tis leftovers as fodder for you tonight." The dog pranced happily beside Ellen as she stepped over the wagon tongue and motioned for Allen to hand her the basket.

"Venison stew, is it?" she heard Allen ask his wife as she walked away.

"I'm surprised you noticed, paying attention to Miss Murphy as you were." Sarah kept her voice teasing, but Ellen heard the worry in it. She'd have to be more careful. She didn't want to tear at the fabric of a marriage.

2

Consideration

November 1844

Journal Entry of Captain Elisha Stephens.

> *A month since meeting Truckee. Several miles traveled in riverbed much to distress of oxen. At fork of Truckee's map. Doctor offers good suggestions for future but takes until midnight to say what could have been said at dawn.*

"At least that Indian was truthful with his map. But now, Capt, don't you think that resting too long strains the rations?" Dr. Townsend countered nearly every comment Capt made, not always contradicting but expounding—like a man who needed to hear his own voice in order to decide rather than making choices in his head.

"It's deciding which way to go next we're about," Capt told him. The doctor frowned. Capt had overheard him tell someone that he, Capt, with his misshapen head, looked like he'd been a forceps baby, pulled and twisted at birth. Capt had accepted his looks, his odd noggin, his hawk-like nose. He'd become strengthened by

25

the bullying when a child. But the doctor's words didn't endear him to the captain.

"Perhaps we should consider taking a small party to explore, see the lay of the land beyond the fork," Dr. Townsend said. "It would give us more information on which to base our decision."

Capt nodded agreement, noting how the doctor preened, looked around for acknowledgment of his good suggestion. "You and Joe Foster make the trek and see what you find. And Greenwood, you'll go as well."

"Yes, yes, of course. A fine group." Dr. Townsend touched the brim of his flat-topped hat.

It was interesting that the doctor first objected to delay, but when he was offered an important role, then waiting didn't matter.

Capt sent them off while he and young Dennis Martin rode the next day along the southern stream. The man was sharp and kept his tongue, didn't babble as the doctor did, probably because some words didn't form like others in his mouth. But his mind noticed things: deer tracks. Timber thickness as the terrain rose. The Indian had said there was a large lake beyond but by how many days he couldn't say. They were already into patches of snow. The timbered topography worked fine for horses. "It's not an option for wagons," Capt said.

"No, sir." Most of his *s*'s sounded like *th*.

They reined their horses toward the company, hoped the western explorers would have better news. That evening, he made sure the wagons and stock would be ready as soon as the other explorers returned.

Mary squatted and squeezed the teats, putting milk into the bucket. When Chica came trotting up, tongue hanging, she directed a spray of warm liquid right into the dog's waiting mouth. Chica belonged to Moses Schallenberger, but everyone had adopted her skinny black-and-white body, her distinctive long tail, white muzzle, and those pyramid ears. John would chastise her if he'd seen her "waste" a drop of milk, but the dog gave her such joy, how could she ignore him. Bó—the Gaelic word for "cow"—had twisted her head to look back, her long tongue reaching into her nose in that way cows did. Mary patted the bovine's head, then bent again into the cow's side while she worked, the scent and sounds familiar and pleasing. They still had sacks of oats and corn to feed the animals, maybe a month's worth, so enough, Mary thought. But supplementing with grass helped. All these little decisions could make a difference. Still, between Bó's calf and their needs, the amount of milk available for them to drink dwindled. Most of the stock was thinner, it seemed to her. And the brown grass lacked much to arrest their weight loss. Capt said he looked for an "open winter," which Mary hoped meant little snow.

She lifted the bucket. Only half full. She'd skim the cream and churn it, then ration the rest for use in hotcakes the boys liked so much. Until this journey, she hadn't thought about food as being anything more than fuel to make bodies strong enough to work. Now she saw the preparation and serving of biscuits and beans as a healing salve. The boys no longer cried themselves to sleep at night as they had the month or more after the company left Iowa. Instead at night beneath their tent, they spoke of Alta California with a hum of excitement. She prayed she'd had a part in that change.

"Good girl, Bó." Mary patted the cow's bony back. "Keep giving us milk. I put it to good use." She tugged at her Aran wool sweater as she headed toward the wagons carrying the bucket. So far, the bad weather had held off, with only thin ice formed on the washbasin in the morning. All was well, according to her brother. A cloud moved across the sun. She felt a chill in the air.

Doc and his party had been gone three days and reported to Capt as snow fell. It came like a visiting aunt, making everything look clean, but it didn't stay to keep it that way. Snowmelt made rivulets through the mud, and midmorning of the next day, it started to snow, again. Capt called the men together. It was November 15. He wanted to keep track of this journey. The doctor, too, wrote in a little book, maybe wanted evidence of poor decision-making on Capt's part. Some men looked for blame; others, like the Murphy clan, just did their jobs, kept moving toward California.

Capt remarked on their sojourn. The wagons would have a hard time making it without cutting big timber to get through, and it was a steep route.

"My way, there's a ridge we have to go up and over," the doctor said. "The wagons can make it, even my two, heavy as they are. On the other side is a lake and meadow, about fifteen miles below the summit. I say we take the western-leading route we've just explored rather than go south."

"We can call that lake Truckee," Joe Foster said. He wore a wide-brimmed hat that snow accumulated on. "In honor of our Indian friend who told us about that route. That water sure sparkled from on top the ridge."

"But that Paiute will never even know of a place named for him," Dr. Townsend complained. "Whereas, labeling it for a member of the party would memorialize the journey—the first company bringing wagons into California. Murphy Lake." He tapped his hat toward Martin Murphy Sr., the patriarch of the family and main funder of this company. "Or even Townsend Lake—" The doctor coughed, looked down at the snow accumulating at his feet. Capt decided the man didn't know the meaning of humility.

"But didn't the Indian tell us that going south would be easier?" Sarah Montgomery spoke up. "Why not do what he suggested?"

"Might be easier for horses," her husband said. "Capt told us wagons couldn't make it. Truckee never took a wagon that route, let alone eleven of them."

"I still want to name the lake Truckee," Joe said. He was a good hand, Capt reminded himself, but could get stuck grabbing at strings when ropes were needed.

"We have more important issues to cover than naming a lake, Joe. The snowfall is a good reminder that we still have challenges—and a month or more to go ahead of us."

Old Greenwood, their pilot, tore off a hunk of tobacco and popped it into his mouth, chewed. "Ah, yep. Looking at those clouds."

"We'll head west in the morning," Capt said. "Make sure everything is secured and ready to go at first light." He hoped he'd made the best decision. But that was part of being a leader . . . assuming the risk of a mistake, though all would suffer if he was wrong.

Maolisa Murphy carried her niece, Baby Indie, over her burgeoning belly as the women dusted up snow with their feet. The company paralleled the stream, keeping it in sight as they eased their way up a bluff, animals pulling; men, women, and children scuffing along through deepening snow. A meadow and sparkling lake were promised on the other side. And then they'd summit the mountain and be in California.

Maolisa's niece started to fuss, and her mother, Ailbe, reached for her daughter. Though sisters-in-law, they both had copper-colored hair whose wet tendrils framed porcelain faces with fine features, arched eyebrows, and blue eyes. They shared a mothering distinction too: Ailbe had given birth on this journey and Maolisa was hoping to *not* give birth until they arrived at Sutter's Fort. Not that Maolisa had ever felt poorly, which was good for a woman in her seventh month with bracing winds pushing at her face and her hems brushing up snow as she trudged. First in Ireland, then Canada, and then in Missouri, she'd been by herself in her labors—except for Junior and their children—and wouldn't have chosen this journey for her next delivery even if she was surrounded by sisters-in-law and had access to a doctor. She'd been surprised to learn she was with child at all and tried to figure the time of conception. She and Junior had joked about it, but now, carrying this extra weight, it wasn't so funny. Her youngest, Mimi, walked between the women, hanging on to her mother's skirts. She wasn't yet three and she stumbled but picked herself up without crying. Maolisa touched her daughter's tuque covering her sunrise-colored hair. "Good girl."

"I'm grateful Indie's so healthy," Ailbe said. Maolisa thought of water—Ailbe's name pronounced "all bay." Ailbe blinked as she spoke, then made the sign of the cross. "Life is a fleeting thing, it is."

Maolisa thought of her four children no longer on this earth, gone and buried, the pain still a cellar of sorrow. And yet she trusted that, despite suffering, she was not alone in her grief.

"I have this . . . feeling sometimes," Ailbe said, a note of caution in her voice. "James says I'm being a moppet." She looked at Maolisa, her tone as though she shared a secret. "I had it when we decided to go west instead of south at that fork. Does that ever happen to you?"

"I never anticipate harm coming my way. It's always an unwanted surprise." Maolisa caressed her stomach absently.

"Oh, I didn't mean to alarm." Ailbe blinked. "It was thoughtless of me to mention it with your . . . I hope it goes easy for you, Sister." The Murphys were woven tight and Maolisa had been stitched into their pattern through the years.

"Oh, I have time yet. This baby isn't due until the New Year if I've figured right."

"'Tis what being organized gains a body—you can trust your days."

"And my labor usually isn't too troubling. Besides, we'll be at Sutter's Fort by then. Your brother has promised it."

"Well, Junior is a certain soul," Ailbe said. She smiled.

Back at Independence Rock, Ailbe had popped her July baby out like a cork drawn from a sauerkraut jug. They had nevertheless stayed a week to let her recover, a grace quite remarkable, the captain being aware of a woman's needs like that. Maolisa hoped she could do as well when her time came and that it wouldn't be while they were on this trail, climbing toward mountains, chasing a creek, delivering a child in a less-than-organized wagon. "What was your premonition like?"

"Just a feelin'. It's never anything more than mist—until something happens and then I say to myself, 'Ah, so this is it.' It's a totally useless gift."

"Except when the future intervenes, you know then God was speaking to you all along."

"And not the fairies. 'Tis true." Ailbe blinked.

"You'd tell if it . . . was about my baby," Maolisa said. She crossed her heart and remembered the Virgin Mary's words, *He hath filled the hungry with good things.* She would remember that.

"I would. Absolutely." Ailbe touched Maolisa's shoulder, her fingers a pleasant pressure, then she pulled away and made the sign of the cross. "No worrying, love." Baby Indie fussed. "Could you help?" Together they placed the youngest member of their troop in a sling-like pouch around Ailbe's neck so she could hold the baby to her as they walked, a knitted blanket covering the child's head.

"When I have vague doubts," Maolisa said, "I make myself pay attention to little things right before me. A sound, something I see, scents. If a frightening thought enters in, I just say 'intrusion,' then concentrate on my feet, like how they feel against the ground or how the wind scrapes my cheeks, the scent of lavender in the soap. Of course, I pray my beads. That helps too."

"A sound . . . you mean like this greedy baby sucking."

"'Tis one of the finest sounds in the universe."

Ailbe smiled and the women walked without talking until she added, "It would be nice if my sights warned me about a new recipe, perhaps to avoid it." The women laughed.

"I guess knowing the future isn't really what I'd want anyway," Maolisa said.

The harness sounds, clangs of chains, the cry of the oxen, men urging their beasts forward, were backdrops to the voices of children and mothers, talking as they walked. Maolisa found the sounds soothing. In the summer, she'd have "stitched as she stepped," but her hands got too cold and stiff now and the pins were too precious to risk dropping. Instead she started to sing a song about a ragman holding a party and later a round that she noticed even Mary Sullivan joined them in. Laughter sprinkled through the company in an effort to keep the round moving, wagon by wagon. Her baby kicked. "You like that, do you?"

At thirty-six years of age, she was still learning new things. Music, too, pressed away worrisome thoughts. She'd remember that when struck with another "intrusion."

3

Decision Points

November 1844

Mary Sullivan would have gone south if anyone had asked her, just as she'd preferred to go to Oregon at that fork in the dusty trail weeks before. Her brother had chosen Alta California, and now here they were in a foot of snow beside a creek with a mountain fortress before them. It had not been a good day.

"You're Contrary Mary. Of course, you'd have gone the other way. West is best," her brother told her when she mumbled about the Oregon road they hadn't taken.

She didn't think of herself as contrary. She just had opinions, but what woman didn't?

At the top of the ridge Dr. Townsend had described, Mary Sullivan looked down upon that exquisite lake sparkling in the distance, welcoming them forward, just as that Indian had told them there'd be, just as the exploring party had seen. Fifteen miles beyond they'd encounter a formidable wall of snow-topped mountains they'd have to find their way through.

As they'd worked going up the bluff, the animals seemed equally taxed going down toward the lake. The Sullivans' lead team, Pierre and Prince, pulled well together and the men helped each other encourage the animals. John kept Mary at a distance from the oxen, but she liked to walk beside them. He allowed little Robert, only eight, and ten-year-old Michael to walk closer. But she was a woman. Still, when the boys wanted to go off and throw snowballs with the Patterson kids or Murphy boys, Mary took their place next to the oxen. She talked to them, told them about her day, encouraged them when they were straining uphill, cooed to them as they eased their way down.

"They don't care, you know," John said, "that you talk to them."

"How do you know? Maybe they speak a separate language, one a tender woman's voice can reach."

John snorted. Her father used to make that sound. So many little things John did that reminded her of their father. She wondered if small acts of hers, little habits or phrases, reminded John or her younger brothers of their mother. She shared her mother's black-as-dirt hair, coal-black eyes, odd for Irish women she'd been told. Once, near Laramie, Mary shook her finger in frustration at the little boys, and she'd looked at her hand and seen her mother's long fingers there. It was both terrifying and comforting in an odd sort of way.

"You can sing these oxen to sleep then tonight with that 'tender woman's voice,'" John mocked.

"I'd be happy to stay out with them and Bó. You can prepare our supper."

"No you won't. You'll get the fire going and the stew on. Then—"

"John." She sighed. "I don't need you to be my father and mother. *We* need to be parents to the little boys." They'd all been orphaned before leaving Iowa and had decided to pursue their parents' last wishes and continue west. By the grace of God, they'd stumbled onto this party of Irish-Canadian-Missourians who had taken them all in.

"I only meant you have woman's work to do and I've got the wagon and animals to take care of. Tomorrow, we head to the mountain." He nodded toward a granite rock in the distance. It sat like a castle in a picture book, with timbered foothills dribbling to bare ground, forming a wide swath covered with snow.

Mary knew she was responsible for the younger Sullivans and feeding herself and John. But she also thought she was worthy of more. At home in Quebec, she'd helped with plowing and putting up grass hay, building fences, all sorts of labor often reserved for men. She did it not because she had to but because she wanted to and her father had agreed. Now John acted not like her father but like her keeper. He wasn't that much older than she was and he certainly couldn't be any wiser. One day, she'd show him so.

Capt rode a horse on this trip, one he now dismounted, removed the bridle, put on the halter, and tied him to the wagon's side. He hung the feed bag over his horse's neck, then put the barley and oats inside while he talked to the gelding. Joe Foster acted as oxman for Capt's wagons that freighted mostly blacksmithing tools—anvils, bellows, and a shallow cauldron for heating coals. He'd used them all on this journey, but he knew the wagons were heavy, and it concerned him that his wagon might be the cause of future delays. His oxen, like all the rest, were lean and tired. The Montgomery wagons and the Townsend wagon also bore extra weight. With the snow, he wasn't sure they could make it. Like all the other parties who had attempted it, they might have to abandon the wagons and go overland. But they had so many more women and children than the 1841 Bidwell party.

It was at the evening camp and Capt took out his journal from his saddlebags. He always reread what he'd written. Probably peppered with misspelled words, but no one else would ever see it. He noted that the party had decided to call it Stephens Lake, and he'd lowered his head, embarrassed by the accolade and honored at the same time. Dr. Townsend had scowled. They'd brought the wagons into the upper end of the shoreline, pulled them into a circle, and met for final preparations for assaulting the mountain, which was how Capt saw it. Once they reached the massive rock, he hoped they'd find a pass through it or they'd have to go over it. Somehow. It was what he was thinking as he heard the spit of moisture in the fire and looked through the flames to see the snowflakes fall again.

"Maybe we'll be lucky and it'll melt like it did before," Joe Foster said. He handed Capt a cup of coffee. They still had beans.

"Maybe. But just to be safe, I think I'll mosey on by the Murphy clan and see if they can put up one of their prayers that has surely gotten us this far." They'd had no trouble, nothing. No Indian skirmishes, no deaths, no lost animals. And no arguments either. He didn't want to tempt fate, but it appeared to be a charmed party.

Sarah used the last of her yarn to finish another pair of socks for Allen. Wool was the very best in this damp weather, keeping feet both dry and warm. The click of the wooden needles soothed. Allen was hard on socks, not that he could help how his feet rubbed against his brogans, making holes at his toes. They had abandoned the moccasins Allen had bought at Fort Hall and now wore the boots they'd brought with them. Could his feet have grown? Perhaps. It didn't matter: wet feet were the very worst thing to happen on such a journey, sore feet bringing a man down faster than a bullet.

"Where are we in the line?" She spoke idly to her husband, who worked the maple on a gunstock. She loved the slow whisper of the rasp across the wood and the scent of the maple being tendered.

"Dr. John has asked for a meeting." Allen hesitated, then said, "Beth isn't doing well in this wet and Townsend thinks we should go back, take the other route and head for that bigger lake the way that Truckee told us. We'd get out of snow country sooner."

She hadn't realized Beth was worse. She loved that woman like a second mother.

"Can the wagons go that way? The trees march right down to the edge in places, Capt said. Horses could make it but not a wagon."

"We'd have to cut a trail, I imagine. But we could. Dr. John seems to think it's possible."

"Dr. John didn't explore that route, only the one we're on. Here's your sock." She rolled it into a ball and tossed it to him. "Catch."

He ducked. "Sarah. I'm working here."

"I see that. You're so serious." He'd been willing to joke with Ellen.

"This rifle with this stock smoothed to a sheen—with no gouges caused by a wayward wife tossing a sock—will bring twenty-five dollars or more. Your socks—"

"Are worth their weight in gold. You mark my words." She pointed with her knitting needles. "Having a good pair of socks is more valuable than a smooth-as-satin rifle stock." She put her needles aside. "I'm going to see Beth."

"If you go over there, don't talk to her about the alternate route. No need to upset her," Allen said. "Nothing's been decided."

"We women can carry on a conversation without getting into fits about it. It's you men who start circling like bulls when there isn't a clear answer but each of you has a high opinion of his own."

"We discuss." The rasping continued.

She'd heard them "discuss" how much flour each family should carry, whether buying bacon at a certain price was good or bad. It wasn't always cordial, though she admitted that Capt Stephens had a quiet way about him that ultimately resolved disputes without fists. So far.

"If Doc does recommend that route, would the rest of us follow?"

"I doubt Stephens will want to split the group."

Sarah donned her wool shawl. She had warm socks inside her own boots that she had insisted Allen buy at Fort Hall and was grateful now indeed. She wore moccasins at night in their bedroll where she'd pressed her feet against her husband's, and Allen had said, "At last, my wife has warm feet." She'd thought the captain's instructions—when the Indian footwear was new, to wet them, then put them on to shape them to her feet—was a strange way to contour a pair of slippers. But it had worked. They fit like a second skin.

She tied the lace on her boots and moved to the back of the wagon. "I won't be long."

"Remember. Don't talk about the route."

She smiled at him. She liked the smell of gun oil that permeated their wagon. She waved her gloved fingers at him. "You take care of your business and I'll take care of mine."

"Sarah . . ."

"Allen . . ."

He turned away and shook his head, and she continued on her own way.

"And that's the end of the story of 'The Two Wanderers,'" Mary said. She closed the book of *Grimm's Household Tales* her mother had packed when they left Montreal. She turned the lamp down to save on oil, changing the shadows in their wagon.

"That shoemaker was very mean," Robert said. "He kept getting the tailor into trouble."

"And did you hear the moral of the tale?" Mary kept the book on her lap.

"What's a 'more-all'?" Robert asked. Both boys needed a haircut. Mary just hadn't had the interest to do it. Robert's face had thinned in the months on the trail. He looked tired.

"It's the lesson," Michael told him, sounding the wise ten-year-old. "I think it's to stay happy and you'll outsmart bad people. Oh, and take extra bread when you don't know how many days you'll be traveling." Mary thought about the part of the story where the two wanderers had to decide which route to take. Just as this party's leadership had decided more than once on this journey at junctures. Michael added, "Bringing extra bread will mean you worked harder than you needed to in carryin', but at least you won't grow hungry and have to bargain with a greedy man to fill your stomach along the way."

"I'd rather be the tailor," Robert said. "He was happy all the time."

Their mother had read these stories to her when she was a child. But maybe she shouldn't have asked the question of the lesson. In the story of "Two Wanderers," it was the part about the stork delivering the baby to the king that had created the most vivid image in Mary's mind. She smiled at the belief she'd held as a child about where babies came from. But in this reading, she found something more. "Those are possible lessons."

"What do you think the more-all is, Mary?" Robert asked.

"I'll read the sentence that I think, but your ideas are excellent." Both boys lowered their heads and smiled at each other. In their family, compliments were as babies, rare and joyous. Mary read, "'He who trusts in God and his own fortune will never go amiss.'"

"What's my own fortune?" Robert asked. His little eight-year-old brown eyes stared up at her.

"It's the gathering of all that God has given you, your smiles, your warm hearts, the riches you have of shelter and clothes and food in your stomach. Your special . . . interests. Michael, you love growing things, and Robert, you and animals come together. Those are part of your fortune too that God will weave into your future, so long as you are willing to share your fortune with others."

"Huh," Michael said, adding, "Is there enough bread for another bite tonight? I'm hungry."

"It is your good fortune that I indeed have a bit of hardtack to share."

"Thank you, Mama." Robert looked away. "I'm sorry I said that."

She hugged her youngest brother to her side. "No need. Mama would understand."

"She'd want you to use your fortune to read stories to us." Michael grinned. "Though we can read ourselves."

"Yes, Robert, I believe she would. Now let me get that bread for you."

When they reached Alta California, she'd find a school for the boys, to keep their minds pushing their dreams. That too was part of her duty, but some women's duties were less drudgery than this truly worthy work.

4

Judging

Ellen Murphy wiped her eyes. She hated it when her father berated her in front of her brothers and sisters. Daniel, especially. Her father rarely raised his voice at any of his offspring. They were all heading west because of the children, he'd said. His piercing blue eyes told her more than his measured words that he was angry. They circled the fire, snow falling on her brother Daniel's shoulders as he stood just beyond the tarp. *Men just want to look tough.* She thought him silly; he should come in out of the falling snow.

"I'm disappointed, Ellen."

Worse than anger. "I've done nothing wrong." Ellen whispered her defense. She didn't want people in the other wagons to hear her; hear them upset with her. *Is that Allen Montgomery coming across the circle?* Dr. John intercepted him. They headed toward the horse corral. She could hear the muted sounds of women soothing their children, getting them ready for the night.

"You are not a good model for your sisters."

"I am! Don't I dutifully prepare meals and tend to the mending and washing and pray the rosary, sometimes two or three times a day." She grasped the beads her mother had handed to her on her deathbed only weeks before, the wood smoothed by her fingers. They'd left on this questionable expedition because a priest they hardly even knew advised them but didn't join them to support their souls. "And I pray with them, don't I, Johanna?" Her thirty-year-old sister—the only flaxen-haired among the auburns—nodded her head in agreement. *How am I supposed to be a model for my older sisters?*

"She does, Papa. Prays. I hear her," Johanna added.

Her father's eyes softened as he looked at his youngest daughter, and for a moment Ellen thought she'd be set free from this inquisition. She tried a change of subject.

"I've bacon to fry," Ellen said. "May I be excused, Da?"

"No, you may not."

Daniel grinned. Ellen felt her face grow hot at his pleasure with her discomfort. It was like having two fathers, with Daniel the more self-righteous.

"Your brothers' wives are embarrassed by your behavior. As a married woman, I expected more from you."

"I'm not married now. I'm a widow." She lowered her eyes. "I accept help from Joe Foster, who is kind to me, nothing else. That I laugh with the ox men—all who are single—should be no concern to anyone. I'm right where everyone can see me, all the time except in the wagon." She lifted her half-gloved hand to the green-sided vehicle with its canvas, still as the falling snow. "Have I not suffered enough with the death of my husband? Am I not allowed to smile and laugh? Surely the Lord does not intend for us to grieve loved ones forever."

"It's not even been a year," Daniel reminded her. Her father's favorite, he was allowed all sorts of leeway in judging others.

"And I wear black."

Daniel scoffed. "You wear your hair down like—"

"It's too thick to pile up each day. Mere boys don't understand." Unruly curls didn't fit well under a bonnet and were impossible to braid.

"I'm not a mere boy. I'm a—"

"Jesus would have wept at such unkindness between loving children," her father said.

"Jesus also danced and enjoyed food with his friends and—" Ellen's voice broke.

"Don't even think about comparing yourself to our Lord!"

"Daniel."

At last, Papa chastises him as well as me.

"We must all compare ourselves, to live more like him."

"It's Allen Montgomery we're concerned about." Daniel came in under the tarp, removed his hat, and ran his hands through his red hair. They could almost be twins, she and Daniel, with those freckles and bushy red eyebrows, their "chaos of curls."

"Has Sarah expressed concern? We're friends." A stab of guilt pierced Ellen's chest. "I will apologize if she thinks I've done something wrong. I am so sorry, Papa, I am only finding joy again."

"It is Dr. Townsend who has expressed concern. After all, Matthew was not just your husband, he was Dr. Townsend's brother." Her father added, "It grieves him to see you acting like a filly."

Dr. John. She should have known.

"Then I will apologize to Dr. John and explain that I do not intend to besmirch his brother's memory. Matthew loved livin' then, didn't he? He would want me to enjoy meself." She knew that last was a lie. Matthew did love life all right, but he cared little whether Ellen enjoyed hers, did what he could to make sure she didn't.

"I think that would be wise." Her father's eyes softened. "The good doctor has held his tongue this entire journey but came to me after watching you . . . teasing Mr. Montgomery, as he described it."

"And acting the filly," Daniel added, arms crossed over his chest.

"Daniel. It is not ours to continue to judge once a contrition has been noted, a mediation found."

Daniel lowered his eyes. He no longer held the smile.

Escape, that's what Ellen needed. Escape from her judgmental brother, her pious father, the wagging tongues of her sisters-in-law, the needs of her siblings, her nattering brother-in-law. She could hardly wait to get to Alta California, where she'd be able to start a life and not be hovered over by Daniel, who used her to build up his good graces with her father. Dr. John might have been concerned, but she was pretty certain it was Daniel who drew his attention to her happy moments. Would a woman ever have a life of her own?

"I'll apologize at once," Ellen said. "Express my deepest regrets to me friend Sarah and to the good doctor as well." She wanted to add, *Does that suit you all, my captors, my inquisitors?* She looked at her sisters—old maids, they were called. What tragedy lay ahead for them simply because they were born girls instead of boys. Instead, in silence she lifted her skirts to push through the ever-increasing snow. No one called her back.

Mary Sullivan tucked her brothers in for the night, wondering if she could follow her brother John to the Murphy wagon chosen for the discussion. It would be nice to hear the facts and evidence firsthand instead of it being filtered for her by her brother. She thought they ought to move forward toward the mountain despite the snow. It would only get deeper. What was Capt waiting for?

"Mama! Mama!" Robert called out. Another nightmare.

"It's all right. Ye aren't alone." She sat beside him, brushed his dark hair from his frightened eyes. No, her place was here now.

She unwound her circular braids, brushed hair that came to her waist. Then she wound it back into a single braid. She curled up beside her brother, who mindlessly rubbed the end of her braid between his fingers. John would be back soon. Whatever the decision, she would have to wait to hear it. A woman's lot.

"'Tis all right to join ye?"

Sarah opened the cords of the canvas. "Ellen. Please. Come in."

Sarah helped her inside the Townsend wagon, then made room in the narrow space between the barrels and crates and stacks of colored bolts of material. Beth lay on a cot, looking as pale as the snow outside pushing up against the wagon wheels.

"I've come to apologize to you, Beth—and Sarah. My father and Daniel seem to think I have misbehaved by laughing with you all." She took a deep breath. "With Allen especially. I meant no ill, truly."

Sarah could see Ellen's discomfort. *She's been crying.* Reddish blotches dotted her freckled cheeks. Even distraught, Ellen was beautiful.

"They're exaggerating," Sarah said. "Sit. Have tea. I've just put a warm brick under Beth's feet."

Ellen's eyes and fingers traced the quilt stitching. "I have to find Dr. John and confess to him too. I guess he thinks I've tarnished Matthew's memory by finding a few moments to laugh or dance or just be grateful to be alive." Tears seeped from her eyes and she dabbed at them with her shawl. "If I don't laugh sometimes, I feel like life will pass me by."

"He's off talking with Capt Stephens—*gasp*—and the other men." Beth Townsend lay on a narrow bed, a nine-patch quilt dwarfed her. Talking strained.

"I expect your father and brothers will join them, trying to decide what course we should take once the snow stops." Sarah wished she was there in the center of the conversation.

"What sort of choice?" Beth asked.

Sarah cringed. She wasn't supposed to say anything. "Ah, whether to turn back and go the other route or not." She wouldn't mention that it was Beth's health at the center.

"Turning back?" Ellen asked.

Sarah had never seen Ellen without a warming smile, not on this entire journey. She'd even forgotten that Ellen was a widow. Maybe that's what Ellen's father objected to.

"No one here finds fault with you." Sarah wanted no more talk about routes. She stood, turned the spigot on the copper samovar. She had rekindled the Townsend fire Dr. John had let go to coals and heated the water. She handed Ellen a tin cup, steam rising from it with the scent of peppermint.

They drank in silence, inhaling the mist. Then Ellen twisted around so she could face her former sister-in-law. "How are you feeling, Beth?" Sarah wondered for a moment if Ellen was still considered a relative with the death of her husband. She noticed she didn't call Beth "Sister."

"Not strong." The same answer to that universal question. Sarah thought she needed to find another way to assess her mentor's condition.

"Your color is better today, though," Sarah said.

"I must apologize to you too, Beth," Ellen said.

"You've done nothing—*gasp*—to harm me." Beth patted Ellen's hand.

"These men," Ellen continued. "Why can't they come to us instead of carryin' a grievance. Has Dr. John said anything to you about me, Sarah?"

"Not a word."

"'Tis death I'd welcome if *you* thought I breached a bond between you and your Allen." Tears poured again. "I only wanted to laugh."

"Since we're being honest," Sarah said, "I sometimes do envy you, Ellen. You're lovely. And you're starting a new life with pluck. That confidence is attractive to men. Like my husband—though I have not a doubt about his faithfulness." She giggled. "He takes too much time braiding and oiling his mustache ends to find time to be unfaithful." Then she added something she hadn't meant to say. "I want to find ways to make him notice me more—not notice you less."

"But you're wise and kind and pay attention to others and—"

"I'm not seeking compliments." Sarah felt her face grow warm. "I'm making my own apology here, for being envious."

"Both you girls—*gasp*—speak ill of yourselves with no need." The effort to talk caused Beth to cough, and Sarah rose to help her sit up, pat her back. "I'll speak to John—*gasp*—complaining to your father."

"Maybe he's still grieving Matthew's death," Sarah said.

"I guess he thinks I don't." Ellen dabbed her fingers on her wet cheeks.

"He did so want—*gasp*—Matthew to be a part of our trek west. —*gasp*—The loss of the store. My constant illness. All disappointments to him."

Sarah said, "You never complain though you easily could." She took another sip of tea. "What do you think they'll decide?"

"It's annoying to wait to be told, isn't it?"

"What if the snow doesn't stop?" Ellen had stood and now faced Beth and Sarah both still sitting on the bed. "What if it keeps falling?"

Sarah looked up. The canvas above them sagged with the weight of the snow already. She swallowed. "The most logical thing is to do what Truckee told us," Sarah said. "Go back. Follow that stream. Find that large lake, then go around it, heading south." She was doing what Allen had asked her not to, in front of Beth.

"There's talk of that?" Beth asked.

"Some. I like the idea of following a river away from that granite monster out there," Sarah said. "The rivers all flow toward the Pacific, from what Old Greenwood says." She should return to their wagons, use the shovel handle to poke up against the canvas and knock off some of the snow so Allen wouldn't have to.

"Though none have ever been through this part of the Sierra Nevada, my da says. What do any of them know?"

"My hands are—*gasp*—so cold."

"Let's warm them together." Ellen sat. She covered Beth's hands, then reached for Sarah's, who cupped her fingers in the palms of her friend, both wearing gloves with the fingers free. Ellen blew on Beth's hands to warm them.

"What do you say we intrude upon the meeting with Capt Stephens and the men?" Sarah said. "I'd like to hear the arguments and maybe even offer a thought or two." She heard the enthusiasm in her own voice.

"You go. Find out," Beth said. "John rarely tells me—*gasp*—anything."

"I'll go, but I'm not speaking up," Ellen said. "'Tis a short rope me da has me on, and me brother waits to twist the hemp into a bracelet, if not a noose."

"Surely not so treacherous as that?" Sarah said.

"Family can be perilous indeed."

"Just make the right decision. I hold the youngest member of this party, James Miller, and I intend to bring her into California alive and well." Ailbe Miller patted her four-month-old infant's bottom, the babe asleep on her chest.

"My intention too," her husband said. "We'll try to figure things out." He hesitated before leaving their wagon. "The snow seems to be letting up."

Ailbe smiled at her good husband. "You find grain in a horse dropping and see it as a gift to replant."

"Ah, Ailbe, me love, you make me sound a mite foolish." James wrapped a wool scarf around his neck, swinging the fringed ends with a flourish.

"You're not silly, just more hopeful than most. It's a blessing, James."

"It gets me through the rougher days."

Some of Aible's sisters chuckled at her husband's optimism, suggesting he was stuttle, as the Irish called a foolish soul, but she'd been drawn to his good nature, his constant ability to help her see the world through glasses that reflected light rather than ones that darkened. She'd never known him to be discouraged and wasn't sure she'd know what to do if he ever was. She'd been blessed in finding this good man. Her thoughts turned to her beautiful sister, Ellen. Never happy in marriage and now widowed. Matthew Townsend had been a handsome man with big ideas that had ended on a fiery night.

"What are ye shaking yer head about?"

"Just thinking of Matthew and Ellen, love. Such sadness."

"Now see, you can't dwell on those places. They'll bring you down. Think of the higher mountains. Ellen's smiling and having her own *craic*."

"Papa thinks a bit too much craic."

"She needs a little fun. All you Murphy girls do. You're much too serious."

"I'm the mother of five. Fun isn't necessarily in my basket of essentials." She adjusted her lace cap.

"Should be. How else will you have goodies to take out when you need them if you don't put goodies in first."

"Now you are being stuttle," she said, but she laughed. "Go on, then. Add your sparkled lenses to the visions going on over there. Take William with you. He's of an age now."

"Can I, Pa?" The boy's eager smile lit his pale face. He pulled himself away from the younger siblings, who squabbled over a stuffed leather ball. The four-year-old wanted to throw it; the two-year-old wanted to chew on it.

"He can learn about decisions and how good men make them."

James motioned to William, and the boy loosened the cords that kept the canvas tight against the weather. Both hopped out and James retied the opening. "We'll be back when the tide's turned."

It was funny to think of the ocean in this distant place still far from the Pacific. Ailbe settled the scuffling, prepared to nurse Indie. "I pray you'll be an independent thinker when you've grown. And maybe a happy one, like your father." James did have a way of brushing away worries. She just hoped he didn't brush over harsh realities on the way to his happy trail.

5

Separation

Isabella Patterson, tall and straight-backed as a hickory stick—or so her father always said—made her way to the Murphy fires where her father and the other men talked. As much as the Greenwood boys—they were both grown men stocky and strong with broken teeth and smelly—sent a wave of fear down her back, they were wise in the ways of the wilderness, which is where they all were. She wanted to hear what they had to say about their current status. She arrived at the fire and was pleased to see Ellen Murphy and Sarah Montgomery there as well. A few women to witness these discussions was good. She dipped her bonnet toward them and wondered if she might get Sarah to knit her one of those tuques with flaps to keep her ears warm. Ellen wore a heavy Irish sweater. One of those would be nice too. Those northerners were equipped for this snow. Their wagons were better furnished than the Hitchcock-Patterson rig. And the Murphys and Martins and Millers all helped each other. Well, they helped her family too.

"We could go back and follow the Truckee south," Capt Stephens said, "leave wagons here until spring. But it's forward toward the mountain or back a few days' time and follow the river, that's the choice."

Allen Montgomery spoke up. "Either way is forward—"

"But irrelevant, Allen." Dr. Townsend cut his younger friend off. "We must decide between following that Indian's advice, take the river south, or go with these seasoned mountain men, none of whom have ever crossed in this particular place but who know Sierra snow. I, for one, am not in favor of leaving our wagons. There's bragging rights if we bring the wagons in."

"You've heard all the arguments," Capt said. "I'd like to see which way you're all leaning. You men," he added. "Not that the ladies aren't wise, but this is a man's vote we're taking."

Chica barked at that. "She's a female taking issue," Moses Schallenberger said. Everyone laughed. Isabella thought the dog's happy bark was meant for Sarah, whom the dog seemed to just discover was in the crowd as she wagged her tail and trotted to the young woman, hoping to be picked up, which Sarah did.

"What's your pleasure, gentlemen? Continue west, raise your hands?" He counted. "Go cross country to pick up Truckee?" He counted again. "Looks like continuing west has it. I'm inclined that direction myself."

"If a woman might speak?" Isabella said. "Now that the choice has been made."

"'Course. Go ahead."

"Why can't we do both? Split the party and those who want to follow the river do so while the rest take the pass."

"Not a good idea to separate." This was Old Greenwood. "We all need to stick together."

"But there are different circumstances for each of us."

"She's right. I worry about Mrs. Townsend," Sarah said. "Do you think she can make that hard crossing, Dr. John?"

"Who's to say the river route will be any better," Allen said. Isabella noticed he scowled at his wife.

"She's already having trouble breathing and we'll be going

higher, where the air is thinner yet," Sarah said. "And didn't Truckee say we'd get to a lower altitude sooner by circling that larger lake he described?"

"River route does go south," Capt Stephens said. "But no wagons can go there."

Isabella wondered how wagons would make it over that granite face in the distance, a fortress so steep the snow broke off from it, revealing its ominous façade.

"What if Beth were to go on horseback with a few others," Ellen Murphy asked. "Your French-Canadian servants, Dr. John." She nodded toward the two men standing quiet, away from the firelight. "And another good hunter to help."

"Our servants, yes." Dr. John seemed to be warming to the idea. Isabella couldn't remember how he'd voted. "Yes, Oliver and François, you two know river travel and could look after Beth."

"Wouldn't you go with her?" Sarah asked.

"I've got the wagons to think of. All our supplies are in them. I'd need to stay with the valuables."

Your wife isn't a valuable? Isabella thought of her husband, Andrew. He would never have considered sending her one way while he went another. He had gone on without her—but that wasn't his choice.

A few more offered ideas, and then Capt Stephens said they should go back to their families and discuss the option of splitting up the party, with some going south, and return in an hour.

"That was a good suggestion, Mrs. Patterson, but you see now, our decision is delayed," Dr. Townsend said.

"It gives us time to involve the ladies," she said. "It's our lives too."

Sarah came back from the meeting, along with Allen and John and Beth's brother, Moses, who brought Chica, of course. "You will go, Beth," Dr. John announced. "You'll be much better off riding a horse than trudging through these snows. And the altitude will be better for you, and François and Oliver will assist." The dog bounded up on the bed next to Beth, wet feet and all. They were crowded, standing shoulder to bent shoulder in this Townsend wagon, looking down on Beth.

"You need to teach that dog better manners," Dr. John said. Beth roused herself to sitting and wiped the dog's feet with a towel.

"Yes, sir," Moses said. But he didn't try to remove the dog, whom Beth now stroked. Chica's tongue hung out happily as her bright eyes looked from human to human.

How vulnerable Beth must feel with people standing over her, Sarah thought. The dog likely gave her comfort.

"I wouldn't want to—*gasp*—interfere with *your* plans, John." Sarah heard the sarcasm in Beth's voice and it surprised her.

"You won't. I'll still go with the wagons. Sarah can go with you."

Sarah turned with a jerk of her head toward Dr. John.

"Oh, hey, wait a minute." Allen stopped twirling his mustache. "I'm not leaving my wagons either, not with all those guns and pistols and ammunition. It's our future in there. No, I'm going where the mountains are. And Sarah's going with me."

Sarah was pleased that he wanted her along with him but would have liked to have been asked her opinion—and maybe even mentioned before his "guns and pistols."

"But Beth has to have a woman go with her," Sarah said.

"You won't be coming, John?" Beth coughed.

"No, no. You'll be fine. Oliver and François know how to take care of you. And they know rivers."

"We won't be on the river, John, but—*gasp*—beside it. Or crossing it. Can they manage wilderness travel—*gasp*—without Capt Stephens's guidance?"

Sarah could tell Beth was upset. She'd be too.

"We'll send your brother along then."

"I think you'll need me with the wagons, sir." Moses's voice cracked.

"Yes, yes, that's likely. Well, another woman then."

They all remained silent.

"What about your sister-in-law, Ellen." This was Allen's suggestion.

Not Sarah. Sarah and Ellen had just gotten over a bridge. She wanted to see where the rest of that trail led.

"And maybe a couple of her brothers, Bernard or John. They're tough. They could help clear the trails and hunt."

"I doubt they'd leave their father's wagons."

"But there are more Murphy boys and the drivers to take care of them. And the sons-in-law too," Allen said.

"Maybe." Dr. John took a draw on his pipe he'd tapped and lit. "I'll talk with Martin. See what he thinks. He may want to take the river route himself. And then there's the Sullivans. Maybe Miss Sullivan would want to travel with you, my dear. I'd pay her, of course."

"What do you want to do, Beth?" Sarah watched as Beth's face gained color but not from better health, she didn't think. She was upset. Dr. John didn't even notice.

"I'll do whatever—*gasp*—John wants."

"That's my girl." He raised his pipe at her as a kind of toast. She coughed at the smoke.

She'd never let herself be like that, Sarah decided. It was one thing to accommodate in a marriage, but that didn't mean that one person's needs could be ignored. She didn't know, of course, but Beth might be fearful of traveling without her husband. Sarah would be. Or she might be worried over his future. She might be thinking of her own mortality, she'd been sick for so long. Once Beth had said to Sarah that she wondered if she could go on, and Sarah had selfishly said, "Do it for us, for Dr. John and for Moses and for me and others who love you." And the woman had faltered on, ever weaker, always sacrificing her own needs for those of others.

"I'll speak with the Murphys. Then we'll decide. Sarah, you'll have to go if Ellen Murphy or the Sullivan girl won't."

Sarah waited for Allen to say something to Dr. John in her defense. He had before. But he didn't. So, she did. "I think we'll shoot that pistol when the target is closer." Yes, she and Allen would talk about this—when they were alone.

"Yes! I'll go." They were at her father's fire. Ellen saw leaving as an opportunity to get away from her father's hovering, Dr. John's frowns, and most of all, her brother Daniel's judging. And she'd prove herself useful in the process. "I love Beth. No offense, Dr. John, but Beth was the most welcoming member of your family, aside from Matthew, of course."

Actually, Moses had been inviting too. It was Dr. John who she found to be cool to her. It ought to have been a warning about his brother, her husband, but she'd fallen so deeply in love with Matthew by then she'd failed to notice the temperament of his brother. They weren't cruel men, John and Matthew, but very self-centered, always in a negotiation for something. Matthew had courted her with gifts and treasures, and she hadn't realized that these were almost bribes rather than offerings meant to express his love and devotion. They were manipulations for something more than her praise at his thoughtfulness. She was to be the prize on his arm, the beauty at his side, the woman working at his mercantile.

"Good. That's settled then. Because you're my brother's wife, I expect to pay Ellen's way, of course."

He said it slyly, waiting, she thought, for her da to object.

"That won't be necessary," Martin Murphy said. "But I would like you to provide her horse and of course wages and horses for John and Daniel, who will be going with their sister and your wife."

What? Daniel is coming too?

"Of course. The party will need good men to help break the trail."

"John is going?" Ellen couldn't believe it. "And Daniel? Papa, won't you need them with you?"

"Wait a minute, Papa." Daniel acted like he'd just heard his fate. "Ellen's right. You'll need me here. John can go."

John frowned. He rarely spoke up for himself, yet of all her brothers he was the most skilled in hunting, the humblest about it too.

"I've got Junior and James and Bernard not committed to wife and children. Johanna and Margaret can take over the cooking. We'll be fine. And I'll feel better knowing you've got a chaperone with you. There being unmarried men along."

As if Beth's servants would interest me in any way.

"John, if you're willing to travel with us, I think along with the servants, we'll do fine without Daniel." Ellen sidled next to her father, took his elbow. "Really. We'll travel light, Da. One change of clothing. We'll have plenty of help with John along."

"I agree with her," Daniel said. "Why should I be punished?"

Ha! Who's being punished? For the first time she wished Daniel luck with his argument. She even said a prayer that her father would listen to his most outspoken son. Otherwise, she'd never have a life of her own.

"I would worry about you less, Mary." John Sullivan had returned from the meeting and had decided for his sister.

"But we have no horses for me to ride, nor the boys either."

"We boys can remain. You go with Mrs. Townsend and Miss Murphy. I've decided."

It didn't make any sense to Mary to ship her off like a chunk of cheese. Why? To get her out of the way? But then why not send the boys as well?

"No."

"No? You're defying me?" He stood bent over to glare at her while she sat, his dark hair falling over his blue eyes. He pushed it back. "You will do as you're told."

"I'm making my own decision, Brother. You cannot force me onto a horse. I'm responsible for the little boys as much as you, and I'm responsible for myself." Her voice shook, but she continued. Stood, to feel less like a small mouse with a large cat outside her hole ready to pounce. "I've sat back long enough letting you decide whether we headed west or back to Montreal or whether Oregon or California. And now, I've chosen the route I think is best to keep with us what little we have left of Mama and Papa, and that's their wagon and the things in it."

"I'll look after it."

"While you work the oxen, cook, and tend the boys? I think not."

He sat down, then stood up. He grimaced and stuck his lower lip out. He clasped his hands together. The little boys, awakened by the chatter, stared from Mary to John, huddled together like puppies seeking warmth from each other. "I have to decide what's best and—"

"John, it's decided. We go where you go. If you want us to be part of the Horseback Party, then you'll be riding with us too. If you're staying with the wagon, then so are we. We are in this together. Share the burden, Papa would say."

He lowered his shoulders. Mary patted his back. *I ought to pat my own.* Why hadn't she stood up to him like this before? Was that all it took, speaking firmly? Or maybe he was tired of being the decider. Maybe grief had wrapped itself around his heart, and he just now saw that he was not alone. She'd pushed this choice but there really wasn't any other. They had no horses. The boys couldn't walk or they'd hold the others back. They had to put their trust in God and their fortune. Wasn't that the "more-all" of their story now? Perhaps had always been.

6

Departure

"But it's our lives," Sarah wailed. "He can't dictate to us. He isn't even family." Sarah plopped down on their bed. They'd had to sleep the last night inside, as the wind had picked up and blew snow into the tent where they'd been huddled beneath the tarp.

"He helped fund our trip."

This was news to Sarah. "I thought we did that, you by selling your gun shop and me sewing up a storm before we left. I almost wore a thimble out stitching dresses for Holt County matrons. I even had a few commissions in Council Bluffs when everyone was waiting to depart, remember?"

"You worked very hard. I agree. And so did I. But I couldn't sell all the weapons. I needed stock for California. Dr. John made me a loan." Allen pushed his brown hair, parted in the middle, behind his ears. His mustache ends jiggled. "He wanted us both along. Beth did too. That's why if he insists you go, then you go."

"I don't think that's fair, Allen."

"What gave you the idea that life is fair? It's a series of diminishing returns."

"That's not true. 'Dost thou love life? Then do not squander time, for that is the stuff life is made of.'"

"Profound."

"Benjamin Franklin."

Allen snorted. "You and *Poor Richard's Almanac*. Beth spoils you reading that scribe to you. You didn't waste space by bringing some of those issues along, did you?"

She didn't answer. Instead she said, "It saddens me that you have so little hope."

"Oh, I have hope. It's just that I expect the worst and then I'm not disappointed. I mean, here we are, stalled in the shadow of mountains, more than a foot of snow on the ground and more coming down. There's urgency, here, Sarah. No time for arguing. We're splitting up."

"But you'd still send me. Against my wishes."

"I don't think separating is wise, if you want to know the truth. But we're not losing critical people by sending Mrs. Townsend south on horseback. Nor you. Frankly, I think all the women ought to go on horseback out of here."

"And what would you do with their children? You make no sense sometimes." She tightened the wool shawl around her. "I can't believe you don't want me at your side."

He shrugged. "I'd be sad to not have you warm my bed at night. But I also think you'd be safer. We have a choice. I'll go with the wagons, you can help out a friend and beat me to Alta California. All around, it's a good bet."

Her heart felt heavy. Yes, they were talking about a decision, but she could see that she had no real say in it. Or maybe even all that important of a place in Allen's life. Except to warm his bed at night.

As though it was a good omen, the snow stopped in the morning, the sky as blue as the slowly freezing lake. The brilliance of the snow all around them and the mountain peaks sparkling in the distance burned Ellen's eyes. She watched the men help Beth toward the painted horse she'd be riding. The Townsends had gotten the sturdy animal in a trade back at Fort Hall from a Blackfeet Indian there. Beth had ridden the spotted pony once before. Each woman—Beth and Ellen—took only one change of dress, few other essentials.

Sarah Montgomery had given Beth a sweater she'd knitted, along with a woolen tuque she now pulled down over Beth's ears. *Will this woman survive the trip?* It was questionable in Ellen's mind, and she wondered that Dr. John was so cavalier about her journey.

"There you go, my dear. You're light as a snowflake, so old Spotty here will hardly know you're on him." Dr. John chuckled as he held his wife's hand in his, looking up at her mounted on a man's saddle. "You'll do just fine with the cadre of protectors. Won't she?" He looked around and Ellen nodded along with the servants. It was almost as if he was relieved of the burden of his ill wife. That probably wasn't fair of Ellen, but still, he seemed too cheerful, too solicitous, making her think that, like Matthew, he was getting something for this, more than having Beth's best interest at heart.

And then there was Daniel. How had she been punished with her jailer as a traveling companion when she thought she would finally be out from under his control?

"I think you should take Chica with you, Sister." Moses held the dog in his arms. "She can ride across the pommel."

"Oh, but she'll miss you terribly. It isn't—*gasp*—necessary, Moses."

"Just be a nuisance on the trail," Daniel said.

"She can alert you to trouble. Mountain cats, who knows what else. I'd feel better if you had her along."

Ellen thought she saw tears in the boy's eyes. He was showing more concern and love than Beth's husband was.

"Moses. Take the dog away, for heaven's sake," Dr. John said.

Moses pulled the small dog back to his chest.

"'Tis a fine idea," Ellen said. "She's a good little Chica, and who knows, she might chase up a fox or two we can fix for dinner." The servants were good hunters, from what John had told her. And her brothers were too. She'd give them that. A dog could help. She'd be extra warmth for Beth too, if nothing else. "We'll make a pair, we will."

Moses perked up, smiled, and that single dimple sank deep in his right cheek, one that matched his sister Beth's.

"She just might. It'd do me a favor. I'm not sure how she'll manage the higher snow and cold where we're headed. I can't keep those wool socks on her. She tugs them off with her teeth."

"Not a smart dog," Dr. John said. "And not good to have to manage. Beth has enough to worry about."

"I'll look after Chica." Ellen clapped her hands and the dog bounded from Moses to her. She scooped the animal up and groaned. The dog weighed as much as a Christmas turkey. Chica licked her face. "We'll get along just fine."

"If it will help your worrying, Moses, then—*gasp*—we should bring her." Beth spoke the words with defiance in her tone, a strength Ellen hadn't heard before.

"Elizabeth, it isn't wise," Dr. John said. "You ask too much of the hunters to have to worry about a dog."

"Let us get—*gasp*—under way," Beth said. Her dimple formed too as she smiled. "Thank you, Sarah, for the tuque and sweater. Thank you, Moses, for your sacrifice in giving up Chica's presence and—*gasp*—thank you, my protectors and companions, especially Ellen."

Why, the woman sounded almost strong. Maybe she'd had her limit with Dr. John's domineering and deciding. "We women will make our mark sprintin' into Sutter's Fort preparin' its residents—'tis Sutter, right, Captain Stephens?" Their leader nodded. "Good." Ellen said. "We'll make our way to Sutter's and tell them to look for your bonny faces later, for surely we'll be there before ye."

"Don't be tempting fate," Dr. John said. "It'll take you longer."

"It is an unknown," Beth said. Her words were clear and strong and she wasn't gasping and hadn't coughed. Maybe the separation was a good thing, for Ellen as well, despite Daniel's intention to keep her in a box he'd built for her in his mind. She might be heading to the safest place she could be, away from Dr. John and his brother's memory and toward a real, new life.

Her father led a prayer of traveling mercies and Ellen mounted her horse. Moses handed up the dog and he lay across the pommel. She hadn't ridden much, but like Beth and her Spotty, Ellen intended to establish a relationship with Moses's dog and the horse she rode named Joker. Moses had given up more than just his dog.

Mary Sullivan waved as the small party of six—all on horseback, leading two pack animals—began pushing through a foot of snow, headed overland to intercept the river they'd once camped beside. The remaining larger party now prepared for the trek toward the mountains. The Greenwoods had been sent out to see about finding a cleft in the distant rock. The other men would hunt that day and then start out with the wagons. Mary felt as tired as Beth had looked, though at the end the woman had rallied. Mary needed to rally herself and she would if she could ever get warm. Every quilt she'd brought along covered her at night and she slept with her younger brothers for the warmth. They were all cold-blooded Sullivans, she decided, except for John. Her older brother didn't even like wearing a cap.

She set the Dutch oven over the flames. Stew was their staple, along with the biscuits she stirred up. She put the flour lumps on top of the cover, heard the sizzle. Good, the cast iron pot was hot. She held her gloved hands over the flames to warm them, careful not to drop moisture from the wool onto the biscuits. When was the last time she'd been warm? At her mother's side back in Iowa, just before the woman died, incense sending a fragrance that ever after brought her mother's memory to mind.

Mary hated feeling weak. She'd been a sickly child. To help heal her, her parents emigrated from Ireland to Canada, where food supplies were more stable. And it had helped. She hadn't had the bone aches after that. But she was still always cold. California was supposed to be warm. She longed for that to be true.

But then her mother became ill and then her father, and they'd both died within a day of each other. Cholera. If only they hadn't left Montreal, Mary had lamented. But John, the eldest, had said after the burial, "What's done was done." Someone else owned their farm now. "We are still going west," John had decided. "It's what Mama and Papa wanted."

It was pure luck or maybe divine intervention that they'd met the Murphys and Townsends and their French servants, the latter making them feel at home, as the Sullivans and François and Oliver spoke French more than English. Many of the Murphys spoke French too. They'd joined people who had become like family, even if Mary felt separated.

But now two of those welcoming faces followed the Truckee River, away. *We should have joined them.* She shook her head. *What's done is done.* Sometimes she thought of her life as a thin, scratchy book held between the bookends of regret and fear. She needed to rewrite that book, make it sturdier. And find new bookends for sure.

"Miss Sullivan." One of the Patterson children in the wagon behind theirs called out to her while her biscuits browned. "May Robert and Michael join our meal?"

"That will be fine." Her younger brothers enjoyed the Pattersons. Mary saw Mrs. Patterson as a loving mother who was inventive in giving the children activities to occupy their time, even in this challenging weather.

"And can they stay the night in our tent?" The Pattersons' six-year-old made the request.

"What does your mother say, *fille?*"

A silence followed, then the reply. "She says they are welcome for as long as they'd like."

Not the night. Non. Mary needed to be there if they had nightmares. And she welcomed their warmth in the bedding. Or maybe this was to be the first day in her new resolve not to be so weak, to stand up for them and herself. It had worked once. Why not again? "We'll see," she told the Patterson child. "For now, go make snowmen. I will bring my bread to share." Later, she'd make corn cakes to put in their pockets for the day they started up the grade. And perhaps without the little boys around, she and her brother could talk as partners in this endeavor and find a new bridge between grief and new beginnings.

7

The Language of Snow

Sarah slid down a deep valley of snow chased by an avalanche, the mound rolling, rolling, gaining speed as she scrambled, her heart pounding, her breath a gasp for air, for life. The sound deafened. Where was Allen? The thought flitted through her mind as the cold mound descended upon her, shaking her body as she cried out for help, tearing the words from the depths of her soul before tumbling her into oblivion.

"Sarah! Sarah!" Something shook her. *Allen.* "You're dreaming, darlin'. What was chasing you?"

She sat up, sweating. She'd had other dreams of dying but none before because of snow. It was the nature of this journey, surrounded as they were by the white. It had snowed the whole day after the Townsend party left. More than two feet covered the ground and little had melted in the cold.

"I . . . I was in an avalanche. I couldn't outrun it."

"Capt Stephens says no one can outrun one. Head off to the side if you can. Remember, he was telling us about that, with fresh snow on frozen snow. All sorts of things can set an avalanche off.

Even us shooting something to eat, he says. The sound of the gunfire can make the mountains move."

"I'm not interested right now in getting avalanche facts, Allen." She took a deep breath, checked her pulse with her fingers. "My heart has slowed at least."

Allen patted her back. "Rough," he said. "I don't dream, so I don't really know, but I hated seeing you tremble and call out."

"Did I get the word 'help' out?"

Allen shook his head. "Nope. Just a kind of groan, but you were fighting me as I tried to shake you awake."

"I thought it was the avalanche speaking to me. Suffocating me."

She lay back down, shivering more from the memory than the cold air. Allen pulled the bedroll up over them, curled up beside her again.

"Guess you're feeling overwhelmed for some reason."

"Let's see. We're miles from civilization and a warm stove. We're surrounded by mountains and the snow is so deep my calves ache as though I'd run a race for hours just going from here to the latrine. Our horses are lean and exhausted. My good friend Beth has gone off on another trail and I'm worried about her. Yes, I feel overwhelmed."

"You've got me."

She turned to face him. "Yes, I do. And I even tried to call out to you, worried over your safety in my dream."

"That's nice to know." He kissed her. "Always pleasant to be the subject of a woman's dreams."

She didn't correct his assumption that *he* was the main part of the dream. The snow was. It was becoming a character all of its own and not one she wanted to spend much more time with. But it was clear she would be. She remembered that day the month before when she'd felt nestled inside a sanctuary, hopeful that the good journey would just continue on. Well, they were still alive and there'd been no avalanche. She'd hang on to that.

"The grade's steep. Not sure the heaviest wagons can make it at all."

Seventeen-year-old Moses Schallenberger listened to the Greenwoods' report, wondered what Capt Stephens would say. The animals were weak, that was certain, and several of the wagons carried heavier cargo than others. Montgomery's with his weapons and ammunition, Capt's with his blacksmithing supplies, and Dr. John's with the bolts of silks, satins, and velvets, and dishes, enough to stock a store. Heavy shovels. He even had a plow. They'd been sent back to their wagons for a meal after listening to the report. The men would gather later supposedly after conferring with their families. Mr. Hitchcock and the Greenwoods would rest their horses, then head back up, still seeking that cleft in the rock wide enough for wagons to go through.

Moses was glad he'd sent Chica along with his sister, but he missed that little face, her breath panting beside him while he cooked now for Dr. John. He missed Joker too. Dr. John bent over his book.

"'Sleep hath its own world . . . and dreams in their development have a breath, and tears, and torture, and the touch of joy.'"

"Sir?"

"Reading Lord Byron, Moses. You ought to do that too. This one is called *The Dream*. He goes on to say that dreams 'leave a weight upon our waking thoughts, they take a weight from off our waking toils.' Do you dream, Moses?"

"No, sir. Not when I'm sleeping anyway. I have thoughts of the future, but Mr. Byron might not be thinking of those."

"Lord Byron," Dr. John corrected.

"Right."

Moses's brother-in-law stood beside him now, the little book he'd been reading from put back in his pocket. "The poet is talking about that place of its own reality between 'death and existence.'

But I suppose your dreaming of the future is not a bad thing. I do that myself from time to time."

Moses thought Doc did a fair amount of dreaming about his silks and other valuables he planned to sell in California. And he talked a lot about "other ideas" he had for his future, but was sly about commenting on what those might be. His sister loved the man. He tried to.

"I've some alum that might help those outbreaks on your face, boy."

Moses's hands went immediately to his cheeks.

"Oh, don't touch them. Just makes them worse. Probably the poor nutrition we have on this trip. It'll be over soon," he said. "And you can get back to cleaning better."

Moses knew he blushed. "What else does he say about dreaming?" *Anything to change the subject from my pimples.* He even had a pox inside his dimple.

"Let's see." He pulled the book out again. "'A change came over the spirit of my dream.' Lord Byron starts several verses of this poem with that phrase. An interesting structure for a poem."

"I suppose that would be true even for daydreams," Moses offered.

"What's that?"

"That change comes over the spirit of a dream. Even daydreams that I guess are just wishes. Or hopes. But things change them."

"That's quite insightful, Moses. Yes, they do indeed change as we face the consequences of what each day brings us. I suppose hanging on to a dream despite that can require change."

Had his brother-in-law looked at him with new respect? Yes, he had. It wasn't as good as a lick from Chica, but it was something pleasant from a brother-in-law who usually wasn't.

If the baby comes early, Maolisa Murphy thought, this would be a memorable place for it to happen. They could call a boy baby

Stephen and honor both their leader and the lake. It wouldn't necessarily be like Ellen Independence born at Independence Rock on the Fourth of July, but still significant. And saying the child's name would remind her of this pristine site so quiet, all covered in white. It was almost sacred. Would Indians have rested here, set their tepees or huts, whatever they called their homes? Yes, the snow was deep, but it was absolutely awe-inspiring to see the vast white world of which they were but a dot on the terrain. The Horseback Party—as she thought of them—missed this. She prayed for their success.

She felt a small jab against her rib. "Whoa, baby. Getting restless?"

Maolisa was much bigger than she'd been at this stage in previous pregnancies. She hadn't been eating as well, given the conditions, so her girth surprised her. They burned up every morsel of fuel put into their bodies and she'd made sure the children all had sufficient sustenance. She was glad they'd prepared so many dried fruits like bleached apples. Pickled beans had filled a wooden barrel. She appreciated the different taste of the pickled foods—crunchy texture too. She'd already rationed those and there weren't many more. Dried venison was their staple, but it lacked flavor in her mind. Still, she ate it. Junior reminded her that she had to think of the baby she carried as well and to not deprive herself. She noticed that he did, though. They'd better be less than a month from Sutter's or they'd arrive starving—if they arrived at all.

Something about the lake gave her new hope. It was serenity at this altitude with snow-studded mountains around it, trees so heavy with foot-high stacks like sugared cones. One could barely see the branches. They acted as sentinels to the lake edge. It was enchanting. Gun-gray rocks dotted the shoreline. Those rocks had been there for generations. Solid. Steady.

Was the human spirit capable of continuing when one's body knew exhaustion it had never known before? Could a magical landscape bring sustenance?

No one had ever been in this valley staring at this lake in the winter with wagons. She lumbered toward the water's edge and picked up a rock. She'd make it a keepsake. It was black as a moonless night and smooth. She turned it over in her palm, rubbed its rounded edges. Then, changing her mind, she skipped it across the ice, something she'd done as a child on Lac Saint-Jean. Her husband called her a proper housewife, but that didn't preclude skipping a few stones now and then.

Horseback Party

They lifted Beth from Spotty, the servants carrying her to a place they'd cleared as best they could, settling her on the blanket-covered snowpack. Ellen was already there. Daniel had started a fire. Thank goodness he was good at that. Ellen had packed snow inside the kettle to melt and heat for tea and coffee. Chica leapt like a cat, hopping up with her middle arching higher than her feet, then bounding down as her way to make it through the snow. The dog had brought them to laughter more than once, the sun highlighting her black hair like little strings of silk. The dog knew tricks, or at least Ellen thought she did. After they had a meal that first night, the dog had sat in front of her and stared, tongue hanging out until Ellen put her hand out like she wanted to shake it. The dog spun around in a circle, then sat and plopped a paw into Ellen's hand. She shook it and the dog put her paw on the ground, staring. Ellen did it again and the dog spun around, plopped her bottom on the ground and gave up her paw. It could go on all night, Ellen suspected. She'd have to find some new tricks to teach her—or wait for the dog to tell her what else Moses had taught her.

"How are you feeling?" Ellen asked. Beth stayed silent. "Beth?" She turned to look at the older woman.

"I'm assessing. It seems to me I have to find a more particular

70

answer to that never-ending question besides 'Not so strong.' After all, I've made it this far." She coughed. "How are you feeling?"

"No one ever asks me that. Let me pause too." She closed her eyes and imagined a light flowing down her body to her toes. No spots needing special reflection. "I'm good too. But let's not ask my feet." The women laughed.

Daniel came from hobbling the horses. He'd hung feed bags over their heads and put grain into them. "Don't you have something hot yet? The men are exhausted and hungry."

"Water's hot. I'll put the peas in. There's jerked venison and some pemmican. The bacon is frozen so I've got to chop at the slab. Unless you want to as you're in a hurry."

"That's woman's work."

"Yes, it is and we do a fine job of it, don't we, Beth. You boys would starve without us."

Daniel scowled while John put his hand out for the knife. "I'll chop off the bacon. I rather like cooking. In case someday I don't have a good sister cooking for me. Or a wife."

Daniel gave a disgusted gesture, pushing away the air, and sat against one of the saddles he'd pulled from the horses. Ellen was grateful to have astride saddles like the men's. Still, Ellen rode in the line behind Beth each day to watch and make sure she didn't slip or fall.

The men had used their axes several times to knock away tall shrubs and small trees in their way. They were riding up, following the river that wasn't as wide here. They camped at the side of what appeared to be a good-sized hill, maybe a mountain. Trees of various sizes had marked their ascent and glistened with snow. Daniel thought they would reach the summit in the morning, given the stream's narrowing. "Whatever feeds this river has to be springs in the mountain or maybe that big lake Truckee drew in the sand."

"Does it mean we're going to be able to go—*gasp*—down after this?" Beth asked him.

He nodded. "I'd like to think so. This is grueling, but at least we're not hauling wagons."

"I appreciate your coming with us, Mr. Murphy." Beth was so kind.

"Wasn't my choice but turns out it's not so bad."

Ellen smelled the cooked peas. Along with the bacon John had carved off the slab, they'd have a hearty meal, if not varied. Daniel and John and the servants ate. Oliver had offered to cook and she'd let him on a later day when she was even more fatigued. Everyone ate, content. Even Daniel hadn't insulted her efforts.

She dreamed about her father that night. He walked in a meadow. A lake lay beyond. He looked contented. The good feeling stayed with her in the morning, perfuming her day so that she whistled as she fixed their biscuits.

They rode to the top of the ridge, Joker lunging the last few feet. Before them lay a wide, glistening lake with blue-green water sparkling, a jewel set in alabaster. "It must be very deep to not be frozen," Ellen said.

"It's . . . breathtaking," Beth said. The altitude affected her. She struggled with her breathing. *Had she yesterday?* They needed to find their route around this lake and descend quickly or who knew how Beth would answer her question that evening of "How are you feeling?" Or if she even could.

Snow started to fall from a gray sky as they began their ride around the rim. Ellen thought it was telling her to hurry up. She was listening.

8

Assessments

It was as though the elements stalked them, Capt thought, giving just enough time to catch their breaths, only to be thwarted into a profound discouragement.

"Gather them all, Joe." Captain Stephens sent his driver to the wagons to give the men the grim truth: The more heavily loaded wagons had to be abandoned. The animals couldn't pull them through the deep snow above the tree line toward the summit. That meant his wagons, Townsend's, and Montgomery's two carrying the rifles and ammunition must remain. Five wagons filled with people—women and children—would summit. Those vehicles would be needed for shelter and to carry essentials. Townsend and Moses were alone now and each had a horse. Though Moses had loaned his to Ellen Murphy, he had an Indian pony as a back-up. A generous kid. Those bolts of material Townsend had hauled west were pretty to look at and pleasant to touch, but together they were rocks of weight for the oxen. Capt had his own riding horse and pack animal and another for Joe. He'd put the freed-up oxen onto the other wagons to help pull. The Montgomerys had neither riding animals nor pack animals, so they'd have to be accommodated by other families. That's why he'd told Joe to invite everyone to the gathering, women included. He figured Sarah Montgomery would be his biggest headache.

"We weren't surprised by your summons," Isabella Patterson said. She stomped her feet on the tarp they'd laid down. Her father stood beside her, a quiet man. Capt wondered how it was that quiet begat chatty in offspring. Not having any children, he couldn't imagine how those generational differences worked their way out. Old Greenwood, Caleb, was taciturn and tough while his boys were slick and sly. He shook his head, welcomed the others without really addressing Mrs. Patterson's comment. Time enough to hear her opinion.

"I've been thinking," Capt said, looking about at the tired faces. "We're here beside this lake—"

"Stephens Lake," Joe said.

"But the sun continues to elude us and we stand again with snow falling on our shoulders and snow at our feet and snow over the wheel hubs and snow, well, everywhere. We've made little gains. Frankly, it's my assessment that we need to consolidate—unless you can come up with other solutions."

"What do you mean by consolidate?" This was Sarah Montgomery.

"He means put some things in other wagons so we can leave a wagon or two behind," Allen told her.

"That's right, Montgomery. Your wagon, I suspect."

He lifted his chin as though to acknowledge Capt's statement. Capt waited for his wife to blow up, but she kept her tongue. Thinking about it, he supposed.

"My wagon, too. One has the anvil and a knife sharpener, all heavy. The other carries my blacksmith tools and traps. Too much for the oxen now, we'll need animals to pull to get the remaining wagons to the summit."

"I thought there was only one more pass to go over. Wasn't this it?" Mary Sullivan spoke up now. "I thought when we saw the lake we'd see California."

"Then I've misled you," Capt said. "A major pass is made up of many ups and downs before we howdy that granite tower. We'll have to go around, if the Greenwoods find us a cleft. Once on the other side there'll be a few more ridges, but each will be of lower altitude and we'll eventually be down out of the snow."

"As long as you can see higher ridges in the west, we ain't yet at the pass," Hitchcock said. He'd trapped in the Shining Mountains, so he knew about demanding landscapes.

"But we're in Alta California?" Mary Sullivan asked.

"Probably." Capt waited, hoping Townsend would see that his rigs were an issue as well. The good doctor didn't, so Capt added, "I also think, Dr. John, that your wagon will need to stay behind."

"Mine? But it has my medical equipment and treatments. We'll continue to need those all the way to the sea."

"It's more the fabrics, those heavy satins and silks—"

"Silks weigh nothing."

"Your oxen would disagree if they could speak. And we need those animals to team up with others to bring the true valuables of this journey forward—the people, women and children."

"And those not yet arrived," Maolisa Murphy said.

"I . . . I can't see my way to abandon all my valuables."

"We could come back in the spring and get them, couldn't we, Capt?" Moses's voice cracked as he said that. The boy swallowed. "No one's going to come by and take anything. Only crazy people are out in this snow anyway."

"You can examine our heads without your doctor equipment," Martin Murphy Sr. quipped. A few of the men chuckled. "Capt's right. The rest of us can consolidate."

"Sullivan, Patterson, Martin, and Murphy's two, those'll be the wagons we summit." Capt pointed toward each name spoken, the fringe of buckskin hanging off his leather gloves.

"And where will we go?" Sarah said. "Every other wagon is already full and now you're asking people to make room for more?"

"You can come in ours," Mary Sullivan offered. That little mouse of a woman who looked older than Mrs. Patterson with all her kids had a generous heart. Or maybe she was lonely. It didn't matter. The offer had been made. "John and the boys, we can make room for two more."

"Joe and I will simply pack from here on," Capt said. "A pack animal can be yours to ride, Mrs. Montgomery." He was grateful now that they'd bought extra ponies back at Fort Hall.

"Moses and Townsend, maybe you can split up, go to different wagons. Or just pack like Joe and me here, like the Greenwoods." The boy looked so frail he hoped he'd get an offer for a wagon and not just have to rough it with a horse camp. Still, he was a good hunter. Maybe he was just wiry and not frail at all. He wasn't sure who would want Townsend. The man had healing skills, but he also saw himself as the center of the sun, never seemed to realize he burned as well as illuminated—now and then.

"Moses, you're welcome to come under my clucking," Mrs. Patterson said.

"Maybe a Murphy could take on Dr. John. You ox men, Bray, Calvin, Flomboy, Harbin, you'll all keep on as you are." Those men were spread throughout the wagons but slept mostly under their tents near the stock until this deep snow threatened their natural bedding spots. Capt had not anticipated such deep snow.

"We'll invite you to our victuals such as they are, Doc," James Miller said. "With a new baby at hand, one can always use a doctor close by."

"Now see here, I think your assessment is in error." Townsend had found his tongue. "We should decide as a group."

"I agree," Allen Montgomery said. "We're being punished for carrying the most goods in our wagons. I've supplied weapons and ammunition for the hunters. We'll need that even more than medicines—no offense intended, Doc."

"Only a small amount taken," Townsend said. "But Allen's right. We carry the most valuable materials and yet you want us to leave things behind, have to come back next spring to get them, if the Indians haven't discovered them by then. Another dangerous journey. Expensive too. Delays our businesses once we arrive."

"The question is about getting there alive," Capt said. "Your animals are weakened. I see no other way but that you'll have to abandon them eventually in this demanding snow either because your animals die or are too weak to pull the weight over the mountains. Can't you see how thin they are?"

"So are all the other animals. Why pick on ours?" Montgomery said.

"I don't think he's trying to punish us, Allen. He's just looking out for everyone's good."

Capt nodded toward Mrs. Montgomery. She did seem to understand. "What alternative would you propose?" Capt said.

Silence. Only the snap of moisture hitting a low fire broke it. Then Moses spoke. "We could leave the wagons here, at the lake, and some of us stay with them. That way, no one could steal anything. We'd have weapons to hunt with. There'd be fewer people to shuttle into new wagon groups. Maybe we could even build a shelter, take a day or two to cut some logs. I'd stay."

The boy had guts. Or he was looking for a way out from under the toe of Townsend.

"It's an option." Capt said. "Any others?"

"I'd stay too." This from Montgomery.

His wife chimed in. "What? We would not."

"Not you. You go ahead with the Sullivans. I'd remain with my guns. Come spring, you could make sure a relief party returned with oxen enough to haul us out. You'd do that, wouldn't you, Capt? That would free up more horses too. We wouldn't need any staying here. Sarah, you could use one of those."

Capt didn't know about wives and all, but he could see by the look on Mrs. Montgomery's face that this conversation wouldn't end here in this public place. There'd be strong words at their wagon tonight, spoken in harsh whispers but no less intense than if they were all alone and could yell loud enough to wake a hibernating bear.

"I'm not sure you're strong enough, Moses, though I admire your willingness." Townsend's words brought a deep color to Moses's face.

"Right. I've more grit than I might appear, sir. You can trust me to do my best for you. You always done right by me, you and my sister. This is my way of giving back."

"I'm just not sure your best will be—"

"I could watch over your wagons, Capt," Joe Foster piped up. Capt hadn't thought of anyone remaining with his wagons, though it held all his worldly goods. He'd blacksmithed years before for the Potawatomi and other tribes, hired by the government to help out. It was all he'd ever known until he started trapping and exploring. Taking a wagon of goods with him had been an investment. Joe staying with those goods wasn't something he'd considered. But that would make a good trio, or at least a good double with Joe and Montgomery. Moses might be more of a burden than a help, but he was certainly enthusiastic. And he was a good hunter, despite a couple of bad choices that had almost cost them the entire party back with the Sioux. The memory caused a hesitation he soon dismissed.

"You three willing to do that?"

Montgomery, Moses, and Joe all nodded their assent.

"Let's sleep on it," Sarah Montgomery said. "Such a big decision needs a little more time."

Capt nodded. He'd give her that. She was the most affected in some ways because she was the only one without a real say in this matter. She and the Sullivan girl. The men would decide.

"And maybe time for prayer," Martin Murphy said. "That however we are separated, our Father will watch over us and unite us all in this land before the one beyond."

"Amen," all the Murphys and Millers and Sullivans said as they made the sign of the cross over their hearts.

Amen, indeed.

———

"You would abandon me for your guns?"

"Don't be dramatic. I'm not abandoning you. Start looking for what essentials you want to take with you instead of berating me."

"You were always going to take care of me."

"I am. And I'm trusting you to take care of me too, make sure they drive oxen back in the spring. Maybe you could even do that, be the first ox woman." He tapped her nose with her finger.

"Don't patronize me. I'm serious."

"What would you have me do, darlin'?"

"Get into the Sullivan wagon with me and help the party make it to Sutter's. We could both drive oxen back in the spring."

He shook his head. "Look. The weapons are simply too valuable to leave behind. And I understand about the weight. The animals are weakened. Maybe I should have ordered English shotguns and rifles in, had them shipped to San Francisco, but what's the likelihood they would arrive, ever, or not be stolen before I got there? This was the best way."

"But what if something happens to you? What am I supposed to do?"

"Find another husband to take care of you."

Her eyes filled with tears. He pulled her to his chest, rubbed her back as she sobbed. She hated it that he only seemed to pay real attention to what she was feeling when she lost control and cried. Crying made her weak in his eyes so he could "lift her up" rather than speak to her as another adult to come to some grownup resolution. She struggled being a grown-up too, apparently, because so many of their major disagreements ended up this way.

"You'll be fine. You and Mary Sullivan can talk women things, while I'll be there with those two numbskulls."

"They're good men, Allen. Don't diminish them."

"Schallenberger is hardly a man. What is he, seventeen, maybe?"

"Age has nothing to do with it." She might be sensitive to such an argument because she was not much older than Moses was.

"Suppose not. Look, darlin', it's only a temporary separation."

"Why don't I stay too?" She perked up, drew her head away from his chest.

"Naw. Too harsh for you. Besides, three men alone will be freer to make decisions without being hampered by the presence of a lady."

She couldn't imagine what choices her presence would interfere with unless it was the men's modesty in relieving themselves . . . or the freedom of flatulence that a woman's presence constricted. She caught herself smiling at that thought.

"You're finding some humor in this. Good."

"I just imagined you having to pucker up, so to speak, after eating peas and beans as those boys, as you think of them, might not like your habits."

"Very funny." She'd forgotten that he was sensitive about his bowels. No, she hadn't forgotten. She was being mean when what she wanted to do was cry again—for her loss, for his ease at sending her off. Maybe he was doing it to protect her—in due course, in time. She only hoped they'd have another time.

"What if you don't . . . make it."

"I haven't a second thought about that. Of course I'll live. We have water and rifles. The game will come. I've not a worry about that. And we won't end up killing each other either."

"I hadn't thought that to be a concern."

"They'll soon recognize my experience as a natural leader and we'll settle into a routine. Why, I can even work on that maple stock, get it ready to finish in the spring. Might try checking a rifle stock too. Be less work than what you'll have to face, darlin'."

"Which is why I ought to be with you." Her argument felt weaker now, though. He'd already moved on into making it a lark, his staying behind. That was the difference: he was choosing to stay behind while she was told to go.

Horseback Party

The horse party camped the next evening on the ridge above the lake. The horses had strained in the deep snow, and Oliver and François had tromped ahead of them breaking the drifts. The little spotted pony pushed with his chest and Beth's feet had dragged through the snow piles. Ellen worried that the woman was growing frailer before their eyes.

"How are you feeling, Beth?"

Seated beneath a tent covering, Beth looked perplexed, then said, "I'm assessing." She was quiet. "My legs are sore, but they still hold me up. My eyes ache from the snow, but I can still see. I'm short of breath, but I can take in the air. Let's see . . . I'm tired as an overworked nurse in my husband's surgery, but I'm still able to sit up and take nourishment."

Daniel laughed. "Da says that when someone asks how he's doing. 'Able to sit up and take nourishment' is always his answer."

"I hope he's saying that today," Ellen said. "I'd forgotten that little phrase of his."

"You moved out and got married."

Why is he so angry about everything?

"Just don't tell any stories on me," John said.

"You're too young to have good fodder for a story," Daniel told him. They all laughed then, a moment of comradery on a mountain peak. The servants began preparing something to eat; the animals were attended to without complaint. Daniel even picked Chica up and plopped her around his neck like a scarf. The dog panted happily, barking as they approached the horses, and Daniel set the dog free. Chica sank, her ears brushing snow, as Daniel picked her up again.

Perhaps, Ellen thought, she should do "the assessment," evaluating Daniel. He had strengths. He wasn't always a judge. He built fires. He tended the stock well. He could read landscapes he'd never been in before. And he didn't always grouse. She must remind herself that he had merits. As did they all.

"Do you have an extra shawl?" Daniel asked Ellen.

"Whatever would you want it for?"

"I want to make a pouch for Chica. Snow beads build up in her paws."

"I've been thawing them with my bare hands." Why was she feeling defensive? Maybe because Daniel had thought of a solution that she hadn't?

"I have one," Beth said. "You can tie knots to your heart's content and put little Chica inside, when she tires of bouncing in the snow or you tire of melting the snow pearls, Ellen."

Daniel twisted and tied until he had a bag that could hang on the saddle horn. They plopped a not too happy Chica inside. "She'll like it better after she's had cold feet," Ellen said.

Ellen added "kindness" to her assessment of Daniel during the evening rituals accomplished despite the cold and cumbersome snow. She had time to think of her family and prayed, something she hadn't been as faithful with as she might have. Time didn't move steady as a clock's ticktock but instead melded all the minutes and hours into a single block called "quest to keep each other alive."

9

Protecting Treasures

Maolisa shivered in the cold inside her wagon. She made a mental list of what she might leave behind and what she couldn't do without. Junior returned to get his axe. "We'll cut logs, build a structure for the three who are staying. Move the materials inside and put the canvases on as a roof, maybe hides. Poor oxen won't get a day of rest. They'll have to help haul the logs and then raise them."

"Should we leave our little stove?" Maolisa didn't want to but felt compelled to offer. It wouldn't do to be selfish when others were sacrificing so much. She'd talk with Sarah Montgomery today, offer her tea and conversation, so she'd know she was welcome in any of the remaining wagons. Poor woman. Another single man staying behind might have been better, but Sarah's husband had all those guns he worried over.

"No. It's the only real weight we have, so if ye need to, ye can set it aside later. But for now, keep the stove. So long as we can find things to burn, green branches even, we can keep our little ones warm. And yourself." He leaned in to kiss her, lingered. Thirteen years of marriage and he still liked to smooch. "And our baby." He patted her burgeoning belly, then pulled down his tuque over his ears.

"We could invite Dr. John to ride with us. A new mother might well use the assistance of a good doctor."

"We'd be awfully jammered with so many."

"Same as Ailbe and James, who invited him, I hear."

"But you're carrying the sixth, Maolisa. You do enough for everyone, making sure the little ones have pemmican if nothing else. Ye made up enough for an army afore we left."

She nodded. "You take some of that now and be careful chopping wood. I don't want to tend a one-armed man nor find a foot bleeding at the toe."

"These brogans would resist." He was so proud of his boots. They'd spent good money on footwear and she was glad now. Especially in this horrifically deep snow.

"Off with you then. And no accidents."

She felt a little selfish about his boots. Keeping one's feet dry and free of blisters was a treasure few knew they ought to seek after. Guilt nudged her as she watched Mary Sullivan with her younger siblings trudge to the latrine area. They were waifs almost, orphans for certain. Mary Sullivan wore a tuque and spoke French with ease, and they had some Quebec connections but traveled without any extended family like the Murphys had. Even the Montgomerys had family, adopted as they were, by the Townsends. She sent a prayer for Elizabeth Townsend and her sister-in-law, Ellen Murphy.

Maybe while the men built a cabin, she could use their little stove to bake bread for the Sullivans. She had flour, salt, and water aplenty. One ought never be idle. People started imagining things going wrong in idleness. She crossed herself and set to work.

Horseback Party

Ellen wondered if the rest of the party might actually be following behind them. After all, if they tried to take wagons over the pass and couldn't, wouldn't they then take the horse party's route? It would make the most sense. She'd twisted in her saddle to look behind her, but all she saw were the servants and pack animals and the vast white of snow-laden trees drawn like an artist's rendering against an azure sky. She turned back, ducked beneath an evergreen branch, hoping not to knock snow onto her neck. She looked forward to their evening camp—which they made not far from a deep tree well that snowdrifts had formed around the base of the big pines. Branches laden with white had kept the snow from building up too close to the trunk. The ground was fairly level and wind had brushed some of the snowfall aside. Still, they had to be careful about those tree wells. The snow at the base was eight feet below them in places. The sight reminded them that, like a giant wedding cake, they rode atop layers of snow.

"Hey! Give that back." Ellen reached for the red tuque that Joker, Moses's horse, had pulled off her head as she bent over to get the grain bag. They were camped for the night, the third since they'd left the main party. The horse waved the woolen hat like a flag between his teeth. "Come on." She laughed until he tossed the hat to Chica, who picked it from the snow and like a hopping rabbit, bounded off with it, circling around. "You two. Chica!" The dog leapt through the snow, fluffy as whipped cream. Then he circled back to her and gave up the prize. She pulled it tightly onto her head, cold having settled in an instant onto her ears without it. She bent again to the grain bag, only to have Joker grab the hat again, wave it in his teeth, then toss it to the dog.

Now she was annoyed.

Tired, cold, irritated, wanting to grain her horse, then sink onto the tarp the servants spread onto the snow. But no, she had to play with the pets. She rubbed Joker's velvet nose, spoke to him, and he nuzzled her. "Chica wants attention, do you?" The dog sprung back and she bent to pet him, retrieved her hat. It was hard on all of them, this journey. So easy to forget that these two were more than beasts to be used. They needed tending too.

At first the horse party had ridden near the top of the ridge, seeing the lake while they rode. The water filled the bottom of a cauldron, as John called it. Ellen thought it sparkled like a bowl in a basin sunk into a washstand. That day, they'd ridden just below the lip, often at a steep side angle, easing their way around, hoping to pick up another river heading south. Even she sometimes felt she was going to slip off the sides. She'd be sure to tell Moses when she saw him again how grateful she was for the use of such a surefooted animal as Joker.

"Come here, Chica." The dog sped past her, but Ellen foiled her plot with her hand. "You'd rather play than eat, you two. No wonder Moses calls you Joker." The horse lifted his head up and down as though agreeing with her, snapping his halter, then curled his lips up over his teeth and looked like he would laugh. She didn't know horses had a sense of humor. Maybe he could teach lessons to her brother. Maybe *she* needed that lesson herself. She was usually so cheery. The terrain had scraped her of it, the cold air hurting her lungs when she inhaled. Poor Beth must be miserable. Ellen breathed into the nostrils of Joker. "You're a good boy," she said. She patted his neck, his hair thickened by the cold. "Let's get you fed."

Back at the camp, Daniel's morose temperament added to Ellen's malaise. Being around him felt like a fog that rose from the lake, dark and wispy. Gray clouds scudded across the sky. Perhaps he felt the weight of responsibility for them all. Or maybe he was still angry that he'd been sent to be her keeper. She was easy enough to deal with. She couldn't get into any trouble here, trying to stay alive, keeping Beth's spirits up. He just cast a spell over them all. If they ever found a private moment, she'd ask him about it.

The alliance of horse and dog ended when Joker crunched in his grain bag. Ellen headed to where the rest of them sat. Beth's eyes lit up when Ellen asked how Spotty was to ride.

"Not like my rocking chair, but good."

Oliver melted snow and prepared to put the heated water and tea into the copper samovar. Beth had insisted on bringing the awkward Russian item with them. She hadn't asked for much and Ellen had overheard her telling Dr. John that he didn't ever use it and she would. They'd have tea, dried elk, and hard biscuits for supper. It was what they'd had the last evening too. And when they broke their fast that morning. Just not the hot tea, which was a glorious luxury they reserved for themselves in the evening.

"Spotty's backside is better than walking," Beth added. "I don't think the saddle fits him well, though. I feel precarious on it, if you—*gasp*—want to know the truth."

"Maybe we should stop now and then to tighten the cinch. Spotty has lost some girth."

"The saddle fits fine," Daniel said.

"I'm sure you're right, Mr. Murphy." Beth never called him Daniel. Neither did she disagree with anything he said. She looked at Ellen with eyes that told her silence might be best at this moment.

Ellen turned the little brass handle at the base of the samovar. The scent of the black tea with maybe a hint of something she couldn't name filled her nostrils. "We're at a Russian teahouse," she said. "There are tapestries of gorgeous colors, silks and satins, wools of splendor and dancers in flowing gowns to entertain us while we drink our tea and eat . . . caviar."

Daniel snorted, but John said, "Wouldn't vodka be better than tea for entertainment?"

"Oh, but surely vodka softens the senses," Ellen said. "Not that I would ever know, 'tis certain."

"We wouldn't want to miss out on caviar's taste," Beth said. "Though I find it somewhat bitter myself."

"I've never tasted it," Ellen said. "Nor vodka."

"Didn't Matthew sell vodka and other spirits at the mercantile?" John asked.

"Oh, did he? I don't remember." She sipped. "Maybe we should tell stories of real parties we've attended, say what we liked most about them. François, in Quebec, how did you celebrate St. John the Baptist day?"

"Always very warm," François said. "*Juin,* twenty the five, always. Very festive." He spoke in English as Ellen had, for Beth's sake.

"June. Yes, I can hardly wait. I miss summer," Ellen said. "When we find it again, I'll never live with snow. Old Greenwood says California is like eternal summer."

"It'll be our home forever as well," Beth said. "This tea is warming me through and through. Thank you, Oliver. And for the jerky. A feast, fit for a queen."

"*Oui, madame.* The *mademoiselle,* she likes the tea with the ginger flavor?"

"That's what that is. Ginger. *Oui.* It's very good," Ellen said. "You're so sweet to have brought it with you. Hmm." She grinned at the servant, whose ruddy face turned a deeper brown. Both men had once worked for her and Matthew before Matthew's death and Beth's greater need for assistance. She'd known them in Quebec and they'd come with the Murphys when the family moved to Missouri. A little older than she was, both servants were enthusiastic, strong. Gentlemen.

"She's a madame, not a mademoiselle," Daniel corrected.

"*Oui,* I am forgetful." Oliver looked away.

"I was married, but now I'm not, so I am perfectly content to be known as a single lady."

"Then act like a lady," Daniel said. "Instead of a cow in heat."

Beth gasped.

Ellen's eyes grew wide as his words stabbed. She took a deep breath. "Our mother would never have said such a thing for merely acknowledging another's kindness about tea. Now, I would like to return to imagining Quebec in June with cakes and pastries and Mama singing with Papa to the accompaniment of the bodhran." She sipped her tea, her hands shaking. "Oh, how they loved to dance, remember, John?" Her brother nodded. "Once she jumped so high her petticoat exposed her knees and everyone hooted. We all giggled, even you, Daniel, if you remember it."

Daniel looked at the tin mug he cupped in his hands but nodded his assent.

"We used to laugh often, before Mama passed. I think she'd want us to do that again. Even animals play." Ellen told them then about the hat and Chica—now lying beneath the overhead tarp—and the tricks the two animals had played on her.

"I will roll up in my bedroll with that happy thought," Beth told her. The days were so short now, darkness had fallen on them. "If you'll help me." Ellen rose to assist the woman to relieve herself a short distance from the camp, holding her skirts out to screen her from the men. They returned and Ellen wrapped Beth in her wool. She snugged Beth's head with a knitted tuque. "Thank you for your help." She inhaled. *Is her breathing getting better?* "And taking our thoughts to dancing and June, and that Joker and Chica have formed an alliance, all an excellent end to the day." She patted Ellen's hand, held it, and squeezed it.

"I just wish Daniel wasn't so grumpy."

"Something haunts your brother," Beth said. "He carries anger, swallows it, licks his lips without knowing he is eating himself. He is in need of laughter. He doesn't know what wealth lies within it. Be patient with him."

Ellen nodded. She spread out her own bedroll, lamented the strong scent of her own body with days passed without washing. Horse smells on her gloves. Her lips felt dry, but she was too tired to care. Chica pushed her way between Ellen and Beth. Ellen spoke her prayers, trusting that God would not mind that she did not kneel. She asked for blessings and sought her dear Lord's providence and protection. She did a shortened version of the rosary. Chica licked her chin and Ellen smiled.

In all her years of living—twenty now—Ellen hadn't thought that spreading kindness was any kind of gift, but like Joker making her laugh and Chica making her smile, it was. She would feast on joy, unlike Daniel, who ate anger. And she'd start counting up treasures, small ones, like jokester pets and hot ginger tea poured from a samovar in the middle of the wilderness.

"We'll build our own shelter," Moses said. "Let's get the wagons you're taking up over the summit."

Sarah wouldn't even be able to see where she was leaving her husband? Just the terrain? It might be her last look at him.

"We can make short shrift of a shelter. Say that fast three times." The men chuckled at Martin Murphy's jest.

"I think Moses is right," Capt said. "We've got sunshine. Let's take advantage of it and move these wagons up and through."

Sarah had gone from being hurt to sad to furious to exhausted. She'd spent the day with the other women, shifting and sorting. They began the trek up the mountain but didn't get far, so Sarah had the night to spend with her husband. The last evening. How could Allen set her adrift with the others, impose her upon the Sullivans or the Pattersons? Yes, she could help Isabella with her brood, but she had hoped to start a brood of her own with a husband at her side. They hadn't even been married a year!

What if after they left him behind she found out she carried a child? She couldn't assume anything by her monthly patterns. Their food had been limited and their exertion so great that the timing of her flow had no predictability. The Murphy women said as much about their monthlies. Maybe she should tell Allen she was with child, maybe then he'd see the need to keep her with him, there, in this meadow beside a lake beneath trees dusted with snow. But no, he'd point to Maolisa looking like she could deliver any day and say that she was wisely going forward with a party where the doctor could tend her.

She had no arguments left. She'd try silence.

"I know you're upset, Sarah. But I'm too tired to argue anymore." He'd come to the wagon, sank onto the bed exhausted. She hadn't said a word.

She jabbed her needle into the fabric that would one day be a quilt. A Log Cabin pattern with matching strips of fabric stacking up like the logs on each side of the cabin they'd build after she was gone. *How ironic. I've designed a quilt to be a constant reminder of Allen's existing in a rough structure he prefers over living beside his wife.* How high would they make their shelter? Would Allen have to bend to stand? What about chinking? What would they use?

Should she take the unfinished quilt with her?

She fed him silence, then saw that he fought to stay awake. She was torn between seeing his weariness and wanting to comfort him and resenting that he could sleep while she was so obviously upset. Wasn't this their last night together?

"Allen. Allen." Her voice gained strength.

"What? Oh, sorry." He wiped at his eyes, pulled his hands over his bearded face. "Thank you for the meal."

"Help me not see that you care more about your guns than about me," she said. "Just help me understand that."

"What?" He shook his head, sighed, patted the bed that she might sit beside him. It was harder for him to dismiss her when she was in front of him, challenging. Sitting beside each other dissipated the outrage into the air without hitting each other in the face. Sarah stood.

"It's about our future. I'm sending you where you'll be safer than with me. Can't you understand that?"

"But why wouldn't you want me with you?"

"I do, I do. But it will be hard enough to feed ourselves, keep warm. I'd be worrying about you every minute if you were stuck with the three of us."

"You'd worry about me?" She hadn't actually thought of that.

"Of course. The guns, the extra ox shoes, the axes, things I hoped to start our life with, happen to be the heaviest of any of the valuables. If it wasn't for that, I'd trudge on, but staying means in the spring, when the snow melts, Capt will send a relief party back. You'll go on ahead and find the perfect site for our own cabin we'll build together. In California. Now, can we get some rest?"

"But what if—" She hesitated, fearing that speaking a possibility made it more real. "What if you . . . die?"

"The others will bury me, and when Townsend and Capt bring back oxen to rescue us, you can come with them. You'll mark my grave or find me happily waiting for you, though skinnier I suspect. Either way, you'll move forward, be a wealthy woman."

He diminishes my worries.

"As if your treasures were of more value than you."

"They're only worth anything for what they can do for us, for you—if you're required to go on alone. You won't be alone, darlin'. You'll have Beth and Dr. John and they'll help you start a new life. But this is morbid talk, Sarah. You'll make it and so will I."

"You don't worry about my dying?"

"Do you think I don't? That's why you can't stay behind with us. You'll do better in a group. Capt will take you under his wing. I've already talked to him about it."

He really was looking out for her. She sat down beside him. "I've some salve for those hands," she said. He nodded and she pressed the paste against his knuckles, dabbed at his cheeks, forehead. He even had a cut on his ear.

"That one hurts the most," he said. "But it bled good. I have to watch how I'm pushing the wagons."

He turned to her and she smiled back. His eyes watered and he held her then, drops of tears falling on her cheeks too. He kissed them away. "I'll miss you terribly," he whispered. "Please know that. But I know you'll be safer than staying here."

She nodded, acceptance settling like a threadbare cloak over her shoulders: it offered comfort but without the warmth. The real treasure was this moment when she felt loved and cared for more than she had since the day they'd married. She guessed it would be her anniversary gift.

10

Faith and Forward

Capt could see the lake behind them. The six wagons they'd left were but dots in the distance. When the three Wagon Guards finished helping them through this pass, they'd return to the guns and silks and blacksmith tools and make some kind of shelter out of them. He waited to hear from Greenwood and his sons, who had been gone for two days, praying with the Murphys that the pilot would find a way through the mountain wide enough for an ox, if not a wagon. It was their best hope.

They'd dragged the five remaining wagons up the ridge, steep as a tent's side. The terrain forced a straightforward track through the mud and slush, with no worries of the wagons rolling backward. Everyone stomped through the snow, but at least the sky was clear. Then today, they faced that stone wall thirty feet high and had to stop. They waited for the Greenwoods.

They built a fire, stood around it in the cold, the sun out, near setting, giving little warmth in nearly four feet of snow. Capt noticed most faces had wrinkles between the eyes from squinting against the brilliant white world surrounding them. "It's obvious. Guess I don't have to say it. Your suggestions, gentlemen."

"I thought you'd been through this country, Stephens." He expected Townsend to be the first to complain. "How did we end up here at this staggering rock face?"

Old Man Martin responded. "The fact of how we got here makes no difference. We're here. What do we do about it is the issue."

"Much obliged for your support, though sorry it's needed."

"*Oui, nous sommes ici*, my friends. What is, is," Martin Murphy Sr., the clan leader said, his breath like smoke. "We must face the reality of what is before us." Martin Murphy's faith had brought him to this place, family in tow. He understood—Capt hoped.

"Wait until the Greenwoods return, that's all we can do," one of the Murphy sons said. "I don't see how getting these things up and over that rock face makes sense, even if we could do it. Use up too much energy. I say leave everything but what we can carry with us and go around by foot."

The bodies of women and children buried in the snow flashed before Capt's eyes. He blinked it away.

"There has to be some option besides that," James Miller said.

Martin Murphy said, "I believe we are here at the Lord's command, so he will not leave us without a way through."

"Maybe we should go back to the lake," Sarah Montgomery said. "We could build shelters there and wait out the winter with Allen and Joe and Moses."

Capt looked in that direction. "I've considered that. Who knows when spring will come? We'll end up eating our stock if we go back. We don't have enough ammunition to hunt straight through until the alpine flowers bloom. And we've seen no tracks. Elk and deer have already left this high country when there is this much snow."

"Perhaps we could go afoot, some ride the horses," Isaac Hitchcock offered. This man had spent time in the wilds, so Capt took his suggestions seriously. Still . . .

"Too many women and children. They wouldn't survive." Capt felt a jolt in his stomach when he said those words. It was his job to bring these people through. They were counting on him to keep them alive and bring wagons with them.

"And we get no closer to our destination, the purpose of this journey." The doctor spoke again. "You promised to get wagons into California. We voted you the leader."

"And so he is. We must listen to him." Martin Murphy's sharp words—rare for him—silenced the good doctor, though Capt thought not for long. "Do you have an idea, Captain?"

Capt could feel the chill on his body with them stopped like this, sweat and cold mixing a deathlike liquor. "If Greenwoods find a cleft, we'll take the animals through, lower chains and ropes and use the animals to haul the empty wagons up over the rock. We'll have to carry all our goods. It'll take a couple of days."

A period of silence filled the vastness. Then Martin Murphy nodded. "Don't seem humanly possible to do such a thing, but all things are possible through him that trusts the Lord."

"We could send out another search party." This from Mary Sullivan. When had she shown up? "It would give us more information."

Capt shook his head. "Greenwoods are the best. If they fail us, we will abandon the wagons and follow the horse party route." They'd have to turn back: all of them, reload, regroup, return, take the women and children the way the Townsend and Murphy women had gone and hope the children would survive. "We'll wait until morning to decide, hoping Old Greenwood and his boys are back with good news." With that, the group disbanded.

Captain Stephens had believed they were making gains within this mountain of rock and snow. He estimated they were at nearly the 8,000-foot altitude. The children were silent, something that concerned him. Probably cold but also worn out from the harder breathing and fighting the snow. Their mothers too, carrying them to lighten the load on the animals as they trudged along.

These families supported each other and that gave him strength as well.

He finished the coffee Joe heated for him. At least he didn't have to say goodbye to the young man just yet. "I'm gonna talk to Martin." The senior Murphy's steady faith comforted Capt. Joe nodded. On the way Capt decided he'd ask the old man to say a prayer or two for the Greenwoods, that they'd find a passage through the mountain and make their own feet like hind's feet, able to stand upon a fierce rock—or find a way through one. An icy wind bit at his bearded face. He tied his wool scarf around his face so only his eyes showed. He really didn't want to turn back.

"A reprieve from saying goodbye," Mary Sullivan told Sarah. The two women had squatted beside the Sullivan wagon, a small fire offering little warmth. Allen had gone off to talk at another fire. Mary tried to imagine what the impending separation would be like for the young wife.

"If I thought it meant more time to change Allen's mind, I'd be grateful. But he's almost anxious to get back to his guns, ready to build that cabin and start life without his wife around." Sarah sighed. "He acts like it's one of his hunting trips where men will shoot and eat and tell themselves stories. If we all decide to take the horse party route, he'll be disappointed, I think."

"Men like to challenge themselves. My brother told me he wished he was staying too."

"He does? He'd let you be on your own?"

"He wanted me to take my younger brothers and go with Miss Murphy and Mrs. Townsend. He would have allowed that separation. But I . . . overruled him." Mary ducked her head. *I mustn't sound prideful.* "He won't let me be on my own unless it's his way. But he also won't let me forget that he has to 'take care of me.' I take care of myself."

"We women all do." Sarah brushed snow from the hem of her

heavy skirt, pulled up her socks. "I like a challenge myself now and then, but to learn something new, get my brain working rather than making my body earn bunions and blisters."

"Surviving the winter in a makeshift cabin in the wilderness probably does involve both mind and matter," Mary said. "Your Allen will discover that."

They stared at the rock ahead, framed by the wagon's opening.

"Formidable," Mary said. "I hate the thought of turning back."

"Indeed."

"I think that's the Greenwoods," Mary said and she stood. "And there are only two."

Seeing Old Greenwood with a grin caused Capt's relief—short-lived though it was. "It ain't wide but we led the horses through it and there was a little room, so the ox's horns'll scrape the sides but they can make it. Won't like it. Have to be gentled through. Probably good that they're thinner than when we started," Old Greenwood added.

"We rode by it twice," his son said. "Pa and us'n headed here to bring the bad news when Britain looked behind. The light hit the rock funny, made a shadow. We turned back to check it out and there it was. Like a door stuffed with snow but opening just a crack."

"Praise God." Martin Murphy crossed his heart. Capt nodded. He'd have to take this praying thing more seriously.

"We left Britain there, so's we wouldn't lose sight of the cleft again."

"How far from here is it?" James Miller asked.

"Mile, mile and a half around the base."

"That's doable for the women and children. And the depth of the opening?"

"Forty-fifty feet through the narrows, then it widens. We wound our way up to the top."

"We just abandon all the wagons?" Townsend spoke up.

"No. We drop chains from the top," Capt said. "Haul each wagon up that way."

"Believe so." Old Greenwood spit his tobacco.

All eyes turned again to the rock face.

"We'd best get going," Capt said. "Unload. Everything will be carried, but we get the oxen through first. Start with the strongest."

"Those would be ours," Mary Sullivan said. "And I'm going to lead them."

Mary knew what she had to do. She'd stood awaiting her fate by decisions of the men, as was her usual pattern. She stomped her feet to keep warm, checked on her younger brothers. Even children—boys at least—were closer to the inner circle of men talking than the women were allowed to be. They'd get told the result when all decisions were made. Seemed foolish to her to ignore half the members of the group. Sarah had had to speak up to offer her suggestion and it hadn't been heeded. Mary didn't expect it to be.

But faced with an inhuman task, she'd found a challenge worthy of a Sullivan. If they succeeded, there'd be stories of great endurance to tell. She guessed the entire trip could be such a story, but the idea of them getting wagons up and over that rock face was an astonishing achievement. She felt . . . invigorated, odd as that seemed to her. The preceding demanding days had been drudgery, but this, this would be a remarkable feat—if they accomplished it. *What choice do we have?*

"Let your brother John lead," Capt shouted after her. But she'd already headed toward their wagon and began unhitching Pierre.

"Mary. You can't. Let me take them." John tried to push her aside.

"You bring Prince or take the harness. Pierre and I are going through." John was speechless. She supposed that radical actions did silence men unaccustomed to dealing with a woman with a singular cause.

"My brother's bringing the mate," she announced as she led the animal by the captain standing with his mouth open. She carried grain in a bag over her shoulder—they didn't have much left. "Point the way," she told the younger Greenwood.

"Just follow our tracks," he said.

Sometimes one just had to take the ox by the horns, she thought, and smiled.

The animal followed her as she tugged on the lead rope, and she heard the sounds of others getting their stock moving. She wasn't tired at all. She hadn't been as awakened by anything like this except that summer she had taken a canoe on the Gatineau River after John told her she couldn't. Or rather she shouldn't.

"You're a fool," he'd said. They'd stood at the shoreline where the river ran smooth, but she could hear the rush of rapids farther along before the river joined up with the Ottawa in western Quebec.

"We could both go, see who gets through the rapids first."

"Why is everything a competition with you?" John scowled.

"It isn't. Not really. I just like the . . . excitement. It beats looking for eggs and feeding chickens."

"You'll have that. Those rapids twist and fall, swirl around rocks and threaten any craft bold enough to try to pierce their watery flesh."

"Have you ever run them?"

"No. Foolish, like I said." He'd kicked at pebbles on the shoreline. Was he actually worried about her?

"Well, I'm going to do it."

"Mama and Papa won't like it."

"They'll never know."

"If you die, they'll figure it out."

Mary was a strong swimmer, so if she did get plunged into the water, she was sure she could survive, let the current carry her into calmer water and slosh her way to the tree-and-rock-lined shore. But yes, there was the risk of losing her life.

It had been a harrowing ride, water splashing, the roar of the water plunging over rocks pounding in her ears. The current shot like an arrow through narrow channels that threatened to spin her and her craft around. Her heart pounded and she wanted to whoop with the sheer ecstasy of facing danger. She didn't think about death.

And she'd succeeded.

She'd lost all that drive to feel life fully when her parents had died. An enemy she had no power over had won. Riding the river rapids had been the last time she'd felt excitement. Everything since then had simply been work. Grief. Giving in, letting John have his way about what they'd do—coming west, which fork in the trail to take. She hadn't blamed him for the struggle on this journey. She'd been . . . apathetic.

The ox bawled and balked. "Come on, Pierre," she said. The snow was fluffy and her thighs were tired. She yanked her skirt hem up into her waistband, making a pants-like arrangement. It would be easier to clamber through. Ahead stood Britain, the Greenwood brother.

"You lost?"

"Just the first to arrive. I'll follow you." They entered the shadowed granite lane. The ox's horns did scrape the sides and Pierre resisted. "Come on, boy. It's all right. I'm right here." She scratched the ridge between his eyes. "Come." She used her firmest voice. Pierre moved again. Just needed a little encouragement. Mary smacked her lips with the glycerin she'd put on that morning. Such a little thing, the scent of it. She'd forgotten small treasures like the smell of a river rock in spring or the racing of her heart when she canoed through calm waters but could see white water in the distance, could feel her craft moving more swiftly, being pulled toward as-yet-unseen waters she had no control over. Just like now.

Pierre sped up. When paired, Pierre had carried an extra iron pad around his neck, and Mary could see the scars from equipment meant to keep him from open sores. Mary had treated them, but it was Captain Stephens, weeks before, who had pounded out an iron neck piece to lay beneath it that had saved the beloved ox.

"Mama and Papa," she said. "You never knew it, but once, I conquered a river rapid. And now I'll defeat a mountain." Pierre bawled again, but he kept following her, one foot in front of the other. It was how they'd all meet the next challenge.

11

We Are Here, I Am Here

Sarah thought Mary Sullivan looked as sweet as butterscotch when she grinned—which she had as she led her ox first toward the cleft. Mary hadn't even waited for their wagon to be called. She headed out before anyone could stop her. That was probably the best way to make something happen: act and deal with the consequences later.

Sarah began unloading the Sullivan supplies, removing her own things first. She noticed men unhitching the forward wagons after pulling as close to the base of the mountain as they could. The Sullivan vehicle pitched at an angle several back from the front. All but a few oxen would be taken through the cleft, leaving one team to pull each wagon closer to the base. Sarah carried food packs, quilts (those were essentials), sweaters. Some of the Sullivan essentials she removed and piled in the snow. She'd come back for them later. She encouraged the little boys with their shoulder sacks to wait. Then after Allen dragged harnesses through the cleft, she and the boys entered the dark, narrow alley.

Sarah's stomach growled and she longed for a flake or two of maple sugar, but she couldn't take any out of the mouths of the

Sullivan boys, or anyone else for that matter. The Canadians had brought maple cones with them and Mary Sullivan had been generous with sharing the brown pyramids. When they got to California, Sarah determined she'd never be without maple sugar. Nor butterscotch. She'd packed butterscotch candies but had none left. She couldn't believe she'd eaten them all, but then sometimes she did mindless things without realizing it, especially around food. Even worse was that she never felt full, never knew when her meal was "over." Maybe she was pregnant? No, it was more that she didn't know how to end her eating. *Or maybe end anything? What do I hang on to?* These past weeks, with rations being questioned given the delays on the trail, she'd paid more attention to what she was eating, savoring it as the larders shrank. Once she had a flake of maple sugar, though, she always wanted more. She shook her head. She had to stop, think about something else. Then Allen came to her mind again and how she'd soon be missing him. She ached so hard that thinking of food seemed easier.

Isabella Patterson shifted her load carried at her hips and held her breath when they lowered the first chains, lengths to equal the drop over the side of the ridge. Men standing below, her father included, latched the chain to the wagon tongue, securing it with ropes too. She'd have thought they'd put the chains under the wagon like a harness, but the men knew how to make this work. Then the oxen above—she didn't know how many—began the laborious task of inching the wagon up the side of the rock face, wooden wheels screeching against the stone. She could hear the men shouting to the poor beasts to "Pull! Pull! Pull!"—as they never had before. If a link broke or it slipped, the wagon would crash to the bottom in splinters, so the rest of the party had to remain back a ways. The wheels clanked against the rock face, scraping up the side like brown beetles inching along.

Ailbe held her infant, little Ellen Independence, while standing beside goods from their wagon not yet carried around and up. The Miller wagon would be next.

Like everyone else's, the Miller goods would be hand carried. Featherbeds. Sheet-iron stoves. Trunks of clothing. Food boxes— lighter now than at any time on their journey. Bags of rice, corn- meal, what bacon they had left. Dried venison. All were stacked in a pile surrounded by snow that an occasional blast of wind whipped up so one could barely see. Isabella sighed and lifted her bag of flour onto her shoulder. "Lydia, Isaac, what can you carry?"

Two of her children dragged a box of clothing by rope han- dles. Once at the cleft, she'd have to pull it on through behind her. She watched the wagon scrape upward. Isabella thought of her dear husband, Andrew. He would have loved this spectacle, this act of man taming the landscape, conquering it. He'd say it was an American way of doing things, seeing something that needed to be done and not wasting time lamenting how the situ- ation had come to pass, laying no blame, simply reclaiming a goal. He had quoted the lyrical words of the poet Von Goethe who said that once one made a commitment to something, then "Providence moves and things begin to happen one might other- wise never could have imagined." Who could have imagined they'd be here at this juncture, facing this test? Her Andrew would have approved of how the group responded, with inven- tion and bravery.

How she missed that man! He was always creating things for her, humming at his work, doing everything he could to bring the eight children from his first marriage into the fold of their own five over the years. It had been awkward at times. He was older than her by quite a few years. His oldest child, Judson, was even older than she was when they married. More than once when Isabella and Andrew had walked on the streets of Jackson, Missouri, people had tipped their hat and said things like "Lovely daughter you have there, Patterson." She'd been mortified at first, but Andrew didn't seem to mind. He actually beamed, and once he'd said to her, "It's amazing to me that a woman like you would find solace with a man like me."

Solace. That was what she sought now. She didn't dare let herself think too far ahead to what they'd face in California. Of course, they had to get there first, but solace would be so lovely.

Her father had spent time in the mountains, trapping, though not into the California of the Spanish. It was odd that he had returned into her life just as Andrew left it. He'd helped her negotiate the estate, as Andrew had failed to leave a will and there were many claims by his first family—which is how she thought of those eight earlier offspring. They hadn't been unkind, but every dollar they took wrenched morsels from her children's mouths. Her father had been a godsend and she had trusted him when he said they could find land in the West, make a new life. She could midwife as she had in Missouri and in Tennessee before that. As Andrew had found satisfaction in his unique encounters, she had sought fulfillment in helping a woman deliver a child, being a part of those first signs of life. And she'd been gifted with that very opportunity with Ailbe Miller's baby born at Independence Rock on July fourth. She still remembered the first breath of the infant separate from her mother's when she'd done the unorthodox thing—she'd tickled the child's feet and the baby had gasped, took in air in surprise, rather than pain making her cry as a spank would have done.

"She'll be a happy child," Isabella had told Mrs. Miller, who had responded with a smile of her own and a "Well, I never . . ."

It was one of Isabella's trademarks, that tickling over spanking, and she believed pregnant women sought her out because of it. A gasp of surprise into life. And out. Andrew had looked up, a smile formed on his face before he said his last "Fare thee well" and then he was gone.

She heard the scrape of wheels against the rock face, men shouting. Then in what seemed like hours but was only part of one, the first wagon disappeared up and over the summit's edge.

Why wasn't anyone clapping with the success? Maybe they were waiting until all the wagons were claimed on top, but it was never too early to cheer.

She wouldn't wait. "Hallelujah!"

"What's wrong?" This from Dennis Martin, who had walked up beside her. "Are you all right, Mrs. Patterson?"

"I am indeed. I just think we should shout hurrah or hallelujah, don't you think? The first wagon survived its new trial."

Dennis shouted too then, and the men getting ready with the next wagon turned to him.

"Celebrate it!" Dennis said. "One down. Four to go."

It was like being a midwife, Isabella thought. One has to celebrate all along the journey and not just when the infant arrived.

Horseback Party

Ellen led Joker in the snow, insisting she could take her turn in the rotation of breaking the trail for the others. Before lay vast pillows of white, mounds and valleys darkened by shadows as clouds moved across the sky. Who knew how deep the snow was here? She poked with a branch before leading the animals forward. She tapped for something solid beneath them. Were avalanches possible in lands where deep snow met with fresh fluffy snow? She took a step forward, tapped with a stick, the rein held loosely in her hand. She'd been testing the terrain like that all day. *Safe. Step. Safe. Step.*

Joker' pulled back, slipped, knocked her off balance. "Whoa, whoa!" The reins burned through her hands as the big horse fell to his side, then slid down a steep angle to within a few feet of the edge of a tree well.

"Are you all right?" Daniel yelled from the end of the pack line.

Ellen's heart pounded, the cold air hurt her lungs as she shouted, "I'm going after him."

The rest of the group could see what had happened. The horse struggled and pushed, made grunting sounds but not squealing as though in pain. If he continued, he'd go into the well.

"Easy, Joker, easy." What had spooked him? It didn't matter.

"*Non*, let me." Oliver was the first to reach her.

"He knows me," Ellen insisted. "I'll see if I can get him calm enough to check him over, try to lead him back up."

He couldn't break a leg, he just couldn't. Moses would be devastated, but so would she. He was the strongest horse and had pushed the snow, making all of their paths easier. She started down, slipping, snow up to her waist, easing her way around the now broken lip of snow that had given out from his weight. She moved with care, hoping not to end up sliding as Joker had. Her boots sank into the white, her woolen skirt a nuisance. She wouldn't let herself think about what they'd do if the horse was fatally injured. "I'll be there, Joker. I'll be there."

When she reached him, sweat formed a white sheath on his neck. His eyes were wide, frightened, his head lifting, then lying back in the snow. Ellen clucked soft sounds, knelt, touched the horse's mane as he struggled, nickered. "No, no. Just be still." He lay on his side, nostrils opening and closing like a blacksmith's bellows. He pushed to get up again. "Shh-shh." Kneeling beside him, she ran her hand down his chest, his flank, his forelegs, talking all the while, then eased her way around to his rump to check his back legs, speaking as though to a frightened child. His tail lay cropped close almost under him, a sign of his fright, if not his pain. One false move and he could knock her over with his force right into that tree well. She could fall in and it would be a misery to get her out—assuming snow didn't follow her and suffocate her. She guessed it was eight feet deep. But not as big a misery as getting Joker out if he slid in.

She heard Daniel yell, "No!" She looked up and saw Chica bounding down through the fluff. The dog stopped at the horse's nose. Joker tried again to stand, but his eyes lost some of the fear he'd held from when Ellen had first touched him. His nose quivered. "I know, I'm scared too," she said. "Chica. Sit." As though the dog knew the danger they were in, she sat.

Ellen worked her way back toward Joker's head, never taking her mittened fingers from his skin. She knew the horse would struggle to rise, try to push his front legs up. She hoped she could calm him enough to get him standing—if he was able—with little disruption to what was around them. Then she'd lead him away from this tree well and on lower, downhill, at an angle until he was settled and maybe they'd find a level place to camp. If nothing was broken. Maybe the rest of the horse party would come down then too, making a wide berth around the section of snow that had collapsed. *Please, please let him be all right, let me lead him out. Keep the others from danger.*

"Come on, big boy. Step back, Chica." As long as the dog stayed near Joker's head, the little dog could distract the horse, keep him focused uphill, which was where Ellen now made her way. She reached for the reins, dark ribbons woven through white. She tugged gently on them. "Come on. You can stand now. It's all right. Good boy, that's a good boy."

Joker lunged to rise, pushed with his forelegs and the thrust of him and his own fear made his movements unpredictable. When he charged forward it was faster than Ellen had expected, the snow like quicksand, sucking at her and she couldn't jump out of the way. She felt her arm jerk as she held the reins and then she was lifted by the animal's head and shoulder, tossed aside like her old rag doll. She let loose of the reins and didn't even have time to scream as she put her hands out to stop her fall. Into the tree well. *Thud.* Followed by pain.

She heard more than saw Joker plunge out of her sight, heard Chica barking, then both were gone. At least she'd dropped the reins and hadn't dragged him down in with her. She gasped, tried to calm her own breathing. She wanted to cry.

"Are you alright?" John yelled.

"We'll get you out, mademoiselle," François shouted.

"Get the horse!" Daniel said.

Daniel would think that the horse was more important than she was and he was right. The horse carried more than her: her packs held grain in the saddlebags for the other animals, carried her bedclothes and the tent she and Beth used nightly. Joker was scared and in new territory. They might spend hours or days looking for him—if they found him at all. She couldn't think about that. She had to consider this position she was in. *"Je suis là."* I am here. *With a broken arm, from the feel of it.* There was nothing to be done except pray that François or her brother John or someone could find Joker. All, hopefully before dark.

"Darlin', don't be crying." Allen patted Sarah's back as she leaned into his chest. *For the last time.*

"I guess I've every right to cry, you making me a widow." She stepped away, wiped at her eyes with her bare hands. Her mittens hung on a yarn strung over her shoulder and under her cape so she wouldn't lose them.

"You're not a widow. It's just a temporary separation is all. We'll meet up in the spring and both have stories to tell. Here, put your mittens back on. Don't want to freeze your fingers off."

"What would it matter?"

"Sarah, Sarah." He tugged the mittens on, then reached for her again. "I'm doing this for us." She nodded, the movement offsetting her red-dyed wool tuque. "Believe me, please."

"What choice do I have?" She hiccuped. "Just . . . stay alive. Please." She felt like a loose thread in a world where being stitched together was all that mattered.

"I will."

Joe Foster and Moses tromped by and nodded toward Allen. "I've got to go," he said. With cold lips, he kissed her hard one last time. She gave all the warmth she could with her kiss back, wanted to hold him there forever. But then she stepped away. She'd separate first, to show him she was strong. He touched her nose, then turned and hurried after the two other Wagon Guards. He turned back once and she waved. "Bye," she shouted, but a gust of wind took her words into a whisper.

———

Maolisa Murphy, big as a water trough, carried her two-year-old Mimi on her hip while BD clung to her skirts as they stomped along the path worn now by oxen hooves, horses, and men, women, and children carrying what couldn't be loaded onto the backs of animals. She felt . . . disheveled. It had been disruptive enough of her routines just to come on this journey, and she'd kept as organized a "household" as one could in a four-by-ten-foot space. But this . . . paring down to even less, was troubling. She supposed the group didn't each need a Dutch pot. They didn't *each* need a reflector oven. Those were heavy items and it wasn't as though they were a separate family now. Everyone was in this together. She'd realized that when Mrs. Townsend and her sister-in-law Ellen had ridden off and the remainder—everyone—had wished them well, said their farewells and waved goodbye. That horse party formed a new family, and that meant all those left behind were part of another.

And she felt that keenly as Isabella Patterson walked with Maolisa's children, her own big enough to carry objects while Isabella carried BD now and then. "I thank you so much," Maolisa told her. "I don't think BD could make it much longer without your help."

"Happy to help. My own Lydia's a good assistant, aren't you, Lydia?" The Patterson girl turned and nodded agreement. She'd been trudging along in front of Maolisa, carrying the salt bag, what was left of several families adding to one supply container. They'd done the same for saleratus, beans, and coffee. Coffee beans had been ground, and the little grinder she adored, one given her by her own mother, had been left behind. Maybe it could be picked up in the spring when they came back for the wagons and the three men left at the lake.

She had to stop frequently. The trail wasn't exactly level and it rose a few feet, so at times she felt like she was carrying a barn up from a riverbank. She had actually looked longingly at the chains bearing the wagons up and over. Maybe they could haul her up that same way. But they hadn't. She'd eased through the cleft and up to the summit like everyone else. She hadn't mentioned her longing for a shortcut using chains. Junior would have thought her daft and risking the baby to be hauled up in such a way. Very unladylike too, she imagined.

"I wish we could have been in a wagon, Mama. Let them pull us up into the sky," a younger Patterson girl said. The children all had a trace of English accent like their mother's.

"You put the very words I was thinking into my ears," Maolisa told the girl. The Pattersons all had hair as black as tar. "Only I was thinking, just put that rope under my arms and lift me up."

"We could use one of those hot-air balloons," Lydia said. She had actually turned around and walked backward, facing Maolisa and her mother. Oh, to be so agile as to walk backward in the snow and not fall down.

"That we could," Isabella said.

"Big birds," BD said. He tugged on Isabella's skirt, catching himself as he stumbled.

"Yes, those hawks have noticed us, haven't they?" Isabella said. They were through the shadowed cleft and dragging themselves toward the gathering of wagons and animals at the top. The wind had picked up. Mary Sullivan stood beside the men, talking to the animals harnessed together to pull up the wagons. Poor girl had been working all day at the task.

"Miss Sullivan says her name means 'hawk-eye.' I'd like a name that meant something," Lydia said. That these children could carry on conversations when she had all she could do to breathe amazed Maolisa. Oh, the joy of youth.

"In Gaelic, Patterson means in part 'descendant from the little curly-headed one,'" Isabella told her.

"It does? I'll tell Miss Sullivan that." She reached to her woolen hat, as though touching her own curly hair.

Maolisa put her child down, pressed both hands against her back. She couldn't understand why she was so large now. She still had two months to go. Maybe she carried twins.

Isabella pulled her cape around her and then bent to lift BD again. "There you go. Climb up onto my hip. Pretend you're flying."

"You're a very slow bird," BD said.

"Barney! That's not nice to say. I'm sorry, Isabella."

"Don't be. He's right. I am a slow bird. But I'm still going, that's what matters."

"Yes, it does." Maolisa stopped then and looked back behind them. Miller children, Sarah Montgomery, Ann Jane—sisters and sisters-in-law—all snaked their way toward the open space on top of a mountain. Mary saw a river of grace. Dressed mostly in grays but for the reddish Irish capes of Johanna and Ann Jane and the blue-dyed wools of Sarah Montgomery's knitted sweaters, the family that followed lifted her spirits. All who had started were still alive. All had found a way to encourage each other. She hoped she contributed to that, hadn't become so self-centered with this babe-to-be-born that she'd neglected to be kind and generous. Her eyes teared up with the sight of them all. They were family now in the truest sense of the word. Their presence kept worry at bay—for the moment. She'd seen the supplies, all out in the open as people combined what they had. There was reason to worry.

12

Settling

Mary Sullivan sat on her bed in the wagon now on top of the mountain, while Sarah prepared a cold meal for them and the little boys. Her brother John was with the captain, almost taking Joe Foster's place helping Capt. Maybe he didn't want to express his frustration with his sister's bold behavior, at least not in front of Sarah.

Her daring invigorated her, while it infuriated John. She wondered, though, at the fleetingness of fulfillment, how it had to be constantly restored. At least for her. At this moment, she was just plain tired. No ability to repair either her brother's upset nor her own weakness at needing invigoration.

"You must be exhausted," Sarah said. She wore a heavy sweater knitted of dyed wool over her plain gray dress and clunky brogans.

"Aren't we all."

"I've worn this same sweater for the last week," Sarah said.

"You don't have to apologize to me for fashion faux pas." Mary had hiked her skirts between her legs and tacked them into her waistband. No one had batted an eye at her wearing something resembling a man's pants—except for John. It was just more practical when leading oxen and later as she helped the men maneuver the cold and wet-stiffened harnesses.

On top of the mountain, there'd been no trees to act as braces against the weight of the wagons being raised, so the animals bore the brunt of the effort, all while wearing heavy yokes and straining through snow. Without trees, there were no dry, dead lower branches for cook fires. They'd also had a cold camp after the three wagons had been lifted and restocked, with more items abandoned.

Mary rubbed her arms for warmth, grateful for the sweater her mother had knit for her. She felt . . . weak to need such comfort, then realized how warmth banished weakness. The hard work of snow stomping had actually brought enough heat into her body that she considered removing that sweater. But she hadn't. They had not brought sheep with them. Probably wise. They would have died in this weather or already have been stew.

"You certainly surprised everyone," Sarah said. Mary reached for a piece of hardtack. "I hope you don't mind my saying it, but you look so frail. I've worried about you. I even told my husband." Sarah's eyes widened as she mentioned her mate. "And yet you just charged right on up the mountain, first."

"That rock face seems to have brought out my granite side," Mary said. She adjusted her tuque, tucked her rounded braids up under the wool.

"Let's get those wet clothes off you into something dry."

Mary could barely lift her arms over her head they were so sore. The tenderness with which Sarah treated her made Mary think of her mother, the kindest woman she'd ever known. She hated it that someone said "God needed another angel, that's why he took her." Surely God had enough angels that he didn't need to take the Sullivans'.

After these past days, Mary felt as though she traveled through two worlds—a world of men and animals and another of women and children. It was a side of her she hadn't considered. Or maybe she had, that time of canoeing in Quebec. Racing the rapids was more like moving oxen up the mountain, while knitting or quilting, or even looking after the plant seeds her mother had carted from Canada, these were activities that didn't get her heart pounding. She'd never excelled at them. It was a regret she carried that she hadn't perfected one of those feminine ways before her mother died, just to show her that she could. But her quilt blocks looked like a four-year-old stitched them. Her cooking was perfunctory too, not something she enjoyed though her brothers didn't complain. In fact, on this entire trip, she hadn't found any domestic tasks as invigorating as bringing those oxen up the mountain.

The sound of a child's laughter from another wagon reached them. Her own little brothers were nodding off even as wafer crumbs dribbled at their cheeks.

"Sorry there's no coffee or anything hot. Nothing to burn. But we have hardtack." Sarah handed her the biscuit as firm as rock. She sat and took a bite herself, using her back teeth, like a dog might, to rip at the hardness. She chewed. "This is good." Sarah held the biscuit up. "You'll have to show me how you made it."

"My mother prepared them. I've never been good at making hardtack or getting saleratus to rise the way my mother could. Nor stitching." She lowered her eyes. "I never even tried knitting."

"We all have our gifts," Sarah said.

There's probably something wrong with me that my body demands physical challenge to satisfy, while necessary functions of daily living leave me fatigued.

"I guess I haven't found my gift yet. I'll have to keep looking."

"Oh, I think this mountain showed us at least one of your strong offerings."

"I wasn't able enough to keep my mother and father alive." She looked up at Sarah, surprised herself with that comment. She hadn't known she'd thought it true, but now that she'd blurted it out, she did. She'd failed them, not having doctored them into wellness. Both their parents, happy and healthy at sunrise, gone by sunset.

"Cholera, didn't you say it was?" Sarah asked.

"Yes." Several had died just days before they'd left Iowa. "Our parents brought us from Ireland to the Provinces. And we lived well there. But Papa and John decided there'd be better things in California." She'd stopped adding the "Alta." She and her mother hadn't wanted to leave. If only Mary had been stronger then, resisted the men of the family.

"Maybe they tired of the longer darkened days."

"At least they didn't have to endure this winter. I suppose I ought to be grateful for that."

"See, there's another gift you have, finding the good in the deep of despair. That encourages me." Sarah tore off another chunk of her hardtack.

Mary chewed hers slowly too, making it last. Maybe carrying on despite grief was a hidden gift.

Capt thought about his farewell to Joe. The young man's face was a mass of black beard and his eyes teared up with Capt's words of gratitude about Joe's willingness to remain with Capt's wagons at the lake. "We'll be back in the spring to get you."

"Yes, sir. I'll be here."

"I know you will." He'd grabbed the boy's hand, put his other over the top, nodded his head. "All right, let's get this party on its way."

Short and sweet farewells, but the boy was like a son to him. Capt didn't know how you said goodbye to a child, so he'd been gruffer than he'd intended. He guessed he fought back his own tears. And that first night when he'd made camp without the boy—the young man—he'd missed him anew. Dennis Martin, not much older than Joe, had come by and offered his cold biscuit to share. John Sullivan had wandered in like a waif too. Dennis was one of the Irish-Canadians traveling with his elderly father and brother and a sister married into the Murphy clan, Ann Jane Martin Murphy. Poor woman. She had a hook nose like Capt's.

He'd thought he could keep all the Murphys-Millers-Martins straight after spending this much time together, but every now and then he'd realize that someone's wife was another clansman's sister. They were hardy souls, these Irish. He couldn't have picked a better group to lead—no, to travel with.

The first morning on top of the mountain, the reloaded wagons lined up anew—they'd only brought three up and over, the animals too tired to pull up the remaining two. Plus, Capt felt the demand to hurry on. Snow fell on them. Maybe some of the men should have returned to help the boys build their shelter, but they couldn't afford the time. Nor the energy it would take. He heard a woman singing a lullaby, one of those Irish tunes of *too-aloo-a-lura* that made him want to sway to the rhythm. Maybe that inhuman lifting of wagons to the summit was the last of their trials. He hoped so, hoped the same for Joe and his companions.

Wagon Guards

Moses, Allen, and Joe chopped saplings buried in deep snow. They attached them to the ox, asking the beast to drag their bounty toward their makeshift camp. Moses kept up with the more hardened men, urging the animal to do its work. The sky was duck-feather gray as they shoveled snow. They tore strands of green they gave to the two old cows left behind with them, animals too weak to go on. One of the cows had gotten sick. Moses didn't know what it was, but they'd butchered it when it died and ate it, then used the hide to cover the roof of their cabin. Moses wasn't worried. They were all good hunters. They'd have plenty of food.

While Moses didn't think it was necessary for them to have a leader as such, organization mattered. Someone like Capt Stephens looking out for them, fine. But with just the three men? Allen had suggested that he assume the position after the first night alone when they'd huddled together in featherbeds and under Allen's wife's quilts inside the wagon. Allen Montgomery was a lucky man to have a wife willing to leave behind such luxuries as feathers and fabric.

"We should designate a leader," Allen had said. "There'll be times when we disagree about what should be done or how to handle a particular problem, and while we should each state our position or concerns, we will inevitably come to a place of dissension solved only by a leader's final decision."

"We could vote," Joe Foster said.

"That doesn't always work when one person has greater knowledge, let's suppose, and then might get outvoted out of sentiment rather than experience. Not wise. Capt Stephens needed to take ultimate control, deciding it was best that we three remain here with the valuables. Voting on that would have been useless. No, sometimes there has to be someone willing to live with the responsibility of authority."

"But Capt always listened."

"As will I, Joe. We're in agreement then?" Moses and Joe shared glances. "I take your muteness as yeses." Moses didn't see himself as a leader. He suspected Joe didn't either, so why not Allen?

They'd made a frame for the saplings using wood from the wagons. Dr. John had packed an extra floor in his wagon and they lifted those boards to use as posts they laid the trees between, stacking them up to a height of six feet. Moses spied a couple of rifles and a small box between the boards but had no time to explore what was in it. He'd look later.

They spent the next day doing the same—finding saplings, dragging them back, stacking them. Branches were latched onto the saplings too. When four walls making eight feet in width were finished, with an opening for a door completed, they focused on a chimney of sorts. They didn't get it finished by the end of the second day. That's when the snow started falling, again. No designated leader could make it stop.

13

Little Gifts

Horseback Party

A well was a good name for the narrow, cold cylinder of snow Ellen had fallen into. She estimated that the walls rose six to seven feet high, the wind having pushed drifts up around the top. Snow-covered branches arched over, reaching the edge and protecting the inside from the accumulation of snow but filtering light too. Prickly cones the size of Daniel's boot length rested on needles that covered the floor. At least she was out of the wind. Her teeth chattered and pain seared through her all the way to her neck when she tried to straighten her arm. Perhaps it was just bruised. Yes, she'd tell herself that, even though she knew it was a lie. Pain could make a person tell stories to their bodies just to get them through.

Daniel's face peered over the side. He was lying on his belly. "Are you hurt?"

"Yes. My arm."

He swore. "How did you get in such a fix?"

"You saw what happened. It wasn't my fault. 'Tis no reason to be foul," Ellen said. Her teeth chattered. "Just go after Joker.

I'll be fine here through the night if you toss me a bedroll." She wouldn't be fine without a fire, without warmth, but she wouldn't beg him or let him know how scared she was.

"We need to get you out of there," John said. He now lay on his belly beside his brother. "François has gone after Joker."

"What about Beth?"

"Oliver is with her. She's fine," John said.

"Toss me a rope and haul me out of here then. My fingers are going numb."

"I just can't believe you let this happen." Daniel again.

"Look, Brother. *Je suis là*. Let go of how it happened and think of what we must do next," Ellen said. She tried to keep her temper despite Daniel's scorn. "Go to the other side, downhill, maybe."

"Why don't we break off the edge?" John said. "We'll push the snow into the well."

"Bury me?"

"Of course not." Daniel rubbed his face, his thinking gesture. "You pack the snow down, Ellen, stomp on it. Then we'll break some more off. If you keep packing it, you'll build up steps, almost. Just a few feet higher and we'll more easily get a rope around you and tug you up."

"It'll be better for your arm too," John said. "I'll get our shovel."

Steps. Up and out. It could work, more easily than attaching her to a rope and having one of her brothers' animals pull her out. Getting the rope under her arms would be a misery with the pain. Then they'd have to figure out what do to about that. She felt tears start. *Non!* She must not think beyond this moment or she'd collapse into sobs. She couldn't even think about Joker, lost and frightened in a strange place.

Ellen stood back when the first push of snow fell into the well. They'd pause and she would come forward and stomp, each footstep shooting pain up to her shoulder. She wished she had a heavy pair of clogs to tap the snow down. "Ready," she'd call up, step back close to the tree trunk, and wait for the next cascade of snow to come down. Each stomp made her arm throb. Once she slipped on the snow and fell over this new edge she'd built up inside the well. She gasped in pain. She'd had to ask them to wait. Which they did. She struggled to get up onto her step as it became higher, decided to make a sort of ramp for herself.

Then the shout. John first and then she heard François's voice. "What is it?"

"Chica brings Joker!"

She'd forgotten all about the dog! Poor thing. But she'd gone after Joker. She remembered that now, had briefly thought it was bad, that she chased the already frightened horse.

"The little *chien*, she has rein in her mouth and she leads the horse to me as I track them in the snow." François's voice vibrated with excitement and success. He leaned over the side. "It is well, mademoiselle. He is oh-kay, your horse. He is bruised but not broken. It is oh-kay."

"Yes. *Oui*, yes. It is good. Thank you, Lord, and François too."

His smile warmed her. "Now, we get you out. Maybe Joker helps, *oui*?"

"Maybe."

In the end, the men pulled her themselves, John coming down into the snow well to put the rope around her and help lift her up while the others tugged. Even Beth was there when they pulled Ellen over the side to the sound of Chica's bark, Beth's clapping, and the shouts of accomplishment. John put the rope around his own body, then walked himself up and out while Joker held the rope taut.

"Well, hello, little Chica." The dog licked Ellen's face as she sat, gathering strength for the next challenge—treating her arm. "And *bonjour* to you, my fine horse." Joker hung his head but moved toward her with a low nicker she took as contrition. Then he reached for her tuque. "No you don't. Not now." She clamped her hand on her head but that took the support from her left arm and she yelped.

"We need to make camp," Daniel said. "Now that this un-expected ordeal is over." He smiled, then covered it with "That's what I get for letting you go first. A girl simply can't lead."

She didn't rise to his disgust with her. Instead, she allowed her-self a few deep breaths before standing. "We'll have to figure out what to do about my arm. Make a sling perhaps."

"I will get the tent set up," Beth said.

Ellen looked at her. It wasn't likely she could do that as frail as she was, but the gesture meant a great deal to her. "Thank you. Oliver can assist."

"*Oui*. It will be my pleasure. There is a good place, where the little dog caught up with your horse. Level. No tree holes as you found, mademoiselle. It is not far."

They lifted Ellen onto Joker. He did seem fine, just tired. They headed downward following the horse's path until they found the clearing edged by trees.

"Both of you will rest now. I will set up the tent before the sun goes down." Oliver smiled at her as he helped her sit on the small folding stool she had brought along. Beth had one as well.

François assisted Beth, and the two women sat and watched the setting sun. Rest. Beth undid Chica's shawl and wrapped it around Ellen. "Don't want you going into shock." Beth hugged her gently. She wasn't alone, no longer scared of the bone-setting ahead. The dog licked her face. She was grateful for little gifts.

Wagon Guards

"Can't you hold that crosscut right?" Allen's words reminded Moses of Dr. John and his constant pushing for improvements or at least that Moses would do more things the doctor's way. It was their third day alone at the lake. They had waited for the snow to stop, but it had fallen for two straight days. This morning, they'd gone out hunting as soon as they finished the main structure but had seen no game. Now they were cutting logs for the chimney and dead lower branches of trees so they could keep the fire going longer before feeding it with smaller branches and limbs. They had matches but not that many.

"I'm using it as I was taught. Can't be too many ways to cut a log," Moses said.

"This isn't an axe, it's a two-man saw," Allen said. "We have to work together."

"What did you think I was trying to do?" Moses's voice cracked as he defended himself.

"Joe! Come take over for Moses. I'll be here all day unless I get someone who knows how to use a crosscut."

Moses wanted to say *And what else do you have to do?* He kept his mouth shut. He'd learned that worked best with Dr. John too. Silence and doing it his way.

Joe wiggled his bushy eyebrows at Moses as he came forward. "Capt told me there's an Indian tribe that makes a couple thinking of marrying work a saw, and if they can't find the rhythm to cut wood together, the elders won't allow the marriage."

Allen snorted. "This ain't any engagement party, I can tell you that."

Moses smiled. He liked that story. "No, but it does say something about people finding give-and-take if they're going to live together. And we do have to do that. At least for a while."

Allen sighed. "Yeah, OK."

"But I will happily hand over my end of the engagement saw to you, Mr. Foster." Moses bowed, swept his arm out as though bringing Joe to a finely laid table.

Joe bowed back, the men exchanged places, and Moses soon heard the *swish, swish, swish, swish* of the saw. Joe did hold it a little differently, and they didn't have to stop as Allen had with Moses.

Maybe he *was* the problem.

With several logs hauled back with their one sad ox, Moses

began notching to stack for the chimney they wanted ten feet high on the outside of the cabin. From the lake side, they dug loose larger rocks frozen into the ground that would act as the jambs and the chimney back. The rocks would heat up but keep from catching the logs on fire.

They left a door hole open at the opposite end. If it got too cold, Moses said they might hang some of Dr. John's fabrics. Or if some critter wandered in, they'd have it for breakfast. They were snug as a bug as could be, which was good because it began to snow again, such thick flakes they couldn't even see the lake. At least the weather had waited until they had a chimney. Small gift.

It had been the most grueling days of the entire trip. Capt Stephens had to not only lead this party through the impossible, but he had to tamp down the growing unease he carried in his own heart that they would not make it after all. Almost minute by minute he forced himself to put regrets aside, but it wasn't easy watching the women strain, children cry, animals bawl. The neat cows the Millers had brought—knowing there would be an infant born on this journey—had long ago stopped giving milk. The youngest—number fifty-one of the party—took all the nutrients from her mother. Both still lived. He was grateful for that. He just had to get the rest of them safely to California, where Mrs. Murphy could deliver her child in warmth. But the snow . . . so deep now and unceasing. Animals pulled through four to five feet.

Capt stopped to take a breath, turned back to check on the company. He surveyed the remaining wagons. At the pass, they'd combined the supplies. That way they had to hoist up fewer wagons. They'd started out with eleven wagons after the split at Fort Hall. They'd left six wagons at the lake with the boys and two at the base of the mountain, leaving them with three to service forty-two people: twenty-six men, eight women, and the remainder, children. They'd have to start slaughtering oxen for food, another reason to not bring all the wagons. At least now they moved toward lower elevations. The snow wouldn't be as deep. They could make it to Sutter's Fort by Christmas, he was certain. Well, God willing, he was certain.

Everyone walked now, the snow like white gunpowder, light and fine. But deep. And not frozen so snowshoes wouldn't help. He looked for a river. The old Indian, Truckee, had said there'd be one. *Had he called it Yuba?* It would be their watery guide taking them to Sutter's.

"I hadn't thought we could do it, Capt." Townsend led his horse up beside him. Usually the doctor stayed farther back, letting others break the trail. The snow here was at the oxen's chest, so they pulled wagons and pushed snow at the same time. The horses needed the trail broken for them and most had to be coaxed. Women and children brought up the rear. The youngest were inside the wagons for only short rides, pushed in amongst the tents and boxes and bags.

Townsend would want something. The man was a wanting sort of soul.

"One never knows until one tries," Capt said. "An old Indian once told me, 'When you come to a wide chasm—jump. It's not as wide as you think.' We had no alternative but to jump and so we did."

"Yes, yes, but that was still a difficult decision, especially leaving wagons behind." Both men breathed hard. "Do you imagine bringing stock back, in the spring, and lifting the ones you left?"

Capt noted that the successful part was a "we," but the leaving behind of wagons, that decision the doctor laid at Capt's feet.

"Hadn't thought that far. Just want to get this party to California. And come back for the boys, of course."

"Yes, well, I've been thinking that we should consider the return trip. Never too early to plan ahead, I always say." He cleared his throat, jerked the reins of the horse he led. "I certainly need my wagons of supplies and Montgomery will want his, of course.

And yours are there. But now there are some Martin and Murphy wagons too that will need rescuing from the mountain base."

"Something to think about. Later."

"Yes. However, I wanted to note that we contracted with you to get our wagons through to California, and now, you see, that won't be the case unless we come back. You get my point."

"I get your point. You can bring it up again when we're in Mexico territory. But for now, I'm keeping my contract to bring *people* through."

"Already not quite meeting the letter of that document though, either, not with the boys' fate unknown."

"Don't forget to count your wife's party."

"Oh, yes, of course. Just things to ponder, my good man."

What can I say to that?

"I'll just move aside here and let you get on with your work. I just thought we ought to have this little chat."

The man would probably sue him for the loss of his goods, which he seemed more concerned about than his wife's welfare. That wasn't fair, Capt told himself. Perhaps the man was worried about his investment because that was less certain than his wife's making it with her servants and the Murphy boys. But was the horseback party more likely to reach safety sooner? He hoped so. He felt responsible for all of them, even the ones no longer in his sight. The doctor just grated on him, especially since Capt knew he might well be right. At least the thin air kept the doctor's charges short and less frequent. He counted that as a small blessing.

14

Bonjour and Farewell

Horseback Party

"You mustn't move, if you can help it," Beth Townsend told Ellen. The men had built a small fire that promised warmth. But the pain in her shoulder wouldn't let her stop shaking. It throbbed and her fingers now were totally numb, as though she'd slept on them, and the tingling had turned to stone. Beth had packed snow inside a towel and put it on her shoulder so she was even colder. Ellen held her elbow, her forearm across her belly in a sling of a scarf François had made for her as soon as they made camp. Every step had felt like a knife entering her shoulder. The laudanum hadn't taken effect yet.

"I'm sorry. It just hurts."

Beth patted Ellen's good arm. "I know. It's the shock of it all."

Ellen had never broken a bone before and she assumed her shoulder was broken. Beth had carefully removed her cape and sweater to her bare skin. "Bruising," she said. "It's dislocated, not broken, I think." She draped her cape back over Ellen's shoulder. She flinched even at such little weight.

John bent inside the tent, handed Ellen tea too hot to sip, but holding the tin cup felt good through her mittened hand. She inhaled the now familiar ginger-scented tea while Beth defended her diagnosis.

"I've seen the doctor put a shoulder bone back in place often enough that I believe I can do it." Beth had tenderly moved her fingertips over Ellen's arm and shoulder, making the assessment. "Lay down on your back. Let me take off the cape."

"It's so cold. And I'm . . . exposed." She felt her face grow warm with her brother's eyes on her. How could she be worried about having him see her in her chemise?

"No time for modesty," Beth said. She took Ellen's tea from her hand. "We'll get this over with, then cover you back up." She looked at John. "Stay close. I may need you."

As Beth knelt, she picked up Ellen's arm to a gasp as she gently stretched it out ninety degrees. *Oh, it hurt!*

Beth braced her feet against Ellen's ribs. "Breathe easy."

"That's a wish."

Beth began a slow, steady pull on her arm, tugging away from Ellen's body.

Nothing happened.

She tried again, to Ellen's cry of pain.

"I . . . I may not be strong enough," Beth said.

"Let me." Daniel bullied his way into the tent, past John, who had been waiting patiently.

"No, no, no. You'll yank it," Ellen said.

Daniel frowned. If she didn't hurt so much, she might even say he looked wounded.

"I'll direct him. Have you done this before?" Beth asked.

"Once," Daniel said. "I did it to myself."

She'd have to hear that story. Daniel picked up her arm, more tender than she expected. He began a slow but steady pull. "Oh, oh, oh . . ." She felt nauseous with the pain. "Stop, please, stop." Then she heard the *pop*. The pain didn't go completely away, but it got better.

Beth patted Daniel's back, then covered Ellen. "Well done. Now the sling again, John. I know the doctor says a dislocated shoulder can mean torn ligaments, even broken blood vessels, causing bleeding inside. We can pray that's not so for you. The laudanum should help you sleep at least."

"Thank you," Ellen said. "I'm sorry to have doubted ye."

Daniel nodded once, then rose up from his knees. "I'll tend the horses." Fortunately, they still had grain to give them.

"Did you check over Joker? Are his legs all right?" Ellen mumbled, thinking John was with her yet in the tent. Oliver answered.

"He is doing excellent, mademoiselle. And now you will too."

She burped and giggled. Chica came in and lay beside her, head on paws. With her good arm, Ellen reached across to pet the dog. She wouldn't think about how difficult it was going to be carrying on with the use of only one hand. She'd be little help to Beth or the rest of them. She'd worry about that later. She let the smoothness of the laudanum take her to a warm place at last without pain.

Snow fell, light as whispers. Maolisa Murphy could see ahead of them, trees dressed in white collars over green gowns. The ground lay like a bleached apron, soon dirtied by the tracks of oxen, horses, people, feet dragging. Heads bowed into the effort. But they were moving downhill, the most hopeful angle.

Maolisa gasped at the sharp pain that stabbed her back. She set Mimi down in the snow. The toddler cried immediately. "Shush, shush. I'll pick you up again. Mama needs a minute." She arched her back to relieve the discomfort, her eyes scanning where the other children were.

Ann Jane, round as a rutabaga, waddled over carrying Ide, her youngest. A gray wool scarf was wrapped around Ann Jane's head and neck, so all Maolisa could see was the woman's blue eyes, with weather-worn wrinkles disappearing in the scarf folds—and her distinctive hook nose.

"I can carry them both." Wool muffled Ann Jane's words, so she pulled her scarf from her mouth. "For a little while. May as well make use of these hips, thank you, blessed Jesus." She raised her eyes heavenward and crossed herself.

"If you can lift her into the wagon for a time, that would help."

Junior made his way toward them. "Are you all right, Pet?"

"I just had a sharp pain. Go along. I'm fine." Maolisa smiled at her husband. "Truly."

He rejoined Patrick in pushing a wagon up and over a rock. The company moved at a beetle's pace over a terrain of snow with rock noses peeking out, shaded by trees with needles as long as her child's foot. "I'm still two months away from delivery," Maolisa said. "I don't want this baby to die." Tears formed in her eyes.

"No, no." Ann Jane had her own tears.

"Ah, Ann. How thoughtless of me. Your beautiful boy. So sorry." Ann Jane's newborn had died and been buried at Council Bluffs. She'd endured this entire journey carrying grief as well as little Ide in her arms. "Sean was such a beautiful boy." Ann Jane nodded. "You must miss him terribly."

"Aye. 'Tis a hard day waking up to meself and his da watching without his first son cuddling at the breast." With one hand she scooped up her niece and plopped her on her hip. Maolisa listened with relief as her child stopped crying and kicked her feet of snow.

They caught up with the Murphy wagon.

"Here you go." Ann Jane hefted the toddler through the opening. "Oh, Maolisa." She turned from her first look in the wagon. "Everything is so organized. How did you do that with so many items condensed and all the children?"

"I can't stand clutter," Maolisa said. "Finding places for everything eases my search when Junior comes asking for this or that." The child settled with her stocking doll. Maolisa said, "I thank you kindly for your help to me despite your grievous loss."

Ann Jane nodded. "Helping others seems to ease a bit of the heart pain." She brushed snow from her cape's hemline. I've been without him now for almost as long as I carried him. So few memories."

"The best memories. He was safe, sound, and contented."

Ann Jane nodded and took a deep breath. "How's your back now?"

"It just protested. I hope it wasn't from carrying Mimi. I never had sharp pains with the other children, but then many things are different about this one. We've been on the move all this time and exerting in different ways. And boy or girl, this one is larger than any of my others."

"Maybe that means she'll be stronger."

"I can hope."

"Or twins." Ann Jane said it like it was a secret.

"Oh please, rescue me from that!" Maolisa laughed.

"Do you have a name picked out, if it's a girl?" The two women pushed forward. Both of them squinted against the whiteness, blinked off snow from their eyelashes. They were moving back into timber country, which Maolisa took as a sign they were getting closer to their destinations. Junior had said they'd be at Sutter's by Christmas. At least that was the hope. *And surely, this is December, isn't it? No.* She'd kept track. It was November twenty-ninth.

"No name picked. Some derivative of Mary, I suppose. As Maolisa is. As Mimi is. We'll have time."

"This is no place to give birth to a baby."

Ann Jane's words were more prayer than report.

15

Yuba

December 1844

Capt spied the river, or at least the willows and aspen trees he was sure marked some sort of stream. He rode ahead, ducking beneath branches, his fur hat catching on one now and then. He could hear the freshet, water streaming over rocks. A small fork likely near the headwaters. The sound sang to him. This was the Yuba River. It had to be. They were close now. They'd camp here for the night, then move out, following the stream sometimes, crossing it now and then, as it likely meandered.

He thought about the Horseback Party. He hoped the two women and four men had found the river as the Indian had drawn on his sand map.

"You'll be glad your women stacked the frozen jerky, put it where it's accessible, as we'll be drawing on it," he told several of the men as he rode back along the inching line of wagons. "But by my estimation, not for long. We've got us a river. Maybe some fresh fish."

He rode, filling people in and advising they'd be stopping for the evening, early. Mrs. Murphy looked relieved. All the women did.

If he could find himself a wife the likes of these sturdy women, he might give up his wandering ways. But for now, he was grateful he didn't have the responsibility of any one woman. No, he felt responsible for eight!

Wagon Guards

Moses had let the fire go out. He hadn't meant to; just slept right through, warmed by his bedroll.

Allen threw a moppet fit (as his sister would have called it) when he woke up to an even colder cabin than the one they'd gone to bed in.

"You can't even keep a fire going? We'll freeze to death, boy. Do we need two people to stay awake, set guards? Who am I here with, a bunch of coots?" He'd ranted for a while, getting himself worked up. Moses was glad he hadn't lent fuel to Allen's flame by defending himself.

"You slept too, Montgomery. And we didn't freeze to death," Joe said, hands warmed at the fire.

"I'm sorry, sir," Moses said. And he was. "At least Joe was able to get a fire going fast. And we've got meat to eat."

Smoke seeped into the sparse cabin as it found its way up through the chimney. *Fire.* It felt so good. Moses watched Allen stand before the mirror piece they'd hung, twist the ends of his mustache into tiny braids framing the man's jaw.

During a break in the snowfall, Allen had killed one thin deer, dressed it out, leaving the guts where he'd shot it so coyotes or wolves would find it farther from the cabin. Joe had hunted too, closer to the lake. "I suppose if varmints are interested, they can follow our trail, though," Moses said. He tugged on one antler; Allen held the other. "I hope it ain't sick. It's awful skinny and alone like this."

"No option but to try to eat it. Roasted we should be all right." He looked up at the sky. "More snow I'm thinkin'."

Moses had been concerned about weather and wondered if the storm had hit the summit and the western slope Capt's party traveled along. It was hard enough for the three of them, in good shape, in a shelter, not moving. He thought of the children. Poor little things.

Back at the cabin, they removed the hide and Allen cut the loin out, telling Moses how to do it as though Moses had never hunted or killed a deer before.

"I know how," he said.

"Oh, sure. That's right. I was just remembering how you lost the rifle I gave you to use when we took that buffalo. Left the loin behind then too."

Moses remembered the event with Allen equally being the coot. Allen and John Murphy hadn't been able to find where they'd left the buffalo they'd taken either, that prairie grass was so high, nearly as tall as their chests, and as far as the eye could see, nothing stood out to show them where they'd felled their prey and left guns behind. They'd had to spend the night away from the larger party—they still had Oregon-bound wagons with them then.

"I prefer to forget that humiliating day," Moses said. "I'd think you would too." If Moses ever became a leader, he wouldn't keep bringing up old mistakes.

They roasted the deer meat on skewers laid across a grill from the Townsend wagon. An occasional fat glob dropped and spit into the flames, but Allen pointed out that venison didn't have much fat to offer, which was too bad. "A body needs fat to survive. It's essential. Maybe we'll get a goose we can shoot. Goose fat's good. It'll really sizzle in a fire."

Moses remembered that people often came by Capt and Joe's fire to get coals to help start their own. It saved on matches. Capt told stories of hearth fires in Georgia and how one member of the family would be the keeper of the flame, making sure it never went out. Others in the hollers could come with their shovels to carry a coal back home for their stoves. Generous, Moses had thought, to give coals away. He felt ashamed he'd let their fire get cold.

Capt had told a story of people heading west and one old gramma not wanting to go. They couldn't get her to say why not— she'd had some sort of seizure that had left her speechless, and she couldn't cipher. She wouldn't budge. They'd loaded everything in her cabin so she had nothing left but her shovel and a rocking chair they would carry her in and set outside next to a fire she tended. The family was almost ready to go without her when she shook the shovel at them. Her sons thought she was angry. But one young child said, "She cain't say fare thee well to her flames."

They found a way to take her coals in a tin bucket. She followed that bucket right into the wagon and was content the whole way, or so Capt told it. Capt said that it was the hardest thing for many old folks to leave their fires behind at the time of their dying. They always wanted reassurance of knowing who would carry on that task of keeping the flames fired up. Hopefully forgiving now and then the coot who had let the fire once go out.

Horseback Party

Ellen rode up past Beth's horse to where Daniel had stopped, worried over yet another disaster causing him to halt. "What is it?"

"That's the river we were looking for," Daniel said. "I don't know its name, but it's going southwest and that's the direction we're headed."

"Thank the good Lord," Beth said. She rode Spotty behind him in the string that day.

He made the sign of the cross, then removed his tuque and spun it around on his finger. "We'll find Sutter's Fort and kill time there until the others arrive."

"If they aren't there first," Ellen said. She did wonder if they'd reach the fort before the main party. She might like a little time to greet the Californios—as the Missouri priest had called the wealthy Spanish-speaking landholders of Alta California. They might like music and dance. Which she would be able to do once her arm was fully healed. For a few hours each day she removed the sling, and oh, how it did hurt when she straightened that limb. Beth told her she had to carry something heavy then, like a cast iron pot. She thought her arm would come out of the socket all over again the first time she tried to lift the Dutch oven lid.

She'd become proficient reining in Joker with her right hand instead of directing him with a rein in each. He seemed to like the way she gave him cues with both reins moving in the same direction.

"We just follow these river?" Oliver used English, but his "this" and "these" sounded similar. English was a difficult language to learn, Ellen found. She at least had had lessons while being married to Matthew, but the Townsend servants had to learn on their own. She wondered if the Californios spoke English as well as Spanish.

"*Oui.* It'll take us out of these mountains, and once we're there, we should start seeing haciendas and remudas."

"Why Daniel Murphy, I do believe you're happy."

"And why shouldn't I be?" He scowled.

I should have kept still. "You should be, of course. Just nice to see your smile."

"You don't give me much to smile about," he said, but she thought he might have had a little lift to the corners of his lips when he said it.

"I guess I don't. And still, you put up with me."

"I do. Let's check the horses' feet, make sure there's no build-up of ice in them."

He was good about changing the subject. *Must be a Murphy trait.*

François came to her, as he had these last days, and helped her dismount. Everything was more difficult with one hand immobilized. He then helped Beth step down, and the two women hugged their capes around themselves, secured their hoods over their tuques, while the men checked the animals' feet.

"It sounds like we're almost there," Beth said. She pulled Ellen's cape up closer to her chin line, tucked in the dark blue wool scarf Ellen wore around her neck. "That color goes so well with your flame-colored hair."

"Does it? I like blue. And yes, Daniel thinks we're not far away now, and he's no brother to optimism, so it's hopeful."

"I hope we'll be there—wherever there is—by Christmas. I pray that the others have already arrived and we'll celebrate our first Christmas in California. I can just imagine the feast." Ellen heard Beth's stomach growl. The women laughed.

They hadn't starved, no. But the food was lean, mostly the jerky they'd made, the hardtack they'd purchased at Fort Hall when what they'd packed for the trip had run out. Some families still had what they'd made before they left. She would have liked to eat something her mother had prepared before dying. She shook her head.

"And what will you want to eat?"

"A big fat goose. Some mutton. And perhaps they have pigs in California and we can have bacon and hams and hog's feet."

Beth's enthusiasm—and the strength of her voice—made Ellen laugh out loud and Beth joined in.

The men lifted their heads from their horses' hooves to hear what the sound was.

Ellen removed her tuque and swung it on her finger as Daniel had his. "We're planning Christmas dinner," she shouted. And so, they were.

"We're on the right track, Capt." Old Greenwood had approached quiet as a grave, broke the silence with his gravelly voice. His greasy hair hung down beneath his fur cap, a coon's tail dragging off the back. They were circled in a wide bend at the river. The snow was maybe a half-foot deep here, but there was green next to the water and the animals had drunk their fill and ripped at the grass. They might even stay an extra day to get them a little nutrient. But no, they had to keep going.

"Glad you agree. This is the Yuba, I'm pretty sure that's what that old Indian signed."

"Head out early?"

"Soon as daylight. Days are getting shorter."

"That they are."

"Should be easier going from here on." The two men, the most experienced in this country, stood staring at the fire. Each man had lived on the hard ground of a transient, fur trader, trapper. Hitchcock had too, the father of the Patterson clan. But Capt's paths had crossed now and then with Old Greenwood, at rendezvous in the Shining Mountains. It comforted him to think that Old Greenwood concurred that they were now onto an easier slope toward Sutter's. "I hope that's true for the Townsend party."

"Expect those women are in good hands." Old Greenwood didn't say it as a question, a question Captain Stephens still had. "Murphy boys are sturdy. Liked watching that John use his sling to bring down fowl. Those French Canadians are strong too."

Capt nodded. They stared awhile longer at the low flame. The captain heard the coffee boil. He offered up the pot and Old Greenwood unlatched a tin cup he carried tied with rawhide onto his greasy buckskins. He wiped it out with a handful of snow and his dirty gloves. The Greenwoods had no wagon, brought everything in saddlebags or carried by their horses and pack animals. The men sipped in silence. The old man's presence reassured the captain. Then Old Greenwood nodded and returned to his sons and his camp.

It was like the old fox could read his mind sometimes. He appreciated the word of confidence. So different from the words Townsend always left him with.

Wagon Guards

Moses's stomach burned like the inside of a stove. The meat hadn't tasted funny and he'd eaten his fill. The others had no problem with it. But something grabbed at his gut and he moaned, prayed even. He'd never had such pain. He tried not to be loud, wake the others, but the cramps came in waves. He panted. In between he thought he'd get up, go out to the supplies Dr. John had left. Ipecac. It was almost dawn. If he could walk, he might find it. There was a bottle of it out there. It would make him vomit. He crawled toward the door opening. Looked up but saw only snow halfway up the doorway, spilling into the cabin.

Mary Sullivan took to the landscape, challenging as it was. She described it as fierce, the snow depth, the cold, the demand on her body to push wagons, urge oxen on. When they made camp, she returned to her old routines: handing out food. Reading to the boys. Disagreeing with John, who was still grousing about her having led oxen through the rock cleft with her skirts tucked up into her waistband. He was more discreet with his criticisms with Sarah living among them.

Oddly, Mary felt less tired at the end of the days when she'd been most physically taxed, when she had to saw branches for burning, had to push at the wagon back or stomp through snow to yank at the harnesses of Pierre and Prince. Only that one day, when they'd had to kill Bó's calf, the cow giving no more milk and the baby starving, only that day did the physical demands of helping John butcher the animal leave her crying instead of quickened. She made herself smile when she served her family the veal that evening. It was the least she could do to honor the being that gave them nourishment. She knew the larder grew smaller and she'd started to worry about how far they still were from

Sutter's Fort. They just had to keep going. She prayed there'd be no more delays.

"Martin. Wake up." She only called Junior by his given name when Maolisa was worried. And she was. "Junior! Oooh no! Not now."

"What is it, love?" Junior pulled out of his sleep.

"Pains. And, oh Lord, I've made water. Oh, 'Holy is his name.'"

"You've done it before, Pet. No need to worry."

"She's early. Very early."

"Oh, ye know it's a girl, do ye."

"Don't argue with me, Martin. Get the towels. There." She pointed.

He opened the trunk. "You're a thoughtful housekeeper, Mrs. Murphy. Putting what we'll need close for when we need it. Anticipatin' this, were ye, love?"

"Just do it!"

He lit a lamp, ran his hands through his dark hair, the curls sticking up like rose meringue.

She panted and he did as he was ordered, then woke the children sleeping like sardines and made them sit on the floorboards, huddled together. "Mama's got a baby coming. She needs the bed." He returned to help her, rubbed her back as she sat, knees up, a quilt over them to protect the children from seeing what they shouldn't.

"She's so early."

"Now, Pet. Maybe you calculated wrong."

"Don't tell me what I've done or not correctly."

She shouldn't argue. He could be right. It was cold and this baby would do so much better if she had miscalculated and it arrived at least as big as a ham.

"Oh, oh, oh!"

"Should I get Mrs. Patterson?"

"There's na time."

"Now, Maolisa, maybe there is."

"No!"

"Let it happen then, Mrs. Murphy. You can do it."

And she did.

The arrival of the little girl took just minutes more until Maolisa held the tiny, wiggling form. Maybe six pounds, same size as her others. The babe appeared fully formed. The infant wailed, then looked about.

"Welcome to the world."

"Eliza we'll call her."

"It makes me sad to name her after our lost child. Maybe Elizabeth, for my sister," Maolisa offered.

"Elizabeth it is. We'll come up with a middle name, call her Lizzie for short. Would that please ye, Maolisa?"

She nodded. The placenta came then, and Junior cut the cord, then donned his boots and carried the mass out to the latrine area they always set up in camp. When he returned, she said, "Maybe I did miscalculate. She's certainly hardy enough. Good lungs. Just pray now that my milk comes in and that she can latch on. She's got your eyes, Junior. Big and blue." Maolisa looked up at him. "And hopefully your good and accommodating nature. I'm sorry I was short with ye."

"What man wouldn't be accommodatin' with a wife as ordering—I mean as organized—as you."

She smiled at him, then lay her head down, stretched out with Lizzie on her breast. "*Bonjour*, little one. Let's give her the middle name Yuba, that's what Capt called this river, wasn't it?"

"Give her a landscape name? Elizabeth Yuba Murphy it shall be."

One more added to the Murphy-Stephens-Townsend party. One more to make it to Alta California for Christmas.

16

Landscape Hurdles

Horseback Party

For Ellen, this journey west had become more rugged than when they'd followed the Truckee upriver to that lake and around it. This stream they met now ran wider and deeper and raced more swiftly than the Truckee too. They'd ridden both downstream and up seeking a place to cross. Snowcapped rocks bordered some banks; dense trees marched to the river's edge at other places. This open area appeared best, though no islands offered respite in the crossing.

"We'll have to swim it," John said. They all waited at the bank. Chica stood openmouthed, ears forward, staring at something unseen in the water's rush.

"You lead," Daniel told John.

"Joker's a bigger animal. Maybe I should go over first." Ellen patted Joker's neck. "We can put Chica in front of me."

"Not with your arm. Daniel's right," John said. "I ride him over, see which boulders we can maneuver around, find some sort of footing for where to take out." Ellen had confidence in John. He was a better hunter than Daniel, though she'd never say that out loud. And he was more . . . thoughtful, was the word she chose, when dealing with the animals, quieter in his movements. He was stronger too.

"All right. You ride Joker."

"Beth, you'll take your Indian pony next." Daniel doing the ordering now. "He was pretty surefooted on the Truckee crossings."

"He's a good swimmer," Beth offered. "In fact, let François and me go first."

"Are you strong enough?" Ellen asked.

"I believe so. And I'll take Chica."

"She's right about Spotty. He is a strong pony," John said. He stroked his beard in thought. "I'll ride Spotty. Beth, you're on Joker."

Beth spoke up. "We should ride whom we're used to."

"'Tis wise," Ellen said. *Good for Beth.*

"Joker's the biggest animal and maybe it's not so deep that he doesn't have to swim. Spotty surely will lose footing." John sounded firm. Daniel hesitated, then concurred, but Beth was mounting Spotty.

Like a shy boy at his first river swim, John and Joker eased down the bank, tentative then into the swirl of water. The current lifted his horse's tail downstream as Joker's chest pushed forward. The surefooted animal moved across the water, swimming, the current pushing at him like a restless sea against a ship.

"François will bring Chica when he comes," Ellen said. Beth nodded, then pressed her legs against Spotty's sides and he plunged in. She whooped, and in what seemed like seconds to Ellen, Beth's horse began to swim, his back pushed downstream but his front legs pulled with power as the two angled across the current. They passed John on Joker and the little horse reached the other side first, shaking water beads from his body. Joker lunged up the riverbank, rivulets streaming from his flanks. Ellen let out a gasp of held breath.

John tied Joker to a tree, then helped Beth off. He mounted Spotty and the little pony plunged back into the river.

"Let's do this," he told his sister when they arrived. He helped

Ellen mount, gentled her bad shoulder as they worked their way back into the stream. John stayed on foot, yelping at the cold, and when the water got deep, he grabbed the pony's tail and let himself be pulled, shouting to Ellen, "Hang on."

Like the others, Ellen had tied her shoestrings to drape her boots over her shoulders. Bare feet dragged in the frigid water as she urged the little horse onward.

"That," Beth said when Ellen arrived on the bank, her skirts dripping wet, "was thrilling, wasn't it?"

Ellen laughed. "Now that I'm safely here, yes, it was grand. Let's get a fire started. I'm putting on my wool socks."

John signaled the others to begin their crossings, reaching for reins as soon as the animals made it. Chica jumped from François's arms and trotted to Ellen, the dog's pink tongue hanging in a happy pant.

Only Daniel and his horse were left. Ellen had squatted at the fire and stood now, beside John.

"What's he waiting for?" *Had he paused like this at other crossings?* This was the swiftest stream they'd encountered.

"I don't know. His horse is pretty strong."

Ellen drew something from deep in their past. "Can Daniel swim?"

"I can," John said. "Surely, he can too. Come on, Daniel," he shouted. "The water's fine!"

Daniel waved his hand back at them, seemed to rethink something, then mounted. It wasn't until after he plunged into the river running fast as a mill race that Ellen noticed that something had been left behind on shore.

Wagon Guards

Moses had located saleratus and vinegar. He mixed them, panting in pain, added melted snow, and when it fizzed up, he drank.

The ipecac would have been better, but he couldn't haul himself to the stacks of boxes from the wagons. When the snow stopped falling, he'd see if there were medicine kits left behind, easier to get to. When his stomach stopped hurting.

Relief. The concoction helped. The cramps eased and he made another dose and drank it about the time that Joe and Allen woke up.

"You guys OK?" Moses asked.

"Sure enough. Aren't you?" Allen spoke through a yawn.

"My stomach's better now, but it's been a cramp all night long." Joe stretched, added a log to the fire.

"You kept the fire going, kid."

"I did." Moses didn't like Allen calling him a kid, but right now he felt like one, a kid missing his mother—and his sister—who would have mixed up that elixir of vinegar and soda and added a little sugar to it to make him feel better, faster. But he'd done all right taking care of himself.

"Whoa! Look at the doorway." Allen stood before the mass of white that had awed Moses in the dawn. Allen reached for the shovel and began digging a trench through it. He didn't get far. "I thought maybe it was just a drift up against the door, but there must be five feet of snow over everything. So much for our plan to hunt today."

"I hope this storm didn't catch the others," Joe said. He had lifted a piece of last night's meat and held it in his hand to thaw it.

"Maybe this'll melt," Moses said.

"Maybe," Allen said, but he didn't sound hopeful

Their last ox bawled and Joe shook his head. "There's no food to be had for him. He'll starve. He's almost dead now."

Moses wondered if Joe's description of the ox didn't also describe their own.

"It'll stop," Martin told Capt. "Meanwhile, this gives the animals a chance to rest and my new granddaughter a chance to stay

145

in one place to build up resistance to the cold." The men were gathered at a common fire, a tarp pulled out from one of the wagons offering little shelter from the heavy snowfall that had kept them there two days already.

"We'll give it another day. Then we have to move out." Capt hated being the bearer of news that challenged them all, but they couldn't remain. They had to keep moving. The snow fell so thick it was like looking through white curtains.

"Agreed," the senior Murphy said.

Silence followed. Then Dennis Martin said out loud what Capt had actually considered in his sleepless night. "Could be we need to think about letting the wagons stay here, using them as shelter for the women, and we men walk out to get help back for them all with more food and refreshed animals." It took a moment for people to understand that Dennis had said "shelter," his lisp disguising his words. Capt guessed maybe he'd taken some teasing as a kid and that had kept him quiet. But he spoke the truth now.

"That thought had occurred to me," Old Greenwood said. "Leave the cattle here. They'd have plenty to eat. Slaughter before we leave. Pick up the hides in the spring. One man or two stay with them to help hunt after we've gone."

"We could build a shelter of some sort." This from James Miller. He was the father of the other infant, Ellen Independence, and several other children so Capt thought his contemplating this idea was a good sign.

"Oh, my Maolisa, she'll never agree to this, not with a newborn." Junior Murphy knew his wife, and Capt expected there'd be tense words spoken between them. Between all the married men. He hadn't even considered what the single women would say or if they'd put up a fuss. Well, they'd just have to go along with what was decided as best for them. The married ones would as well.

"Maybe you'll have to stay with her then, son," the senior Murphy said.

Isaac Hitchcock said, "You and me too, Martin. We're the old ones." He jested and the elder Martin lifted his walking stick as though he concurred.

Capt thought Isaac Hitchcock would be good to have along. He knew rough country and could get them into the valley as well as anyone could. Maybe Capt should hand over the whole expedition to him and Greenwood, stay behind himself looking after the women. But no, he'd been chosen their leader and that meant to the very end.

"I'll let Sarah know," Townsend said. "She won't like this. I can settle her down."

"Let's take a vote first," Capt said. "Who's in favor of heading on foot out of here, building a shelter first for the women and children?" All hands went up. "Who is willing to remain with them to hunt as needed?"

There was only a slight hesitation and then James Miller said, "Me and my boy William will stay. Along with Hitchcock and Martin, of course."

"I'd like to go," Old Man Martin said.

"Now, Da, your bones are brittle," Dennis told him.

"You'll be good help to us," James said. "Stay." He clapped the elder on his shoulder.

"Maybe you can be there when I tell my Maolisa, keep her from hurting on me," Junior Murphy said. "She'll have another reason to remember the Yuba now, and it won't be quite such a pleasant memory as having a healthy babe arrive."

"I'll tell my sister Ailbe if you'll tell my wife, Ann Jane," James Murphy said. "They might kill us, but they won't kill the next of kin." The men laughed. It sounded shaky to Capt.

"We're agreed then, James and Old Man Martin stay? And all the women. Your sister included, Sullivan."

John Sullivan nodded. Murmurs of assent moved around the fire. Capt was grateful that for once neither the Sullivan woman, the Montgomery woman, nor the Patterson widow were here to protest. "And Dr. John, I appreciate your offer to tell Mrs.

Montgomery, but it's my duty to inform those without their husbands. Meanwhile, let's start thinking of how to put the shelter together for how many?" He started counting.

"Eight women," Dennis Martin said. "And," he hesitated, "seventeen boys and girls. Counting the new baby."

Horseback Party

"What took you so long, Daniel?" Ellen was hungry now that all were safely on shore.

Ellen's brother threw his leg over the horse's neck and jumped off, his pants like the other men's, wet to the thigh. "I don't like water, I just don't. Especially deep water."

"Can you swim?" Beth asked. She stood with her back to the fire, her hands behind her, her black skirt almost dry. The women had taken just one change of clothing with them, and Beth's wool skirt had its share of smudges and dirt, but so did Ellen's second dress.

"I know how to swim, but I don't like to." Daniel looked away. "I'm here. We're all here."

"Yes, we are. But there's a pack saddle or something left over there." Ellen pointed.

"What?" Daniel turned around.

Ellen didn't say, "How could you let this happen," as he'd said to her when she'd been knocked into the tree well.

"Maybe there's nothing critical in there."

"It ese the kitchen pack," Oliver said. "The samovar, tea, saleratus, salt. Eet has the medicines too."

"I'll take Spotty and go back and get it," John said. "He's rested."

"You just got dry," Daniel said. "It was my mistake."

"Hey, brother, let me do it. I'm a better swimmer than you anyway." John's arms were the size of Ellen's thighs. She'd watched him practice with his sling, loading stones in the pouch, flinging it toward a target.

148

"All right." Ellen knew he must really dislike the water to let John claim the better swimmer status without protest.

"Need to borrow your little horse, Mrs. Townsend."

"He's willing, I'm sure. Carry on."

Spotty stood with his head down. He'd already made the river crossing four times, but he had been able to rest a little. Ellen hoped it was enough.

John mounted the pony and they slid down the muddy slope into the water. Was it her imagination or did the river seem a little higher? Could it have come up in so short a time? The weather had been warmer. Perhaps the snow they'd ridden through days before had melted now, raised the creeks and streams.

Ellen held her breath and let it out just as John and Spotty were midway. The pony slipped, maybe at a boulder they'd been able to see before, but now, with a higher, faster force, something twisted him and his head went under, tipping John into the turbulence.

"John!" Ellen yelled. His head struck a rock, then it spit him away, gave him to the river where he bobbed downstream, not even trying to swim. *Unconscious?*

Horse and man separated, the current threw each against more rocks, their heads sinking. John flailed, came up, tried to swim, but he was forced against another stone. Ellen couldn't hear his head hit it but she saw it, felt it in her stomach. John stopped struggling.

Chica barked, then raced along the shoreline. "What can we do?" Beth stood at the water's edge.

"Follow them downstream," Daniel shouted, and they ran, the bank a bramble of rocks and brush beneath towering trees. Ellen picked up her skirts, grateful she'd put her boots back on. She looked for John to reach, grasp, pull himself out of the water. She feared his body would wash up, feared more if it didn't. Every part of her being prayed that he would live, prayed that they'd find him.

And around the bend, they did.

17

Strength of Spirit

Wintering Women

"You have no right," Mary told her brother.

"I agree," Sarah said. John Sullivan and Dr. Townsend and Capt surrounded her and Mary as they stood in the snow, stomping their feet beside the Yuba River, making yet another choice. Mary hugged her arms around herself, the cold air numbing her cheeks and lips. They were the misfits, women controlled by domineering men who were neither husbands nor fathers.

"I've made the decision as is my right, Mary," the doctor said.

He'd been spending too much time with Captain Stephens, who just affirmed the power of men. She had the same goal as them—getting to Sutter's Fort—so why couldn't the discussion of how and who involve her too?

"No." Sarah Montgomery raised her voice. "You cannot do this to us. First Allen sends me off, then you want me, all of us women, to stay here and wait to be rescued? Hope to be saved in the spring? No, I'm going with you."

"I am too," Mary said.

"What about our brothers? You'd leave them here without you? No," John said. "They are your responsibility as you are mine."

"We'll bring a relief party as soon as we can," Capt said. His calming voice did little to quiet the women. "You'll be safer here than riding out with us men."

"And we can't afford to risk your holding us back." The doctor nodded to Mary and patted Sarah's back as though she were an aging dog. Sarah sloughed off his touch, stepped closer to Mary.

"Safer," Sarah said. "I don't know what that means anymore."

Mary's heart pounded like a mad spinner stomping on the treadle. "No, no, no, no." She'd never expressed herself in public this way. *Would Mama be upset?* Sarah reached out and put her arm around her, bringing tears to her eyes.

"First Beth and Ellen are sent away. Then my Allen is left with wagons rather than his wife. And now you will abandon your sisters and wives? And your children? What kind of protection is that?"

Mary tugged at a loose thread. Their lives were unraveling just like her sweater. They'd come so far, choice after choice. She was tired of choosing. She was just exhausted.

"We'll come back with food and healthier animals to rescue you," Dr. Townsend said. "You'll expend less energy staying here. Plenty to eat. We'll slaughter cattle before we go. And James Miller and his boy and Mr. Martin agreed to stay behind, to hunt."

"You can help with drying the meat," John told her. "Be useful here."

"They'll need your good head, Miss Sullivan," Capt said. "The many children, mothers of little ones. Your help will be welcomed."

"I'm apparently too weak to ride out with you men, so I'm not sure my strength will be noticed." She sounded sarcastic, but she didn't care.

"It is your strength of spirit that will hold people together," Capt said.

Why he would have thought she had a gathering spirit was

beyond her, and she started to ask when the good doctor interrupted. "Sarah's already been temporarily abandoned by Montgomery." He pointed with his chin toward her. "And she's survived that great inconvenience, which will be a model to the other women who might miss their dear ones."

"*Might* miss them?" Sarah said.

"You'll remind them of what you've already endured," Capt said. "You can help those who struggle with this decision of what's best for them. Both of you women."

"Why is it that what's best for us is always what someone else wants, whether we women want it or not?" Mary said.

"It's the way of things, dear." Dr. Townsend's words were like being patted on the head.

For the first time in her life Mary wanted to slug someone— namely the good doctor. But she didn't. It was her "strength of spirit" she imagined that must have kept her clenched fists at her side.

"Stay," Maolisa Murphy pleaded. What stronger argument did she have than this newborn suckling at her breast? They huddled in their wagon while wind whipped against the canvas, billowing it in and out like sheets thwarted on a sagging line.

"We're constructing a shelter for you out of logs and the wagons. The oxen, though skinny I know, will be here for food. You'll have a regular abattoir right at your door." He grinned.

The image of living in a slaughterhouse was not one she wanted to carry while she fed her daughter. "Your attempt at levity is not appreciated."

"I know, Pet. I'm not makin' light of the situation. In fact, it's because it's dire that we've decided this is the best. We'll be leading horses, hoping we can get to where the snow isn't so deep, drive a couple of cows with us. Ride when we can. We've snowshoes for when we can use them."

"We put everything into this effort, Junior. The cows—what will be left for us to start over with if we consume them and don't even have hides to sell?" She knew she sounded frantic.

"We'll come back soon as we can, Pet. We'll have our good wits and the Lord's blessing to start over with."

Are those tears? My husband, crying?

She heard the lament in his voice. This was a terrible choice to have to make, she knew that. Not having brought every possible tool along didn't mean they hadn't planned well. They had expected to be through the mountains before bad weather hit. They didn't expect to have a newborn here, now. Her husband looked bereft. "Who would have thought there'd be mountains with snow so deep in 'warm and wonderful California'?" Maolisa touched her husband's bearded cheek. "We'll have to let our Missouri priest know one day that treacherous mountains stood between our home and his Catholic haven—along with deserts and rolling plains and rivers to cross and terrible weather and now . . . separation."

"Aye."

Maolisa changed breasts for little Lizzie Yuba. She shouldn't be nursing when she was upset; it would sour her milk.

"Capt says we are in California now and Lizzie's the first American born here. Something to be proud of, Maolisa."

"A hollow accolade, if I might say." She stroked the child's cheeks with the back of her finger. Their other little ones clustered among the stored items of Maolisa's well-kept wagon that would now be torn apart for a larger shelter, she imagined. The children must have sensed the moment, for they crawled on their father's lap. BD hung across his back.

"See my whistle, Papa?" Their five-year-old attempted to gain his father's attention while the two older boys, perhaps more aware of the gravity of their parents' conversation, stared into a silence Maolisa would long remember.

"I hate leavin' ye, Pet. I do. But it's best."

She sighed. "Build a shelter. Lead them out and bring back a rescue party. We will do what we can. Look at this 'premature' baby." Her sapphire eyes stared at this world she'd been brought into. "She's survived." *Premature.* The child must have been conceived in March, just as they left Missouri, not in May as they left Iowa.

Junior grinned. "They're sweet as honeysuckle at her age."

"And you're right, I must have miscalculated."

"We brought a bit of Missouri with us then." His voice caught.

"And she will grow up in California. Go. We women know how to adapt as we must. Now, be gone with ye." She wouldn't let him see her cry.

Wagon Guards

It was a bleached world remaining unchanged throughout the day. The next morning, Moses shoveled his way to where they had tied the ox, though he wondered now why they'd bothered. The animal was as snowbound as they were, and soon they'd have to butcher it. It made him sad to think of the animals giving up their lives for them after they'd worked so hard. Taking elk or deer or bears—if they were lucky—was more the natural order of things. But animals they'd come to know, to love even—well, consuming them was almost sacrilegious, though he wasn't exactly sure what that word even meant.

He was glad Chica had gone with his sister and that Joker had too. Eating horsemeat was even worse than eating an ox. At least they didn't have that decision to make, having been left no horses.

The bovine bawled as he approached. Moses sank into the snow with each step, though he could make his way to the animal. He shoveled near the droppings that steamed in the snow. Maybe he could scrape up something green closer to the lake where the snow wasn't quite as deep as where they'd built their shelter. Put off the killing for another day. At least his stomach wasn't hurting anymore. Still, he was pretty weak, but then as Allen kept telling him, he was "just a boy" and boys are more susceptible to tainted meat—if that's what had done him in.

He shoveled a path to the lake, scraped snow away down to the ground, a narrow tunnel five feet deep. Not much there. But Moses returned to the ox he called Bill, led him down the path he'd dug to see if it might be able to take nourishment. He'd been sent out to gather more wood, which fortunately the group had dragged close to the cabin. He'd have to scrape away snow from the pile of logs and chop on them. Smoke rose from the chimney, so the fire hadn't gone out yet. But he'd best get back. He thought about letting Bill roam free. Where could the ox go? But he didn't. If the men couldn't hunt or even find game, this bovine would be it, sacrificing its life for them. He'd never live down the fact that he'd let the animal loose to be coyote meat. That is, if they all lived.

He re-staked Bill. Finished brushing snow off its back. The ox bawled again. Moses rubbed the space between Bill's short horns. "All our stomachs are empty as a gun barrel. Wish it wasn't so. Weren't so." He corrected himself and smiled, thinking of his sister. Boy, he hoped she was all right.

Horseback Party

Ellen ran toward the apparition—no, body—caught by a branch hanging out over the river. The raging stream had given John Murphy up. Alive or dead, she didn't know. There was no sign of Spotty.

As they approached, she saw that somehow John was caught by or clung to branches of a willow, the water swirling around him not far from the bank. He had been conscious enough to grab the branch, hold on—but his head lolled to the side.

He must be conscious. "John! We're here." *No response.*

"I'll get ropes." Daniel turned, but Oliver had already brought up Joker and another horse and untied the rawhide looped on the saddle. "Wrap it around the tree," Daniel ordered. "Ellen, give him that second rope. Oliver, tie it around that tree too."

Daniel put the end of the first rope around his middle, then grabbed the second rope while Oliver knotted the other end around a tree away from the bank. Ellen noticed that Oliver's hands shook. "I'm going in," Daniel said. His fingers clumsily tied the knot.

Ellen shouted, "We're here, John." *Is he even alive?* She touched Daniel's arm. "Maybe François or Oliver would be . . . better. They're more rested, know rivers."

"It was my fault I left the pack there. I'm going."

"Daniel's coming for you. Hang on," Beth's words pierced the sound of rushing water. John's eyes opened, then slowly closed— then opened again as Chica barked and barked, back and forth on the shoreline, her sharp retort forcing John's eyes to blink.

Daniel took a deep breath and waded into the water chest deep, arms out, holding the rope no longer slack but tight. He slipped, caught himself. Even in this eddy the current was strong. "He's coming, John," Ellen shouted.

Sizing things up, François said, "We tie one rawhide to these horse? So they do not tangle when we pull?"

"Yes!" Ellen said. "Daniel, the rope you're holding, Joker will hold it taut. Just get it around John."

Daniel ducked his body beneath the water.

In what seemed to Ellen an interminable time, he shot out of the river, spitting but with the loop of his rope now around John's chest.

"Pull it tight!" Oliver backed Joker up and Daniel said something to John, who let his body drop into Daniel's arms. His head slipped beneath the water, but Daniel lifted his brother, held his head like a baby cradled.

"Pull!" Daniel said, and Oliver backed Joker up while François, at the tree rope, began pulling the men toward the shore. Ellen and Beth dragged John up the bank as Daniel pushed from the river.

As John lay splayed in the mud, eyes closed like the dead, Ellen rubbed his cheeks; Beth, his hands. "John, can you hear me? Oh please. Wake up." *Please, please, please.* Crying wouldn't help, but she couldn't stop the tears.

Oliver helped Daniel from the water and he panted beside her, arms over his knees as he sat, caught his breath. Water glistened off his red hair, ran down his neck.

"Let's turn John on his side," Beth said.

Oliver assisted and with Ellen's one-arm help—she was closest to him—they turned John. He groaned. Blood oozed from a wound above his temple, but the activity awoke something in him and he coughed, then spat water. He started to shake.

"Start a fire," Ellen said.

"I will bring a coal." François draped a saddle blanket over John. It wasn't quite dry at the edges but was available and warm against the river's cold. "We will get a flame and he will live." He ran back to where they'd left the packs and the fire.

Ellen wiped her tears with her cape hem. She rubbed John's arms, hands. "You were very brave, Daniel."

"This time."

Ellen wondered when he hadn't been as brave. It didn't matter. He had done what had to be done. "This is the time that counts," Ellen said.

Chica's barking had stopped with John on the bank, but she started up again, then ran farther downstream.

"Chica! Come back!"

What more? A mountain lion? A wolf?

Wintering Women

"Rough" was the word Mary Sullivan used to describe the structure the men whipped together in two days. Wagon tongues, side boards, floorboards, canvas, all put into commission for new purposes. Saplings, then tarps and fresh cowhides acted as the roof, latched over the center ridge. They chopped a few trees, used the animals to drag them to the structure not far from the Yuba. Mary hoped they'd be rescued by the time the snow melted and raised that river likely to the heights where the structure rose in the snow. Rocks were provided and served as a crude chimney liner. James Miller said they could finish that after the men left. Mary agreed. They should just leave and trust their women.

While she helped with butchering and building, Mary considered heading out with the men anyway. Would they stop her? How could they? John would try. But Sarah bent over like a week-old bean and Mary couldn't see leaving Sarah behind. They were friends now and friends stuck together.

"We can figure out the rest of this," Mary told her brother. "If you think we're brave enough to stay here, then we're smart enough to figure out what else needs to be done and do it ourselves. Just leave, why don't you?"

She hadn't meant to sound angry, but she was. The challenge of a lifetime awaited those men, riding—and walking—through snows toward Sutter's Fort by a trail none of them knew, bringing about a rescue. She would have liked to have been a part of that.

At least the Irish-Canadians had brought snowshoes. She had a pair as well, though the little boys didn't. She doubted any of the children had them. But between those who had them heading out, they could help break a trail for the horses, who would have to work so hard on no food—if the snow was frozen enough to hold their weight at all.

"Townsend has no snowshoes." John walked up to her, rubbing his hands at the fire. "Guess he didn't think to bring them."

"Brought all his fancy supplies instead."

John tugged at his red yarn tuque. "People in Missouri had little use for snowshoes." He pulled the wool from his head. "Look, Mary. I . . ." He ran his hands through his hair the color of old leather. "I don't think you'll need your snowshoes and they're big enough for the doctor."

"Won't he ride his horse?"

"When he can. Mostly we're taking mounts to pack. There's no food for the animals. And they can't push through this deep snow easily. We'll make better time walking. With snowshoes."

"I need them, John. To gather wood. Going to the latrine will certainly be easier with shoes. What about the Murphy women, they surely have them to loan."

"Mostly the men. You were the practical woman."

"And now I'm to go without." She crossed her arms over her chest. "It isn't fair, John. I'll need them to help those of us being left behind. Maybe he can make a pair."

"Mary Sullivan. Turning aside a man's need, are ye? What would Papa say? You honor our parents when you comply with my wishes."

"Do I? Maybe I honor them more by doing what I think is best, even if it isn't what you want." *How can I ever know?* "Oh, all right. Take them. Maybe the good doctor will reward me with some pretty silk one day."

"I'll see to it," her brother said. He grinned. "And if he doesn't, I will."

She didn't want silk or satin. She wanted to go forward. Instead, she'd once again been held back.

18

She Stays at Home

Cross-Country Men to Sutter's Fort

December 6, 1844. Capt Stephens wrote the date in his little journal, holding his hand over the page to protect it from the falling snow. He thought of when he'd started writing those notes to himself. It had been back among the Chippewa, good people he had come to respect and even love, especially one. He wondered if that was why he and Caleb Greenwood got on so well, because Old Greenwood had wooed and married his Batchica Youngcault, as fine a native woman as the Capt had ever met. Except for Capt's Abeque, a Potawatomie woman, whose name meant She Who Stays Home. And she had remained behind, keeping his hearth fires burning while he moved with his blacksmithing tools among the far-flung tribes and forts. If she had been along on this trek, would Abeque stay with the Wintering Women—as he thought of them? Or would she, like Mrs. Patterson, insist that they all remain as one party, abandon the wagons but tromp through the snow together? His Abeque was sturdy, with strong hands made so by how she wielded a knife to separate heavy buffalo hide from muscle, cut and roasted the flesh, dried what she wished, used every sinew and bone, then massaged the hide into a soft underbelly of a blanket or into the very coat and hat he still wore—all that remained of her many gifts she'd given him.

Yet her hands softly eased aches from his back after hours spent shoeing the fort's horses, and they cupped the tiny fingers of her nieces and nephews, teaching them to write on the birch scrolls she delicately stripped from the white-bark trees. Yes, she would survive a trip like the one they were undertaking. But she would also have kept the children and women alive, his Abeque, She Who Stays Home.

Capt watched Townsend tromp toward him, practicing the snowshoe walk as Capt put his notes away.

"I left behind a paper ream with Moses. Perhaps he'll write of what those boys are handling, but I have plenty. I brought pages with me to make my own account. Paper weight is quite an interesting study—which of course I undertook before we left Missouri—and it has—"

"Yes, that's good. With my notes and yours, we are well positioned to account for the last part of this journey. And the women may wish some to help occupy the children."

"Why, I hadn't thought of that. Very perceptive of you, Captain." He shook his finger at him. "Very perceptive. Entertaining the children will be important. But I wouldn't want to miss any notetaking. I'll want it all for my book."

Capt grunted. Had he known about the doctor's intention to write a book? No matter. If Capt ever wrote a tome, it would not be of this journey split now four ways. No, he would write of his days with the Potawatomie. How he wished he had brought some of Abeque's birch scrolls with him, just for the feel of them and knowing she had touched them once. But as was the custom, when she died, he'd given all of her things away.

"You're not as hardened with those snowshoes. Maybe you might consider staying behind, to help with the ladies."

"Oh, no. I'll be of more use as we real men push hard toward Sutter's."

And, Capt thought, the good doctor wouldn't want to write a chapter in his book of staying behind while the "real" men displayed their strong spirits tromping out to bring a rescue party to the women and children. Travelers are more interesting storytellers, he supposed, than those who stay at home.

Horseback Party

"Look what I've found." Beth led the little horse while Chica barked her happy bark. The pup twirled in her joy. The pony limped and shivered with his injuries as François reached for the animal's mane and mumbled in his ear.

For Ellen, the relief of John's surviving was like finding a rock to stand on in the middle of a flooding river. Just seeing him before her, his eyes glassy but getting focused, and Daniel, exhausted, still breathing hard but there, warming at the fire, these were answered prayers. Oliver had fanned the flames, bringing coals from the spot where the initial crossings had been made. And now, here was Spotty, wounded but walking.

John asked to be helped to sitting, held his head with both hands.

"That pony knows tender loving care," Beth said. "And he knew where to find it again."

"A lot of horses might have just kept on running—if they even made it to shore." Daniel stroked the pony.

"He is a fine animal," François said. His hands ran down Spotty's side, gently assessing the damage.

John coughed. Ellen touched his wet hair, lifted her skirt hem to wipe the blood dribbling down his temple. She couldn't stop smiling, so grateful that he had survived, that Daniel had been successful in the rescue. Well, it had been a team effort.

"Last I remembered," John croaked, "was seeing a hanging branch, and reaching out to me, the hand of God, it was, or an angel. I latched on like a dying man reaches for water."

"And you had plenty of water," Daniel said. The laughter brought relief.

"Daniel saved you," Beth said.

John coughed again as he sat up and Daniel turned to him. "It was my fault you needed to be rescued. And the medicine is still on the other side." He shivered too. John's head hung between his knees. "I'll take Joker, after I'm rested and we're dried off. I'll get that pack. It's my fault you were back on Spotty."

"No blame assigned," John said.

"I'll take Joker," Ellen said. "He's used to me."

Daniel shook his head. "Enough of us are banged up because of me. Scraped pretty bad." He spoke of Spotty. "This cut is bleeding." He lifted a flap of hide and pressed it back in place on Spotty's chest. The animal's shivered. Blood oozed out over Daniel's fingers.

"We have to get the medicine pack. And I know Joker best."

"Ellen, you—"

"I understand, Daniel, I do. Seems we both want to redeem ourselves. Maybe the river will go down."

"François, you take Joker," Daniel said.

Ellen touched Daniel's arm. "And like it or not, I'm the better horsewoman, especially on this animal."

"She's right, Dan." John found his voice.

"Then it's decided. François, come with me and be my lighthouse where we can aim toward you on our way back." She wouldn't let herself wonder if she could make her way. She'd done it already. Once.

"Oui, mademoiselle." François's eyes looked to Daniel, and Ellen was relieved to see her brother lower his head and nod agreement, even though it was in defeat. *He must really be exhausted to allow me to do this.*

"Good. Get these boys warmed up," she directed Oliver. Beth

was already pulling at John's wet boots. Ellen inhaled a deep breath. She'd gotten what she wanted. Now to prove that she could do it.

Wintering Women

Ailbe thought the structure proved a poor church for the prayers spoken as the men prepared to leave. Apparently, so did the others as Martin Murphy said they should all step outside for prayers and final goodbyes. Sporadic gusts of wind pushed against them, women in their shawls or heavy sweaters; men burdened with the packs they hoped would keep them alive but not weigh so heavily they'd be weakened on their journey. At least the snow had slowed. They could see trees in the distance, tiny beacons through a landscape of white.

Each man had packed ten pounds of meat taken from the slaughtered cows. Eight days of preparation had brought them all to this moment.

Martin Murphy led the prayer, asking for traveling mercies and more, mercies and blessings on those who remained behind. Ailbe lowered her head, prayed the men would reach safety and when the snow melted just a little bit, they'd come back with fresh animals to haul the rebuilt wagons on to Sutter's Fort and their new lives. She spoke a special prayer of gratitude that her James remained behind.

Prayers spoken, she heard Ann Jane tell her father, Old Man Martin, "You can't make it, Pa. You'd hold them back worrying on you and you'd feel terrible about that, now wouldn't you?"

"I've but fifty-six years on these bones," the older man said. "It was me who brought you from Ireland. Me—just as much as Murphy—who wanted Catholic churches and a Catholic education in California. I've brought you this far. Seems a sin to let a faithful follower remain."

"You haven't been well, Pa," Dennis said. He patted his father's shoulder, the one that hung lower than his other, his arm listless. Ailbe considered Dennis one of the kindest of men. Maybe his speech problems made him more aware of the need for gentleness in a soul.

The men milled about, saying their goodbyes.

"Don't get it," Mr. Martin complained.

Ailbe moved beside him, her baby in her arms. "We'll need your faithfulness here, to encourage us. Remind us that we're in God's hands. And it won't be forever."

He grunted. "Old Hitchcock, he gets to go, but me, younger than him, I'm stuck here?"

"He knows the country," James Miller told him.

"How come he didn't know we'd have to drive wagons up rock faces and build cabins so ramshackle I wouldn't put my hogs in it, let alone my kin." He'd gotten crankier on this journey, while Mr. Hitchcock—in his late sixties—had gotten more jovial. Maybe it didn't matter how many years you had but how well you carried them. Some people were old at fifty, found less to be hopeful about, more life behind than before. His plan to find hope and newness in the West had been thwarted by this calamity of weather. It galled him, Ailbe could tell, that he couldn't make the trek out with the seventeen men prepared to go—including her father and brothers. Maybe she could convince him that they'd benefit from a wise, kind old farmer like him to assist them. People needed to feel useful regardless of their years.

"We're off then, Da," Dennis Martin said. "I'll miss ye like the moon misses the sun, sure that on the morrow they'll meet again." It was one of the longest sentences Ailbe had heard the young man speak.

Ailbe heard a soft whisper as almost all made the sign of the cross over their hearts. She didn't share the depth of faith of her husband and the other Murphys. She knew bad things could happen. Still she invited the Lord to reveal himself to the men and the women, to fill the empty places in all their hearts.

Isabella Patterson didn't have much faith in the prayers the men prayed. She would find her strength somewhere else, perhaps in the way she survived this new ordeal, kept her children alive. Hadn't she remodeled herself after marrying Andrew? After she became a mother overnight? Hadn't she adapted to trying to win over eight children bereft of their mother's death and angered—she came to feel—by their father's sudden marriage to her? Yes, she'd endured a great deal already in her life and she had adapted. She would do that now in this most challenging of situations.

Isabella hugged her girls to her. "Looks like we're to have more time together than we ever imagined." Both girls nodded. *Silent as fence posts.* Isabella took a deep breath. It had been months since they'd seen a fence post. She'd sing the praises of the first one she saw when they reached the California valley, that sign of civilization. Fence posts defined borders and they kept conflict at bay.

Mary Sullivan and Sarah Montgomery stood arm in arm as though holding each other up. Mary's brother John wore a bright-colored tuque that now had ear flaps. Isabella thought they looked like puppy ears flopping in the breeze. Sarah made the adaptation for John's hat, and in the days when they'd moved supplies from wagons to the shelter, Sarah had found moments to knit. She might get Sarah to show her how she'd done that, take up knitting and make caps for her children. *That won't work.* She chastised herself. She had no yarn. Raw material was necessary to make those changes.

Isabella watched the men finish their embraces. She hoped she wasn't saying goodbye for the last time to her father. She'd held him extra tight when she'd helped him don his fur-lined coat, one he'd worn for years, with its grease-stained hide and made him look more like those Greenwood mountain men than the well-spoken, well-read father he was. This saying farewell, it wasn't for the faint-hearted. She'd said goodbye to a man she'd loved and would never see him again in this life. She didn't want the same thing to happen between her father and her. She must stay strong for her children, not let them see her fears. "Farewell," she whispered.

Old Man Martin stomped his way back into the makeshift cabin. His daughter, Ann Jane, would have her hands full with him. She'd been designated his tender, as daughters always were. Well, Isabella hadn't been so named for her father, who was heading off without her. He would have been a bear if she'd have tried to keep him behind.

The men looked like thieves, with only their eyes left showing after wrapping their faces with scarves. Capt Stephens gave the shout, and the men turned their backs to the women and headed out, tromping through the snow. Maolisa Murphy, with her newborn tight to her breast, let out a sob but turned her back so her husband wouldn't hear it. Another gift Isabella had been given: she didn't have a newborn to worry over. She wasn't grieving a lost child, like Ann Jane, nor having to tend a grumpy father. And she'd already cried the tears of grief that Sarah Montgomery cried, saying goodbye to a husband, but she'd see him again. All the wives would be hoping for such. They'd begun this together, this trek across the continent, but now each was on a new journey, one demanding a commitment going beyond anything they'd been called upon to do before—and hopefully ever after. Yes, she'd encourage these women—and two men—and seventeen children who were staying at home—such as it was. She'd do what she could to be a good steward to her pain and loss, use them not to carry grief but to fuel the hearth fires of this new place.

19

To Carry On

Wagon Guards

They spent two days making snowshoes. The act made Moses hopeful. They were taking action, doing what his sister always said one must do: carry on.

Allen and Joe cut the bow from one of the wagons, a hickory strip that had long ago been soaked to bring it to a bend to hold the canvas on the wagon. With effort and some of Allen's tools, each man made a curve they crisscrossed with rawhide to be the web they'd stand on. Then they wrapped more rawhide around their ankles to secure their heels to the webbing.

"Kind of awkward for walking," Moses said. He stomped around, lifting one leg up then down, as though wearing a box on each foot.

"But it'll get us out to get some meat." Joe lifted his rifle over his shoulder, practiced walking. "Besides, we're nearly out of wood. We'll head out with our axes and guns. If we're lucky, we'll bring dinner and a log or two. Practice with these things." None had ever worn snowshoes.

The ox's bawl was ever present and Moses knew the animal

was starving. He was ready to put it out of its misery, but it was their last resort. Once they slaughtered the ox, that would be the end of their food supply until they found game.

They spent the day searching. They noted tracks of coyotes and foxes but never saw an animal. And no evidence of elk or deer or anything edible. Not even mice, though Moses wondered if he could eat a mouse. He supposed if he had to, he could.

The next day they brought axes and only Moses carried a gun. They chopped down a tree to haul back for fuel. It had needles and the ox either wasn't interested or was so weak now, it couldn't chew anymore.

By the fourth day after the storm that had kept them inside for almost a week, they all knew what they had to do.

"I'll do it," Moses said. "I'm the one who volunteered to stay with the wagons. You agreed to keep me company. I'll do that dirty work."

"We'll let you," Joe said.

Moses put on his snowshoes, loaded his gun with black powder, tamped the wad, added the lead ball, then tromped out. His stomach hurt and his thighs ached like he'd run a thirty-mile race, not that he ever had. Maybe his gut ached because he knew what he had to do without even eating much. He'd had a small bit of beef they had dried from the first ox they'd killed. He kept taking the saleratus mixture, but that would soon be gone. What would he do then? Maybe eating good, fresh meat would help him—and them all.

He tromped to where the ox had worked a path around itself, the snow packed lower than the remaining drifts. Moses slid into the corral, walked over and patted the ox, ran his hands along the short horns. The ox bawled. "I'm sure sorry about this," Moses said. "I really wanted you to see California too. I guess I should have listened to Dr. John and not let myself get to know you." He felt tears burn behind his nose. "Shouldn't ever have named you, should I have? Bill. But I thank you for your life and hard duty.

And I promise to make good use of all you'll give us." He stood in front of him, put his head to the ox's, and before he knew what was happening, the big animal stopped bawling—and licked his cheek, the rough tongue a caress. He felt like a Judas goat. Moses bawled himself then. "I'm so sorry, Bill. I'm just so sorry." *How can I do this?*

He was a man now, and men did what they had to. He wiped his nose, thumbed at his tears, and stepped to Bill's side, then away, pointed the rifle at the ox's temple and pulled the trigger. He wept. And he carried on.

Wintering Women

Sarah was hungry before the men even left. They'd butchered six oxen so the women would have food. They'd also dried much of one of the oxen for meat for the men to carry. Sarah had wondered how they'd calculate how much meat eight women and seventeen children would go through in a day. She hoped Mr. Miller and maybe Old Man Martin—if he was able—would find game for them. They'd been slaughtering oxen since leaving Allen and Joe and Moses at Stephens Lake. The absence of game was like scum on an otherwise promising body of water: it was a world belonging to wild things and yet they'd seen nothing wild. They were surrounded by wilderness that surely housed hundreds of elk and deer, maybe even buffalo—what she wouldn't give for a piece of roasted buffalo meat—but the wild things refused to appear.

She must not dwell on what she could not control.

The women had decided to try to stake out corners as their own, or sides as the case might be. If it wasn't so cold, she would have slept in the Sullivan wagon, which was partially intact, serving as storage, a large canvas lying over the butter churns, axes, even that rocking chair that Beth Townsend sat in long ago. It was really only a few weeks as she calculated. Sarah herself had hung onto that chair, carried it up and around the rock face where they hauled up the wagons. She'd carried the two volumes of Webster's *Dictionary of the English Language* too, even though she couldn't read a word. One day she would. It was her indulgence, one she defied Allen in bringing. He'd said the books were too heavy. She didn't care. She saw them as a promise to herself. She put the books at her "home."

Once they found their spots in the cabin and made a common area of sorts, she'd suggest bringing the rocking chair inside. Surely the mothers of the babies would like rocking in it now and then. Sarah wouldn't mind sitting in it once in a while herself. After all, she knew its story. And maybe she'd find someone willing to teach her to read. Allen had never been able to take the time.

"Could you hold the baby for me, for just a moment?" Ailbe asked Mary Sullivan. "James and William and Mr. Martin are going to go out and see if they find any signs of game. I think my dear husband is anxious to be free of all these children." She smiled.

"Maybe I should send my little brothers with you."

"You could. I need to help William get his snowshoes on." Mary raised her eyebrows. "I know he's twelve and he'll moan, 'Oh, Mama,' but I want to pamper my boy a little." When Mary reached out for now five-month-old Ellen Independence, the child launched herself into Mary's arms.

"She's a really good baby." Mary bounced the child on her hip, making faces at the child's chubby face. "I haven't heard her wail once this morning."

"She is as long as she's well fed," her mother said. "And that's up to me."

"And the rest of us. We'll make sure that you and Maolisa get enough to eat. Ration if we must."

"Oh, I don't think it will come to that. The men will be back with a relief party long before, surely." She looked toward the west, her eyes with a faraway sheen. She blinked several times, then shook her head as though emerging from sleep.

"What is it?"

"Oh, nothing, love," Ailbe told her. She fussed with the baby then, wiped her mouth of drool. "I sometimes have these seeings, a feeling really, about something in the future. James says I'm silly indeed and he's right. They rarely come to pass."

"The Murphys never show the slightest worry. I'm . . . it's admirable."

"Oh, pah, not so worthy. We all have little cautions, our wonderings. But it helps to have a belief that we're on this journey for a reason."

"Because the men said you had to come."

"Yes, they say such things, but we each must make it our own decree. Otherwise when things go wrong—and they always do— we'd blame our men. Instead, we find our own hope. My James will say, 'We go left here,' and I make my case for turning right. When he won't budge, I take it as an opportunity to try a new way—his way. And if later it turns out left wasn't such a good idea, perhaps we can turn back to see what challenges my way would bring. If not, I trust God is with us whatever choice we make. It's what I draw on in the hard times. That I'm not alone and that God wants good things for us at the end." Ailbe leaned in. "Truth is, I'd rather be happy than right." She tweaked her daughter's nose. "I'll be off to help my William. Thank you, love, for lookin' after the wee one."

Thank you.

The baby grabbed at Mary's braids, pulled a loose strand to her mouth. "I believe you could use a nappy."

"In that bag." Ailbe pointed from her perch helping William.

Mary walked across the narrow cabin to her own bedroll, where she laid the baby down, pulled up the little girl's dress, and untied the diaper knots at the baby's sides. Indie cooed. She could enjoy this time stuck here—or blessed to be here—with an infant. Her future would all depend on the choices she made, like being happy rather than trying to always best her brother.

Cross-Country Men to Sutter's Fort

Capt Stephens was glad they'd brought all the horses with them. The animals slowed them somewhat being led, as they didn't easily push through deep drifts. But they were traveling downward and surely in a day or two they'd be in terrain where snow wasn't thigh-deep, where patches of green pressed through the white covering the universe. He wondered if this deep snow level was common in these mountains in December. *It is still December, isn't it?* He'd have to confirm that when they stopped and made a snow camp.

The horses also made it possible for some of the men to simply carry themselves, with packs burdening the animals. Townsend wasn't all that strong, though he'd been a farmer, he said, back in Missouri to supplement his doctoring. The snowshoeing tired him more than the others, Capt surmised by his quieter demeanor. And Mr. Hitchcock too seemed to appreciate that his horse was carrying his rifle and a bedroll and a small bag of corn for their effort so he only had to carry himself. Even the Greenwoods were walking, but their mounts plodded behind, heads low, tails still. It was a survival march for all of them. He recognized that truth and he carried the burden of getting them through.

He'd come to appreciate all these men, but some more than others. The Martin boys, Patrick and Dennis, were both stalwart, never uttering a complaint of any kind while being encouraging. He watched as Dennis offered to put Townsend's pack on his horse, as Townsend's animals were all off with Mrs. Townsend and what he called the horse party. Townsend had readily accepted. There were other things he saw too, acts of kindness that kept the men's spirits up—sharing a pull of tobacco, offering up dry socks. He realized that half of being a captain of any sort meant not just making good decisions but keeping up morale, letting them know that the future held good things. He hoped there'd be someone forming a temporary leadership among the women. They were more dependent than this party of men, moving, acting, getting somewhere. What had Milton written about how to spend his blinded life? "They also serve who only stand and wait." That was those women. It was up to him to make sure they were not abandoned, but meanwhile, they'd have to survive on their own. He hoped someone at the cabin could bring them to encouraging places.

And there were the wagon boys—Joe, Moses, and Allen. How were they faring? His troops were now split into quarters, and each was asked to take steps forward in their own way. Only this party, men and horses plodding through snow, was in his command now. He couldn't think about the others. He could only consider these men, men who had to make it, as they would be the ones to return to rescue all the others. The four branches of the once fluid, flowing river would have to ride the waves alone—as best they could.

PART II

20

Forward

Horseback Party

"Better you suggest that than me," Ellen said. "Daniel will get all wrathy."

"I'll tell him." They'd walked back to the site of the crossing, where coals still glowed and they could see the left-behind container. Patches of snow dotted the riverbank, lay deeper in wooded areas where the sun didn't reach, but a warm breeze had taken most of the snow, buoyed their spirits. The horses ripped at small shoots of grass, and Ellen knew that could make them ill if they got too much. It was a balance to keep the animals fed while not allowing them to overeat. The little grain they had left wouldn't be enough without the grass though. *The horses all look so skinny.* At least the weather cooperated, with clouds like horsetails wisping across an opaque sky.

François had set up a tent and the women had gone beyond it to take care of their personal needs, which is where they were when Beth made her suggestion and Ellen concurred with the decision.

Ellen stripped off her dress. They were fortunate that the saddle packs that had survived the crossings held their clothing. She donned one of John's shirts, kept her pantaloons on, the ruffles reaching to her ankles. She wrapped a blanket around her shoulders, the movement causing a sharp pain. *Am I being foolish?*

"The moccasins will be good too," Beth said, handing a pair to Ellen.

"I'm ready," she said. Beth nodded her approval and went out in front of her.

"Is Joker rested enough?" Beth asked.

"*Oui*, madame," François answered. "Is mademoiselle ready to—Oh!" He looked away.

"Think nothing of it, François. This is serious work we're about."

"You—you can't do this." Daniel's voice rose and Chica barked as though something was wrong.

"I'm covered head to foot," Ellen said. She pushed her way past him, didn't glance at John lying just inside his tent, the flap open. "I hesitate to bring up the fact that I wouldn't have to do this if you hadn't forgotten—"

Daniel's expression went from domineering to crestfallen. "I know, I know. I . . . have no excuse. But you can't go, Ellen. Your arm, you haven't the strength. We should wait until the river stops rising and the horses are more rested."

"No time," Ellen said. "We need the laudanum now, for John."

"Sister. Please. Don't . . . don't be foolish. Don't be like I was."

The sadness in his voice stopped her. Tears filled his eyes. "Just . . . you're not the strongest swimmer. Listen, please."

His frown amidst the freckles and the stillness of his body told Ellen that her brother felt something she'd never seen before. *What's going on?*

"I should go, mademoiselle." In French, François made his argument of his ability to swim, his mount being the most rested of all the horses.

Ellen translated his words for Beth, and as she did, she realized the wisdom of his proposal.

"François makes good sense," Ellen said.

"No," Daniel said. "It's my duty."

"You've shown your bravery, not just by rescuing John but by . . . I know there's something more, something you're not saying," Ellen continued. "But doing what makes sense, that's an act of valor too." She pulled the horse blanket around her, aware of her exposure now. "You put my own false pluck to shame. We have to make the right assessment for the right reason. We wait. And when the river stops rising, we'll accept François's offer." Daniel lowered his eyes and nodded agreement. "Good." She shivered. "Now if you'll excuse me, I shall dress for our meal. I believe we're having hardtack and ginger tea."

She swirled in her pantaloons, throwing the blanket like a fringed shawl out into the atmosphere. As she put her dress back on, she thought of how easy it was to convince herself to do something that another could do more wisely. Had she wanted to show bravery? Or win the approval of her brother? Even without an injured shoulder, she had no business trying to swim this rising stream on Joker. *Ignoring the truth can get me into trouble.*

As they waited through the afternoon, watching the muddied bank reveal darker evidence of the river's slow drop, the group talked. There'd been fires where they shared stories, but this noon break was different. Ellen said, "I've been thinking. My talents, if I have any, are in encouraging others, not in being a heroine. 'Twas foolish of me to think I should be the one to go back and get that pack."

"We've all made poor choices," Beth said. "And we make the best of them."

"We were swimming." Daniel's tone caused Ellen and others to turn to him, his words as though arriving from a distance. "There were four or five of us boys, nine or ten years old, swimming on a summer day. There must have been a cloudburst upriver." He stared straight ahead. "We didn't notice that the current pushed harder or that the river rose around us. When we did, we rushed to get out and sloshed our way to the bank." No one interrupted Daniel as he scoured his past. "My friend Jorge shouted that he couldn't move. We were close to the shore and water didn't even come to his knees. I turned around and could see him standing like in a baby's bath. It wasn't deep at all. I laughed at him. He cried out while I pulled at grass and scrambled free up the bank. He must have lost his balance. I turned, saw the current grab at him as he struggled to stand, and couldn't do anything. I—I was frozen."

Daniel looked at Ellen. "I knew I should go in for him, but I couldn't." He looked away. "It was another of our friends who pushed past me and plunged back in. He fought the river for him, though I was closer." Daniel pushed at pebbles with a stick then. "The others said the strongest swimmer had made the right call. Jorge was safe. That was all that mattered, they said. But I'd been a coward."

"You were just a boy when that happened," Beth said. "Today you acted nobly."

"You saved your brother." Ellen touched his arm. Daniel didn't jerk away. "Letting François return for the pack, that takes courage too. Knowing when you can't do a thing."

"Not the Murphy way, though."

Should I tell them? Perhaps this was the time. "Ye remember the fire, Matthew's mercantile going up in flames?" Ellen said.

Daniel frowned. "I had nothing to do with that."

"I know." Ellen patted his arm. "But I did." She took a deep breath. "The privy called one night and I was careful not to wake Matthew. It wasn't hard. He slept the sleep of the dead served by rum. Beth knows." Ellen looked to her friend, who nodded. "I'm saying nothing new of that. But that night I set the candle on a shelf by the door beside greasy rags I had not put away. I should have taken the light outside, but the moon shone bright as a gold piece, enough to shine a town. I left the door open at my privy perch and finished, and I watched foxes playing in the moonlight.

And then the light got brighter and I began to feel warm, and when I turned to look, I saw the mercantile in flames." Ellen swallowed and Beth moved closer to her. "Our rooms above raged in orange. I heard him scream at the window. I told him to jump!" It was as though it happened right in front of her, again. "But he didn't and I didn't save him."

"You can't be certain it was your candle, Ellen," Beth said. "Matthew may have lit one himself. Perhaps that's why the upstairs became enflamed so quickly."

"My shame is still that I did not act. I made a coward's choice."

"I didn't know," Daniel said.

"We never know another's demons," Ellen said. She cast a tentative smile to him. "But maybe sharing them is a way of smashing up their powers."

"I think you might be right," Daniel said.

His admission was so rare Ellen had nothing more to say.

Wintering Women

Isabella Patterson and her brood were assigned the wall space opposite Sarah and Mary Sullivan. James Miller had created the designations, making sure that his family had one of the two warmest corners. Well, they had little Indie, so that made sense. But there'd been words spoken between him and Maolisa, who had a gift for organizing. The Patterson corner space offered nestling. Being out in the open between Ailbe and James and Ann Jane and her father made Isabella feel like there was no room at all for any privacy in talking with her girls, who were nearly women themselves. Thirteen-year-old Isaac brooded about not being mentioned as a possible hunter by Mr. Miller, granting credit to his own boy who was a year younger. Isabella would build her boy up, remind him that men liked to hunt with those they knew, that his rejection had nothing to do with him or his abilities at all. The truth was, Isaac hadn't hunted but one time with his grandfather and never with his father, who was so tender he'd carry spiders outside rather than squash them at the privy.

She sighed. "Are you all right, Mama?" Lydia asked. "You've been a-sighing all morning."

"Have I? That's not a very good use of my breath, now is it?" Lydia smiled back at her. "It's just the settling in that's bringing on the sighs. I'll be fine once I feel like our little nest is made."

"Nesting is what we women do well." This from Ann Jane, who couldn't avoid overhearing anything that Isabella said. "We tend and befriend. Here, Da." She handed her father his cap. He frowned but allowed her to adjust it over his mostly bald head. "I'm sure Mr. Miller will appreciate your help."

Mr. Martin grunted. "He should. He's lucky I stayed behind." He maneuvered his way around the piles of bedding and clothing and trunks and children. Isabella estimated their cabin was ten feet by twenty, long and narrow. Isabella's son had set up a tent for the younger children, who giggled inside, while Mr. Martin headed toward the door that had once been part of a wagon floor. The Millers left, leaving a blast of cold air behind them. Mr. Martin grunted at the hide hinges swinging on the wooden covering that had once been a wagon seat.

Whispering, Ann Jane said, "He can't shoot much anymore with that bad shoulder, but he can help haul in a deer if they find one. And he's good with a knife for butchering."

Ann Jane sounded defensive for him. Isabella understood that. She felt protective of her son while wishing her own father had stayed behind. "He's a good man," Isabella said. "I'm not sure how my father would have handled being left with all of us."

"We'll have to take a lesson from them," Ann Jane said. "Make the best of what we have." She parted her brown hair in the center like most of the women. "Including figuring out how to make our spaces . . . cozy. I want to light a candle it's so dark in here."

Isabella noted that the unchinked logs let light through but cold air too.

"The wind will blow the candles out," Lydia said.

What could they chink the logs with? "We could cover some of the walls with hides, but maybe stuffing the cracks with clothes for now would help," Isabella said. "And when we want a little light, it would be easier to remove a pantaloon than try to roll up a hide."

"That's a good idea," Maolisa Murphy said. Her area was tidier than the rest of the cabin sections. Her older children already flipped winks into a tin cup while the younger ones tossed a canvas-covered ball. "It's not exactly a cabinet for clothing, but we can find that child's britches when we need to." She laughed. "We'll adapt."

"Manage, I call it," Isabella said. "Manage children in new places. Manage old folks and their moods. Manage food. Manage tears. One day, I fully expect to have to manage my own funeral."

"Not anytime soon, I hope," Maolisa said. All three women and Lydia laughed, but discomfort settled on their faces too. *Death is an approaching visitor.* "I've already arranged for one funeral on this journey, and I don't intend to have to do another." Mimi had picked up a clump of snow-dirt trying to melt near her feet. She squeezed it between her fingers, examined the white, muddy mixture as though it were the most interesting invention she'd ever seen. At least Isabella didn't have young children to consider as she watched Maolisa wipe the child's hands and mouth where the "interesting invention" had ended up.

It occurred to Isabella that if they divided the limited space by age group of children, putting older children together with adults off to the sides, they might be better off, able to help those with younger children. But for now, the thought of merging families and eliminating a border around her own kin was one too many adaptations, even for Isabella.

Wagon Guards

"It's a big decision," Allen Montgomery said. "But I say we do it." He sliced another chunk of meat and stuck a sharpened branch through it, then laid it on the griddle away from the direct heat but so that the meat would roast slowly until almost dry.

"We said we'd stay with the wagons," Moses said.

"But we didn't know then that we could find no game, half starving. What do you suggest we do when old Bill here is eaten up?" Allen said.

Moses winced. He still had trouble thinking they'd be consuming his ox. But staying alive counted for more than sentiment, he supposed.

"I think Capt will understand," Joe Foster said. "We all assumed we three could hunt our hearts out and be fat as ticks come spring. Capt always said you had to have a plan, but you also have to be able to change it when you get new information. To not do that is foolhardy."

"We've got new information all right," Allen said. He skewered another slice of meat, turned the other pieces over. Sizzle and aroma made Moses's belly ache in craving.

"No game. Great pain," Joe said.

Moses sighed. "All right. I guess you guys know best." *You being grown men and all and me being just a boy.* "What's your plan then?"

"We'll dry and carry ten pounds each. Probably only use half of Bill. We should be able to carry enough to get us over the summit where the wagons went and follow the trail they made. As we get to lower altitudes, there has to be meat on the hoof," Allen said. Moses did like his confidence, even though it seemed like speculation rather than that "new information" he touted.

"Let's eat a good meal tonight. I hate to leave any of old—I mean, any meat behind," Joe said. "But we need to go now while we still have strength."

Moses nodded. That made sense. He just felt he was failing his sister and her husband by not remaining to keep his word like he said he would. But who was going to steal any of this? No one was within miles and miles of them. And if Allen was willing to leave his arms and ammunition behind, then who was he to worry over satins and silks?

"All right. We head out in the morning. Now let's get us some vittles," Joe said. "I'm starving."

"Not sure starving is the best word to use here." Moses didn't like *that* kind of new information at all.

21

Plans

Wintering Women

Maolisa had always been able to make a home out of nothing, but the chaos of this cabin strained her resolve. Children crying in between bouts of laughter. Women's tense voices interrupted by shouts of directions to a toddler. The scent of tallow marked the constant worry over active children—especially BD—knocking over the flame in an accidental burst of energy chasing his older brothers while they barked back at him for ruining their game of pickup sticks. She couldn't begrudge them, but she also couldn't let go of the worry. She nursed Yuba in the midst of the rush, grateful that Mary Sullivan had offered to entertain the children now and then. Mimi had taken to the young woman whom Maolisa thought had fewer feminine graces than some but she had a kind heart. And her rush to lead their ox team to the top of the summit before even her brother showed her courage and resolve. Maolisa didn't even mind that Mary almost always pulled her hems up into her waistband for easier walking. The Sullivan girl liked playing Jacob's Ladder, a toy lifted from the bag of flour where she'd buried it for her brothers. It was a game Maolisa associated with boys. Still, why couldn't girls do things frequented by boys? Can't a woman stand out with her physical strength as a man might, without losing her femininity? She remembered the slight build of Moses Schallenberger, which in no way diminished his manliness, or perhaps she should say boyhood. He and Mary Sullivan were about the same age. Surely the world was large enough to accommodate all kinds of physical abilities and passions. Wasn't that one of the very reasons they had left Canada for Missouri and then nearly a year ago to make their way toward California, to allow their own children to respond to the Lord's call however that seemed fit?

Yuba nuzzled deeper into her mother, who still gripped annoyance, an easier emotion to deal with than the empty feeling she had when Junior told her he was going to go with the men. And did. She would find resolution in time. *Don't I always?* She made herself think happier thoughts so that Yuba received blessings from her mother's milk rather than angst. Maolisa always did step over annoyance, even anger, in time; but with such a new baby and with uncertainty weighing like a storm off the Irish coast of their homeland, she had hoped Junior would have seen her need to have him remain. He assumed that he could better serve by going forward and bringing back help. Wind whistled through their cabin walls despite the hides and now clothing stuffed as chinking. The pantaloons pushed between the boards made her smile.

The hinged door leaked wind and sound. Some tempests can't be hoped away, though.

She must remember other gales she'd weathered. Literal ones in County Wexford and those on the sea they'd crossed to County Dorchester in Canada when she was twelve. Her family had happily reunited with the Murphys, with whom Maolisa had grown up. A storm followed by a welcome calm. They went together. She had to remember that.

Junior lived in Canada, and within four years, the two had seen what their parents had known would be—each other as lifelong mates. She had never shared with Junior—or anyone else—any other desire of her heart, slipping naturally into the worlds of wife and mother. But she remembered that once she'd wanted to be called *múinteoir*—teacher. She had wanted to instruct not only children of their own making but others, to have a wider touch than just the minds of her own flesh and blood. She wasn't sure why she'd not expressed the desire to Junior. Perhaps a passionate love had blinded her to her own wishes. Junior was a persuasive man, not that loving him required any persuasion. But marrying so young had, and she supposed she accepted the reading of the wedding banns when she did as much to please her father as to bring pleasure to Junior and her own desires to love and cherish her husband.

He was a dear. That's what she had to remember. And he would not have left them if he hadn't believed it was the best thing for them all. Courage could look like that, doing for others. "You'll make the most of your time here, Pet. I know ye will," he'd said.

"You men and your confidence in women when it suits you. It can be a strain."

"I've not confidence in *all* these women, but I have it in you. You'll get this place organized and in ship-deck shape, everything battened down. They'll need you." He'd whispered that last as though even a final intimacy couldn't be heard by everyone else in the vicinity.

"I need you." But her words fell upon shoulders already lifting his pack, tugging on the reins of his horse, then one last fleeting kiss to her and to Yuba, Mimi, BD, James, Martin III, and Patrick before he turned his back on her. On them.

She would forgive him. She always did.

The sounds of quarreling between her own sons took her to where Mary Sullivan's coal black hair was being tugged at by Mimi, keeping her from addressing the howls of her boys, now joined by Melinda Patterson's girlish retort and another niece's wail. Mary Sullivan needed help. Maolisa gave a hard push in the rocking chair and rose up, baby in tow. Rationing food took its toll on the children. That and being stuck inside. Maolisa was needed. Maybe dear Junior was right after all.

―――――

Horseback Party

"I do believe you are as healthy as an Irish slinger, Sister." Ellen scrubbed Beth's hair at yet another river's banks. François had been successful in retrieving the forgotten pack and John had steadily gained back his balance.

"I wouldn't have imagined I would ever feel so strong," Beth said. "Ah-h-h! That's so cold."

"A cool rinse, 'tis good for the hair," Ellen said. "Without rose water, we have to make do." She pulled the wooden hair pick and carefully tugged at Beth's snarls. Sun beat warmly on their faces. "I know it's December, but it feels more like April. If this is California, I'm never leaving."

"Maybe it's the weather but you know, I wonder if no longer being jostled around in a wagon hasn't been the real cure for me. Maybe Spotty's companionship too. I've never ridden much, but we're a team now."

"He let you sew that patch up on his chest. 'Tis a fine thing many horses would not allow without something to deaden the pain."

"He trusted me. And I did it without anyone looking over my shoulder barking advice." Beth lowered her eyes. "I'm sorry. I ought not to grouse about John." She shook her head of the wet. "I like the animals. It's something I've never done, work with them. I didn't know I had the interest nor the talent. Assisting my husband with human wounds . . . I never thought about our horses or dogs."

"My father said herds of horses roam California, brought in

by the Spanish. Maybe you could learn how to doctor them while Dr. John stitches up their owners."

"Wouldn't that be interesting."

"I hope you don't mind my saying this, but you seem more . . . relaxed without Dr. John's . . . helpfulness. That can be healing too," Ellen said.

"Can't it just so." Beth turned to look at Ellen, giggled with her delicate fingers over her mouth. Her single dimple deepened.

"I hope you can sustain your independence once you're re-united. I couldn't, with Matthew. He wore me down like a rasp on a hoof, bit by bit. I didn't even notice at first until finally I was a woman reduced."

Ellen handed Beth the wooden comb, announcing that the snags were out. Beth twisted her hair into a braid she let hang over her shoulder. She looked younger. "I'm sorry I didn't realize what was happening with you and Matthew."

"It would have been hard for anyone else to see. I didn't recognize it for quite a while." Now it was Ellen's turn to look away. Bad memories always made her seek escape. "I had such fun with customers at the mercantile. I loved making them laugh and, yes, flirting but harmlessly. Matthew didn't see it that way." Ellen yanked on her curls, bunching them into a braid whether they wanted to be restrained or not. "He'd fallen in love with my 'life-delight,' he'd called it, but once the banns were read and the wedding date set, he began to rasp away at the delight—and my life. I was too naïve to see it."

"We should have visited with you both more often. John and Matthew were closer when they were younger." Beth sighed. "John was so busy on the farm and doctoring and I'd lost the two babies, so was weakened. I just didn't—I'm sorry."

"I . . . I never knew about the babies, Beth." Ellen stopped her braiding and stared. "How hard for you."

"It was. But we'll try again, now that I'm healthier. It'll be such a surprise to John when we meet at Sutter's Fort. He hoped the trip would result in good things for us and so it has."

"Do you think they're at the fort already?"

"I'd hope so. We've found springlike weather before Christmas. They're not that far distant from us, are they? As the crow flies?"

"I've no idea. We've been privileged to have game so handy. I haven't been this full since that time when the Indian marked this path."

"They had a good team of hunters with Moses, that Joe Foster and the Montgomery man. Best in the bunch. I can't believe they've lost a pound. Ready? Let's head back." Beth's steps were even lighter, no more dragging as she had so much of the journey before this separation.

As they moved in comfortable silence, Ellen imagined her new life in California. There wasn't much a widow was allowed to do except win over a good man. There'd be plenty of them in that Mexican Territory: dark, Spanish-descended men with cattle ranches and haciendas and big hearts. But she had her sights on something else. Her brothers might not approve nor her father, but it would be a waste if she didn't take advantage of the lessons she'd learned from being married to a businessman.

The two women finished their toilet and walked arm in arm back toward the campsite. The aroma of rosemary and fowl reached them before they could see what the men served for supper: a once-fat grouse.

"John's sling, it gets credit for our dinner tonight," François said. John dipped his head and blushed.

"Oliver, you've prepared another masterpiece." Ellen sat on a blanket, leaning against her saddle. "Will you be a chef once we reach the fort?"

"I will be chef for the Townsends," he said. "If they have me."

"Oh, we'll have you," Beth told him. "Your gifts are as good if not better in the kitchen than being careful of my health on this sojourn."

Oliver's face turned a deeper hue. "*Oui*, madame. It has been my pleasure." He bowed.

"Maybe you'll open an eatery," John said. "I've thought of that."

"Have you? I'm surprised, though I shouldn't be, I guess. You and Daniel, all us Murphys are enterprising." Ellen chewed on the thigh bone of the grouse. "This is so moist." Chica lay a distance from the campfire, white face, black nose resting on paws, staring at Ellen. She expected a bit of that meat herself.

"I suspect we've all got plans," Daniel said.

"What's yours, Daniel?" Ellen wondered if he'd share.

"I plan to make a stake in the mountains, look for diamonds or gold."

John said. "I want a good business venture, that's my plan. I might have a place for you, Oliver, in *my* restaurant." He tapped his chest.

"There's risk in business too, Brother." Daniel pulled skin from the grouse's chest, tossed it to Chica, who caught it in a single leap.

"What about you, Ellen?"

Was Daniel actually interested in her future? She hoped they'd turned a page in their lives together.

"Oh"—she fluffed the end of her braid between her fingers—"I expect I'll go onstage. Form a theater company."

"What?" Beth, John, and Daniel spoke in unison.

She laughed. "No, I expect the Murphy clan to spend the summer seeking a handsome Spanish vaquero as my suitor. A fine Catholic man, as Papa would want for me."

"You deserve a good husband," Daniel said.

"Thank you."

"But you probably don't need one. You're pretty capable on your own."

"Why, thank you again." His comments brought happy surprise.

She did have a goal to continue her independence, one that just might begin as soon as she met up again with Dr. John. She only had to find a way to convince him it was his idea. That kind of man always needed to believe he was running things even when he wasn't. She'd once thought Daniel was such a man, but as her brother had changed in how he saw her, she was beginning to transform the way she saw him.

Wagon Guards

The cramps began again not long after they ate their last meal before heading out. Moses wondered if maybe it wasn't the food but rather the anticipation of some future event that made his gut twist.

"Will you be able in the morning?" Light from the fireplace cast a ghostly look to Joe's face as he sat on the three-legged stool across from Moses. Allen checked over the rifle he planned to take. He'd oiled the others and wrapped them in cloth with such tenderness Moses thought he was putting babies to bed.

"Yes, sir, I believe I will be. I've taken the saleratus and vinegar and put a mixture in a canteen. Make sure you don't drink out of it by mistake." He grinned, hoped Joe could tell that he jested.

"I'd spit it out first swallow," Joe said.

"It tastes pretty foul, but it works. I expect I'll be up and ready by sunrise."

Moses hadn't slept well, tossing and turning with the cramps. He pulled his knees up toward his chest, wrapped a hot rock with a quilt left behind and placed it on his belly. The heat felt good and he drifted off to sleep before the rays of morning flooded the doorway.

At sunrise, his stomach felt queasy, but he stirred the fire, fixed the grain coffee, and cut fresh meat for roasting. They'd be eating dried until they arrived at the fort, so a last meal of fresh meat would taste good. He had to bring the leftover half a cow closer to the fire, as it froze during the night. He chopped off a chunk and put it in the pan.

Joe and Allen rose, made their outside journey, returned, and ate what Moses had cut up for them, already fried. The evening before, they'd brought inside everything they thought the weather might affect. Dr. John's books, remaining clothes of theirs and those left by the women. They'd dragged trunks inside, things with documents they didn't bother to read. The cabin felt more closed in than before, less room to maneuver. No longer home.

"Guess we're ready, right, boys?" Allen said. They donned their snowshoes, their coats, and the packs they'd roped that they'd carry on their backs. Moses struggled with his snowshoes, tying the heels tight to the rawhide web; getting his toes tied too, lacing rawhide over his boots. When he stood, his stomach lurched, but he was ready.

They started off.

Moses turned back to look only once. He stared at the lake, the cabin, the patch in the snow that Bill had made. The remains of wagons they'd cannibalized to make their cabin. Treetops pierced the bluest sky he'd ever seen and he inhaled the scent of pines. He'd remember this place. And they'd be back in the spring. Allen had said so himself.

The slope up from the lake proved tiring, but Moses persisted, last in the line. The snow often couldn't hold his weight even spread out by the shoes and he'd sink down a foot, then have to lift his entire leg up and out. He'd done that while gathering wood, but they'd also made paths over time. Here, there were no trails, just the goal of the rock face where they'd lifted the wagons up and over. That was their hope, to reach that summit by nightfall. Fifteen miles. When they'd hiked back, it had been before the big snowfall that had kept them in the cabin for days, snow so deep they'd had to shovel their way out through the door, the only natural light in their cabin blocked by the deep drifts. Here, he sank into the snow and each step was like lifting a calf when he roped one, laying it on its side to tie up the hooves so they could brand it.

When the sun was overhead, the cramps began again. Moses reached for his swig of saleratus and vinegar, paused to let it settle. "Go on," he yelled to the men ahead of him. "I'll catch up." He started out only to double over again with pain. Now his legs cramped too. He watched the men stall, waiting for him. "I guess this boy isn't in as good a shape as you men." Moses made a joke out of it, but it was how he felt. They rested for a moment but not moving started to chill their sweat and Allen said, "We have to keep going. We can make it to the summit. Here, let me carry your pack, Moses."

"No. I need to hoist my own load. But thanks."

They carried on but within a very short time, Moses felt his legs give way, his gut ached like he'd been poisoned, if that was what poisoning was like. He collapsed from fatigue and yet another round of cramps. "Just keep going. Make camp by the abandoned wagons. I'll find you."

"I hate to leave you," Joe said. He stood over Moses, his body a shadow.

"Go on. Build a fire. I'll be along."

The two men looked at each other, then at Moses. "All right," Allen said. "But give me your pack. We'll get the fire started."

They turned toward the summit and Moses was both relieved that he had a moment more to rest and frightened that he might not be able to get up, and now, his pack was with Allen.

The moon rose in the night sky. Moses didn't take the time to open his clock piece. He stood. A flicker of light called out to him ahead, and after what seemed like hours, he fell into the camp Allen and Joe had set up.

"I was about to come looking for you," Joe said.

Moses squatted on his heels. Allen took dried beef from Moses's pack and handed it to him. Moses chewed slowly. "I've had some time to ponder," he said. "I don't think I can make it. And you will have to abandon me at some point because I'll hold you back."

"Naw, you can do it," Joe said. "Let us carry your pack and you just walk."

"Even that's a strain. The spasms haven't gone away. They go from ow! to agony in minutes and it takes longer to rest each time. It just won't work."

"What are you planning we should do?" Allen said. He sounded gruff. "Shoot you, like you did Bill?"

"Hey," Joe said.

"Hope that's not my fate," Moses said. "I propose to go back to the cabin. I've got the remaining beef. That'll hold me a few days. And maybe by then there'll be game again and I'll get by. Got salt and plenty of water. A fellow can go a long time without food if he has water." His voice broke at that last, and he wasn't sure it was the "growing vocals," as his sister called it, or if it meant he was close to tears. Maybe a little of both.

"We'll consider it in the morning," Allen said. "Let's get some rest now."

Joe and Allen had chopped pine boughs for their beds, made another platform of branches and boughs to hold the fire. But it didn't really keep them warm. Sleep was a restless dance. Joe rose once or twice to push more of the treetop they'd cut down into the flames. Moses watched in the firelight. *Am I making the right choice?*

In the morning, the fire had melted an area of about fifteen feet around it. But the fire itself had disappeared. Moses looked over the well the melt had created. The fire still burned, but now it was fifteen feet below them.

"Good thing we've nothing to cook," Joe said. He took a bite of jerky, chewed it.

"We'd need one of those long-handled paddles the stone bakers use," Moses said. His breath floated in the frosty air, dancing around before him. At least the frozen ground meant he didn't have to use his snowshoes. Maybe he could go on with them. But before he could say so, another gut pain assaulted him. *No. I can't hold them back.*

196

"You—you go on."

"Are you sure about this, Moses?" Allen asked.

"Yes, sir, I am. If the snow ever melts enough—" He grabbed his side, inhaled quickly. "I'll try to walk out later too, but I can't risk holding you back."

"You know we'd try to help," Joe said. He frowned. "I just don't think Capt would want us to leave you."

"But you can't help my gut. You skedaddle with a clear conscience. It's my decision." He swallowed. He hadn't been scared before, but now he was.

Both men nodded. They lifted their packs, their rifles and jerky. Moses stood, holding his gut with one arm, the other held a rifle barrel with the stock of the gun like a cane. Allen reached for Moses's other hand to shake it. "Goodbye," he said. Joe did the same, but he hugged him too.

Moses vowed he wouldn't let tears fill his eyes, but the looks both men gave him made him wonder if they were the last he'd ever witness, their goodbyes the final human sounds he'd ever hear. He watched them both make their way toward the summit, seeking that cut in the rock that would take them to the others. Then he picked up his pack and turned back toward the lake lost in a world of white.

The frozen snow was a boon. He could walk without the snowshoes. He said a prayer of thanks for the gift of freezing, slinging the bag over his shoulder. He stopped to hold his stomach, started up again. *Will I make it?* He didn't know. He hoped to reach the cabin before dark. He wiped his nose with the back of his mitten, turned to look at Joe and Allen but saw only their tracks. He flicked away the tears of farewell.

22

Where the Shoes Take Us

Wintering Women

The scent of wet wool, of children needing bathing, the absence of cooking smells, bore into Maolisa. She had to do something. Not even two days and already tempers flared. When they'd been moving toward a goal, it had been easier to overlook little irritations, an annoying laugh, a story told more than once, a dry cough.

"Tonight, let's put the children into one area—except for our babies." Maolisa nodded at her sister-in-law, Ailbe. "Men and boys together. Divide the older girls where they aren't taunted by the toddlers or BD, who has a habit of getting in everyone's way, I know. And I apologize. I don't know where he got such contrary ways."

"You really don't know where he got it from, Maolisa?" Ailbe said it with a kind of cackle that cut through the sounds of frustrated children, but Maolisa didn't know if her sister-in-law complained or cajoled.

"I guess I am contrary but only for the good of all." Maolisa thought maybe she was a little overbearing at times since other Murphy women had become mute. "And I do apologize for my

BD. It likely won't get better. You can bet that when the first snake of spring appears, he'll put it down the front of his closest cousin, boy or girl."

"We won't be here when snakes arrive," Mary Sullivan said. "At least I won't be." She dabbed glycerin on her wind-chapped cheek. I agree with your idea, maybe there'll be fewer scuffles." Mary's eyes appeared red, though Maolisa had never seen her crying.

Isabella cleared her throat. "I too think the plan to put the children into one large bedded area near the fire is a good one. The rest of us can fan out behind them, find a little space to call our own. Create some borders."

"I don't think there's much to claim as ours," Sarah said. She sounded irritated.

"It presents some small level of order, though," Maolisa said. "Little ones closest to the fire's warmth. Older ones to the side. When the children are awake, that can also be the space where we set up our table, such as it is." James Miller had brought in wagon baseboards and rolled in four butter churns to act as table legs. At the time they left Missouri and again when they'd carried them up to the summit, Maolisa had thought each having a churn when all the neat cows had stopped giving milk was a poor idea, but now, yes, four churns had come in handy. She would dig into her rounded trunk and pull out a bedsheet to use as a cloth. A little civilization in the midst of the wilderness. They could take the table apart and use the churns as sitting stools. They certainly weren't needed to make butter.

She kept returning to Sarah's voice of irritation. Everyone was annoyed. It was bad enough traveling in wagons with everything overheard, but now they were even closer, with conditions more stressful than before. There wasn't a place to get away from each other. No one dared go walking in the snowy woods. She'd talk with Sarah and try to find out what was the most recent cause of distress. As if the possibility of starving to death wasn't enough of a reason. *I must not think of starvation.*

The plan went into place, and as the wee ones settled in their bedrolls, mothers listened to a dozen bedtime prayers. The women migrated toward the back of the cabin. They sat on the floor they'd covered with blankets, then wrapped themselves with quilts. Sarah worked on a quilt patch she said would become part of a Medallion square. Maolisa nursed Yuba, lamented to herself how little milk she had to give. *Can I keep this baby alive? Intrusive thought.* It gave no optimism and drained what little hope she had. She hummed a lullaby, hoping the rhythm would calm herself as well as her child. Being settled is what she needed, more than order.

The women had organized their children, and now came the long hours of darkness with thoughts of missing men and uncertain futures. At home in Quebec, Mary Sullivan would have lit a candle and read, but she needed to preserve the tallow they had left, so the women rotated who would provide pale light during the long evening, pushing down unwelcome thoughts. Reading was a luxury at night now. Mary struggled with the intrusion of regrets and censuring thoughts. What could they all talk about that wouldn't make any of them punish themselves for having arrived in this desolate place and time, for not being able to move forward, for having to wait?

"I have an idea," Mary posed, the notion arriving as comforting as the sounds of water lapping at a summer lake. "Why don't we get to know each other a little more, talk about where we came from?"

"Like how I got to be the size of a rutabaga?" Ann Jane said. The others laughed with her, but Mary didn't like to see people make fun of how they looked. She'd seen children tease each other—they'd teased her for her big "boyish" feet and her height as she'd towered over shorter children her own age. It was worse when self-inflicted.

"I was thinking stories of our past, maybe where our shoes

have walked," Mary said. "I came from Ireland, a place I loved. My shoes have walked where Vikings walked. Dublin. A grand city it is."

"Many of us have walked in Dublin," Maolisa said. "Where else have your shoes taken you?"

"Into a canoe on the Gatineau River." Mary surprised herself with that comment.

Young Lydia Patterson oohed at that.

"By yourself?" Johanna Murphy asked. She was one of the single Murphy aunts.

"Oh yes. While my brother snorted on the shoreline all worrisome." Several of the women laughed.

"Men do seem to worry over us when we try to do what they do," Sarah said.

"After that, these shoes took me through Michigan and Wisconsin Territory to reach Council Bluffs." Mary lifted her leg straight out before her. *Large feet give me greater balance.* It was the first time Mary admired her feet. "My boots have been on water and land and jumped over rock walls so high I thought I was flying. As a child." Mary Sullivan quieted. "They've taken me to Mass and kneeling for Extreme Unction given at the same time to my mother and father." She stared at her shoes. "Cholera. My boots have walked me into rooms where people I loved died." Ann Jane sat next to her and she patted Mary's knee. "And now they've taken me here, sharing space with each of you."

"I'm glad you're here," Sarah said. "I'd have been homeless without your offer to share your wagon."

"Which is now a part of this humble cabin," Ailbe said. "Housing us all. We're grateful."

"My shoes took me to a gravesite in the Iowa dirt," Ann Jane said. "I put my baby Sean in that ground. With his little booties still on his feet. The only shoes he'll ever know."

"We lost a daughter to malaria," Ailbe said. She made the sign of the cross over her heart. "It's one of the reasons we headed to

California—if that's where we are. Where have your boots been, Sarah?"

Sarah put her quilt patch down. Mary wondered how she could have seen to stitch in the poor light anyway. "I was born in Ohio, so I suppose my first steps were taken there. Then we moved to Indiana. My father had itchy feet. That's what my mother said. I guess I do too." She tapped the toes of her moccasins against each other. "After that it was Missouri and then, let's see, Iowa, where we joined up with all of you. The plains across and now California, assuming we're here." Her stomach growled, but no one said a word about it. "They took me down an aisle toward marriage and they walked me away. Not from marriage," she added quickly. "Away from, well, where Allen and the wagons got left."

"They'll walk you to him in the spring," Isabella said.

Sarah nodded. "I hope so."

"What about you, Maolisa?" This came from Ann Jane.

"My shoes? They've walked to a lot of midwives, that's certain." The women laughed. "Eight times before we left Missouri. Four babies didn't survive." She patted the youngest member of this company. "I still can't believe it. Eight babes before I turned thirty-four and this last one in the direst of weather conditions. Yet she lives, little Lizzie Yuba." Beth Townsend's rocking chair creaked as Maolisa comforted her infant. "These shoes have taken me to a simple cabin with a dozen midwives." She spread her arms around. "All of you."

"Me included," James Miller chimed in.

"I wouldn't have thought you'd wanted to be part of a women's circle," Maolisa said. "But if you do, then, yes. You count."

"First time I've been named a midwife." James chuckled.

"When Indie was born you were off hunting," his wife told him. "So, this will be your one and only midwife claim, that you were around for a niece's arrival."

James Miller and Old Man Martin were at the edges of the semicircle of women, along with William and the oldest Patterson boy and Mary Sullivan's brothers. There wasn't really any other place for them to go.

Ann Jane's father looked like he slept, but he opened one eye. "An interesting way to hear a person's story," he said then sat up. "Now my boots, oh my. They've been to the mountains in the far west. They've walked the banks of the Missouri. They've helped me gather driftwood to build a fire on the beach of Oregon Territory. 'Course they were mostly moccasins, not leather-soled by the cobbler's hands. And with any luck, these boots will take me to California. If I can get the swelling in my legs to stop so I can get the dang boots back on."

"Now, Da," Ann Jane said.

"Stepped in a lot of—"

"Da! There are children."

The women laughed and Mary noticed Mr. Martin smiled too.

"For a minute you sounded like my father," Isabella Patterson said.

"I wish me and these boots were with him, with all those other men. No offense, James."

"None taken," James said. "Kinda wish I could have gone with them too. But I had another assignment, just as important."

Maolisa said, "May the good Lord be with those men."

Mary sensed a shift in the mood. "Anyone else?"

No one spoke, then Maolisa said, "All these different shoes and boots together in one place. We've been strong enough to make it this far. I'm feeling confident we'll be setting our feet at Sutter's Fort before too long."

A small child called out "Mama," and several heads turned.

"It's my Kate," Ann Jane said. She pushed herself up. Mary didn't think she looked much like a rutabaga anymore. Her dress hung on her so long it needed hemming up so she wouldn't step on it. Her apron strings wrapped twice around her.

Ann Jane's movement took the others away from the circle and they too rose to nestle themselves among their children to find sleep.

"That passed some time," Maolisa told Mary as she undid her braid for a good brushing. "Thank you for offering the idea. Maybe it's something we can do each evening, to fill the time."

"And we know a little more about each other," Mary said. "Maybe even about ourselves." Despite her shyness, she had braved sharing a part of her past, choosing her escapade on the Gatineau River. No one had found it unladylike or brazen. Mary looked around. She saw lowered shoulders. Faces not so grim. Talking about where they'd come from had brought them closer to here, where they were but with more joy and less fear.

Maolisa began to sing a lullaby and the others joined in with her *Too-ra-loo-ra-loo-ra*. Music was a blessing. So were stories, shared.

Cross-Country Men to Sutter's Fort

Capt noticed Dr. John struggling in the snowshoes the Sullivan woman had loaned him while he led one of the Murphy horses. "Can we halt, for a man to catch his breath?"

"We have to keep moving, Doc. You've got to push yourself a little harder."

The image of the women waving to them from the cabin drove Capt. They had plenty of food, surely. And without much exertion, the food could be stretched for two weeks or more, giving them time to reach Sutter's and then return with healthier animals to bring the women out.

And James Miller was as good a hunter as any of the men. He'd be highly motivated with his family right there, all those children with hungry eyes looking up at them.

The men followed the river through the great silence, their boots making no noise, muffled by the snow. Around them the landscape played tricks on their eyes—a cluster of trees luring them for a resting place, only to skip steps ahead just when they thought they'd reached it. In places, because the terrain proved rugged, they'd had to leave the water's edge and walk overland, moving through timber. His horse wasn't always that happy about where he'd had to lead him.

The third day out, they halted to eat jerky and let the horses paw at the snow to find a blade of grass or two. Capt speculated about how they'd get those wagons through here when the time came. But they would. After the assault at the summit, he believed this party could do anything.

"I've . . . we've got to stop." Townsend leaned over, his gloved hands on his thighs. "I . . . I can't continue without rest."

"And we can't hold up but for a moment, Doc. Look about. Everyone is tired. Exhausted. Think of the women waiting for us. Think of your wife perhaps struggling as much or more." He didn't like to use guilt, but sometimes it motivated people. "Think of the book you'll write about this trial, Doc. You'll want your 'I can do it' attitude to be the star of such a tome, wouldn't you? It'll be a read about daring, bravery, maybe even catapult you into, I don't know, public office."

Townsend lifted his head. "Public office?"

"We're going into a foreign land. You might be the one to speak for our immigrant voices. Be a strong say, especially if we could all report how much you encouraged us onward. A man like me isn't so well spoken as you. Why, you might even become governor."

"Yes, yes, that's true. Well . . ." He clapped his gloves together. "Let's get on with it then, boys, shall we? I can take the lead for a time if you'd like, Capt. Put these borrowed snowshoes to their best use."

Capt bowed low to Townsend. "At your service," he said.

"Indeed." Townsend led his horse around the captain's mount and struck southwest.

Capt patted his animal's neck. One never knew where renewed vigor could be drawn from. The promise of fame seemed to work just fine for Townsend.

23

Confession

Horseback Party

"Are those calves?" Ellen squinted. They rode down into a wide valley spread before them like a green carpet. What a difference a few days made. There'd been those tasty grouse everywhere and then no signs of game, neither four-footed nor fowl. Their jerky was long gone, yet here grazed fat calves. Ellen's stomach growled. They were out of flour, out of peas, out of meat.

"Yearlings is my guess," Daniel said. Their group still followed a river and the boys had expected to see deer at least, but they hadn't.

"Best we take one," John said. "We've got to eat."

"Isn't that cattle rustling or something?" Beth rode Spotty up beside Ellen.

"Maybe we can find who owns them if we keep going, offer to work for our supper." Ellen was as hungry as the rest of them, but rustling? What would their father say about that?

Daniel loaded his gun, took aim, and shot. Both women startled, as did Spotty, but Beth held him in check. Chica barked.

"Holy rosary! Give us a warning next time," Ellen said.

The animal dropped several yards in front of them. Other cows with horns spread like open arms and calves moved farther away but didn't seem startled by the noise nor the presence of these intruders. Good, Ellen thought. Maybe there'd still be a few around if they had to shoot another.

Two days later they killed the second calf. "Maybe cattle keep the other game away," John said. They rode through balmy country now. Birds warbled in the trees that held leaves, as though they'd never known about snow, and orange blooms dotted the hillside. The sun felt warm on the travelers' faces and the women donned hats they'd tied to their saddles, put away their tuques.

"There. Isn't that a structure?" Beth's voice rose in an animated range. "Yes, I'm sure it is."

Ellen squinted again. Sun on snow had ached her eyes. They still felt tired. No one had a spyglass with them, but it did indeed look like a low house in the distance. "People." She'd never thought seeing strangers would make her so happy.

They quickened their pace, let the horses munch less, pulled at their reins until the structure became a barn and then an adobe house with outbuildings. Chica barked, and instead of her own echo, another dog answered.

"Hello, the house!" John shouted when they'd passed through a gate. A dog trotted out to them, tail up. Chica sniffed a greeting to the other dog's raised hair and low growl.

"There, there," Beth said, as much to calm the dog as herself, Ellen decided. "We're friends."

And then a woman came out onto the wide veranda, wiping her hands in an apron. She couldn't have been more than twenty. Slim, with bright blue eyes, wearing a colorful skirt and snow-white blouse with pretty blue ties at the shortened sleeves. When she began to talk, she carried an English accent. "What a proper joy. Wherever did you come from?" She looked behind them to the foothills and the mountains.

"Missouri. The States," Beth said.

"And Ireland and Quebec before that," Ellen added.

"Positively delightful." The woman tugged at blonde strands of hair escaping from her combs. "I crossed the great sea myself a few years back. My husband will be so happy to see you. He's out on the slope with the cattle. Or did you run into him?"

"No, ma'am. We haven't seen another soul since we left our party back at a lake more than a month ago."

"You're welcome, indeed. We're the Sinclairs. Please—Stub, stop growling. That dog is just chipper. He's a herder, should be out with his father." She scolded the blue-gray dog. Chica stood between Ellen and Beth's horses, her tail between her legs. "Imagine, a dog and all of you coming from so far. And over those mountains in December."

"What day is it, Mrs. Sinclair?" Ellen asked.

"The fifteenth. Christmas is around the corner. What day did you think it was?"

"None of us was certain."

"Maria and I were just getting supper on for the hands. Are you hungry? Oh, surely you are. You've got to tell us your story. Are there more coming? Listen to me asking a dozen questions. I'm as bad as Stub, making a fuss without welcoming you inside." She grabbed her dog's collar and towed him aside. "You'll only have to repeat yourselves when John gets here. I'll try to hold my tongue. Please, come in now, welcome to our home."

She let loose her dog, who backed away, scattering chickens as he skulked and circled. Chica plopped her bottom down in the dust and panted, then whined as Stub slipped under the veranda. Ellen could see dark eyes looking out at them as they dismounted.

"You can water your horses in that tank over there. I'll get the vaqueros to help." She rang a metal triangle hanging on the porch and several men emerged from behind the barn, another low building Ellen learned later was a bunkhouse. "Give these folks a hand," she ordered. "They've come from the States. My, my, what a surprise."

"How far are we from Sutter's Fort?" Daniel asked. He watched as three men led their horses away.

"John Sutter is our neighbor. He's just a short way south, maybe two miles. You'll have to cross the American again. Did you follow the river down?"

"We didn't have a name for it," Ellen said. "But maybe we should keep on riding to the fort." She felt guilty eating more of the Sinclairs' food.

"You have to eat. Come along."

"Our hunger is fed by seeing Californians at last," Beth said. "Thank you."

Ellen was anxious to talk with Ailbe again, to see how Ellen Independence had survived the trip. There'd be a baby born soon to Maolisa Murphy, and oh, wouldn't Dr. John be amazed when he saw how healthy Beth was. She thought of quiet Mary Sullivan, the Patterson woman. And seeing Sarah, laughing together again. She'd missed them all, and now she could allow herself to feel that loss when the promise of their presence was close. Yes, this was a time for celebration, no doubt about that.

Stub barked again as John Sinclair rode up, another dog trotting along. "They've come from the States," his wife said.

He was a tall, lanky man with bowed legs. "Welcome." He said it like "Wylcome" and Ellen heard a Scot in his history. He reached to shake the hands of the men. He took off his hat, held it over his chest, and nodded to Beth and Ellen. "Ladies," he said.

"They'd come along the American River," his wife said. "All the way from Quebec."

"The American dinnae begin in Quebec," he teased.

"You know what I mean."

"Not all of us came from Quebec and not lately," Daniel said. "My sister exaggerates. We left our home in Missouri March 1. My father and my brothers and families."

"Are they behind ye?"

"No sir, they brought wagons and are headed toward Sutter's."

"Wagons, you say? Over the mountains? Well. Bidwell tried it. He had to abandon them."

"Capt Stephens won't," John said.

"We can talk of the trials, aye. Let's get you some vittles first. Ye must be starved."

Ellen kept a smile on her face, didn't dare look at her brothers, knowing just how well fed they all were—thanks to the Sinclairs.

Ellen told Chica to "stay" on the veranda, then they entered the frame house to an open room with wide chairs covered with cracked leather and a table that could easily serve fifteen. Greenery that looked like chives grew in a pot at the window. A stone fireplace took up one entire wall, while a plant with a red bloom crowned the center of the table. It was civilization once again.

They sat to a meal of beef and greens, deviled eggs. *Eggs!* Dried fruits plumped up with water, Ellen guessed, were in bowls at each place, along with dishes of applesauce. Mrs. Sinclair and Maria, a young Mexican girl, moved platters and brought out several more. The vaqueros joined them, but Oliver and François held back, having returned from tending the horses.

"Wylcome to Rancho del Paso," John Sinclair's voice boomed. "There's plenty of room at our table." He invited the two men to sit. Would Oliver and François return to their servant status in this new country or remain as the equals they were?

"Oliver's been our cook and François is my . . . servant," Beth said. Ellen thought she hesitated.

"All the same at this table," John Sinclair said. "Wylcome."

"'Tis delicious. It's got . . . what are these?" Ellen lifted her fork, showing what looked like shredded beef with finger-length pods of various shades of red and green.

"Chili peppers. We stew the beef in them."

"*Esta es birria*," Maria offered.

"Yes, we call it *birria*. It's quite tasty with goat too," Mrs. Sinclair added.

The dish had at first stung Ellen's tongue, but the more she ate, the more the flavor rolled in her mouth. "I could eat a wagonload of this."

"What are your cattle going for these days, if you don't mind my asking," Daniel said. He looked at Ellen and she wondered if they were going to confess now. They should. They'd have to disclose what they'd done at some point; offer to pay for what they'd eaten.

"A yearling might get us twenty dollars. Hides are worth more than the beef."

John coughed. Ellen caught her own swallow and reached for water, pretending it was the *birria* that caused it.

"Well, sir," John said. He put his fork down. "It's mighty fine beef you've got."

"And we've had the pleasure of eating some before," Ellen said. Daniel frowned.

"'Tis right to tell, Daniel. Papa would want us to." She turned to Mr. Sinclair. "'Tis a confession we have to make."

"Game was scarce the last few days," John said. "And, well, sir, looks like we've robbed you of some dollars by eating a couple of your yearlings."

"Did you now." Sinclair leaned back in his chair, dabbed at his long-handled mustache with his linen napkin,

"We can pay you back," John said. "Me and my brother, Oliver, François, we can work. Just no cash 'til our da and the rest of the party arrive, which they may have already."

"Son, I hope they made it, but the wagons, I don't know."

"We'll stay and work, sir. They were really good."

"Mrs. Townsend and I can help you, Mrs. Sinclair." Ellen turned to her. "With whatever chores you assign. We know how to wash clothes, though to look at us you might not believe that."

Mrs. Sinclair laughed and she looked to her husband. He said, "You boys don't worry. Or your ladyships, either." John Sinclair lifted his glass of water to them all. "Here's ta ye. Ye crossed the *paso*, we're happy to offer hospitality to the Americans. Quite a feat coming over that rock in winter."

"Thank you, sir. But we'll find a way to repay you soon as we can."

"I was a foreigner myself once."

"John came from Scotland, then to Oregon Territory," Mrs. Sinclair said.

"Eighteen-thirty-two with National Wyeth," John said. "Went to the Sandwich Islands, got shipwrecked. Ended up here in '39 with Sutter, hoping to create our own little colony. Mary here"—he reached for her hand—"she came from England and headed by wagon train to Oregon."

"My dad went to that territory, but I came here, met John and—"

"Swept her off her feet, I did," John said. They passed kind glances between them and Ellen felt a twinge of envy. One day, she hoped a good man would look at her the way John Sinclair looked at his wife. "But we're still the outsiders in this place."

"But there are towns with churches and schools, aren't there?" Beth asked.

"'Tis why we make the trek," Ellen added as Maria plopped berry pies on the table with a serving ladle. Ellen wasn't sure she remembered how to use one. "Civilization. Stores and all of that."

"And Catholic missions, oh yes."

"There's some tension ye should know of too," John Sinclair said. "Ye'll learn of it soon enough. A new Mexican governor was just appointed with both military and civil powers. The locals are loyal to Micheltorena, the former magistrate, so there has been resistance. We non-Mexicans, well, we got on well with Micheltorena. Now we have this new ruler assigned from miles away who vows to send *us* scampering, says we're intruders, though we've built up this territory in nothing but helpful ways."

The sounds of chewing and forks on ceramic plates kept them occupied until Sinclair added, "We have a confession to make too: we're happy not just to see new faces, but real pleased to see you carry rifles. Worth more than the beef you ate." He grinned. "But sad to say you've just crossed the country and cleared the mountains and entered a war zone. Better eat up. You're going to need the strength."

Wintering Women

It made her feel vulnerable, but Sarah would never get anywhere if she didn't leave the safety of her shore. Mary Sullivan had inspired her by doing things others didn't expect. Maybe, in time, if she built her confidence, Allen would find that more appealing than someone always needing his encouragement and support. But getting to that point carried risk: of looking foolish; of maybe even failing.

"What have you got there?" Maolisa asked Sarah.

"Dictionaries." She'd lugged Webster's two volumes across the continent. "I thought maybe we could have school—for the children."

"That would make my little brothers groan," Mary Sullivan said. "But it's a good idea. I'll gather up the primary ones. We can make it fun. Open one at random, Sarah. Read a word. Any word and we'll talk about what it means."

Maolisa adjusted the sleeping baby she carried in a shawl draped around her neck and back for supporting the baby at her chest. She had the rocking chair for the moment.

Sarah held the books to her chest, hesitated, grateful that Isabella offered her thoughts. "Those dictionaries are almost like reading the Bible," Isabella said. "Webster put so many references to Scripture and stories in there, with illustrations, you feel like you've been to church after reading it."

"The man learned twenty-seven languages in order to compile the words and meanings," Maolisa Murphy added. "I used them in Missouri where we lived without a school."

"He took away the English 'colour' and gave us 'color.'" Isabella spelled out the two words as she brought seven-year-old Melinda to her side. The Pattersons stared over Sarah's shoulder at the colorful illustrations. "Made it an American spelling."

"Go ahead, Sarah. Pick a word," Mary Sullivan said. "Let the class begin."

"I . . . someone else will have to read it and teach it—to me too." Sarah handed the book up to Isabella. "I love words but I don't know how to read."

Isabella put her hand to her throat, jerked her head back. "Why, you sound like a professor with your words and grammar. I can't believe you're illiterate."

Sarah winced at the harsh word that sounded close to *idiot*. "I'm a good listener. And I memorize," Sarah said. "I guess I recognize a few words by sight, like *poison* on a bottle or *halt* next to a gate. But I want to learn how to read all the words in these books."

Mary Sullivan hugged her, a Webster book pressed between them. "I'll give you private lessons if you like. We'll get you caught up to the little ones who know their alphabet already. And maybe you'd teach me to quilt or knit. Neither one found favor in my fingers. I'd quit trying, but if you'll instruct, maybe by the time we reach Sutter's Fort, I'll have honored my mother by learning a woman's art."

"It would be my pleasure. Let's look up that word."

"*Pleasure* means 'desire,'" Ailbe said. "And that's a word in Proverbs, telling us that 'Desire accomplished is sweet to the soul.' Isn't that lovely?"

"Yes, it is," Sarah said. She had many desires to realize. Learning to read was just one.

24

A Way Out

Wagon Guard

Moses made it back to their cabin at sunset. Depleted, drained, exhausted beyond any memory, he had to lift both legs up and over the doorjamb with his hands to get inside. The step wasn't even a foot tall. He just couldn't step over it like a man. He fell to the floor skiffed with a layer of loose snow. He knew he'd have to get warm or he'd die. He rolled onto his knees, sat, removed the snowshoes, the effort greater than if he'd climbed a mountain. At least that was how it felt. He rested a bit more, shivered, then forced himself to crawl to the fireplace. He found a match, so grateful they had saved a few. He lifted a book, tore a page out, and crumpled it. Pulled a few bark chips into a pile over it, then lit the paper. The flame took and he fed it with dried branches, then a log, so grateful to see the fire lap at the bark, the wood, eat into its center giving off heat. So thankful. He lay next to the fire. So appreciative of warmth. Shelter. Life. He'd figure out what to do in the morning. He fell asleep.

While he wouldn't have thought he could even stand after all that exertion, when morning came, he felt renewed strength. He saw the meat, that quarter of Bill left, frozen solid, and he vowed not to eat any until he'd taken his gun and gone out to see if he could find any game. Once out in the snow again, those snowshoes strapped to his toes and ankles, he saw nothing but tracks. Foxes. Coyotes. No deer. Nothing he could follow. The effort warmed him and it seemed like the day warmed too. Maybe the snow would melt and he could try to leave after all, take the same route as Allen and Joe. But those were false hopes, he knew that. He still had to stop often to manage the cramps.

But surprisingly, knowing there was still a meal or two left made it possible for him not to eat it. And when thoughts of hunger gnawed at him, he quelled them with marking the day as another that he had not eaten, had saved himself from starving because there was a last meal that awaited him.

That second day back with no luck hunting, again, he pawed open one of Dr. John's trunks and there found a book of poems by Byron. He opened it at random to one titled "To Thomas Moore." Moses wasn't sure who Thomas Moore was, but he read the short poem, stopping at the second stanza.

> Here's a sign to those who love me,
> And a smile to those who hate;
> And, whatever sky's above me,
> Here's a heart for any fate.

Did he have such a heart, one to endure anything set before him? That Thomas Moore must have been such to have Byron—Lord Byron, Dr. John would have corrected him—write a poem of him. And then the fourth stanza:

> Were't the last drop in the well,
> As I gasp'd upon the brink,
> 'Ere my fainting spirit fell,
> 'Tis to thee that I would drink.

Who would I drink to with my last drop?

To his sister who had given him so much, had taken him in when their mother died. He'd drink to her. Fortunately, he had plenty of water to toast her. But that "fainting spirit" part, that was more familiar. And maybe it would be good to think about others when one's spirit fell, to remind himself that there were more beside his sister who he hoped had a heart for any fate, would make it through. He'd have to eat the beef eventually, he knew that. He couldn't go that many more days without eating something. He'd take that last bite and have it be a toast to his sister, praying as he did that she had lived, taking Chica as solace and Joker given up for pretty Ellen Murphy. If he lived through this, he vowed he'd find out who Tom Moore was, and if he was still alive, he'd tell him that the poem about him kept him going, at least for one more night.

Wintering Women

Sarah's fingers felt stiff as sticks, especially in the mornings. They had no tea or coffee, but holding the tin cups with steaming water eventually warmed her hands, actions that took her mind from food, separation, decisions that might mean life or death. She remembered sitting around a campfire back on the plains before the Oregon party had split off. Allen had been especially attentive and had not only steamed her tea but had walked to another wagon and secured a mug of milk for it. He'd even scraped a couple of flakes of maple sugar into it. He didn't often add the sugar, as he said it made her corpulent. *I'm not plump anymore.* He often used words she didn't know and couldn't look up because she didn't know how to read, but she imagined what those blooms meant by the soil that surrounded them. She'd asked Beth Townsend what "corpulent" meant and felt a sting of embarrassment that Allen had described her that way.

"You surely don't think—*gasp*—that you're plump," Beth had said in her raspy voice.

"Allen seems to think I am." Sarah squeezed her upper arm. *It doesn't feel fleshy.*

"Goodness. A little gust of wind could—*gasp*—blow you away." She missed Beth.

Sarah had taken in Allen's assessment and set aside Beth's, whose body really could be pushed over by a breeze.

She remembered a day in late summer when the fiddles had serenaded the sunset that burned of reds and golds, and he'd handed her the sweetened tea and sat beside her while she drank it.

"I've been talking to some of the others thinking about going to Oregon."

So that's it. He's buttering me up for a change he wants to make.

"And I wondered what you'd think of that, our shucking California for Oregon. There are rumors, they say, there've been some uprisings in California. Old Hitchcock told us. But Oregon's peaceful. "

"We're traveling with the Townsends," Sarah said. "They've been good to us. And you said you even owed money to Dr. John. You couldn't walk away from a debt."

"I could. I mean I wouldn't not pay. We'd stay in touch and I'd pay him back when things got established. Land is free in Oregon. We just take it from the Indians. In California, the land's owned by the Mexican government and we'd have to buy it from someone else or get the government to grant it to us. They might not do that to foreigners. Could be burdensome."

Her stomach lurched. It always did when she sensed a conflict with Allen. "I . . . think we should continue as we agreed. The Townsends can help us. Dr. John's educated and can deal with lawyers and whatnot. I don't think separating is a good idea at all." She'd sipped her tea. "But thank you for talking with me about it. It's nice to have a conversation about our future and not just 'What's for supper?' or 'Can you darn my socks?' Having conversations about things that really matter, that's good." He'd nodded and she'd taken that as assent. But when they reached the choosing place, with a sign she thought must say "Oregon" and "California" with arrows of direction, Allen again approached her.

"Look at all who's going north. Some of our friends."

"But not the Townsends." She'd sewed a patch onto his britches. Something about Allen's pushing annoyed her and she decided to stand firm. "I'm California bound. If you go to Oregon, you go without me."

She'd later gotten Dr. John to cajole Allen to continue with them to Alta California. That's probably what worked. Dr. John had big ideas to match Allen's dreams.

But right now, in this cold and drafty cabin, she had second thoughts. All she had here was a tin cup and a dictionary she couldn't read. Allen had jested that those who couldn't read the sign went to California. "Only the literate ones headed to Oregon."

She didn't give him the satisfaction of knowing his words had pained her. In this gathering of winter women, she knew that he was wrong. Everyone here knew how to read—except for her. She wished she was in Oregon with Allen, sipping real tea and not just hot water. On the other hand, here, she was learning to read.

"I know this isn't a great time." Mary Sullivan interrupted Sarah's thoughts. "But do you have enough yarn left to show me some simple knitting stitches? I may as well learn something new. It might take my thoughts off my stomach."

"I'm not sure anything except food can do that, but it might help me too. A fair exchange for your teaching me words. I haven't much yarn left, though. The blanket I knitted for Yuba used up the last of it."

"And the flaps you put in John's tuque." Mary sighed.

"You don't happen to have an extra sweater you're not wearing, do you?" Sarah asked. "Maybe one stuck between the logs?"

"Are you cold? I'll get my other one for you."

"No, I'm no colder today than yesterday in my wool. But I thought, if you were willing, we could take your sweater apart and reknit it."

Mary looked at her as though she'd seen rescuers walk right through their cabin door. Her eyes sparkled. "That would be lovely."

She returned shortly with the coarse wool sweater.

"It was my mother's made with Aran wool, the lanolin still in it."

Sarah held the green sweater warm across her knees as she began to unravel the heavy yarn. "Wrap it around your fingers. We'll make it into a ball. The lanolin might make your hands feel smoother."

"Taking things apart to re-create them," Mary said.

"That's happening to us too," Sarah said. "We're having to remake ourselves."

"You're doing your best." Ailbe encouraged her husband. "If there's no game, there's no game." Baby Indie sat in a pile of down comforters and quilts on the floor so she wouldn't topple over while her parents whispered, though they likely didn't need to. There were cries and wails even with the Patterson girls urging the children to sing or play little games. Mr. Martin had taken out his bodhran and BD Murphy danced to the beat. Ailbe hoped the other children might join in instead of whining.

"I can't abide the sounds of the babes cryin' as they are," James said. "I think William and I should head out after the men and bring back rescue."

"No." Ailbe felt her chest tighten. *Men always want to do something; they can't see that their presence is what a wife needs most.*

"There'd be more to eat of the last cows if William and I took a small amount of jerky and went for help."

"You're not thinking straight. They've only been gone two weeks." *It seems like months.*

"And we're down to two cows. If I don't take what we can from those last two, I won't have strength enough to make it. We're still looking at another week before they bring back supplies. We won't last much after that."

"People can go several days without eating, James. They won't like it, but they can. I can. And if you leave, who'll hunt for us in case we should be fortunate enough to find game?"

He stared at the floor.

"You see? There has to be someone to keep hunting. The act itself gives us hope."

"Old Man Martin, even with his bad arm. Or Sarah Montgomery. Her husband's a gunsmith. She must know something about guns."

"Perhaps, but knowing how one works doesn't mean she knows how to hunt. That's a separate skill, James, honed after years of experience."

"Little good it's done me. Us."

"James. Don't."

He sat up straighter. "What about Mary Sullivan? She's tough and probably a fast learner. She handled herself at the summit. She might be willing to carry on 'specially since it's her Pierre and Prince who will be the last to go."

Ailbe Miller looked at the Sullivan girl being shown how to knit by Sarah Montgomery. In exchange, Mary had been teaching her the alphabet while the older children—already steeped in language learning—giggled, often repeating the letters with her. Sarah was good-natured about it anyway, Ailbe thought. And it gave the children something to do besides complain about the smells left by the two babies filling their nappies several times a day. She'd started setting the napkins outside until she could wash them, but then they froze, contents and all. She scraped them, then reused them, though she had no more glycerin to put on the babies' bottoms, and they surely couldn't scorch flour in the cast-iron frying pan to make a diaper-rash powder.

"Give it another day, James. Maybe a deer will wander this way. We can try fishing again."

"You won't begrudge me speaking to the lass about shooting when she's not learning how to knit."

"No, I won't interfere. Talking is better than leaving and gives me more time to hold you here."

He kissed Indie's fine hair the color of early dawn and stood. "Guess I'll find out a little about knittin'."

"It's almost finished." Mary held up her Aran wool sweater. "If I hadn't had to redo slipped stitches, I'd have been finished in time for Christmas." The cabinmates had gathered to celebrate the birth of Jesus. "My dear mother would be proud. Or . . . at least encouraged that I could put a sweater together with you sitting beside me each stitch of the way."

"You're doing a fine job, Mary." Sarah grinned, a smile that looked gaunt in her thinning face. "Almost completed. And I have a confession to make. There was a tiny bit of yarn left over since you're so much . . . thinner than you were. I think you can use this." She handed Mary one of the Webster books, opened it, and showed her the knitted bookmark inside.

"It has an owl's face on it," Mary said. "It's . . . beautiful." Mary ran her fingers over the flat, soft surface. "But you're learning to read so quickly, you'll need this for your books."

"I kept one for myself, I hope you don't mind." Sarah pushed it back toward Mary. "Allen would be disgusted if he knew I'd carried the books all this way." She sighed. "I made a small bookmark for each of you, actually," Sarah's voice perked up. "Your sweater gave to everyone, Mary."

She handed a cross bookmark to Maolisa, a rosette with a string on it to Ailbe. For the aunts and Ann Jane, she had knitted tiny bags to fit a rosary inside, smaller than their palms. "I guess I should have been thinking of the children, but it was each of you women who touched my heart, helped me deal with the sadness and worry of my Allen."

Ailbe said, "A word of Scripture, something the Virgin said. 'He hath filled the hungry with good things.' Such satisfying friends we've found. Thank you, Sarah." She fingered the rosette.

"And I have a porcelain thimble with the most exquisite painting of a rose on it," Isabella said. "Which I was planning to give to you, Sarah, with my thanks for helping Lydia with her quilting." She fingered the flat bookmark Sarah had given her made to look like a plum pudding. It wasn't knitted but rather stitched and quilted with little embroidered knots to resemble raisins.

"But we have all given each other stories," Mary said. "I've looked forward to our evenings of sharing. And learned things too, not just entertained. I wouldn't have thought that my first Christmas without my parents or my older brother would have been so memorable."

"Now we have to think of something for the children," Maolisa said.

"Let's begin with the Christmas story," Ann Jane said. "Da, you could read it to us."

Mr. Martin nodded his head.

"Could we act the story out for the children? They might like that," Sarah said.

"Or better, let them perform it for us," Maolisa said. "We'll rehearse and make costumes. We can use the table sheet."

"I know just who we can use to play the part of baby Jesus," Ailbe said, nodding toward Yuba. "We'll tell the Christmas story and make it a new one here in our wilderness."

They'd feed the hungry with good things—something old with a new twist to warm them—just like her sweater, Mary thought. With yarn leftover for bookmarks.

25

Filling Up

Wagon Guard

"Lost your bearing and I'm sorry but guess you were sent to me."
Moses lifted his gun to his shoulder and shot the crow, stopping
the cawing midflight. He tromped through a layer of new powder
snow to pick up his dinner. It was the first bird he'd seen since
he'd been back to the cabin. He noticed coyote tracks and foxes
crisscrossing. It looked like they were coming to the edge of the
lake. He never saw them in the flesh, but he dreamed about them,
roasted their meat in his sleep, ate his fill, then awoke to the growl
of his stomach.

He plucked the feathers from the crow, cut the body into pieces,
and fried it. "Bless these thy gifts we're about to receive from thy
bounty. Really, bless it," Moses said. "Let it fill me up." He inhaled,
took his first bite of the stringy fowl.

It was . . . terrible. He tried to come up with other words to
describe the dreadful, revolting, disagreeable, awful taste. "I won't
complain," he decided after getting his brain to stop coming up
with foul words—he laughed at his own pun. "It's foul fowl fuel.
That's how I need to think of it and I thank God for its wayward

flight to my stomach." He'd taken to talking out loud. Hearing his own voice gave him assurance he still existed. He scraped a little more meat from Bill's thigh bone and fried it in the pan, giving a bit more flavor to his once winged supper.

With the crow consumed, he decided to look at the pile of items left from Capt Stephens's wagon. Joe had brought most of those boxes and packs inside. He eased one off the top. Farrier tools: rasps, hammers, nippers, clinchers, pullers, and cutters. He'd have to consider if any of Capt's treasures could be useful in his isolation.

The second box made him shout. "Oh, wow, thank you, Capt." *Traps.* "I can trap that coyote and those foxes." *Can't I?*

He tried to remember any conversations he'd overheard about setting traps, where to place them, how to manage the heavy springs. "Think, Moses. What can you use for bait?"

He looked around the cabin. Nothing here. But outside lay the brains of the two beasts who had given their lives for Allen, Joe, and Moses. "Ol' Bill will save me yet again." He nearly cried.

He only had to load the bait and not cut off his own hand in the process. If he messed it up, it'd be his doom.

He remembered once back on the trail when they'd encountered a large band of Sioux. They'd been friendly enough, using those hand signals to talk with the Greenwoods. They camped near them, though they'd been wary in the night, ever watchful. In the morning, he couldn't find Joker's halter. It was a fine leather one. He looked about and then saw it on the head of one of the Sioux ponies. He stomped to the Indian standing beside it. Pointed. "Mine," Moses told him. "You've taken my halter."

The Indian ignored him. He tried again, his voice getting louder. "You're a rotten thief. Give me back my halter."

A crowd had gathered to watch the ignoring Indian and the rattled boy. Then Moses lost his temper. "I'll just take it back my way, then." He ran back to get his rifle and returned, lifted to aim, when Capt Stephens and Mr. Murphy and Old Man Hitchcock read the situation and stood between him and the Indian.

"They'll kill us all if you shoot," Capt said. "Give me the gun, boy."

By then the thief's friends had also gathered and there were many more of them. Capt took away Moses's rifle, and Greenwood and the Murphys showered the Indians with beads and other gifts they had to spare. Capt gave them traps—all he had, Moses had thought then—and that pleased them and they'd ridden off without taking any revenge on the wagon party. Joker's best halter had gone with them.

"It ain't fair," Moses complained. "You gave 'em traps and trinkets when they stole my halter!"

"A man has to evaluate each situation. We're in new territory here," Capt had said. "And in this circumstance if they'd decided to respond to what they saw as an insult on the other end of your rifle, we would have died. A man's got to do what's best for all."

Do what's best for all. Moses guessed he'd taken that lesson in to his gut, as that was part of why he'd offered to stay with the wagons. It was best for Allen and Joe to not have the burden of him, either. Capt had shown him how to do what was right, and he'd sacrificed but a halter. More than that if he failed to live until his rescue.

He'd go slow setting the steel jaws. He didn't have anyone here to rescue him if he did something stupid.

Horseback Party

"There's the bridge the Sinclairs told us about." Ellen made the observation as though it was the most precious thing she'd ever seen. "We don't have to swim across." She patted Joker's neck, then rode up beside Beth. John and Daniel led the party with François and Oliver bringing up the rear. "Little Spotty won't have to push himself through chest-high water anymore this afternoon." The midafternoon air felt warm on her face where her straw hat offered welcome shade. Balmy weather gave a lift to her spirits she hadn't known she'd needed.

"So, this is California," Beth said. She inhaled a deep breath, the leather reins loose in her hands. "Look at those bushes. Purple blooms. Wait," she told the others and with ease slipped off Spotty to make a selection. She held the smooth, almost oily leaf to Ellen, who inhaled the bloom. "Flowers in December," she said while Oliver helped her remount. "In California."

Ellen stuck the leaf and branch into Beth's straw hat. "Alta California Province, remember. That's what Mary Sinclair told us. We're not part of America. Sutter's New Helvetia is a colony in Mexico. And it's right in front of us."

"Look over there, those blue blooms. They look like violets." Beth's enthusiasm made Ellen feel festive, excited. She pressed her knees and hurried Joker forward. Would they see the other travelers? Sarah, Moses? Chica trotted by her side with occasional detours to sniff at the violet-like plants growing wild.

The horses *clip-clopped* across the wooden bridge where John Sinclair said the Sacramento and American rivers converged. The dirt trail they rode on arced toward a hill where Sutter's Fort stood as a beacon to the region. At least that's how John Sinclair described it. Sutter had named it New Helvetia after Sutter's Swiss heritage, but Sutter's own name was what the Murphy clan had always known their destination to be.

"Yes. We're in Mexico. But California too." Beth *tsk-tsked* the little pony forward. They passed through a wide gate in the adobe wall that lined the perimeter.

"'Tis a real town," Ellen said. It had been months since they'd seen one. She had visions of a place to stay, eating regularly again, especially those Mexican dishes. She wondered how the rooms would be furnished and if they could remain in them until the rest of the party arrived—if they hadn't already. What would they do if they couldn't? The reality of "arriving" when for months they'd been "journeying" caused a little flip in her stomach.

"Welcome, welcome, one and all." A barrel-chested man with black curly hair cropped around a growing baldness greeted them. "Sutter," he said, holding his hand out to John and Daniel, who had dismounted. To Beth and Ellen he tipped his hat and gave a wide smile. Ellen thought he might be in his forties. He wore a plaid vest, puffy-sleeved shirt, and cuffed trousers.

"Daniel Murphy, my brother John," Daniel said. "And my sister and our doctor's wife."

"Ellen Murphy," Ellen added. It was so like Daniel not to even give the names of the women. "This is Mrs. Townsend and her servants Oliver Manent and François Deland."

Ellen wanted to tell Daniel that this California was different. Here, from what the Sinclairs said, men and women might be considered equal, servants welcomed at their masters' tables.

"We've come from Missouri by way of the Sierras and lately the Sinclairs," Daniel said. "Has the larger party arrived with the wagons?"

"Wagons? Over those mountains? No, nothing like that. Which way did you take?"

"Council Bluffs across the plains to the Oregon divide after Fort Hall, then across a wide, flat desert where we later followed a river to a lake. We separated from the wagons there. They went up over the summit."

"The summit. *Ja*, that will stop them."

"We got some snowfall and Mrs. Townsend's husband, a doctor, felt she'd do better on horseback. An Indian named Truckee told us of the way. Rode a few miles up a ridge to a grand lake," John said.

"It was breathtaking." Ellen fanned herself with her straw hat, it was so warm.

"You were injured?" He nodded toward the sling Ellen kept her left arm in.

"I'm doing well—"

"And then we headed down 'til we found another river to follow to Sinclair's *Rancho del Paso* and now we're here." Daniel had made their seven-month journey into a few short sentences.

"A river crossed a hundred times," John added.

"The wagons headed due west," Daniel said.

Sutter shook his head. "It will trouble them to bring wagons over that mountain. Snows get ten, fifteen feet deep. Who's with them?"

"Captain Elisha Stephens. The Greenwoods. Old Man Hitchcock and Martin," John said.

"I know Greenwoods. And Hitchcock I believe I met here in '39, though we were just getting this place started then." He exchanged *v*'s for *w*'s so "we" came out "vee."

John said, "We began with eleven wagons and fifty in our party, so you see, we're just a paltry little vanguard."

"Fifty-one," Beth said. "We added an infant at Independence Rock on Independence Day."

"True Americans then," Sutter said. "Ja, dat's *Gut*." Ellen had heard that same accent from customers at Matthew's store. "You are welcome here. We need such Americans. With rifles, I see. To defend our lands. I have grant from Mexican governor, but now, they send us new government who wants us all gone."

"Mr. Sinclair explained some of this."

"*Ja*. This is not a good time to be here, but it is good you *are* here. We will need to raise—*ach*, we will talk of these things later, *ja?*"

Ellen wondered what it was he had planned to raise, but she didn't ask. She was too taken in by the activities—people arriving, trappers leaving, bales of furs stacked, the smell of cooked meat, Chica sniffing new pals. There'd be mirrors and she could find more of the hair rinse Mrs. Sinclair had shared. Civilization. She felt filled up to her eyes in gratitude.

"Come, we find the ladies rooms to wait for others—if they come. You have baths if you wish, *ja?* There is a bunkhouse for you men." He pointed toward a long, low building.

"Thank you," Beth said.

"You! Take water to the hostel." Sutter barked orders at tragic-looking brown-skinned men and women with hair like old mops, graying and chopped. They were barely clothed as they hauled water from the well. They shuffled as though to tarry would bring harsh consequences. They didn't look at her. The women carried the buckets. *Is that my bathwater? Are they slaves?* What kind of civilization had they come to?

Wintering Women

"Like you," Mary Sullivan told James, "I've seen no signs, no tracks, no rubbing of antlers on tree branches. We'd have better luck trying to nab fish if we had spears. We're too close to the headwaters, I suspect, maybe too far from spawning grounds."

"Or too early." James sighed, then with firmness said, "I'd take William with me and leave his rifle with you. With a little ammunition so if you did see something, you could maybe shoot it."

"Oh, I could shoot it all right." Mary hesitated to get between a marital pair, but she said, "What does Ailbe think of all this? She can't be in favor of you and William leaving."

"She's not. But she'll do what I think best. And I think it's best if we head out. That's easier to do with you agreeing to hunt."

"Something new to add to my days," Mary said. "Do you know when you'll leave?"

"We'll have to slaughter Prince and Pierre first."

"That was going to happen soon anyway, bless those beasts. But like Ailbe, I'll do what you think is best too. For the good of all of us."

The women had settled into their evening gathering places. Sarah could smell the days without washing, see the tired looks on the women's faces, skin as pale as leeks. Maolisa stayed close to BD and her baby. Sarah noticed the little boy moaned in hunger while he slept. Perhaps they rationed the meat too much. Isabella Patterson stroked the hair of her youngest girl as she tried to find a comfortable place on the floor. Sarah had to think of something to take her mind from hunger, the cold, the wind, and yes, more snow. Mary Sullivan took children to the latrine, making light of the trek, telling stories and creating little competitions in the snowdrifts. Older children helped drag in branches to burn. Once this latest storm passed, they'd have to butcher.

Sarah decided they should welcome what they couldn't avoid. "Let's speak of food," she said. "It's what we're thinking about all the time anyway, isn't it? No sense to avoid it."

"We're not just thinking about food but dreaming about it too. At least I am." Ann Jane's cackling laugh caused Mimi to startle, but she stayed asleep. "I guess that's nothing new for me." She patted her stomach, though now she didn't look much different than the rest of the women, who no longer had fleshy cheeks and whose eyes were more deeply set into their skulls. Sarah hadn't looked into a mirror, but she knew she looked emaciated too. *Emaciated. Withered. Gaunt. Descriptive words for how I feel.* Dr. John had used it to describe a woman who had wasted away, had refused to eat despite her husband's urging. Sarah wouldn't need to be urged. She was so famished. But she thought if they spoke of food in other ways, maybe it would encourage. They might need fortifying of their spirits as much as bolstering their bellies with meat or bread. They could fill their Christmas stockings with stories.

"Let's tell about something we prepared, or a meal we had, that had special meaning to us. I can go first."

"No, let me," Isabella said. Sarah noticed that she'd kept herself with her children mostly, didn't participate in the alphabet lessons or knitting. Her wanting to go first was a good sign.

Isabella took a deep breath. "When Andrew and I married, he brought eight children into our lives with him. I'd had none, so you can imagine, I was a little intimidated."

"Were they all living with you?" Margaret, one of the Murphy aunts, asked. "I'd die having that many people around."

"You've got a lot more than that around you now, Margaret," her sister Johanna said. "And you haven't died yet."

"All the chatter keeps me from thinking too much about what I don't have," Margaret answered. The women nodded like they understood exactly.

"Only six lived with us," Isabella continued. "The oldest two were already married. But my meals meant preparing for eight people. Apparently, I'd passed the cooking tests, as they went along with my stews and spices, though there were a few other tests I didn't get passing grades on. I won't go into those." She pressed her hands down against the floor, resettled herself. "The first meal I prepared after learning I carried our first child proved memorable. Nothing I ate tasted good during that time, but no one had complained. We hadn't yet told the children, and I thought I'd done a good job of hiding my morning discomfort. So we planned a festive Christmas dinner when we'd tell them. I fixed plum pudding in the traditional way my mother had prepared it in England. I boiled the cloth, wrapped the pudding in it, simmered it for three hours two days before." She motioned wrapping a large cloth.

"And the knitted bookmark I made had a plum pudding on it," Sarah said.

"I thought you had eavesdropped on my life with that gift," Isabella said. "I couldn't believe you chose such a thing for me."

"Tell us about the plum pudding," Lydia said.

"Well, I let it hang for two days, then boiled it again for two hours on Christmas Day. When we were ready to eat it, I heated the rum sauce over the flame with my long-handled ladle. Oh, the scents. It was lovely."

"After all that work on the pudding, did you have the strength to eat it?" Mary Sullivan asked, to the women's laughter.

"I thought I did. With pride I watched my new family take their first bites into the nuts and dried fruits and all that sugar and cream. I'd added extra sugar. Sometimes the rum can give it a tart taste. I wanted this sweet. But instead of joy I looked at scrunched faces and puckered lips. Something was wrong. Then I took my bite, chewed—it was very strange—swallowed and ended up running to the privy—but so did all of them!"

"What had you done?"

"Used saleratus instead of sugar. The soda taste was so strong, even the rum sauce didn't block it out."

"Did you tell them about me?" her oldest daughter asked.

"Not that evening. Didn't think it a good time, dear." Lydia nodded at Isabella. "But in the morning when I was still 'sick,' don't you know, they didn't think anything out of the ordinary. I guess they had sympathy for when we—uh—retched together."

"Retching together. What a lovely family image," Ailbe said and everyone laughed again.

Isabella smiled. "I was able to cover my own morning sicknesses for a few more days and then we told them. I think sharing those wretched retching moments might have brought us all closer. But, oh how I hated throwing out that plum pudding. All that work. I haven't made one since."

"You should when we reach Sutter's," Johanna said. "I'd love to have you show me how to make that. With sugar, of course."

"With sugar."

"And what a waste of rum," Mary Sullivan said. "I wish we had some here to warm us. Just a teaspoon full."

There were murmurs of agreement.

"I'm not sure I can top that," Maolisa said. She spoke loudly from where she sat with the children. She looked like a frog on a lily pad of progenies. "I once tried to fry fish in kerosene instead of oil."

"Didn't it catch on fire?" Isabella said.

"If I'd put it on the flame, it well might have. But as I poured it, I smelled it and realized it wasn't from the tin I thought it was.

Children had distracted me. Washing kerosene from fish is a terrible task."

The women chuckled and so did Old Man Martin.

"When our parents died"—Mary Sullivan lifted her chin toward her younger brothers sleeping—"we were in a place foreign to us. Bereft, really. Struggling about whether we should turn back to Quebec or continue on from Council Bluffs. At least, I struggled with that decision. My brother apparently didn't. We had to bury my parents there. Loss scraped across my heart like a scouring pad. But then so many of you came to my brother and me and encouraged us. If you remember, Maolisa, you brought us a mess of fish your father had caught that morning, no hint of kerosene." The women smiled. "And Isabella, your gift was a cake. Not plum pudding."

"You can be grateful for that."

"Ann Jane, you gave us deviled eggs. I didn't know then about your having buried your *bairn*."

Ann Jane nodded. "We all had losses too large to ponder."

"It wasn't so much the food as your acts of kindness that made my brother and me decide to continue on with you. I don't regret that choice. We're locked together for life now, having shared a grieving meal and this vexed journey. What was it you said, Ailbe? 'He hath filled the hungry with good things.' I'll remember that."

"Sarah, you started this," Margaret said. "What about your special meal?"

Sarah had wanted others to share, to discover more about them and their families. Her stories paled in comparison. But she did have one she'd never spoken of. "I know this may seem strange, most of you being Catholic and all, who at the mass take in bread—or Host, I think you call it. But my best meal was at a table, in a little church a friend had invited me to." A log cracked in the fireplace and a flash of light spread over the gathered women. "I wasn't much for church. I'm still not, I suppose. But something happened to me that day. There was talk of hunger and of food that could fill me up forever. It was just a little piece of bread I dipped in a cup of homemade wine. It moved me. It was a different kind of being fed. And I was full that day." She hesitated. "Sometimes I don't know how to end a meal. I mean, I keep eating, like I don't know what being full feels like. But I did that day."

Ann Jane said, "I know what you're saying. How to end a meal or how to end . . . anything. Saying goodbye. Well, it's just stomachwrenching." Sarah thought she spoke of burying her baby in Iowa, but connecting loss to wrenching stomachs reached her heart.

"I wish we had a priest to pray the mass for us," Maolisa said. "Short of that, we must pray for each other."

"We have survived another day," Ailbe said. "And soon, they'll send back help for us. Don't you think so, James?" Her husband didn't answer. He might have been asleep.

"We should talk about preserving foods—foods we wish we had with us." Ann Jane's eyes were bright with memory. "Bleached apples."

"We smoked ours," Mary Sullivan said. "A little sulphur on the hot griddle inside an old butter churn, with a touch of cream of tartar, of course. Then lowering the sliced apples in their basket to just above the heat. We covered it all with a quilt and left it. They came out so white and soft. We kept ours in the churn all winter, taking them out for pies or just to chew. Hmmm, yum."

Several others offered ways they'd made sauerkraut or added a story of a special method of burying potatoes so they wouldn't freeze all winter. Sarah hoped she could remember all these different ways the women had for taking care of their families.

"I for one feel fed tonight," Ailbe said.

Sarah thought of that little piece of filling-bread she'd eaten those years before. Maybe it didn't have to be bread. Maybe it was the tiniest piece of dried beef that was her portion that day, shared with another who felt lonely too, willing to let her stomach—and her soul—be filled up.

$$26$$

Contemplating Reunions

Wagon Guard

Moses's first catch was a coyote. The steel teeth had only caught one leg and the animal had been trying to chew his foot off to get free, so Moses had to shoot the coyote to extract it from the trap. "Thank you, Lord. And Bill," he'd said, eyes raised to the overcast sky. It had been a day since the crow meal and he was hungry.

Moses skinned his fare, saved some of the entrails for future bait, then stretched the hide to dry in the sun. He noticed that if he kept busy he could go longer without eating, as though resisting his hunger was a mark of his courage to continue on.

He cut the meat and cooked it in the stew pot with handfuls of snow that melted. He watched steam rise from the Dutch oven. "You brought me my next meal, Bill," he said. Using pieces of the ox's head had been the bait and it had worked. He had lots more and he'd save some from whatever he caught and use it the next day. After he ate, he could set another trap. It made him feel good to always have another activity to do. It didn't take away the fear of starvation, but the activity gave him a goal, a direction which he needed.

After he ate a few chunks more, he spoke again. "This coyote is worse than the crow. Well, maybe it's a dead-heat tie." He could hardly swallow it but made himself. Success was a good sauce. Finished, he went back out to set the trap again. A full stomach lifted his mood and he allowed himself to appreciate the vast beauty, its stillness, the wonder of a white world.

The sun set as he returned to his cabin, having found fox tracks where he set his trap. He dragged a branch back to burn. Then in the dusk, he took a moment to look for that small box he'd encountered in Dr. John's wagon. He pulled it out of the hidden floorboard. It wasn't any bigger than the palm of his hand. He lifted the cover.

Tacks? A strange thing to put in a precious place. He swirled the metal with his fingers and imagined he might use them to hang up fabric on his rough walls, blocking out some of the cold air and making it a little festive. In the morning he planned to put the tacks to work holding up a magenta velvet and a lavender silk. He let the white linen stay where it was. He saw enough of that color outside.

For his evening reading, Moses chose *Lord Chesterfield's Letters*, a man writing to his traveling son, from what Moses could figure.

> Pray remember to part with all your friends, acquaintances, and mistresses, if you have any, at Paris, in such a manner as may make them not only willing but impatient to see you there again.

Moses thought about his parting with his sister. He was impatient to see her again. He was pleased she'd taken Chica, though he missed the cheering brought by the little dog. His sister was like a mother to him. He knew she hoped to have another family—with Dr. John—one day. If she could get healthier. He thought of his parting with Allen and Joe. They hadn't wanted to leave him, but he never would have made it. The cramps came to him now and then, but he could wait them out here. That wouldn't have worked if he'd continued on with his friends. He trusted that he'd parted well with everyone. And he couldn't imagine Dr. John ever writing to him about such things as friendships, let alone telling him to part with his mistresses well. "Ha. I may not live long enough to even kiss a girl," Moses said. "No, I must not think that way. I will get out of here one day. I will."

He read well into darkness. He found a medical book of Dr. John's and read about stomach cramping. Something about "obstructions." He guessed he couldn't have an obstruction if he didn't have anything inside his gut to get in the way. The treatment involved drinking fluids, exercise, and waiting "if possible." He guessed that crawling and walking fifteen miles through heavy snow, lifting and tromping one leg at a time, would count as exercise, as would setting traps for his supper. If he read until he dropped off, then he'd sleep later in the morning and it made the days seem less long. It was a trick he played on himself. He read until he fell asleep, his arm draped over the book as though it were a lover. Sleeping as much as he could kept both hunger and hopelessness at bay.

Cross-Country Men to Sutter's Fort

A warm breeze brushed their whiskered faces. The men had removed their tuques and fur hats the day before, the weather so much more agreeable near Sutter's Fort. It felt like spring in Missouri, but it must be late December. Maybe they had made it in time for Christmas—at least the men had.

"Capt Stephens, coleader of the Murphy-Stephens wagon train." Capt held his hand out to a portly man who must be Sutter as he'd stepped out from a two-story adobe building that had the Sutter sign over the doorway.

"Wagons? I don't see them." The little man looked at the motley array of the Murphy-Stephens men.

"Townsend too," Dr. John added, stepping up to shake his hand before Mr. Murphy could. "It's a three-named company."

"*Ja*, I see the men, but I don't see wagons. Still, you're welcome here, especially those rifles you carry."

The fort spoke of prosperousness with its adobe buildings, secure perimeter wall, and sturdy bridge they'd ridden across to reach it. People of all stripes wandered about, making purchases, packing fine-looking mules while dogs sniffed and barked. They'd have supplies to take back to the wagons. Capt felt relieved.

"We've left our women and children near the headwaters of what we believe is the Yuba," Mr. Murphy explained.

"And we need to take supplies back to them and bring the wagons out," Capt said.

"That will take some snowmelt," Sutter said. "How much food did you leave the women with?"

"Several oxen and a good hunter," Dr. John said. "Shelter in a crude but suitable cabin."

"I left behind a baby born but a few days old," Martin Murphy Jr. said.

"They were healthy, all?" Sutter asked as though he hadn't heard Martin's concerns.

"Healthy, yes, but the conditions there and the lack of—"

"Excellent, excellent," Sutter said. "Because—"

"Papa!" Capt watched as Ellen Murphy ran toward her father, wearing an inviting smile with her red curls bouncing. "You made it!"

"Aye, that we did, lass." Martin Murphy hugged his daughter as she held him tight. "And 'tis a gift of the Lord that ye've made it too. Everyone?"

"Alive and accounted for, Da." Daniel Murphy, followed by John, joined them to handshakes all around. The cluster of starving horses and tired men attracted other onlookers.

"Where is Mrs. Townsend?" Capt asked. Perhaps he should have waited for the doctor to ask, but her health had been a big concern for the captain.

"Beth's on her way. Wait until you see her, Dr. John. She's a

bloom in December, but that's not so unusual in this country."
Ellen put her arm through her father's. He patted her hand, then
motioned toward a stump he sank on to.

"I'm healthy as an ox," Beth said as she fast-walked toward
them. Capt did indeed think she looked much improved, pink
cheeks instead of pale. "The Murphys took good care of me. You've
raised a fine bunch of offspring, Mr. Murphy." Capt thought the
old man might just have blushed behind his graying beard. Mrs.
Townsend looked rested and cheerful, though now her voice carried
worry. "Where are the others?"

"And the wagons?" Daniel asked.

"We had to leave them," Capt said, the pain of the words surprising him. "We got snowed in at the Yuba River."

"You got wagons over that far?" Sutter asked. "That's *Gut.*"

"We did. We'll have to return in the spring to get them. But
now, we need to send a rescue party for the women and children.
They couldn't have made this last trek. Even with snowshoes and
jerky, it was an ordeal."

"I can see by the look of you," John said.

"And Mrs. Murphy, is she all right?" Mrs. Townsend asked.

"Women have been bringing forth new life without a hitch for
generations, dear." Townsend lifted her hand to kiss it. "She gave
birth to a baby before we left."

Mrs. Townsend pulled her hand away. "We can thank the Lord
for that."

"A newborn wouldn't have survived if we tried to keep everyone
with us." Capt hoped to take the pained look from Mrs. Townsend's
face. "We built a cabin, crude as it was."

"And Moses," she said. "Chica's looking for him. Where is my
brother?"

Townsend cleared his throat. "You mustn't worry, Elizabeth.
Moses and Joe Foster and Allen Montgomery remained behind
at the lake." He tipped his hat to Capt. "After you left, that next

day, snows hit us pretty hard and it was decided to leave some of the valuables in wagons there."

"They were the heaviest laden wagons," Capt assured her.

"You left my brother?"

"He volunteered to stay, dear. Joe and Allen did too."

"Sarah and Allen aren't together?"

"They aren't," Capt said. "Their separation is a generous and brave thing to offer."

"But—*gasp*—Moses is just—*gasp*—a boy."

"It'll make a man of him," Townsend said. "Don't you worry."

Capt knew though, that she would worry until she could see the whites of the boy's eyes.

"We'll send a relief party. Mr. Sutter . . . ?"

Sutter shook his head. "I have news to tell you. I am raising an army, as it must be. The new governor has an armed force sent to remove the old provincial governor and the Americans here. We're joining Micheltorena, the old governor, who has resisted his forced retirement and has refused to give up the palace to the new governor. We hope either victor will let us Americans stay, but we like the governor we have. Some Mexicans want Alta California to be independent of Mexico City, but they don't want it to become an American territory. So, we must fight."

"But we have to rescue our families," John Sullivan said. "I've two brothers and a sister back there."

"Can the brothers hold a gun?" Sutter asked.

"Maybe. They're pretty young, but if they were here they'd sure try."

"Ach! You cannot bring women and children into this place without securing it and these lands for them. It must be made American, taken for Americans, held by Americans. That means you are desperately needed, my friends, for defense. I conscript you all. No one is taking supplies back."

Capt said, "Let's talk about your army, but we must send relief."

He'd felt so pleased that the men had survived, made it to the fort. Now the most important rescue was to be thwarted by a skirmish?

"I can't afford a single man to go back and help. And supplies must be used for defense first. Your women have oxen to eat and game. With shelter. You said this yourselves. They would want you to protect them by going to war."

"I could go, boss. Pete Sherrebeck." He introduced himself to the group. Tipped his hat to the two women. Capt thought he looked sturdy. Likely Swiss too, with his accent.

"How many oxen did you leave them?" Capt answered and Sutter continued his questioning. "And how many are there?"

"Eight women, seventeen children."

"And you left a hunter?"

"My brother-in-law and his twelve-year-old, William," Martin Murphy said. "And an elderly man."

"Then no, Peter, you must not go. No one must leave except to go to war."

Capt kept his eye on the young volunteer—Sherrebeck—who lowered his head. *Maybe I can take one or two back. The Murphys and their servants. They're rested.* Capt's attention returned to Sutter, whose voice rose now as though he were on a summer's fair stage. "We must fight to save our adopted homeland or you will have nothing to bring those precious women and children to. They are safe where they are. They will not be here—without their men to fight for them."

Mr. Murphy made the sign of the cross over his heart. "With the Lord's help." Sutter was making headway.

"Will there be commissions?" Townsend asked.

"What?" Sutter turned to him. "*Ja,* of course. That is expected. Officers are needed for an army. Captains. Lieutenants, corporals. And surgeons."

"Then we are with you," Townsend said, as though he spoke for all of them. "You can't go to war without medical support."

"But, my brother Moses—"

"Is fine. He's fine, Elizabeth. Calm down. Your fussing will upset you."

"I think we need to discuss this matter amongst ourselves," Capt said. "When we're rested."

"*Ja*. Of course. We get you fed. Warm baths. A good night's rest will help you see the great need there is to fight for your freedom, for the right to worship as you choose. I don't know where the priests will stand in this war, but to know we have Americans who worship as they do might sway them to our side." He clapped his hands together. "You bring what America is, the rights of your constitution, to speak, to move about freely, to worship whether kneeling or standing. That is what the Americans bring to Alta California. *Ja*. And to keep it here, you must fight."

Townsend finally took his wife's hand and held it in both of his. It was a tepid reunion, to Capt's mind. If Abeque had been waiting for him after this long journey, he would have swung her off her feet and kissed her roundly.

Sutter directed Sherrebeck, "Get those lazy Indios working. Get these men some food and restore their ammunition. We got ourselves an army."

Sutter ordered the horses watered and jugs carried from the well for welcomed baths. The Stephens-Murphy-Townsend company dispersed. Captain Stephens was no longer in charge.

27

Character

Wintering Women

Stiff, with tiny cuts from working the rawhide, Sarah's fingers ached. She attributed the pain and clumsiness to hunger. Her nails, once strong, now split. Little to feed them. The watery soup with five dried peas (found in one of the cannibalized wagons and shared) did little for them, even with Maolisa's wormy flour. The Sullivan oxen had been the last meat they'd consumed. Sarah had watched Mary Sullivan sob at the slaughter, but what other choice did they have? That had been a week ago. Not a morsel of meat was left on a single bone, the marrow stripped in fat white tubes and given to the children. The bones barely flavored the hot water they told themselves was soup.

"If you twist it like this, I think the weave will be stronger." Mary Sullivan showed Sarah how to cross the tough strips of hide over each other on the snowshoes Sarah crafted. Mary had snowshoes, but she'd loaned them to Dr. John. Now she made another pair and helped Sarah make a pair as well, the women helping each other, whether learning to read, to knit, and now, to fashion footwear.

Working the sinew onto a frame gave Sarah something to think about besides food. And Allen. It was also a step forward in Sarah's mind. Maybe she could more easily get to the latrine or saunter with Mary, who took the children out into the cold and snow and returned with her spirits lifted. Maolisa had organized washing days where they melted snow in Dutch ovens and scrubbed clothes, rinsing them at the river with hands that nearly froze. The action brought back memories of watching Allen and Ellen at the river's edge. Had it only been a few months?

"Maybe we could walk to Sutter's," Sarah whispered. "Do you think we could?"

"We don't know if the men even made it. It would be risky for us to try." Mary gave a yank on the rawhide. She used her teeth to pull the stringy material tight.

"We may have to rescue ourselves," Sarah said. It was an errant thought. *Errant. Wayward, off the path.*

Then she watched James coming to their corner of the cabin. A child cried and a mother soothed her. There was always a child crying.

"Mrs. Montgomery, Miss Sullivan." He acknowledged them with a lifted chin to each woman. "I've made my decision. A relief party ought to have been back by now. We simply can't wait any longer." The Miller infant let out a wail that Ailbe worked to console. Sarah guessed Ailbe had little milk to give the child, but perhaps the act of sucking gave the baby comfort.

"With these snowshoes finished, we could walk out too," Mary Sullivan said.

"But not everyone can. I'm the strongest and William's got stamina, though it's dripping out of him like a leaky pump. My mind's eased knowing you can load and fire, maybe even track a wounded animal should you need to."

"I know how to shoot too," Sarah said. But she wasn't strong enough now to even carry a rifle. When she stood up, she felt dizzy—but it passed.

"Can't Old Man Martin hunt?" Sarah said. She didn't want his daughter to hear her. "Then we could go with you."

"Too weak," James said. "Even he knows it. No, you women are stronger than us men. Maybe in your minds too, enduring as you all have. Waitin' might be the hardest work. William and I will leave in the morning. Mrs. Miller's given her blessing at long last, though she's as reluctant as a kitten at the barking end of a wild dog."

"I wish I had a kitten to pet," Sarah said. Then she did giggle. "I don't know what's gotten into me. My mind is traveling while my feet are staying put."

But at least James Miller had a plan. Sarah did not.

Wagon Guard

Moses awoke with the sun overhead and his stomach gnawing. He'd eaten the last of old Bill. Consumed the coyote and crow. Now, he was without. Maybe this was how the Israelites felt, each day awaiting the manna. His sojourn here was a good test of his faith—and his trap-setting skill.

He rose, scrubbed snow on his face, heated water, washed, dressed, then donned his snowshoes to check his first trap.

He danced in the snow, whooped his delight, breaking the great quiet, then spoke a prayer of gratitude. "My manna in the wilderness," he said to the fox. He took the animal back to the cabin, gutted, skinned, and then cooked it. It was the best meal he'd ever eaten, better than beef roasts served at Christmas by his sister. Better than turkey. Better than . . . he couldn't find a comparison. He saved pieces to use as bait for the next trap. He wondered if he'd set aside enough to lure in another fox, but then would tell himself he needed to eat too. The fox lasted him two days, and it was on the third day that he caught another one. If he could trap one every few days, he could make it. Until bigger game showed up.

At night, he read more of Lord Chesterfield, deciding that the man was puffy at times but must have loved his son deeply to have written of wisdom as he had. He decided to memorize some of the best passages. He'd recite them and Bible verses and song lyrics and poems from his childhood to keep his mind from sinking. He appreciated the lines about character.

> Without purity of character you can have no dignity of character; and without dignity of character it is impossible to rise in the world. You must be respectable if you are to be respected. . . . In purity of character, and in politeness of manners, labour to excel all, if you wish to equal many.

Moses thought of the character of Dr. John as the candlelight flickered and his fire crackled. There was room for a little more purity, he thought, in the man's actions at least toward his sister. He'd treated Moses all right through the years, but he'd never felt warm toward him. He guessed that was a way to put it. If he was troubled about anything, he didn't make his way to the doctor for advice because he got a lecture instead. When he'd fallen from an apple tree and broken his elbow, it was his sister who had comforted him in the terrible pain while Dr. John waxed on about how Moses needed to be more careful, that he, Dr. John, had never had a broken bone, suggesting that accidents didn't happen to people except by their own foolishness.

Moses thought that if that's the case, what foolishness had gotten him here in this snowbound world, separated from all he loved? Had he been a fool to volunteer to stay with the wagons? To let Joe and Allen leave without him? What did those choices say about his character? He read more, then thought of something his sister had told him not long after the elbow break. He'd gotten into a fistfight with a friend over—he couldn't remember. "Poor choices don't have to define a man's character, Moses," his sister told him. He remembered she'd called him a man, but he was only twelve then. "Unless he fails to gain wisdom from that poor decision. Failure to learn taints character more than the original choice itself. Adversity can destroy or redefine. That option always belongs to us."

He guessed he was learning how to appreciate the willingness of a fox to let itself be trapped so that this man could keep learning lessons. He made the choice to appreciate small joys—like his looking forward to savoring the last of his coffee on Christmas Day. He could control his mind to keep it from the panic he often woke with, wondering if he'd eat that day. He was ever more grateful each night when he had been graced with food.

On what he believed was New Year's Eve, he listened to the wind blowing. His snare would be covered by drifts come morning. But he could remember the tree with the crooked branch that lay like the letter Y on its side, and the way the cabin looked when he turned back to see how far he'd come and the look of three large rocks like patient Magi waiting to cross at the creek's bend. All those points would help him know where he'd set his trap even when he could no longer see it. That was a little like faith too, he supposed. Trusting in what was beyond his sight using other clues to obtain what he sought.

Wintering Women

Isabella woke with a start in the dark cabin. Andrew had come to her in a dream. What had he said? Three words? *Fare thee well.* It wasn't a farewell, as in goodbye, but more a hope for her future, that she might indeed fare well. He had said those very words to her on his deathbed, but she'd mistook them as goodbye. Why now did she understand them differently?

The women had spoken of regrets before turning in to their bedrolls. Perhaps that was what triggered the dream. Sarah regretted not staying with Allen at the wagons. Mary Sullivan regretted not heading out with the men. The Murphy aunts lamented not being married, not having children. Maolisa comforted them, as did Ailbe. "We'll always share ours," the women had said to quiet smiles.

Isabella's own Lydia had squeaked out the words "I regret not growing up before I die." The child had expressed the thought that plagued them all: death. Still, there was something comforting about knowing one would not die in a room by oneself. Maolisa had said then that they ought to light candles every night and pray for the safety of the men who would bring back help. And to pray for each other. "We don't know what's in store for us, but we know that God is present with us. Everything will turn out well," she insisted. "Scripture teaches us."

Isabella wasn't so certain. Oh, she believed that God was with them through thick and thin but things didn't always turn out well. People did get sick and die. They suffered. Age came upon them as a cloak threadbare or heavy. But she had prayed with the women anyway, to gain something from this waiting beside the Yuba River.

Now, awake from her dream with Andrew's admonition to *Fare thee well*, she also knew she must speak her mind to Sarah and Mary and to her own daughter too, to put regrets behind, to forgive the faults so one didn't have to carry the weight into the future. She must not let her own regrets keep her from faring well in the days ahead. She would advise the younger women to do whatever they could to fare well until . . . they couldn't.

At Sutter's Fort

Ellen Murphy walked around the perimeter of marching men while Beth stood with a shawl around her shoulders in the January dawn. Beth dabbed at her eyes as though she'd been crying. Chica trotted beside Ellen, the dog having whined outside Ellen's room and only quieted when Ellen let her in. She wondered what it meant that Chica didn't enjoy Dr. John's company, as the little dog had been quite content in Beth's quarters until the doctor joined her.

"Boys playing at war," Ellen said as she walked up the five steps to where Beth stood overlooking the trainees. That was how Sutter had referred to the men he'd conscripted. He funded his own private war—but not a rescue party.

"Except they intend to actually go to battle, get themselves killed." Beth shook her head. "Isn't this the strangest turn of events? We're here. The men arrive, safe and sound. We attend a Christmas mass at the mission and the present they give us is to abandon the rest of the party—and us—to put themselves in harm's way. It's . . . inexplicable."

"I haven't been able to get even one of Sutter's men to consider sending help. I've used all my charms, as Daniel would say. They want to fight instead. Even Martin Junior. I can't believe he won't return to help his Maolisa and their baby."

"John says every local is employed by the little Swiss man," Beth said. A breeze rustled the bougainvillea, the flash of red vibrant against the beige adobe walls, the blooms and leaves a garland of color twisted around the wooden beams that broke up the sun overhead.

"They all seem to think the number of oxen left with those at the river will be enough." Ellen pulled her shawl with black fringe around her shoulders. "I pray they're right."

"I've wondered if the little Swiss fears competition that will surely happen once John's supplies are brought in and we start our own mercantile." That store had been part of Ellen's dream for the future, but now, perhaps she'd have to consider something else. *Can dreams drift away, then be called back?*

"Does he know about the Montgomery guns? Maybe he'd send help to Moses and the others using our route if for nothing more than the guns."

"But they still couldn't get the wagons out, so what would be the use? Moses would just remain. He can be stubborn like that." She sighed. "I asked Dennis Martin if he'd consider forgoing the war effort to take relief to them. His father's there, for heaven's sake. He said he'd like to but felt his rifle would be best used in defense."

"Sutter's washed all their brains of common sense." Ellen snapped her finger at Chica, who came trotting. "John and Daniel are out there marching with the rest of them. So are Oliver and François."

"None seem too concerned about keeping those who remain behind at the fort safe," Beth said.

"I suggest we arm ourselves just in case."

"They'll take all the guns, surely."

"We'll use kitchen knives if we have to, though will we recognize the so-called enemy?" Mr. Sutter had been so good at describing the peril, even her father believed they must go to war.

The commander called a "halt" and "at ease" and the men relaxed their shoulders, began milling around.

"I feel—*gasp*—so incredibly helpless," Beth said.

"Me too." The two women locked arms in comfort. "We're healthy," Ellen said. "'Tis something." She smiled.

"And isn't that a good thing since our doctor will soon be off to war."

"We may not be able to put together a rescue team, but we also won't have men hovering over our every move, either. Let's get to know this California place before we're sent north to Oregon by an enemy we can't even see."

28

Hello and Goodbye

Wintering Women

The sun was above the horizon the morning Sarah thought she saw things. That had happened lately: a fleeting image of movement across the room as she fell asleep. She wasn't frightened. In the morning she'd asked if others had seen what she had and no one had. "Must be hunger angels," Ailbe told her and Sarah had been grateful no one thought her daft. *Daft. Around the bend. Hysterical. Devoid of mind.*

Sarah had gone out to the latrine using her new snowshoes. James had been gone two days, at the last minute leaving William behind. The young boy was bereft, but his mother had prevailed. "I can't lose both of you," Ailbe told her husband loud enough for the rest to hear. Well, you could hear everything in these close quarters. It was why sometimes Sarah sat in the torn-apart wagons from time to time, just to be alone, her sweater snugly around her. The cold drove her back to the others—or maybe it was the comfort of shared suffering. At night, her breath looked like clouds visible in the moonlight, and sometimes, when the moon hid its face, the stars caused her to pause in wonder at the smallness of their little cabin, the people making do inside, watched over by the eyes of God. Mary said they were in a living purgatory, waiting, and perhaps they were.

She finished her dailys, made water in the snow, rose, and lowered her skirts, then used the shovel to cover her refuse. Finished, she looked up and saw movement. *More angels.* James must have turned back. But he would have come from the west and this activity—it was two men—came from the south. *Indians!* "Indians!" She screamed the warning, turned toward the cabin.

"What is it?" Mary caught her as she threw herself through the door.

"It's Indians. Men. They're coming."

"Are you sure?" Mary grabbed a rifle that leaned next to the door. "Gather the children up. Keep them quiet if you can," Mary said.

Maolisa was the first to respond, shushing children, clucking them into the far corner. "Let's play a silent game," she said and began making up rules she whispered while Sarah followed Mary back out and around the cabin's corner.

"Did they see you? Were they armed?"

"I . . . I don't know. Do you think they did something to Allen? Are we next?"

Mary pushed Sarah behind her, signaled quiet.

The men, Paiute perhaps, continued their movement toward the cabin. If they carried guns, Mary couldn't see them, nor bows and arrows. They walked on snowshoes using an odd gait.

"Go get Mr. Martin," Mary whispered. "Ask him to come out."

"He can't shoot," Sarah said.

"He can talk. With his hands. I saw him do it back when we met Truckee." *So long ago now.*

Almost as though they'd heard, the men halted several yards beyond the disheveled cabin. The clothing they'd used for chinking between branches and logs flapped in the wind and might have looked disturbing to these wilderness visitors. Maybe they'd think them all daft and leave them be. They were far enough away, they looked like sticks stuck up in the snow. Sticks that could move.

"Mr. Martin. Can you sign to them?" He'd slipped out wearing his gray underwear, his daughter's heavy shawl around his narrow shoulders. Ann Jane steadied him. He crouched, nodded, yes. "Ask what they want?"

His bad arm worked well enough to make words. But before he could shout or begin to motion to them, the men turned and angled away from the cabin.

Sarah had rejoined them and Mary felt a sudden emptiness at watching them walk away. Perhaps they could tell them how far away Sutter's Fort was or they might have come by the wagons being guarded. "Maybe they think there are too many of us here," Mary said. "Or maybe they can't see us as tucked down next to the creek as we are."

"Just as well," Mr. Martin said. "No way to know if they're friend or foe."

But then Sarah let out a whoop. "Allen! Allen Montgomery! Don't you walk away from me! That's Allen. I can see it in his stride now. But there are only two of them? Who have they left behind?"

"Allen? Allen? Oh, Allen!" Sarah tromped toward him, stumbled. "It's you!"

"It's us," Joe Foster croaked.

Allen let Sarah help him toward the cabin. He was weak but still upright. His face was so thin and felt so cold when she put her cheeks to his. His beard scratched against her skin and it felt lovely.

"Come. Get warm. Joe, come." They started the short distance to the cabin and Mary said, "Where's Moses?"

"At the lake. He was ill. Didn't think he could make it and didn't want to tardy us," Joe said. "I hope he made it back but I don't know. He didn't look good. We got . . . sort of lost looking for you. More days out. Snow. So glad to find you."

"Had you in her sights, Miss Sullivan did." Mr. Martin patted Joe on his back.

"I wasn't ready to shoot," Mary told them as they clumped their way into the cabin.

"Look who's here." Sarah shouted the news as the frozen men ducked their heads at the doorway. Her eyes always took a moment to adjust from the bright snow glare to the cabin's interior.

Sarah saw hope in the eyes of the women as they gazed upon these men. They'd gotten over the summit and been traveling through the snow. Allen and Joe still had a little food left and that was shared.

"Thank you, thank you."

"The most filling meal I've ever had," Ann Jane said. She honked her laugh.

"It's surprising what we can convince our minds of," Mary agreed.

"Now you're here, you can hunt for us," Sarah said. "You'll have better luck than we have."

"We shot one deer," Joe Foster said. "Poor animal was starving too. We put it out of its misery."

"The snow's so deep that our fire sank each morning," Allen said. "But we've eaten all right."

"We've tried pinecone soup," Mary said. "Gives a little flavor to the water."

Joe nodded, acknowledging her resourcefulness.

"Just knowing you're here and safe. It raises our spirits," Ailbe said. "It means James will make it too. And the others, who left for the fort."

"They all left?" Joe looked around, as though noticing the absence of men for the first time.

"All of them, except my James. He headed out two days ago."

"I'm still here." Mr. Martin spoke up from the hide-covered wall he sat against.

"You're here. We'll get game now," Sarah said. She knew she was focused on food.

"No," Allen said. "We need to keep going. Bring back a relief party."

"We don't know why one hasn't arrived already," Mary said. "Unless they didn't make it."

"No, no, no, you can't say that out loud," Johanna wailed. "Never put the fear into words the devil can hear and make so."

Sarah had no time for the devil. But she too felt a lurch in her stomach with Mary's voicing what the two of them had only whispered.

"Then we are going with you."

"It's too hard, Sarah. The snow has been exhausting and—"

"Your snowshoes are all wrong," Mary said.

Allen looked at his feet.

"The heels shouldn't be secured, only the toes. Like mine." Sarah held her foot up. "And Mary's. The Canadians know how to make them." She was immediately chastened by the look on Allen's face. Had she humiliated him in front of the others?

"But you made them and they got you here," Mary said. "Very . . . resourceful."

Resourceful. Sarah would ask Mary to look that word up. Mary's using it had changed Allen's expression—for the better.

"Anyway," Mary continued. "It'll be easier if we release the heels. You won't get as tired."

"And we can leave with you," Sarah said.

Allen put his arm around her shoulders. "Of course, darlin'."

"I won't let you abandon me again."

That night, Sarah slept better than she had since their journey began. The warmth of her husband, his scent, being able to reach and touch him brought a deep sleep to her life. She dreamed of when they'd met, a wound bringing him to the surgery, the scent of linseed oil on his skin, a romantic connection spinning toward marriage. She heard him get up in the night to go to the latrine. She fell back asleep immediately and didn't rouse when he returned. There was a plan. She dreamed again, this time of a warm hearth burning somewhere in California, a table with food aplenty.

The sun was up when she awoke and stretched. She turned to speak to Allen, but he wasn't there. Joe wasn't in the cabin either. They'd departed before dawn.

"Then we're going too," Ailbe said.

"You can't." Maolisa spoke to her sister-in-law, trying to bring sense. Allen and Joe's arrival and departure had turned them all upside down. Turmoil swirled the cabin's order. "Sarah and Mary Sullivan are young, able. They don't have to worry over children. You do. Please, be reasonable."

"We'll have William with us. I can carry Indie on my back. Kate, Mary, and Martin have snowshoes. We'll make it. I can't stay here."

"You have to wait."

"If we wait, the snow will come in and fill in the men's tracks," Sarah said.

"We need to leave now," Ailbe said. "The girls are right."

Maolisa patted her baby's bottom. *Do we go or stay?* Junior would return to help them, she was certain of it. *If he's alive. What if he isn't?* The risks of getting lost and starving out there had to be worse than dying here. No, they would remain. But it was foolhardy for the Millers to go. She was powerless to stop them.

"Leave little Indie, then. What milk I have, I'll be sure she has a portion. You'll be able to move faster without an infant. There's . . . less risk of frostbite on her little cheeks."

Her sister-in-law hesitated, clutched her child to her, then lurched the six-month-old toward Maolisa's arms. Maolisa was adjusting her infant in one elbow and arranging to take Indie when

Isabella Patterson stepped in. "I can hold one," she said. "Maybe leave Martin. He's barely two, isn't he?"

Ailbe nodded. "But he'll whine terribly. William and I can trade off carrying him."

"I can help," Johanna said. An aunt could carry Martin if necessary, but what would James say about her allowing his sisters to head out like that?

"But who will hunt for us?" Isabella said.

Silence followed. The departing women looked at each other.

"I'm still here." Old Man Martin made his way toward them. "I may be crippled up, but I guess I haven't forgot how to wad a rifle."

"Yes, you can, Da." Ann Jane patted her father's shoulder. "And I can drag in whatever he might shoot." She laughed, that cackling sound. Maolisa had grown to love her laughter, found it a comfort now rather than an annoyance.

"What about us, Sister?" The little Sullivan boys stared with owl eyes at Mary. Mary's younger brothers had joined in the chaos of decision-making, their eyes going back and forth between the women's conversations.

"I can't carry you." Mary squatted down to look at them. "And you haven't had enough food. I . . . you won't make it."

"We'll watch after them, won't we?" Isabella Patterson patted Michael's shoulder. "You can help us here. I thought we might try to make a fishhook, maybe get lucky from the Yuba." The new idea seemed to interest the two boys. It was good they weren't as driven as their older sister, Maolisa thought. At least she had the good sense to leave them behind. She wished Ailbe would leave Martin too.

The bustle and activity of packing followed. The small amounts of meat Allen and Joe had left they divided further still. Warm sweaters and capes. They latched on their snowshoes and the Miller family—minus the youngest—and Mary Sullivan were out the door. Sarah brought up the rear in that parade of souls, their snowshoes leaving crisscrosses in the snow.

Maolisa prayed the rosary, sent up prayers to all the saints, entreated Jesus, then God to please, please keep them safe. What was the point of coming all this way for religious freedom, to start a school so her children could be educated, if within miles of the finish line half the Murphy clan perished? And the Millers were part of the Murphy clan. James Miller didn't know what he was in for when he married Ailbe. She could have told him that the women were headstrong. Resilient, she liked to think.

She made the sign of the cross over her heart, then went about putting things in order in the now slightly less crowded cabin on the Yuba. Tending was how she put her fears at bay.

Men at War

The army, such as it was, rode out on January 1, 1845. Capt made a note of it in his little book. He was torn, but he'd convinced himself that the women and children would be all right. They had plenty of oxen and surely James Miller would have found game. Their fate still concerned him—but so did the prospect of a lost country. If they were driven out by either the new governor's men or after helping Micheltorena stay in power, would they be able to go back and get the women? They could be forced to go north to Oregon even after being on the winning side. The long journey would have been for naught. All that suffering with no gain to show for it. No, they'd go back for the women, just have to abandon the wagons.

Capt Stephens rode in the advance moving south. They'd encountered no resistance. John Murphy rode beside him, filled him in on the horse party journey.

"I almost drowned," John said. "All that effort to rescue me would be a terrible waste if I die getting shot at."

"Do you think the wagons could have made it going where you went?"

"Naw. You did right, Capt, taking them up and over the summit. Sorry the snows buried you at the Yuba."

"Hard picks," Capt said.

"Guess that's what life is about, sir. You've had to make your share of them."

"Appears you and Daniel did too."

"Gotta honor our pa and do it right." He twisted in his saddle, searching for his father and brother, Capt supposed. "Actually, looking back, it wasn't so hard." John faced forward again. Capt couldn't get over the lush country, light rains but still a constant summer. "Guess when you find success in something, all the pain getting there gets washed away."

Capt remembered Abeque saying something like that about women giving birth: they forgot the pain of it. "I hope the women will feel that way when we return to rescue them."

"My sisters are mother bears," John said. "They'll do whatever they have to, to keep all of them alive. I've got no doubts about that."

John's optimism encouraged him. It was what Capt wanted to believe. He had seen the evidence of the Murphy women's fortitude fed by their faith, intelligence, and good nature. And each other, he supposed. Sisters and sisters-in-law made up quite a community. He'd seen it in Abeque's family too. Aunties acted like mothers and all the kids felt loved even in the discipline. He'd wished he and Abeque had had a family. But after she died, he was grateful he didn't have a little one to raise up. The baby girl had gone to heaven with her mother.

He was about to thank John for his encouraging words when a bullet whizzed past his head. "Take cover! Fire from the east!" Capt shouted and the group scattered into the trees.

He'd better put nostalgia aside and pay attention to where he was or encouragement and optimism would be nothing more than words written on his tombstone.

29

Doing What We Can

At Sutter's Fort

What Ellen had wanted to do was talk with Dr. John about being the proprietor of his mercantile. She had experience. She could free him up to do more . . . social things, political. Write his book he was always talking about. Becoming well-known in this new place. But he'd gone off to war before she could broach the subject.

She and Beth spoke of trying to take a rescue team in themselves but knew they couldn't. They'd have to secure horses for those stranded to ride out on and take food in. That assumed they could even find their way into a wilderness they hadn't come through. She'd approached Peter Sherrebeck—left by Sutter to run the mill and store—but he'd told her it wasn't possible to find a team to make the trek. It would have to wait.

It was what women did. Waited for the right husband. Waited to begin a family. Waited for a life to begin.

Despite the war going on, music played each evening in Sutter's courtyard. Bright red flowers bloomed and draped over the veranda. In the pause to begin her life, Ellen eyed the fine Spanish-looking men—none dressed for battle. But she stayed clear of the *señors* dressed in tight embroidered pants, wearing short jackets with wide shoulders. Most dismounted from fine-looking horses decorated with silver cheekpieces, while dark-eyed *señoritas* welcomed the local landowners on the balmy evenings. Ellen dropped her eyes if one of the men smiled at her. She didn't know the rules to flirting here and she was wary of her history. Hadn't she already selected poorly? She hadn't recognized Matthew's bent toward business risk stirred by his love of liquor. She'd judged Daniel's sharp tongue and frowns as bitter fruits without seeing the broken crust they'd been baked in. Perhaps that was why he'd gone off to war so readily, John with him, to find new ways to prove his courage to himself, exchange bitter fruit for sweet heroics. Her older brothers didn't seem to mind being conscripted either, and when she'd argued on behalf of her sisters and nieces and nephews and friends still stranded in the mountains, her brothers had said it was not her place to decide. They would and they had.

She'd never understand men, not ever.

She'd met a fair number of American men coming from the Oregon Territory, but in this California, they'd spread out, unable to buy Sutter's land grants with him off fighting. Some joined the fight against or for Micheltorena, immigrants like her family, trying to make a country they could stay in.

Karl Maria Weber, an immigrant like herself, had been polite to her. He was a good-looking German, and he seemed to know it. He went by the moniker of "Captain," having fought with Sam Houston in the Texas-Mexican war of independence and she noticed that the wealthy locals called him Carlos or *Señor*. He was a "businessman," he'd told her. The business part intrigued Ellen. He'd looked after her and Beth, making sure they could secure what they might need from the fort, though when she ventured a conversation about a relief party, he acted like he didn't understand English.

She was in purgatory, waiting, not a place she bloomed well in, despite being planted there by the very nature of being born a woman.

Señor Weber left before long, taking supplies to the war effort. She wasn't sure which side he fought on. War was so strange. These men meant to change the country, that's what they said. But Ellen could see that the country changed them. And her.

She busied herself trying to communicate with some of the Indian women. They were Wintu people, Peter had told her. They'd been shy at first, but now they smiled when she approached, and one of them—she had yet to learn the woman's name—had shown her how they made the flat bread Mrs. Sinclair called tortillas. The woman's hands worked the dough into thin swirls she placed on a wooden paddle and stuck it into a round-top fireplace outside. She'd laughed out loud at Ellen's poor attempt to do the same, her fingers sticking up through the flat pancake.

To fill their days, Ellen and Beth had ridden about the area. They were told to be wary, that kidnapping was a favorite occupation of the locals to get ransom to fund their resistance.

Ellen offered to work in the Sutter kitchen in exchange for some material she sewed into a linen frock with short sleeves and a scoop neck. The bright red dye appealed to her. But once the dress was finished, she felt listless again.

When the mission bells tolled out a mass, she joined local men and women who walked outside Sutter's walls to the nearby church. She couldn't understand what was being said, though the Latin and the incense, the murmur of the priest's prayers, and the *swish-swish* of slippers on the dirt floors were familiar and brought her a kind of peace. Perhaps this waiting was a gift meant to teach her that a pause or hesitation could be a filling thing.

She walked back, her feet sinking into the soft dirt. She'd been a sickly child and Daniel said their mother hadn't thought she'd survive. Daniel had shared that when the Horseback Party followed the American River, before they killed the Sinclair calves. "Illness is what made the family indulge you. We all feared you'd get sick again and gave in to your every screaming demand."

"I don't remember being a screamer."

"You changed to a beguiler," he said. "Still are. But then you couldn't wait a moment."

She had punched his shoulder. "But you love me anyway, yes?"

"I do." He looked sheepish. He'd changed along the way.

"I'm sorry my actions sometimes upset you," she said.

He nodded, cleared his throat. "You don't seem to miss your husband."

She was about to retort but gave herself a moment to consider. She didn't want a feud. "People grieve in their own way," she said. *Should I tell him?* "Matthew . . . drank. And he was a mean drunk, Daniel. I never wanted to say. But I didn't wish him dead, just that he would go away, let me live in peace."

"Guess he did that by dying in the fire."

She and Daniel had made a truce and she didn't want to sever it ever again.

She didn't remember much of that time of her sickness—she was only seven—but she did remember hearing her mother pray a Novena. She'd prayed the prayers and recorded them in a little book. It was dated 1820 and was one of the precious items Ellen had carried with her all the way from Ireland to Quebec to Missouri. And now to this California place.

With music from the courtyard behind her, Ellen returned to her room. She took the little book out, lit candles, the light flickering on the windowless adobe wall. She began to pray the prayers of her mother in French, some in Gaelic and English. Her mother's Novena had gone for nine days, the traditional time. Ellen would go on longer, she decided. She'd pray the prayers every day until her family was gathered together in this place, until all were returned from the mountains and Stephens Lake, until she knew what it was she was supposed to do next.

But before she prayed the second prayer, she heard a commotion in the courtyard. She stepped out onto the veranda, squinting into the sun, her hands at her forehead for shade. Beth stood at the door of her quarters.

"What is it?" Beth asked.

"It's . . ." Ellen strained her neck to see. "I can't tell." They'd have to wait to know. Again.

Wagon Guard

That day, Moses had a fox in two traps. He'd rummaged through more of Capt's things and found a second steel snare. A bonanza! That morning, he took the first fox and stuffed it in his coat. He started to take out the other, when it darted away from him, not dead, his foot left behind in the teeth.

"Why didn't I bring my rifle?" he said to the wind.

Moses ran back to the cabin, clopping through the snow, grabbed his gun, left the fox, returned to the trap, and followed the other's bloody trail. "There you are." He took aim. But he'd forgotten that he'd left a greasy wad inside the barrel—to prevent rusting—so when he shot, it landed well short of the fox, which now splashed across a creek to the other side.

"Quick, quick, reload, reload." His fingers shook. It might be his last fox. He never knew. He shot again and the fox went down. On the other side of the stream.

Moses laid his gun in the snow and checked the creek. It was about two and a half feet deep. There was no choice. He plunged in. His legs numbed like young saplings, wobbly. He made his way, splashed out, dug down into the snow, and grabbed his breakfast, the fox's long red tail dragging. He carried the animal back into icy water, then out, shivering now, his teeth actually chattering. This time, he found his gun and stomped back to the cabin. He built up the fire, took off his wet clothes, and sat with a blanket around his back. He craved the fat of this game. Not salt—he had plenty of it, but he never needed it. He tossed off the blanket. It was the grease that eased down either side of his mouth when he ate this prey that he hankered.

He tore at the roasted food.

Satisfied, he wished he had a cup of coffee, but he had saved the last bit of the grain and drank it at Christmas, now many weeks previous.

He looked for Lord Byron's poetry when he realized he was full. *Isn't that remarkable.* Maybe he should write a gratitude poem about that.

Wintering Women

Fog rose up from the river, forming a gray veil that filtered the trees and sky, gave no sun to guide them. Mary's brother had taken the compass. She shivered despite her warm sweater and shawl, woolen socks. At the last minute, she'd brought her little brothers with her. She watched them. They weren't shivering. Still, maybe they should turn back. They could follow their own tracks, but going forward . . . they could so easily lose their way in the dense fog. Mary felt the weight of decision. She'd convinced Sarah to go to the fort with her or at least hadn't discouraged her. Sarah's anger at Allen explained some of Sarah's drive. Perhaps it would keep her warm. But Ailbe had also made the choice to leave her infant but brought William with her. Mary's little brothers had come too. "It will leave more food for the others if we join you," Ailbe told her. "We have confidence in you, Mary." *They ought not to.* Mary didn't know how to pray, but she sent up thoughts to whoever might be listening to watch over the children, watch over them all.

The first evening out they'd found pine branches, laid them like a cross and fed the flames through the night. Sarah had torn several pages from her dictionary before they left, and Mary used one of the precious matches to light the paper.

"I just can't believe he'd say that to me and then sneak out." Sarah held her hands to the flames, drank the water heated in the tin coffeepot set off to the side near the coals.

"He probably did it for your own good," Ailbe said. "Sometimes Junior says things to me he thinks will comfort me, but the words don't. They make me feel like a child. Maybe Allen knew if he said you couldn't come with him, it would end in a fight."

"It would have."

"You'll surprise him. And I'll surprise my brother too. We'll make it," Mary Sullivan said. "We will."

She'd been confident then. But this morning, the fog hovered, weighted with discouragement. Maybe it would lift. They could stay by the fire. Wait. Return or head out, hoping the river didn't meander farther away from their destination. Returning would demoralize them, perhaps rob those who waited of the hope their departure had meant. But going forward in the fog, following the creek uncertain of what lay around the bend, that might lead to all their deaths. "We have a decision to make," Mary said. "Should we go back or keep going?"

"Remember the story you read us, Mary, about which fork in the road the tailor and the shoemaker were supposed to take?" Robert's words were cloud puffs in the cold air.

"I do remember that story." But she'd forgotten it until that moment.

"And the 'more-all' was 'He who trusts in God and his own fortune will never go amiss.' That's what you told us, Sister," Michael said. "We'll never go amiss."

How simple that story had seemed then. But here, now, very much could go amiss even if one trusted that it wouldn't.

At Sutter's Fort

"It's James Miller. All that commotion in the courtyard is Ailbe's husband!"

"Oh, are they all there? Moses?" Beth wrapped her shawl around herself and ran down the steps before Ellen could answer.

Ellen followed through the milling people. She heard Beth pleading. "Are they all right? Are the others behind you?"

James collapsed against a barrel. "No one's behind me. They're all there, starving. Why didn't I meet a relief party?" He looked around. "Where's Capt? Where are your brothers, Ellen?"

"They've all gone off to war," Ellen said.

"Dr. John too."

"War? What? There are women and children starving." He stood, his eyes wild as a feral cat's and as desperate.

"Starving?"

"Yes. Starving. No game, nothing. We've eaten every ox we had, every milk cow. We need a relief party. Now."

"Maybe Mr. Sherrebeck will listen to you," Ellen said. "No one listens to us." But maybe . . . her Novenas had been heard.

30

Warmth

Wintering Women

Without the act of eating, including the preparation and satisfaction of serving, Maolisa felt cold inside and out and imagined the rest did as well.

There were still things to do. Gathering wood to burn took longer. Chopping branches and hauling them in took time to help fill the days. Someone had suggested boiling pine needles and Maolisa thought the soup might have given some nutrition, but it was so bitter and two of the children became sick, their discomfort passing when they set aside the pine tea. They'd also tried eating the softness beneath the tree bark, consuming the marrow like that of an ox's bones, life hidden. They'd dug it out, roasted it. Boiled some. She thought it might have reduced her flickering "intrusions"—those thoughts she could do nothing about but that increased her worry. It became a daily task, letting the trees feed them. She suckled her sister-in-law's child, then nursed her own. Little Indie slept, seemingly satiated by the warm water she'd been fed through the tip of a glove Maolisa had cut off. And Yuba, too, slept now, her mother hovering for fear she might stop breathing.

Isabella had suggested they look at the frozen pile of cowhides stacked outside, ones they hadn't latched to the log walls to keep the wind out. "Whatever for?" Ann Jane had asked.

"Remnants." Isabella and her children had begun scraping any bits of flesh stuck to the old hides, morsels they might have missed in the first cleaning. By day's end, they had a little pile of bits and pieces of meat that the children had eaten. "Slowly," Isabella had said. "Imagine it is a large piece of roasted buffalo. Let it roll around on your tongue. Can you smell it? Feel it in your mouth? How does it feel when it goes down your throat? Oh, doesn't it make your tummy feel full?"

Maolisa wondered if a child's imagination could go so far and so deep as to let a scrap of dried meat fill them up, but they had slept after that. And the hide scraping had continued, giving them all a sliver of meat and a fragment of hope. She wondered when they would all set out as James and Mary and Ailbe had. What could have happened that the men had sent no help? Had they miscalculated the distance? Had they all perished? And at what point did those remaining behind force themselves to leave the safety of this rough shelter?

They would boil the hides next and make a soup.

The fire crackled and she rose from the rocking chair, nearly stumbled on the hem of her wrapper now sweeping the floor, since she'd lost so much weight. She prayed the rosary standing before the fire. It gave her order and kept her mind from the hopeless things. At least they had a fire.

That evening, Maolisa said, "Let's think about what was warm in our lives, when we were growing up. Maybe it will take our minds from . . . other things."

"It won't work anymore, Sister," Margaret said. Her once fleshy body had shrunk, was barely wider than a wagon tongue. "We need to talk about how we will deal with death. We should start digging graves now."

Maolisa knew that death was a topic they needed to speak of

but not in the evening, not when darkness made the cabin smaller, light so far away and the cold crept deeper into their bones.

Maolisa patted the shoulder of the aunt who had spoken. "There is time for that. I'll begin. My mother was the warmest person in the world to me. She used to hug me to her side and read to me every night. Bible stories but also stories of animals. My father used to say anything other than Bible stories would 'spoil the mind,' but she ignored him and kept reading. She made up stories for us too. I can still smell her apron with its mix of bread and berry scent, and even now when I smell biscuits baking, I think of her and how she filled us up. She was as warm as a wool sweater to me."

"I'll go next." Ann Jane's daughter slept beside her. "It was a dog. Chippy we called him. I guess I named him. I was trying to say 'Sheep' because that was his work, herding the flocks. Black and white he was. He was often out on the fields, but when he brought the flock in, as soon as Da released him, he'd run to me." Her eyes grew shiny in the firelight. "I came to him with my tears and buried my head in his fur." Her child stirred and Ann Jane reached out to rub her back. They'd all begun sleeping closer to their children after Sarah, Mary, and the Millers left.

"Pets do that," Isabella said. "Let us cry into them. They never judge."

"Can a man join in this jabbering?" Mr. Martin rose up, lying on one elbow for support.

"Of course. We're always happy for a man's perspective, Da."

"Humph. Not always, I'd say."

Maolisa chuckled.

"I had a pet snake as a boy."

"Ick." One of the Patterson children spoke. Apparently savoring a scrap of beef and bark hadn't been enough to put her to sleep.

"Now, wee one, don't you be judging," Mr. Martin said. "Mr. Snake would come out of the weeds when I sat on the back steps to eat my breakfast."

"How did you know it was a him snake?" BD asked. Maolisa's boy wasn't sleeping either.

"Well, now that you ask, I didn't know. I just assumed because he was so agreeable a creature, he must be a boy." He grinned. "I'd tap on the side of my tin and he'd be there. He'd slither onto my lap. Curl up. He was just a bull snake. Usually ate mice, of course."

"Was he warm?"

"Yes, he was. Smooth as silk and reliable too. I couldn't always count on my da. He had a liking for drink, and me ma, well, she left when we were wee, my brothers and me."

"I don't think I knew that, Da."

"Not easy to speak of, girl. Never forgave her for that. Guess I should now, before last rites are given, though there's no priest to do it in this place."

"We're still alive," Maolisa said. "And the Lord willing, there'll be a relief party before last rites are needed. Or better yet, you'll shoot us our dinner, Mr. Martin, and we'll have a warm meal."

"Would like to. Want you ladies to count on me the way I counted on that old snake to be there when I needed him."

"I've never been compared to a snake before," Ann Jane said. The women laughed, and Maolisa felt a shift in the cloak of despair she'd been wearing.

"I'd say who was warm for me growing up was my grandmother," Isabella said. "She was a resilient woman with a faith to change a river's course. She literally kept us warm because she was the keeper of the flame. People traveling by, expanding the territory, neighbors who let their fires go out, knew that it was her fire where they could get coals to take with them. She always said that around the fire was where everything happened. Family members ate there, exchanged barbs and bribes and babies between them."

"It's where the heat is, all right," Maolisa said.

"And where the heat is, that's where our zeal is," Ann Jane added. "Careful, Da. Don't burn your cane." Her father had stood up and wobbled to add a branch to their fire. He accepted her worrying over him, saw it as the care his daughter intended. All their acts—the men leaving, the followers, those scraping bits of hide—they were all meant to tend. Maolisa thought of how often Junior's comments to her she'd taken as criticisms when he'd only meant to show his care. When she saw him again, she'd remember that.

"We'll never be the same when we're through here," Maolisa said. *We'll either be at Sutter's Fort or in heaven.* She decided not to say those words out loud. "But we'll remember how we looked after each other in a time of peril." She nodded toward Isabella and the Martins. "And have warm memories of how we sheltered ourselves, family, and friends."

"Amen to that," Mr. Martin said.

The benediction eased Maolisa's mind of intrusions and she went to sleep beside the babies, as warm as she had ever been.

At Sutter's Fort

Ellen liked to think her Novena had something to do with it. As she and James approached Peter Sherrebeck to make their case, a band of men accustomed to the mountains arrived. Clad in buckskins with fringe, carrying rifles and powder inside bison horns, they looked more animal than man. But they had clear eyes and experience, and when James Miller told them of the women's plight, they listened. James's agitation, his absolute certainty of the need, convinced Sherrebeck to provide supplies, risk Sutter's wrath. Several Indians would ride with them and remain at the various supply depots to guard provisions that would be left in trees along the trail they'd make seeking the headwaters of the Yuba. That way, the group would have food as they made their way back.

"It took me over a week. But with horses, and healthy men, we should be back there in a few days." James's eyes moved back and forth as though seeking safety from some unseen threat.

"Should you attempt to go?" Beth asked. "You don't look well."

"I'm fed. My wife and baby, they aren't. I have to go back."

"Do you think, that is, could someone continue on and look for Moses and the wagon keepers? My brother. He's so young." Beth pulled at the fringe of her shawl.

"Time will tell," James told her. "We will keep that as a side trail, if we can."

The arrangements made, the women listened to James's story of his journey. Ellen thought he needed to repeat what he'd said, justifying his having left them, his gratitude for having arrived. And then a new commotion in the courtyard, at dusk.

Allen Montgomery and Joe Foster straggled in, beards below their chins, faces chiseled out of hunger like hard stone. No braided mustache ends for Allen.

"Where's Moses?" Beth said. "John told me the three of you were left with the wagons at the lake below the summit."

Ellen moved closer to her distraught friend, put her arm around her. What must have happened?

"We were, ma'am," Allen said. "And he started out with us. But he wasn't well and he could only go a little way before he had to rest and clasp his gut."

"He insisted we go on without him." Joe Foster looked down at his feet. Snowshoes were attached to his pack, no longer needed here in this balmy place.

"And you did?" Beth said. "You just left him in the snow?"

They stood in the courtyard, the mountain men chewing tobacco, listening, gathering information about what might lie ahead. James blinked like his Ailbe often did in her nervousness.

"We had no choice. There was no game. We left him with a quarter of beef and the hope he'd be able to hunt. The snow never stopped. We . . . we got lost getting out."

"But as ill as he was, do you even know if he made it back? How far would it have been?" Beth's voice grew firmer. "How could you do that?"

Joe Foster kept his eyes down. "It wasn't an easy choice, ma'am. Moses made it for us. He feared we'd have to abandon him if he continued and that would be worse. He spent the night near the summit with us, then started back."

"He was making it. We saw him. Just going slow. It was all we could do to keep going ourselves." Allen sounded defensive and Ellen could see why he was.

"I . . . I'm appalled," Beth said. "Two grown men leaving a boy behind. You've got to send a rescue party for him." She turned to Mr. Sherrebeck. "Please."

"This party is ready to go for the Millers and Murphys."

"Did you encounter the women? Did you see them?" James wanted to know. "Were they—"

"All alive. We'd have stayed, but it would have been two more starving people."

"We'll consider what else to do about your brother," Peter Sherrebeck said, tightening a cinch on his horse. Even he couldn't look Beth in the eye. "Maybe get someone to go beyond to the lake."

Ellen didn't want to say it and she could see that none of the others did either. It was unlikely Moses still lived. Allen and Joe had been walking over terrible terrain for several weeks. That quarter beef wouldn't have lasted very long—if Moses even made it back to their cabin.

"I've got to do something." Beth caught her sob before fast-walking back to her room. Ellen followed to offer whatever comfort she could, Chica close at her heels.

"All to save his precious satins and silks, his . . . his investments." Beth threw her shawl onto the bed, sat down, stood up. "My brother gave his life for my husband's big ideas. For things. Why did they even need Wagon Guards? Who would be out there to steal velvet and books?" She looked up. "And my tacks. My brother lost for tacks." That last caused her to sob.

"We're not sure he didn't make it, Beth. You know he's a bright boy, a good thinker."

"And incredibly generous to tell those men to go on without him." She looked up, tears streaming. "He probably had appendicitis or who knows what. And they left him." When they thought John had drowned, Ellen's heart had broken in the same way. "I've failed my mother by letting her son die."

"Shh, shh. You don't know that. Remember when we thought John had drowned but he didn't. He used his head and we rescued him from the river. Moses has good common sense. He may be hanging from a willow but we'll get him down. He just needs someone to go back for him. We must pray. And then we'll get another party—even if it's us."

"Find what's left of him, you mean."

Ellen didn't try to argue. Instead she held Beth while she cried and silently spoke another of her mother's prayers.

Wintering Women

They'd spread out, not walking in a line now. The fog had lifted and they'd used the sun to tell them direction as they moved away from the river. *Good decision or bad?* Mary didn't know.

The snow wasn't as deep and the Miller children didn't need to be carried as much. Sarah was grateful. She was so tired. Her legs ached as though she'd climbed a mountain. A cramp worked its way into her thigh and she called out. She sat in the snow to stretch her muscle. The others heard her and stopped. Oh, the words she'd have with Allen when she met up with him. Fury fired her, made her stand and pick up her feet for yet another step when she didn't think she could. She was only thinking of the next step now. *I can make it to that tree. I can make it to that rock.* She marveled at Johanna Murphy, tromping a few feet beside her, carrying her nephew. Ailbe carried a child too. The three-year-old stumbled but didn't complain. Still leading them—though now they had no line, no tracks to follow—was Mary Sullivan. Every now and then she'd shout, "We're almost there!" Her voice was filled with optimism, energy, passion. Her troops would rally. They'd all take another step. *Women are resilient. Spirited. Durable as leather. Strong.* Those were more powerful words to dwell on than words that chastised her husband for his choices.

31

Now My Friends
Are Here to Help

February 1845
At Sutter's Fort

"It's Dennis Martin!" Ellen lifted the heavy iron circle knocker on Beth's door. "He's back from the war!" His arrival announced that the waiting was over. Things would return to normal—whatever that was. Chica danced around Ellen's feet, sensing the change.

Beth swung the door open, grabbing her red-fringed shawl as she did, and both women ran across the courtyard, intercepting Dennis Martin as he headed for the store.

"Is it over? Mr. Martin, are you—is everyone returning?"

"Ladies." He tipped his hat, returned it to guard against the afternoon sun. He looked tired, hadn't shaved for weeks, it appeared. He brushed at his dusty pants and handed the reins of his horse to a Mexican man who led the animal to water. "Capt convinced Sutter we weren't needed no more, so here I am. Must be the first, eh?" He seemed more confident, despite his lisp.

"The war is over." Ellen couldn't keep the joy from her voice.

"For me, at least, ma'am. Could hardly tell who the enemy was and who wasn't." The three moved to an area shaded by bougainvillea while Chica sat in the courtyard and licked her hinterlands. "We went south almost four hundred miles by my figuring," Dennis continued. "Place called Santa Barbara. A sleepy Mexican outpost, but beautiful too."

Ellen thought it was the most words she'd ever heard Dennis Martin speak. The war had given him a new voice.

"My brothers? Did you see them? My father?" Ellen turned to look at the entrance gate, willing her family to come through it.

"Dr. John?" Beth asked.

"Didn't hear of casualties. Just know soon as Capt convinced Sutter it was done that I wanted to get back here and see how others fared."

"James Miller arrived a few days ago," Beth said. "He says those he left behind are in terrible condition."

"Miller's here?" Dennis raised his dark eyebrows. "My da and sister? The children?"

"Still at the Yuba. When he left, they were all alive," Ellen said. "But desperate. After you all went off to fight, we tried to get a relief party put together. We did."

"We should have sent provisions back before we ever went to this fabricated war."

"Time awaits to debate that," Ellen said. "But that field's been plowed. It's what we plant now that matters."

"James isn't here," Beth said. "He left yesterday with a group of willing mountain men from Oregon. They're taking provisions back to the sheltered women, hoping to bring them all out."

"Thank the good Lord for that," Dennis said. But concern clouded his dark eyes.

"Moses is at that lake with the wagons," Beth said.

"Alone. Allen and Joe came without him." Ellen bent down to pet Chica, who had lifted her front paws onto Ellen's brightly colored skirt. Satisfied with the comfort, the little dog ran off to sniff near the water trough.

"They left Moses behind?" Dennis raised his voice, then shook his head. "Who am I to judge."

Or any of us. Allen and Joe hadn't felt strong enough to join the rescue party, but they'd gone off to parts unknown looking for a place to "hang their hats," they'd told Ellen and Beth when Beth had begged them to return for Moses.

"Would you rescue Moses, Dennis? Please. And if he didn't make it . . . bring his body out?" She wiped at her eyes. "Moses is like a son to me. Maybe the only one I'll ever claim. I'd be so grateful."

There was no hesitation. "Yes, ma'am, I will. Just as soon as my horse is rested and we can put provisions together. And maybe I can have a bath. Wouldn't want to scare your brother with this wild-looking man."

"When you're ready, you can take Joker, the horse Moses loaned me."

"But not Chica," Beth said. The little dog heard her name and came trotting. Beth lifted her. "She'll be here with the rest of us to celebrate when you bring Moses home."

Ellen hoped they'd have something to celebrate rather than to mourn.

Wintering Women

The black dots before Mary's eyes didn't go away, but she wasn't sure if it was her mind playing tricks on her again or if it was really horses and riders who approached out of the timber.

Mary answered her own question, waved her arms. She was the only one still strong enough to do so.

"Someone's there?" Sarah could barely speak.

They had wandered. No longer able to hear the river's gurgle, they followed the sun setting in the western horizon. It had been three days since the fog; eight days since they'd left the shelter? Mary thought that was the right number of days. She couldn't be sure.

"I see them," Ailbe said. Then, with glee in her voice, "That's James. I recognize that bright blue tuque, those slightly bent shoulders." She clapped her hands. "William, Kate, there's your da come to rescue us."

There were five riders and each led another horse behind them. There'd be enough mounts for each of them with children in front of others. They were saved. The ordeal was over. They'd have food. Sarah sat in the snow, sobbing. Mary touched her tuque, comforting.

Now my friends are here to help.

The relief Mary felt was unlike any she'd ever known. She had done what she could to save the others and herself, and now someone else would help. She collapsed, her knees bending as she sank beside Sarah. She watched as James dismounted and held his wife, his two children, gratitude wrapped around her like a sweater she never wanted to take off.

"Why didn't you wait? We were coming," James said.

"I had a premonition that you didn't make it. I . . . I couldn't wait any longer." Ailbe clung to him. "And Mary was going. Sarah too."

"But I did make it." He hugged each child, kissed their cheeks. "Where's baby Indie?"

"I . . . I left her with Maolisa. She had more milk than me and . . ." Ailbe started to cry. "I didn't know what to do."

"There, there, you did right." He patted her back. "We'll get you back, then return for the others."

"You can't continue on, now?" Mary tried to stand up. "They're desperate, Mr. Miller. Desperate. We could follow your tracks back to the fort." *Walk out or ride?* Mary was willing to let friends make up her mind.

She looked at the other rescuers, mountain men and another clean-shaven man wearing a heavy wool sweater with cables of yarn that looked like flows of rivers running from his throat to his chest. Her father had worn such a sweater back in Quebec. It might even have been Aran wool.

The younger man spoke now. "We've only so much food and horses. It'll be better if we get you all back. Then we'll provision again and bring out the rest."

"What happened to the other men?" Ailbe asked. "You made it. Did they . . . die?"

"They live," James said. "We'll talk of that later. Let's get some food into you."

The sweater man, as Mary thought of him, dismounted and broke open the bags of biscuits and cooked carrots, dried apples. He and James and the others helped serve people, their big hands dwarfing the bread and fruit each shared. Then they lifted people up onto horses. The younger stranger came to assist Mary, forming his hand into a stirrup for her foot. "And you are, sir?" Mary asked, then boldly added, "I guess I should know the name of a man who touches my feet." She thought of the stories they'd told about where feet had taken them. She had a new chapter to add.

"Peter Sherrebeck," he said. "And you are?"

"Did you meet up with two men, one tall with dark hair and the other smaller?" Sarah interrupted.

"You mean Montgomery and Foster? *Ja*, they sign notes for supplies," Peter added. "I work there, so I know this. They say they have people coming soon and must find places for them to live. They were in need of rest."

Mary hoped Sarah could rest easier knowing Allen had reached the fort.

"And you are . . . light as a snowflake." Peter nearly sent her over the horse, unprepared as he was for her near weightlessness. Mary laughed, and once she landed on her mount, Peter gave a slight bow. "You are settled then, Miss . . . ?"

"Sullivan. Mary Sullivan."

"Miss Sullivan. It is a pleasure to meet a woman who would lead others so far to safety. The women, they say it was you who made the good choices."

She wasn't interested in compliments, especially not with the others yet in jeopardy back at the cabin. But she liked the warmth in this man's eyes. They set out, ducking beneath branches, snow dropping onto their backs. Peter said there were caches of food ahead guarded by Indians. They would have more food before they slept. Hopefulness rode with her, and the peace that draped her heart was like slipping into a warm bath knowing the water would never get cold.

Wintering Women

They chewed rawhide now. That's all Isabella could give her children or herself. They scavenged every morsel, every tidbit of meat from the hides. She had scraped them of fur, given each child a strip, her fingernails so brittle they had splintered in the cutting process. They chewed, creating saliva in their mouths. They tricked their stomachs into thinking they had something in them.

She kept her children separated, in a corner, away from the others, shamed that she had not rationed the food well enough. And she could be there close when the fainting happened. Lydia had fallen twice. They all complained of dizziness. Lydia had lost a clump of hair. They were too weak now to even consider walking out. Only death or rescue remained. She wondered if perhaps her father had died on the journey. Surely, they couldn't be so far from Sutter's Fort to have taken them from mid-December to what must now be mid-February to bring them provisions. It had already been fourteen days since the Miller party had left. She kept a count of the days—assuming she could still think clearly. Why hadn't her father come to rescue them? He was old, yes, but he loved them, had always done what was right for them.

The Murphys hadn't been delivered, either, she had to remember that. That thought gave evidence for her fear that all the men had died. Some terrible disaster—an avalanche, an Indian raid—must have taken them all. Tears squeezed, burning drops from her eyes. *All gone. And we soon to join them.* Fare thee well. She had tried, she had.

Old Man Martin had shot one thin deer shortly after the women left. The animal had been stuck in the snow and starving too, so there was little meat to share. Maolisa had done a better job of rationing, so they still had bits and pieces and they boiled the bones for a watery soup they shared—but there was nothing now, just boiled hides to suck on. The Patterson clan had consumed their portion of the venison, much as she tried to get her children to eat slowly. Maybe it was a good thing they had so little deer meat to eat, as their bellies hadn't rebelled after being empty for so long. Probably because they'd made it into that watery soup. So now, here they were, without even a bone to gnaw on. Chewing hides.

But they could still chew. Isabella forced herself to be hopeful, for the children if nothing else. And hadn't our Lord gone forty days and forty nights without food? If she counted from the last thin deer, they were only twenty-one days out. They could surely go many more . . . though the weeks of starvation before that sacrificial deer might make going forty more on a tiny doe less possible.

When her children asked what dying was like, she said it was like falling asleep, but then none of the children wanted to sleep at night. Maolisa must have heard their questions—her own had asked as well—and she told them that dying must be like falling into the arms of one they loved because everyone one day did that and surely God would have provided a special cradle to rock them from this world into the next. Isabella liked that image: a cradle they would one day return to.

Isabella's children were nothing but bones with bellies wafted out like a gust of wind had taken up residence in their skirts and pants. Isaac had complained that all his teeth felt like they were going to fall out of his head. They weren't dying of thirst, another hopeful thought. They could still stand for a period of time. Would they ever recover?

She didn't know.

What kind of mother was she that she couldn't keep her children from starvation? If she lived, she'd be asking herself that question until the day she died. Which might not be too far away.

At Sutter's Fort

Capt Stephens arrived tired but hopeful. The skirmishes had left no one of his command dead. John Murphy had been kidnapped for a short time but they'd discovered where he was being held in an old barn and his brother Daniel had made a daring rescue and released him. He'd have a story to tell.

Sutter rode behind him a few miles letting neighbors know the skirmish was over. Sinclair had already returned to his property. Several others—the Murphys, Old Hitchcock, the ox drivers who had picked up a rifle and fought—were fanning the countryside now, finding places to live. Even young Sullivan said he felt like he'd made an investment in this new place. The Greenwoods had peeled off fairly early, not interested in fighting for land in Alta California. Those who did want further investment made stops in this verdant central valley as they headed back to Sutter's, hoping to collect some pay for their soldiering.

"They're looking for ideal places to put down roots," he told the women who came out to greet them. Beth asked where the others were. "Your husband will be along in a few days," Capt said.

"I wouldn't want to inconvenience him," she said. Capt raised his eyebrows. "I'm sorry," she said. "But my brother is still there at the lake."

"With the wagons and Joe and Allen. Yes. They'll come out in the spring, I expect."

"No. Mr. Foster and Mr. Montgomery saw fit to walk out now. They're here. Well, in California. They left my brother behind."

Capt leaned back on his horse. "You don't say. Joe's here?"

"I do say. And James Miller came out too. He hadn't been able to find any game. That's what Joe and Allen said too. James has taken a rescue party back for the women—if they're still alive. They ate every bovine they had and without game, they've been starving. I . . . I feel guilty having this luxury for the past two months while they—" Beth couldn't continue. Tears pooled in her eyes.

"What else could we women do?" Ellen tossed her head in defiance, the chaos of curls catching the sun.

Capt Stephens winced. His worst nightmare. The women and children of the party he'd helped lead with his name to it were likely dead. And for what? Did they need to fight this war? He'd been convinced in January. They'd have been driven out, had nothing to bring the families into. Now, very likely, there were none alive to bring.

"When did James leave?"

"More than a week ago. And Dennis Martin has just left to try to bring my brother out. I pray, alive."

Capt dismounted. "Sutter should be right behind me. I'll see what I can do." *What is there left for me to do?* He didn't know. He was a poor leader, he was certain of that. He was glad his Abeque was buried far away so she wouldn't have to hear him when he confessed his shortcomings, growing by the hour.

32

Breaking Bread

Wintering Women

"Hello, the cabin."

Maolisa Murphy thought she was dreaming when she first heard the voice.

"Hello, the cabin." *It's real.*

"Who . . . who's there?" Maolisa set little Ellen Independence down, picked up her tiny baby, and wobbled to the doorway. Her eyes hurt against the sun reflected on the snow. A brisk breeze struck her face, and instinctively, she wrapped her arms around her child, but the breeze proved warm.

"Dennis Martin. I've provisions for you all."

"That you, lad?" Mr. Martin stumbled toward the door as the others slowly rose.

"It's me, Da. It is."

Maolisa looked at the women, the children, seeing what Dennis would see: thin, faces hollowed out like rotting logs, stringy hair, skin as pale as bleached apples. Oh, how she would have loved some smoked apples right now, soft, chewy, full of the flavor of fall, of life.

Dennis put his arm under his father's elbow, steadied him; touched his sister's arm. "I've brought bread and vegetables. Ann Jane, you all right?"

"Now you're here I am."

"Carrots?" Maolisa asked. "I'll start cutting, put them in the water to boil."

"Chew the raw ones with your back teeth," Dennis said. "Make a paste before swallowing."

"Isabella, come help me," Maolisa said. She wanted the woman to join this feast. She and her family had been so cloistered these past many days, she didn't understand why and she hadn't been able to bring them together. She watched the woman attempt to rise, do so, then walk bent over like an old crone. *Do we all look like shepherd's crooks?*

She patted the woman's bony shoulder. "Thank you. Dennis needs our help."

"My children?"

"Of course. There's small amounts," Dennis said, "but if each takes a little, you can all be fed."

Isabella nodded and Maolisa thought Dennis fought back tears as he helped her sit again, looked to where the other Pattersons waited, listless as rain-drenched leaves.

"There's a party coming from behind with more provisions and horses. Can you manage this food here?"

Maolisa nodded.

"I'll be going on for Moses Schallenberger."

"You're leaving, son?"

"I'll be back, Da. Give me a few days. By then, there'll be another rescue group."

Maolisa liked his optimism, but she didn't share it. They weren't out of the woods yet.

"All you men who left in December? My father? You made it?" Isabella asked.

He nodded. "All of them. And Montgomery and Foster made it,

and James Miller too. He brought food. But I never passed him."
He looked around. "His wife, Mrs. Miller. Is she . . ."

"She and the older children and Mary Sullivan left many days
ago, with the Millers," Maolisa said. "You have word of my husband, of Junior?"

"Junior's good. Yes, he's fine. We went to war. I'll explain later.
Eat now."

Yes. Eat. That was what mattered in this moment. Maolisa
tugged the doughy bread and served it, motioning to the Patterson
children, Ann Jane, the others. "Come." She wouldn't eat until
all had had something. While the water boiled with the clumps
of carrots and onions, she broke off chunks of the loaves of bread
so everyone had something immediately, though she still waited.
Dried jerky, cheese, would come after the soup, after the bread.
How good that Dennis had brought not only ground corn and
flour that would take time to prepare but loaves of bread, ready
to consume immediately.

"My father? Capt Stephens?" Isabella asked as she nibbled
bread with her front teeth.

"He is all right." Dennis rubbed his whiskers. "The captain
too. You must wonder why we didn't come right back to get you."
Maolisa nodded. "There was a war, to defend the province. They
wanted to kick us immigrants out. Capt, your da, the rest, all
agreed that we wouldn't have had a safe place to bring you without
our fighting for it. And Sutter wouldn't allow provisions to come
here. Everything went to serve the war."

"But we were starving." Isabella whined the words.

"They didn't know," Maolisa said. She touched Isabella's cold
hand. Junior would not have left them if he hadn't been certain it
was necessary. "They thought we had enough. And in the end, we
did, with help from our friends." She smiled at Dennis Martin. She
lifted her baby to her shoulder. "We'll be at Sutter's soon, Isabella.
You will see your father then. Come help me now, feed this little
flock of enduring souls."

Her eyes scanned the cabin, took in the sustenance she saw—and the clutter. Maybe order wasn't all that important. Survival was. The assurance came to Maolisa as she unloaded the provision bags Dennis left with them before he headed to where Moses was. Each had something to eat so now she could. She blessed her morsel, thanked God for answered prayers. It was when she put the first piece of bread into her mouth that she began to cry.

Wintering Women

Sarah and the others had been given small amounts of jerky and at their first camp, James had handed them bleached apples, so soft that chewing didn't hurt Sarah's teeth. She wanted to devour everything, let the flavors soothe her, the tastes and textures make her swoon with joy. But she knew eating too quickly or too much after a long fast could be fatal. She'd heard of prisoners of wartime, abandoned by their captors with nothing to eat for weeks, when rescued might die of overconsumption. Still, her mind didn't want her to wait. It was force of will, moving the anger into strength to stay alive that permitted her to savor the smallest crumbs of broken biscuit placed on her finger while she held young Martin Miller on her lap and let him lick the biscuit piece. The act was nearly holy in her mind. The bread of life. *Communion.*

Sarah remembered that Mary Sullivan had once looked up that word for her, telling her it had a Latin beginning. "*Com* once meant 'the exchange of burdens.' And *union* means 'together.' I guess when we are joined together in a gathering, we share our troubles. Or should." The two had stood by the Sullivan wagon, their breaths like clouds of smoke in the cold air.

"Like a marriage is supposed to," Sarah said. "Be a blending of the good and bad."

"I wouldn't know about that," Mary said. The conversation had been a part of their effort to stay strong. They'd made themselves go outside trying to keep their strength up by walking a little every day, even in the cold and snow. "I know the word as *Eucharist*, from the French," Mary had told her. "It means 'thanksgiving.'"

Sarah said the word out loud and the others in their rescue camp turned to her. "We are having a small thanksgiving supper."

"'Tis so," James Miller said. He hugged his Ailbe to him.

She lifted her biscuit as a toast to him, the others. Peter Sherrebeck sat close to Mary. She didn't appear to object.

They chewed in silence.

"Maybe another party has already started out," Sarah said. "I'd like to think Allen has reprovisioned and is coming for us."

"That's very likely, Mrs. Montgomery, though I don't know what shape he was in," Peter said.

She remembered Allen had been very thin, his beard long with little hints of gray and shaggy hair pooched out beneath his knitted cap. She didn't know if she preferred to meet up with him out here in the cold while he rescued her or at Sutter's with his beard trimmed and his mustache ends braided, looking rested, while she appeared as miserable as she was, suffering from his desertion.

She stopped the thought, grateful that she could. She must let this food give her strength. She chewed the bread. She ought not serve this precious Eucharist with resentment.

Wagon Guard

Moses's legs ached. He'd had to walk farther from the cabin to set his traps each day. He'd approach, wondering if the meal he'd eaten yesterday had been his last. But once again the good Lord had provided. He carried the fox, the breeze flitting through the dark, almost black fur. He ducked beneath branches and wondered if he couldn't girdle a tree and eat the sap or the soft cambium. Hadn't he read that somewhere in one of Dr. John's books, about eating trees—the needles and that soft growth beneath the bark? That's what he'd do if tomorrow the traps were empty.

As he approached the cabin still covered with a mountain of snow, he thought he saw something. The sky was overcast, so it couldn't be a shadow. Were his eyes playing tricks on him? He'd had a little light-headedness when he stood too quickly. And his hands shook when he used scissors to cut his beard and trim the mustache that hung too far over his upper lip. It took up too much fox food, leaving grease above his lip instead of on it. But now he squinted, and before long the black stick coming down from the pass came closer. It was on snowshoes and moving at a good clip. He wished he could walk on snowshoes with that kind of vigor. *Could it be an Indian?* He dropped his fox and lifted the rifle. He should load it, quickly. But he didn't do anything quickly, and before he knew it the shadow was close enough to shout.

"Hello, the cabin."

English!

Moses didn't recognize the man.

"Dennis Martin, come to visit," he said. Then as he walked closer, Moses could see the wide grin through the brush of beard belonging to one of the Martin boys. "If you're Moses Schallenberger." He laughed then, a big hearty laugh. "And am I glad to see you standing. Your sister will know her prayers were answered, every single one."

"My sister made it then? And Allen and Joe?"

"She did. They did. So far, we think everyone has survived, though the Miller party is not counted for yet. And Mrs. Montgomery and Miss Sullivan who are traveling with them." By then he was beside Moses and he reached his arms around him and held him in a bear hug, lifting him off the ground. Moses began to cry.

"I'm . . . sorry. Golly, I didn't mean to go all weepy like a girl. I—"

"Men cry in gratitude, so don't you be apologizing. I'm teary myself. You've kept yourself alive. Alone. And you're making sense, so you didn't lose your thinking. Oh, the story you'll have to tell."

Dennis looked around then and saw the dozens of bones piled outside the snow-covered cabin.

"Foxes," Moses said. "A boy's best friends."

"A man's, I'd say. How'd you get 'em?"

"I found Capt Stephens's traps. Without them, I'd have only lasted a week. I'd have eaten the pages from Dr. John's books or tried the trees, but I didn't need to. Traps and foxes, one coyote—tasted terrible—and one wayward crow. Don't recommend it."

Dennis ducked inside the open doorway, following Moses, and bent to remove his snowshoes. "We'll hike out tomorrow if you're able. I've brought bread, a few vegetables for our soup."

"They'll be good added to my latest fox meat. But I don't know about snowshoeing out. I . . . couldn't go far on them. I still get so tired." Moses bent to remove them.

"You've got a tie around the ankle. That makes it too hard to walk."

"We all thought that was needed or they'd come off." Moses stepped back. *Doing it wrong this entire time?*

"We Canadians just use toe ties our whole lives. We'll get those adjusted and get out of here. A few days away is the cabin where there's women and kids and my da waiting on further rescue with horses, we hope."

Moses frowned. "Women and children alone?"

"After we summitted that day when you all returned here, a few days later on the Yuba River, we got snowed in. We built a rough cabin, left most of the cows and oxen, and we men headed out, but for my da and James Miller."

"Why, they were just over the ridge from me?"

"Several miles, but yes, over the summit."

"We were worrying about food together—but apart," Moses said. He took the carrots and onions Dennis handed him and put them in the Dutch oven with the fox meat he'd already cut up. He'd been delaying eating. He had taken his time preparing, waiting, saying a prayer over it, then eating slowly so he felt filled up. Now, he had carrots and onions to add.

The aromas filled the little cabin, and when the two men squatted to eat the meal, it was more satisfying because he shared it with someone else. Moses dipped the biscuit Dennis had brought him into the meaty soup. He sucked on it. Moses said, "Food to feed the heart for any fate."

Dennis looked at him with a question in his eyes.

"Lord Byron's poem," Moses said. "Written to someone named Tom Moore. But I like the sound of it. 'A heart for any fate.'"

"Yours is a big heart, Moses," Dennis said.

"Thanks for using yours to rescue me." Moses felt his voice break like he was a kid.

"I'd do it for any good man."

Moses wondered if he'd ever again eat such a glorious meal. And tomorrow he would head out and he would make it this time. He could hardly wait to greet his sister.

33

Food, Clothing,
Shelter, and Love

March 1845
At Sutter's Fort

They rode into Sutter's on the relief horses the mountain men and James had brought with them for their rescue. Sarah began to worry about how she looked, which she knew to be silly, but once basic needs of food, clothing, and shelter were met, one could think about frivolous things. Like how bedraggled they must appear. *Bedraggled. Messy. Unkempt.* Her eyes scanned the gathering crowd for Allen. *Where is he? Is he all right?*

"Oh, oh, oh, they're back!" Ellen Murphy lifted her skirts to run to them when they came through the gateway into the bustling fort. "Beth! They're here!" Chica danced her happy dance around the women's feet.

Beth Townsend flew through a doorway. "Moses?"

"No, ma'am," James Miller said. "We met these wanderers and brought them back. We'll go for the other Murphy women and children and your brother next."

"Yes, no, the Murphy men have left already. I'm surprised you didn't meet up with them. Dennis Martin went ahead too. And Mr. Neil."

Sarah wondered if Allen had joined that relief party. *Why didn't he come back with James? And who is Mr. Neil? It doesn't matter. Arriving is enough.*

"But it is grand news that you are all here, survived. Maybe Moses has too." Beth clapped her hands to her face, and Sarah saw she fought back tears of both relief and disappointment. Sarah knew just how she felt. "Come, girls," Ellen said. "We'll get you baths."

Ellen asked the Indian women in a language Sarah didn't recognize to take up buckets of water for *un baño*. Spanish? This was another country. The women smiled and nodded, dipping buckets into the large cauldrons where water heated over flames all day long in the courtyard. "This way," she told Sarah and Mary. "Bring the little ones." Kate whined as Ellen lifted her from the horse. "Are you hurt?"

"Just hungry," Johanna said. She licked her chapped lips.

"I bet you are. I have some lovely tortillas we will fill with warm beans for you. You can chew while we strip these clothes and sink you into a nice tub of water. Won't that feel good?"

"Yes, Miss Ellen," the three-year-old answered.

"Oh, you remember me, do you? That's good." Ellen looked up then and frowned. "Where's your little sister?"

"The youngest babes were left with Maolisa," Mary said.

"We all thought it best." Sarah took a deep breath. "The Murphys will surely get there before they—"

Sarah's throat caught and she couldn't finish her words, overwhelmed with gratitude for her survival and dread at what they'd left behind. Why was it that the food of goodness was often seasoned with guilt?

"Come along," Beth said. Her words were gentle as snowflakes. "Miss Sullivan and Mrs. Miller, you come now. To our rooms."

"Is . . . Allen here?" Sarah asked.

"Not at the moment," Ellen said. "But he'll be back soon, I'm sure."

"Where . . . where has he gone?"

"He said he was looking for a place for you and him to settle down."

"How long ago?"

"But a few days. Come now, let's get you pampered for that wonderful reunion you'll be having."

"So he didn't go with the Murphy relief party?" Sarah reached for Ellen's arm, needing support to hear the disheartening news.

Ellen patted Sarah's hand. "It'll be all right. He was pretty weak. Both he and Joe were, but they were fine when they left."

Able to go riding off looking for a place to start over. Sarah guessed she should be hopeful. She had food, clothing, and shelter. The necessities for survival. But wasn't love and caring a necessity as well? Wasn't that a requirement for enduring?

"I want to hear everything," Ellen said. Beth had taken Mrs. Miller and Mary Sullivan into her rooms that accommodated two large tubs.

"Wash up the children first," Sarah said. "I've waited this long for a bath, I can wait awhile longer."

"I'll have them bring the wee tubs in," Ellen said. "Wait here." She left to tend to the two little Miller girls. Sarah gazed around the room. A cross hung on one adobe wall, and she saw what looked like an altar with candles and a little book. Ellen really had been praying for them.

"I'm back. Here." She directed the Indian women to fill the tin tub, then helped Sarah strip off the dress that nearly fell apart as they pulled it from her skin.

"I don't think it's worth saving," Sarah said as Ellen handed it to one of the women.

"I agree. It's seen its last scrub." Ellen's voice held lightness. "You'll have to shop at my wardrobe. I have frocks for you to choose from. And underdrawers. Sewing—and helping at Sutter's store now and then—has kept me sane waiting for everyone to arrive."

"Teaching Mary to knit kept me from too many frayed loose ends."

"What matters is you'll survive a washing."

Sarah laughed. "I hope so. You may have to help me get in and out."

"That I'll do." She took Sarah's elbow, assisted as she stepped up and over and slipped into the tub. "Let's get that hair washed too."

"What's left of it. It started coming out in clumps."

"They have the loveliest hats here, big wide brims to thwart the sun. You'll look grand in them. They'll give you time to grow back your hair."

Ellen had an answer for everything and Sarah was grateful. She had survived being abandoned twice. With the help of her friends she could survive anything after this, even Allen's never returning for her. Yes, she would make it on her own if she needed to. Alone—but with the help of her friends.

Wintering Women

It was BD who'd been the crier. "Mama! Mama! Da's here. He brought friends." Maolisa had roused herself, hoping the child hadn't begun to hallucinate, took baby Yuba from her breast. Then she spied him too and the horses and other men. None mattered except Junior. She'd made the sign of the cross, whispered prayers of the rosary, and moved toward him as if in a dream while he dismounted, ran toward her.

Junior lifted Maolisa from her feet and kissed her soundly, right there in front of all those men and the children with eyes big as biscuits. "Ah, I've missed you, Maolisa, me love."

"And I you, Junior Murphy." All the days and weeks of waiting, the moments of chastising him for having left them, the hours of prayers that he lived, all washed away like crumbs left on the table's cloth.

"Oh, careful. We've little Yuba here." The baby's face was scrunched up, ready for a wail, held in the cradle of Maolisa's arm. She wondered how long the infant's hunger would touch her life as she grew older. Would starvation always be a wispy ghost haunting her home, discomfiting their lives?

Junior touched the nose of his newest child, let the baby suck on his finger then, "Where's me wee ones?" He shouted and the children ambled to him, too weak to run. BD grabbed him first and Junior lifted the boy and patted his back as the child hugged him as though to never let him go.

"We ate pine soup, Da. Like eating skunk."

"Did you now. I didn't know pine needles could be eaten or that you've tasted skunk."

"Mama made us go to school. I'm too young for school," BD said.

"Your mother's a good schoolmarm." He winked at Maolisa. "I bet she fixed the lessons just right."

BD let himself be put down but clung to his father's leg while he lifted the other children.

"You brought rations? Let's get them out." This from Mr. Martin.

Patrick Martin moved to assist, handed his father dried beef. "We'll distribute the food. No need for you to worry, Da." He patted his father's shoulder as the man sat slumped.

Mr. Neil, one of the rescuers with a black beard covering his face, tipped his hat at Maolisa, then began opening packs pulled from the horses.

She let the men take control. So tired of making decisions, she listened as they reported news of the Wagon Guards, of the arrival of James and his return for Mary, Sarah, and the others with them. All had survived. *Praise God.*

Junior helped her to a corner, the children following. She sat, nursed Yuba with what little she had to give. Junior gave the other children portions of dried beef. "Eat slowly." To BD he gave sliced apples. He lifted Mimi and James, one in each arm, while Maolisa gripped a piece of jerky in her back teeth. She winced in pain.

"Best you take a mite of bread first, Pet," Junior said.

"Suppose you're right, Husband. But Dennis brought us vegetables and loaves. I need the meat."

"Aye. That you do." He set his children down, shook the hands of his two oldest boys, neither yet reached the age of eight. But they would now. "I'll soak the jerky for you, Pet. Soften it so you can eat it." He set about doing that, then returned.

"Dennis Martin told us you went off to war." Maolisa's strident voice surprised even her. "We ate the insides of trees before he arrived. The Pattersons, bless them all, have lived on chewing rawhide these past two weeks."

"I'm as sorry as I can be, Pet." Junior took her hands that shook after she'd eaten. "We thought it best to defend our new homeland and we thought you had plenty here, that hunting would merely supplement. We didn't know. I'm so, so saddened by your state."

Children giggled. Hard-boiled eggs were peeled and lent their scent. Mr. Neil began a stew. Maolisa felt the pressure of her husband's arm around her shoulder. Time stood still and would not start again until she set aside her disappointment, her hunger, her fears of death. *Intrusive thoughts.* Hadn't they all done what they thought best?

They were safe. Only one more hurdle for this party remained, and that was getting them to Sutter's. Shelter of another kind couldn't be far away.

***

At Sutter's Fort

"Your sweater, Mr. Sherrebeck. Is it of Aran wool?" Mary had come into the store on the pretext of picking up needles, putting the cost on the account her brother John had started for them. She'd noticed Peter, wanted his attention but feared it too.

"*Ja*. Irish wool, the best kind. You wore such a one, *ja*, when you left the Yuba."

She nodded. "My mother made that sweater for me."

"It was very beautiful." He lifted eyebrows the color of the sun. "As is the woman who wore it."

His flattery caused a tightening in her stomach. Was he sincere? How did a woman know for certain? "I unraveled the yarn of one of the sweaters my mother made while in the cabin, and then Mrs. Montgomery taught me how to knit it again. I'm a novice, so it lacks the brilliance of her work. I probably ought to have kept it by her hands."

"This way you wear two generations," he said.

"I hadn't thought of it that way." She touched the round braids at her ears, had made sure the center part of her hair was perfectly straight beneath her hat. His stare caused her to look at the shelves lined with pickle jars and spice tins. She filled the silence. "And how did you come by your fine Aran sweater?"

His cheeks turned pink. "I make it myself."

"You knit?"

"It is a fine way to settle the nerves," he said. "And I like the click and clack of the needles. My mother, she insists I learn and I find I like it."

"That's . . . delightful," Mary said. "You stepped outside the ordinary expectation of what a man's about. Oh," she put her fingers to her mouth. "That was a very bold thing for me to say to a stranger."

"You're no stranger, Mary Sullivan. I know you now ten days." Mary blinked. "*Ja*. I count them." His grin was merry and she liked that no beard hid his shaved-smooth face.

A customer called to Peter. He nodded and left her. She waited, wandered through the store, picked up items, read the labels, put them back precisely. He approached her between the cabinets housing lanterns and ledgers, offered her a string of licorice. His fingers touched hers and she startled at the pleasure.

"I hope you like men who step outside the 'ordinary expectation,' as you say it. I like such in women too."

Can this goodness be happening?

"I need a needle," she said, all business, then. "Mrs. Montgomery is teaching me how to quilt now. I'm working on a nine patch." She cleared her throat. "Do you quilt too, Mr. Sherrebeck?"

"Yust the knitting. Maybe you teach me, *ja?* I'm a good student."

"I'm a better farmer than stitcher."

"Then we make a good pair, though I like my horses. And sheep. The yarn you see, *ja.*" He stood closer to her. The aisles were narrow and her heart beat at her ears. "Would you care to ride out with me, Miss Sullivan? I share what I love of California and you tell me of what pleases you of being here."

"I . . . I would like that very much." Her face felt warm, her hands were wet. She waved her fingers before her face like a fan. "It's warm in here."

"*Ja.* Aran sweaters are best in the mountains."

"Or when you want to please a woman with a story." She didn't know whether to smile or not. This flirting wasn't something she knew about. She'd have to speak with Ellen.

He stepped back. "No story, no. A cool night near the river, is *Sehr Gut* then too. Or when you want to find a way to talk to someone who otherwise makes your tongue tie in a knot."

Her face felt as hot as a hearth fire and she suspected just as red. He lifted her hand in his, and when he did, the sparks from those embers burned bright inside her heart. Another courageous adventure had begun.

Wagon Guard

It started to rain. The snows would melt, the rivers would rise. Moses thought if they were going to leave, they should go soon.

The two checked the traps the following morning and brought back two fat foxes. They dried the meat of one, ate the other.

"I see you have tacks holding up Dr. Townsend's fabrics." Dennis nodded toward the cloth wall linings Moses had improvised.

"They kept a mite of cold out," Moses said. "I should take them down and repack them. He'll want them come spring." He folded the satin with its lavender flowers and the silk hand-painted poppies from the Orient. He put the tacks in their little box. *Should I take them with me?* Dr. John must have thought them precious. Why not. They weighed nothing.

The next morning, they headed out. Moses wore his snowshoes without the heel attached and it amazed him how much easier it was to trek through the terrain.

"Why didn't I think of that?" Moses felt stupid.

"Logic told you the more secure the better. But experience in Quebec told the rest of us how to put them together. How's your stomach?" It sounded like *thomach*.

"Good. It's good. If we go slowly."

"That we can do." They talked little, saving energy for the uphill climb. At the summit, they built a fire and warmed themselves, ate a little, heated water and made coffee. Dennis had brought coffee. Oh, the luxury of it: food, coffee, and a friend. His hopefulness knew no bounds. He was going to see his sister again. He would have a life, maybe one day write a letter to his son the way Lord Chesterfield did to his. He let himself imagine more than food.

Wintering Women

"Why are you looking so glum, Daughter? We're here. We'll get you back." Isabella sat looking up at her father. His stamina belied his years. "You did a wonder here caring for my grandchildren."

"They went without for so long, Daddy. I didn't think of the pine needles until a few days ago, and then, they were so bitter we could hardly consume them."

"Those big pines, Ponderosas, have needles not recommended for consumption, but you did right to try."

"It was chewing the hides. That's when I was the lowest." The texture of the hide—chewy, soft after hours but otherwise stiff—would haunt her forever. "My children . . ." She began to cry. "I shouldn't have brought them here. We should have stayed in Tennessee."

Her father took her hands and pulled her up, looked into her eyes. "Isabella Hitchcock Patterson, no shoulds. I *should* have come back for you. I *should* have known. No. You did what you could. You know that. And we did too."

She became aware of the activity around her—Lydia, listless just moments before, laughed with the bleached apple pieces. She compared the texture to the rawhide—and her brothers laughed! It had taken daring to keep going each day, to invent hope. Mary Sullivan had given them routines, making them go outside to walk for a few minutes in the deep snow—to keep the muscles strong—she'd said. Ann Jane looked after her father with good humor despite his orneriness. And her own daughter had taught the children games to play—Hot Potato, Cock-a-Roosty. Before Mary Sullivan, Ailbe, and Sarah left, there'd been the hours of sharing stories that had passed the time while Mary learned to knit and Sarah studied her letters. *Little acts of hope done because we believed we would survive even while we prepared for dying.*

Could she claim bravery by simply surviving, keeping her children alive? Could any of them? Yes, she decided, she could. Courage was trying again tomorrow.

34

One More River to Cross

Wagon Guard
At Wintering Women's Cabin

"Where is everybody?" Moses had so looked forward to seeing little BD, the Murphys and the Pattersons, Dennis's father. But the cabin door stood open like an empty mouth.

"They must have worried about the snowmelt," Dennis said. He nodded toward the Yuba river rushing, flirting with stepping outside its banks.

"That rain we had didn't help either," Moses said.

They entered the abandoned cabin. "My guess is they've gone overland. I'll look for tracks. You see if they've left any food for us."

Moses laughed. "Would you?"

Moses wished he'd brought a trap with him, as a remembrance, if nothing else. Or had learned how to fling a sling-bullet like John Murphy could, as there were geese in the air.

Moses sat in his sister's rocking chair, listened to the sounds of the ice breaking on the river's edge, a crack like a gunshot repeated. He saw the remains of endurance—children's drawings, candle stubs, a Dutch Oven.

Dennis scouted and returned. "I've got their tracks. Are you rested enough to go? The river's coming up fast."

"You bet. Be pitiful if those foxes gave their lives for me only to have me rushed away by the Yuba." *Should I take the rocking chair? No.* "Let's hang this chair in the tree. If it makes it, it'll be a fine remembrance for my sister when we come back for the wagons this summer." He noticed Webster dictionaries stacked on a butter churn and grabbed them. Stories had helped him brave his solitary time. He suspected these fat tomes had encouraged someone.

At Sutter's Fort

"You've got your alphabet down just fine," Mary told Sarah, who hoped when everyone was safely at Sutter's that Mary could still continue her lessons. Sarah knew she must better herself. Reading would do that. *What if Allen doesn't come back?* Her children would benefit one day if she could read. *Was I foolish for falling in love?* She would learn to read so she could know what was happening. *Other women survived the loss of their husbands. Ellen has. Isabella has. I can too.* She turned her mind to her letters. One day, she would read a newspaper. Weeklies now and then arrived by ship from back east, she was told. It was old news but useful for keeping tabs on what Congress was doing, what wars raged across the sea. Even Yerba Buena didn't have a newspaper and it was the largest city in this part of California. She needed to read so she could make her own judgments about rumors and stated facts. *And reading and writing will help me get a job if I have to, maybe working for a newspaper.* She thought of the irony if she were to be involved in printing letters for a living. Not likely. Quilting and knitting, needles and thread, those were her skills.

"I imagine there is more to reading than simply knowing my letters," Sarah said.

"I bet you can spell out with sounds some of the labels on the tins."

"You mean like milk spelled m-i-l-k?"

"You see?"

"There's a picture of a cow on the can. It's a good guess."

Mary smiled. She was a different person since the journey out. Or maybe it was the time she spent with Peter Sherrebeck that accounted for the change.

"It's also a good start," Mary said. "Let's work a little longer."

Ellen skipped over to where the two women sat beneath an olive tree.

"Let's take a ride, you two." Ellen took the slate from Sarah's hands. "I'm not needed at Sutter's now, since he's returned from the war."

"Is it safe?" Both women spoke in unison. "For us I mean," Sarah said. "As immigrants."

"I suppose there will still be tensions over Americans being here. But 'tis a country more beautiful than wedding flowers and much longer lastin'. When people see we mean no harm, maybe they'll accept us. But 'tis not dangerous. Mr. Weber will act as chaperone. He knows the area."

"Maybe your Mr. Weber knows who might have sheep. For wool, that I can spin and knit sweaters, though with this climate they'll only be worn on the coldest of days."

"Socks are always welcome."

"You're right." Sarah should take apart her own sweater and make man socks. "I'll put a poster up on Sutter's wall or maybe sell direct to him." It was a much more realistic venture than working for a nonexistent newspaper one day. *Venture. Risk.* Soon she'd be able to look up words herself in those pages she'd ripped from the dictionary. Words would comfort her, they always had even before she married Allen. She'd keep learning. She could make her own life—if she had to. And when Allen went back for the wagon, they'd see if the dictionaries had survived. She hoped so.

Wagon Guard

Rain descended, not cold but steady, as they plodded through now-melting snow, rivulets cutting paths through mud following the tracks of horses. "There they are." Ahead Moses saw people he hadn't seen for three months. Some were on horseback, two led pack animals, others rode bareback. They looked like they had stopped to make camp beside a raging stream. "My friends," Moses said. He flung his arms out as though to hug them all. "They're all here."

"They should have horses for us. Your sister was working on Mr. Neil to bring relief—and to find you." Dennis urged him forward.

"I think that's Joker. She sent him along too? God bless her," Moses said. He'd never meant it more.

Little BD saw them first and ran forward. "Mr. Moses! Mr. Moses!" Moses lifted the boy and squeezed him. Ah, the child's arms felt good around his neck. The adults greeted him with much back clapping and surprise, praise and gratitude. John and Daniel Murphy, who had taken the route with his sister, were there. "You're all alive. You're all alive." Moses repeated himself, set the boy down, then rubbed the neck of his pal, Joker, who tugged at Moses's cap. He let the animal take it. "Guess I don't need a wool cap in this weather." But Moses took it back and plopped it between Joker's ears. "It don't look good on you either. Doesn't look good." He corrected himself. "Is Chica all right?"

"Aye," John Murphy said. "She was entertaining as a piglet squeezing in beside his brothers. Chica brought Joker back after he was startled away in the deep snows. Our Ellen fell in a tree well." Moses frowned. "We'll exchange tales once we get your skinny body back to Sutter's."

Moses recognized François and Oliver and Mr. Hitchcock. Where were Capt and Dr. John? He turned back to those crowding around him.

The greeting commotion continued. Moses tickled the chin of

Ellen Independence and cooed at the new baby Mrs. Murphy held. The infant squealed and kept Moses from hearing the shouts.

Several men sprinted back. Daniel Murphy carried the news, breathless. "It's Neil. He got separated and he's on an island but he can't swim."

John Murphy clasped Moses's arm. "If you're able, get Joker. I'll get a mount too and we'll grab a third."

Moses wasn't sure he was strong enough, but if he had a chance to rescue the man his sister had sent along to supply them, then he had to give it a try.

Mr. Neil had taken his six-foot-four-inch frame and climbed a tree on the island that was slowly disappearing in the river. Moses wondered how many times a man could cheat death on one journey. Trying to snowshoe out and turning back. Every day in the cabin. Yet here he was, alive, still meant for something. Even if he gave his life for this man, he would have lived well; his sister could be proud. His heart raced. He leaned forward over Joker's neck. Neither John nor Moses said a word, but they exchanged a look that told them they were plunging into the torrent. At least one of them would make it to Neil and hopefully bring him back. It's what a man did, lay down his life for a friend—even one he had never met.

At Sutter's Fort

"You ought to follow them, Dr. John. Provide medical care." Ellen said. They stood in Sutter's courtyard.

"I . . . could have gone, of course. But food is the primary concern and they took that plus horses," Dr. John said. "Especially if they're in as bad a shape as Allen and Foster suggest—which they may not be. Allen likely exaggerated as an excuse for his not bringing his wife out with him, that she was too emaciated to make the trek."

"He made no effort to go back and get her," Ellen said. "I used to think him quite a fine husband, but now . . ."

"Never judge another's marriage." Dr. John wagged his finger at her.

"'Tis so. But one takes lessons from watching at a distance."

"Still, what a joy it would mean to Moses to know a relative had come to help rescue him," Beth said. "Your patients can spare a few days."

"Now, my dear, men don't think about such things as you women do. He'll know we'll clap him on the back and say, 'Good work, boy.' That's all he'll need from his family."

"Sometimes—*gasp*—your views of what anyone needs are quite—*gasp*—disconcerting, dear husband. If not wrong."

Is her breathing problem returning? Only when Dr. John's around.

Dr. John rambled on. "I am needed here, Beth. How do you suppose we are to survive without means if I don't work for Sutter? Why even Captain Stephens is confident everyone is good and well. He's off marking out the land he bought from Sutter, at a fine price, I might add, since we went to war for him. We have land as well, and when spring arrives, I'll go back for our goods and then we can settle into this fine country."

"I had a way for us to survive, but you left the wagons behind," Beth said. She pooched her lower lip out in a pout.

Ellen wondered if she should walk away from this marital discussion, but she stayed, more curious than ever over what Beth said.

"Yes, we were to operate a store, which we will, come spring."

"Well . . . oh never mind. I'll find out when Moses is rescued, which he'd better be."

And with that, Beth swirled her skirts and left her husband's side. "Join me," she said to Ellen. "I shall take solace in the company of friends and horses."

Advice for me as well.

Wagon Guard

Moses and John had saved Mr. Neil and now all were camped beside the flooding Bear River. Moses found himself a reluctant hero. He'd helped with a rescue after being rescued himself and people marveled that he was in better shape than most of the others.

"We must hear how you did it all alone those months," Ann Jane said.

"You women survived too. There's the real story." Moses pointed with his chin toward BD and other Murphy children. "Had a lot more to feed than I did. And I had books."

"Did you eat 'em?" BD asked. The child sat on a saddle Moses had resting on its pommel, the sheepskin pointing outward to the breeze to dry the sweat. The rain had stopped, the weather balmy as summer in Missouri.

"Thought about it," Moses told him. "But no, I read. A lot. Sure glad my sister taught me how to read. You Murphy kids know your letters, don't you? Pattersons too?" Lots of heads nodded. They were stalled at this river and food was still scarce, so distracting talk was good. Again, Moses wished that he had brought out a trap. He hoped John could bring down a goose.

"I never liked school," one of the Pattersons said. "Mrs. Murphy taught us all kinds of things in fun ways. When we was not so hungry and able to think."

"Weren't so hungry," his mother corrected. Moses thought Mrs. Patterson looked the most changed of all, with her clothes hanging from her shoulders like a coat tree and her eyes so hollowed out.

That evening they gave out rations. The men talked about options—going back and following the Yuba, or going upriver looking for a better place to cross or just waiting. He noticed they talked loud enough that the women could hear and they even listened to suggestions the women made. He'd remember that. He wondered if Dr. John would listen more to his sister after she had survived just fine, or so he'd been told. *Where is Dr. John?* He would have thought he'd have come along to see to the health of these Murphys and Pattersons and him, for that matter. Dr. John was probably busy jawing. *"Talk often but never long."* He'd read that in Lord Chesterfield's letters about conduct. *"Tell stories very seldom . . . and beware of digressions. To have frequent recourse to narrative betrays great want of imagination."* Moses wasn't so sure about that last. Every single person on this westward trip had a narrative to tell and it had nothing to do with a failure of the imagination.

"We stay here. Wait." Martin Murphy Sr. spoke the final decision.

The river kept rising and they moved their camp back. They could barely see the other bank now, the water flattening the landscape to a lake of brown. Mr. Hitchcock concurred, along with Mr. Martin and the younger men. The women seemed mollified. Perhaps they'd become accustomed to hunger while waiting for nature to cease its demands. Once these people had all run together in Moses's head, but now he saw them distinctively: Junior—the father and husband he hoped one day he could be. Mr. Hitchcock, the explorer and survivor and grandfather he could aspire to. Even Mr. Martin, who was kind of a curmudgeon. (There was a word his sister would be proud he knew.) But Mr. Martin played the bodhran and music fed the spirit too.

"You know it's March 1," Mr. Martin said. "A year since we started out from Missouri. And we ain't made it yet."

"We're in California, Da," Dennis said.

"Don't have much to speak for itself, does it?" his father said.

"You'll be happy when we reach Sutter's. It's summer there. You'll love it. No more achy bones from the cold. Bridges or ferries to get us across."

"The cold I can handle, it's this empty stomach that I've wearied over."

"That'll change too." Dennis patted his shoulder.

"You'll all be shedding sweaters soon and wearing sombreros like the Mexicans," Junior told the children. He pantomimed the wide brim. They giggled.

"Can I borrow your knife, Mr. Moses?" BD tugged on Moses's sleeve.

"Sure, but what will you do with it?"

"Make a toothpick," the little boy said.

"Well, aren't you the optimist." Hungry as the boy must be, he still had room to imagine a time when he would need a toothpick. Moses would remember that. It was all right to think about the future if it was a happy call. Maybe that was what having faith was all about.

Wintering Women

They waited. Maolisa scraped her baby's napkin, rinsed it at the water's edge, and spread it on brushes back away from the flooding water. She drew on every strength of faith and fortitude she had to keep their spirits up as they waited for the river to recede. They were so close now, and it was almost worse having had a taste of sustenance only to live again with none.

Two deer had been shot, a couple of grouse taken; but with so many people—fourteen children, plus their parents and rescuers—the rationed morsels hardly whet their appetites. Sutter's horses roamed the area, no cattle, though they'd seen a bloated one, legs up, float by on the flooding river the men called Bear. Men with guns planned to head out this third day to search for game.

"If we can't find any, we'll have to shoot a horse, love," Junior told his wife as he saddled his mount, tightened the cinch.

"Your father won't eat it," Maolisa told him. "You know how he feels."

"He won't know, Pet. I'll make sure he hunts far from me."

"You'd deceive him?"

"It's been three days of waiting without food. And you women are already thin as reeds." He kissed her nose and mounted up. "We'll do what we must."

Maolisa guessed he was right. A little lie might have to be told to serve the greater good. And keeping them all alive was the greater good.

The Bear River still swirled its muddy waters as they made their way downstream and approached the confluence of another river, also in flood stage. Mr. Neil called it the Feather, and Maolisa set about organizing, getting the children to look for things to burn, while Isabella Patterson fetched water they boiled to drink and Ann Jane convinced her father to play a bit on the bodhran as her brother Dennis took out his whistle. A little Irish jig. Just what this party needed, Maolisa thought. She couldn't see a way to make a table, so her cloth stayed rolled up in her bedroll.

A cheer went up when Moses Schallenberger and Patrick brought in game. It was one of Sutter's wild horses Moses had shot. They were already roasting it when Mr. Murphy rode in dejected, without having hunting success himself.

"Well done, boy. Good for you," Mr. Murphy said as he saw the roasting meat. "Looks like a good-sized heifer. I'm sure Sutter won't begrudge us." He rubbed his hands together in anticipation of food.

"Hope not, sir," Moses said. They all passed glances of loyalty to the conspiracy of never letting Mr. Murphy know that he was about to eat a horse. Especially after he ate the roasted meat and claimed it mighty tasty.

Then James Miller spilled the secret—and Mr. Murphy spilled his vittles.

Maolisa didn't know how much nutrition her father-in-law maintained. She felt bad for him, yet grateful that he didn't have to try roasted pine needles or boiled hides as the women had. The taste had not been to her liking, but she had discovered this winter that by faith, one can take steps never before imagined. After all, they'd crossed a continent. She'd delivered a baby into a winter storm, sent her husband off not knowing if he'd return. Her child lived, her husband returned, and because of it, she could dream of something more.

The rivers roiled on out of their banks, but it was part of a river's nature. She had a feeling—she thought of Ailbe and her forebodings—but Maolisa's sense was that God was with them despite the turmoil and trial. They had gotten on a craft called faith and pushed out onto a river. Sometimes the stream flowed calm and restful and sometimes it meandered and swirled the craft about. But it always took them to where they needed to go. Sometimes they'd end up at a ferry landing they hadn't known they were meant to reach. She couldn't organize everything. The future held surprises. She was almost excited about what was next in store.

35

Homecoming

At Sutter's Fort

Sarah had dressed and walked across the courtyard as the sun rose over the flagpole. She loved the early morning in this country with the gentle breeze, bees humming at their blooms and birds chirping as they flitted from California lilac to a manzanita bush. She wore a new wheat-colored muslin dress with a scooped neck and a bright red sash around her waist. California was all about color—in people's skin, in the greenery of growth, in the flourish of fabrics that Sutter sold and kindly gave to these new American women so destitute upon arrival. Sarah had been sewing muslin and calico dresses, embroidering flowers and birds at the hems, on the bodices. It had kept her busy and she delighted in hearing the oohs and aahs from both native women and Americans arriving by ship or south from Oregon Territory.

"*Buenos días,*" she said to one of the native women waiting at the well as Sarah now did. Mary still taught her how to read, and she, Ailbe, Beth, and Ellen and Mary, too, were all learning how to speak the new language, though she couldn't say much more than "good morning" in Spanish. While she waited for her turn to pull up the bucket, she went through the alphabet in her mind, remembering the sounds Mary Sullivan had taught her.

"*A* is for apple," Mary had told her.

"*A* is for animal," Sarah said.

"That's right. *A* is for animal and apricot, though that's a tricky one because some people say ay-pricot and others say ah-pricot—" and they'd be off writing words that Sarah would try to remember that began with that first letter, *a. Anxiety. Aggravated. Abandoned.* But such words were harder to learn to print out because there was no object she could look at to remind her—only an emotion.

The line of women seeking buckets of water moved closer to the well, and Sarah had been about to move on to *b* when she saw riders come through the gate. One sat tall. He had a full beard and short mustache without braids. She'd know him anywhere. "*A* is for Allen," she whispered.

The men dismounted and went in to Sutter's offices. Sarah slipped toward the door, listened, her heart pounding.

"We've seen a large party with horses and children . . . a dozen or more babes. It has to be the rescuers of the Murphy party." Sarah recognized his voice, the deepness of it, the warmth. *What will I say to him?*

"*Gut,* ja. Food is plenty at the Hock Farm. I will send ferry to help them cross. You, take word back to do everything for them. Supplies from here—dried food, blankets, sweets for the children. Food from the farm. Go, go now."

"And dresses for the women," Sarah said as she stepped inside.

"Ja, ja, that's gut."

"Sarah, I—" Allen hesitated, and then he lifted her up and kissed her. "I've missed you." He set her down, hands still on her shoulders.

"And I, you." She didn't say he wouldn't have had to miss her. She didn't chastise him for his absence. Her anger had been spent weeks before. She was wounded, but she was also wiser. She loved him, but love had many dimensions and believing in her own resilience had kept her from disappearing inside herself or becoming isolated on an island she'd let Allen make. She could create her own ferry to cross from abandonment to strength.

"I'll be back in a few days. We'll talk then." He no longer braided his mustache ends. So he had changed too.

"I'm going with you," Sarah said. "You can tell me where you've been along the way and I'll tell you what I've been doing. Like you, I haven't been idle."

"Did he say what condition they were in?" Mary Sullivan asked. Sarah had awakened all the Stephens-Murphy-Townsend party women at the fort and they clustered inside Ailbe's quarters.

"Did they see a baby? My Indie? Does her father have her? James is with them, isn't he?" Ailbe rushed her questions. "Maolisa and her baby. They've made it?"

"Allen didn't say. Only that he was sure it was the rest of us."

The rest of us. What a comforting image, Mary thought. They'd be whole at last, all together. Blood no longer defined the community. She thought of Peter, who was likely preparing the packs the men would take to Sutter's farm called Hock.

Ailbe hugged a sleepy-eyed child to her side.

"I don't know the details," Sarah said. "I only know I'm going with them to the Bear and Feather confluence. That's where they're crossing."

"Is it flooded, like the others are?"

"I imagine so." Ellen wore a colorful dress with stripes of red and yellow running around the hem and a belt to match. She pulled on leather boots. "Carlos said all the rivers are in flood stage."

"Carlos, is it?" Mary teased as Ellen blushed. Karl Weber—sometimes known as Carlos—had spent a fair amount of time with Ellen who rarely mentioned running a mercantile for Dr.

Townsend now. She talked of farming and running a *hacienda.* And here was Mary, the former farmer, now dreaming of a mercantile operated with her soon-to-be husband, Peter Sherrebeck.

"Yes. Carlos. He's educating me about this country." Ellen blushed. "He says the rivers always overflow this time of year because of the snowmelt in the mountains."

"And Moses is with them?" Beth didn't wait for an answer. "I know, Allen didn't know." She put her hand to her heart. "If Dennis Martin made it. If Mr. Neil got them supplies. Then Moses is with them. He has to be."

"I, for one, am going to the Hock Farm," Mary said. "To welcome our family."

"But what of your little brothers?" Johanna asked.

"I'll take them along," Mary said. "They miss the Patterson children." She pulled her long skirt up between her legs and tucked it into her belt so she looked as though she wore Persian pants. Not a woman batted an eye at her impropriety. People did things differently in this California place. "Who's coming with us?" Mary had ridden the forty miles to the Hock Farm with Peter, so she knew the way. After all they'd been through, the Stephens-Murphy-Townsend women could make this last trek easily.

"I am," Ailbe said. "Let's fill the canteens."

"You can't leave me behind," Beth said.

Chica barked at the excitement.

Ailbe's two-year-old turned over in his sleep and moaned.

"I'll have to wait," Ailbe said. Her shoulders sank. "I've the younger ones to tend."

"I can watch them," Johanna said. She tightened her belt around her now slender waist. "You go, Ailbe. All of you go. And bring back Da and the brothers and sisters all. Someone needs to remain behind. To look after things."

Yes. They looked out for each other, paid attention to what another needed. *Family*, Mary thought. *From the Latin word* famalus, *meaning "servant."*

With Mr. Sutter's blessing, they were off. Ellen's Karl came with them, along with Dr. John, riding stiff like he wore a uniform when he didn't. Beth had held her own, badgering him in front of all the women, and he'd finally agreed Beth was strong enough to make it. Ellen had shared looks with the others who had seen Beth's strength grow daily, no longer defined by Dr. John's demands. Allen and the man who had brought the message the day before rode with them. With new, fresh horses, they might arrive before sunset.

Women wouldn't be excluded in this province, Ellen thought. They'd left behind their sidesaddles in Missouri. They'd start businesses as Sarah had with her knitted socks and embroidery. They'd shed dark, heavy clothes here. They were stronger. Why, this province might not even need a Dr. John, they'd be so healthy. Ellen grinned.

"What are you smiling about, my señorita?" Karl said.

"I'm just happy."

Ellen watched as Sarah and Allen rode ahead of them. Sarah held her head tall, her back straight, her blonde hair tied with a red ribbon that cascaded down the golden plait. She looked confident. And when Allen reached across the space between them, offering his hand to her, Sarah hesitated as though to say she was able to go on without his help—but she would accept it anyway. And she did.

Wintering Women

Maolisa clutched her children close. Angry waters surged before them. She was grateful that the Patterson girls lent a hand with her little ones whenever they dismounted, Lydia especially. She saw Ann Jane assist Mr. Martin, who clutched his bodhran, her brothers Dennis and Patrick close at hand. The river's rise was unpredictable and so were little children so long confined by hunger and waiting. Decisions. Try to ford the river? Wait? Some go, some stay?

The party had moved to where they could see a cluster of buildings near the confluence. She saw activity, a commotion. "They're putting a ferry in," Junior told her. He held a telescoping eyepiece. "They've seen us. They're sending help."

"One more crossing." Junior put his arm around her, squeezed her shoulder.

The wooden structure arrived to an uncharted landing. Chains and ropes held it against the surging stream as the survivors boarded the ferry. Horses moved side to side, agitated by the watery bridge, pulling back on reins. People clustered, keeping children from the animals' backsides, gripping little fingers. Fathers like James Miller carried the youngest. Dirty water rushed by as Maolisa clutched her infant in her arms, whispering prayers. Junior kept Maolisa stable with his arm around her, and with the other he held his Mimi. BD clung to his leg. Children stood in front of them both, pressed against her skirts, their eyes staring at the water as the craft shuddered downstream, then pulled back upward with a jerk, straining and jolting the towrope toward a landing on the other shore. Maolisa closed her eyes: *Pray for us sinners, now and at the hour of our death, amen.*

"We've made it, Pet."

Maolisa felt the jolt of the wooden ferry hitting the shore, watched men rush forward to assist. She opened her eyes. "Yes. We have."

"I never doubted for a minute."

"I did. When you didn't come back for us." Junior started to defend but she put her hand on his arm. "You did what had to be done. And so did we."

He nodded and they moved forward on their transport, horses' hooves on wood and children's chatter, the music of the river.

Weary and worn, all set foot on the banks of the Feather River, where people helped them walk up to the adobe buildings, led the horses to corrals, lifted children into strong arms. Maolisa buried her face in Yuba's knitted blanket and let the yarn absorb her tears.

Beth leapt from her horse. "Moses," she shouted. "Is that really you?"

"Bet you recognized Joker before me."

Chica danced around, jumped onto his thighs, and he scooped her up. She licked his cheeks, and he brushed his face and dark beard. "Not sure you'd recognize me, Sister," he said. His hair rested on his shoulders. He thought he resembled pictures of their father when he was young. He picked up his sister, and when he set her back down, she wiped her eyes.

"You have the sweet scent of a survivor," Beth said. "You're a young man, no longer a boy. I have worried so over you. Don't you ever volunteer to stay behind like that, ever, ever again. Whatever John thought was so precious is nothing compared to your life. You remember that."

"I did all right. Look at me," he said. "I'm skinnier, but I can still shoot and even got to help the rescuers rescue. Can't thank you enough for sending Dennis and Mr. Neil, Sister. Not sure I would have made it without them."

"It's what we do, Moses. Look after each other."

Why, she ain't breathing hard at all. Isn't.

Moses looked around. Ellen had found Joker and introduced him to some man standing family-like close.

"Mrs. Miller, Mrs. Montgomery, Miss Sullivan?" His eyes cast around the group. "Where's Capt? Joe and Allen? They surely got out, didn't they?"

"Montgomery's here." This from Peter, who then introduced himself and shook Moses's hand. "Over there." He pointed.

"And Capt's gone south," Dr. John said. "I suppose he knew everyone would make it. And he's agreed to come with us when we go back to get the wagons come summer."

"I wonder, little brother," Beth said. "It's such a little thing. But did you by any chance find a box beneath the floorboards?"

"Why, yes I did."

Dr. John frowned.

"I have it in my pack," Moses said.

Beth clapped her hands.

"What are you going on about?" Dr. John asked.

"My nest egg. You had yours with all your fancy fabrics and I had mine. A box of tacks."

"I used 'em hanging some of that cloth, Doc. Hope you both don't mind."

"You hung my satins and silks? Whatever for?"

"Kept the wind out of the walls."

"Which is exactly why I brought them west," Beth announced.

"And they were pretty to look at, those silks." He smiled. "But why'd you hide 'em under the floorboard, Sister? Tacks aren't valuable."

"Ah, but they are. I didn't want John thinking they were of no use and tossing them aside. So I hid them."

"But however did you know they had worth, my dear?"

His sister turned to her husband. "One of your patients told me, John. I'm a good listener. You should try that more often. Anyway, the patient's relative had written to him that tacks were a rarity, worth their weight in gold in California by women wishing to tack up fabric on their walls. You may have thought they'd buy up your cloth for dresses and skirts, but it's wall cloth they long for. And wooden pegs won't hold them up. Only tacks." His brother-in-law stood speechless. "I also toted Webster's books."

"Oh, those would be Sarah's. She thought they would have floated away. What a nice surprise they'll be."

And then Moses saw Allen, who had taken supplies into the barn and returned, walking toward them. He didn't look the dandy as he used to. He didn't even have a mustache.

"There you are, Montgomery. Hey, did you find out how we

messed up on the snowshoes? Worked twice as hard, we did." Allen had hesitated when he'd first seen Moses, but now he laughed with his old friend. "I might have made it out with you if I'd knowed what I was doing. Knew." His sister grinned.

"You're still here," Allen said. "So, I guess you knew quite a lot."

"Capt's traps, that's what saved me."

"And your good sense," Beth said. "And a hundred prayers. Come along, tell me everything." She gripped his arm, leaned her head into his shoulder as they walked toward the tables spread with beef and pork and chicken in stews of peppers, beans, and tomatoes. "I am so grateful," she said. "So very pleased to hold you close again."

"I'm pretty obliged myself." Moses patted her arm looped through his. They were woven together, Moses thought. "And I'm glad I brought out your nest egg. Or nest tacks."

"Me too!"

He loved his sister. One day he hoped to love another in a different way, but it would be as fierce. Blood-love carries a special strain of strong.

Mary decided she could tell the rescuers from those still suffering from starvation by how differently they stood: redeemers tall and erect; survivors bent as though to surround their stomach's pleading for food.

"Your people are all quite remarkable." Peter walked up beside Mary. They stood together as her brothers reunited with the Patterson brood. Even John had joined them, taking special note of Lydia, Mary thought.

"There was nothing to do but live," Mary said. She thought her mother might have agreed with that, the need to go forward, make the best of things.

"All your life from now on you can say this, *ja*, that what Mary

Sullivan begins—she finishes. And you do it with a flourish." He raised his finger in a swirl rising above his head. "In a new and uncertain place, that is a fine legacy, *ja*. Very fine."

Ahead, Ellen hugged her father while Daniel and John talked amiably with Karl Weber. Mary fully expected Mr. Murphy would give his consent to what Karl would soon be asking him.

Mary's eyes scanned the group, her kin, seeking. She spied Ann Jane, the Martins. Everyone. The fifty-second member of their company slept in Maolisa's arms. Mary felt teary. "Look, Peter." She pointed toward James Miller. "That's the reunion I've been waiting to see."

James, who had spent the most time with the Wintering Women inside their cabin, placed the fifty-first member of the Stephens-Murphy-Townsend party in her mother's arms. The child reached out, laughing. Mary choked back tears. "Only one more reunion to go," she said. "With the Murphy aunts and little ones we left at the fort. Then find Capt Stephens to reassure him that the people of his little wagon train arrived safe and nearly sound."

She didn't wait for Peter to take her hand but grabbed his. He squeezed back and she led him toward the food tables set up by the Sutter workers at the Hock Farm. "Let's eat quickly, then take everyone back to Sutter's, where we'll all be together in one place."

And so they all were, at last.

Epilogue

Mary Sullivan Sherrebeck dismounted her horse. She smiled, thinking of herself as Mary Sherrebeck. She'd come to another fork in the road and had taken the one marked "marriage." She had no regrets being a wife and raising her younger brothers. She stood in front of the cabin the guards had built last winter. Mary wore a man's pants on this adventure, a white muslin wide-sleeved blouse, and she rode her horse astride. She adjusted the wide-brimmed hat held secure in the breeze by a string beneath her chin. She no longer braided her hair in circles at her ears as her mother had. Instead, a coal black bun rested on her neck cradled in a lacy net the color of snow.

Wildflowers bloomed near the lake, circling stumps, like soaring candles, cut down by the Wagon Guards eight feet above the ground. The snow had been that deep. Animal bones lay scattered. Shredded canvas flapped at the cabin sides, no longer a roof nor offering protection for anything inside. Two wagons looked salvageable, having weathered the heavy snow with wheels intact, a tongue unbroken. The Schuttlers' avocado-colored side boards looked like some giant cat had clawed them, chipping off the paint.

The captain, Moses, the Murphy brothers—Junior, Daniel, and

John—and Peter (hired by Dr. Townsend and Allen Montgomery) and several ox men, including Oliver and François, had pushed six teams of oxen before them along with leading several pack animals, hoping to hitch up wagons left at the Yuba and these at the lake. The presence of the Schuttlers gave the company bragging rights for having been the first covered wagons to enter California through the Sierra Nevada by way of the Truckee and Bear rivers. Until they brought the Schuttlers in to Sutter's Fort, though, there'd be no real celebration of that success.

At the Yuba cabin, only one of the three remaining vehicles would be saved and the ox teams and their handlers remained at the headwaters to rebuild it. They'd found Beth's rocking chair hung in a tree and could see the high-water mark letting them know of the flooding. That chair would head to the Townsends.

Mary's party had left the Yuba, trekked over the summit to the lake, a journey of about ten miles. A much easier trip without fifteen feet of snow to impede—and without wagons. The two wagons they'd abandoned at the base would be repaired of snow damage, then hitched to oxen and taken to Sutter's.

Mary had been invited along on this expedition once she suggested that they'd need a cook. She didn't mind the women's work at all. Besides, Peter helped with preparation. She liked being part of the experience, putting a period on the long sentence of their lives begun in Ireland by most of the participants.

Now at Stephens Lake, Mary approached the wagons. No fabrics, no ledgers, no bedding, no plows or dishes inside the doctor's rig; no blacksmith tools, no traps, nor hammers or saws once owned by the captain. No guns or ammunition inside Allen's wagon either. Everything gone.

"Indians shopped here," Capt said. "You Murphys will see dresses and doodads worn at Sutter's one day."

Moses put his hand on a wagon wheel while he chattered happily, pointing out where he'd trapped his first fox, where he'd crossed the creek to get his escaping dinner.

"I'm anxious to see what's left inside," Capt said. He ducked his head through the cabin opening, stepped up and over the threshold. Mary and the others followed, light streaming through the shredded canvas roof covering but one section. The scent was of moisture.

"Would you look at that," Capt said. The others crowded around in the small enclosure. What they saw were a few books scattered about, the bleached bones of foxes, and boxes of ammunition with the tops off but still full of powder. Capt bent to a leather-covered pile of objects in the darkest corner. Capt removed the covering. He looked up at the party peering over his shoulder.

"Well, I'll be," Moses said. "It's Montgomery's store of rifles and pistols."

"Weren't Mr. Montgomery's weapons the very reason Wagon Guards stayed behind?" Mary asked. "Why would the Indians have left them when they took everything else?"

Capt removed his hat and scratched his head. He put his hat back on. "They must not have known how to use them. Not their weapon of choice. They took only what they knew."

"Won't Allen be glad and Dr. John sad," Moses said. He shook his head. "All that's left are the guns. Well, I'm taking a souvenir."

Mary wondered what he'd choose.

He stepped back outside. Oxmen assessed what was left of the wagons and which might be brought out. They'd load the rifles onto pack animals, let the snow-crushed vehicles sink into the landscape. "I'm garnering a wagon wheel. I'll turn it on the hub when I get back, clean it up good, and put glass over the spokes and rim and have myself a table. I'll put a lamp on it, have my cup of coffee, and put my Bible and Byron there to read. I'll say my prayer of gratitude and raise my cup like Byron said to do, to those with a heart for any fate."

Mary was the last in the string of riders. She watched as Moses's wheel bobbed at the top of a pack. They'd take an easier route, not have to go through the mountain crevice. But it was there that she told her husband, "Go on. I'll catch up." She wanted to savor for a moment where she'd taken her stand, pushed ahead to bring the Sullivan ox forward first. Like the story she'd read to her brothers, she'd come to her own fork in the road that day, and it had changed her future. "I hope you're pleased with the decisions your child has made, Mama," Mary said. She gazed at the landscape, memorializing it, something to draw on in times of future trial. Mary patted the neck of her mount, pressed her knees against his sides, and followed the pack string, confident that for whatever lay ahead, she, too, had a heart for any fate.

Author's Notes and Acknowledgments

People often ask me where my stories come from. This one came from a footnote in *The Brazen Overlanders of 1845* by Donna M. Wojcik. Writing of the Bear River country, "they camped in the valley near a log cabin built by 1844 emigrants. . . . Here the snow must have been very deep for some of the trees had been cut off 8 feet from [above] the ground . . . this cabin was occupied the winter of 1844 by women emigrants who were looked after by James Miller." For me the obvious question was, who were those women and what were they doing? A few years later, I began the search to find the answers and uncovered as well this amazing story.

My thanks go to CarolAnne Tsai, who gathered documents and helped me organize the many players on that journey. If the characters are clear and their stories well told, my thanks go to her and my editors Andrea Doering and Barb Barnes and the team at Revell. I'm grateful to Janet Meranda for her exquisite reading for errors, to historian-author Stafford Hazelett for his review with corrections, and to the director and docents of the Sunnyvale Heritage Park Museum for identifying errors in my notes with time to correct them! Still, more may be found and I am responsible for them all. And to divinity student Melissa Temple, a welcome houseguest, thank you for exploring the wintering women questions that might have brought them nurture in their Sierra stay.

I tried to stay with the "shared knowings" discovered through the various accounts, but the women wrote no memoirs about the journey nor the months beside the Yuba, taking the horseback trail (Ellen Murphy and Elizabeth "Beth" Townsend), or later while they were at Sutter's Fort. At the cabin, in reference to the rescue, one comment referred to Mrs. Patterson and her children and their plight the last two weeks as "eating rawhide," but no one wrote of how the women endured, what they did to keep the children occupied, how they kept their spirits up—or didn't.

The decision by the men to become conscripted before sending rescue continues to baffle historians and others, including me. I'm hopeful that my explanation rings true.

Moses Schallenberger, Allen Montgomery, and Joe Foster as guardians of the six wagons holding the greatest wealth and the outcome of their plight is based on Moses's reminiscences. It is in another footnote in historian H. H. Bancroft's editing of those reminiscences that provided the final story of the wagons being brought in to Sutter's Fort in late summer of 1845. It also contains the reference to Moses's souvenir of that trip. References to Lord Byron's poem and *Lord Chesterfield's Letters* are from Moses's account.

Historian and author Stafford Hazelett helped me discover more about that initial footnote said to be made in a reminiscence by "old Greenwood," who had been part of the "Murphy-Stephens-Townsend" party who were the first to bring wagons into California via the Sierra Nevada. Greenwood did have a wife named Batchica, and his two sons were part of the group, and it's said that later they returned to Idaho to trap. More scoping of records led me to *Overland in 1844*, a recounting by Moses Schallenberger written when he was in his fifties. *The Opening of the California Trail: The Story of the Stevens Party from Reminiscences of Moses Schallenberger as Set Down for H. H. Bancroft about 1885* offered insights into motivations, accounts of the Horseback Party, and John Murphy's near drowning. The editor commented about why the men went to war; Dr. Townsend's tendency to think well of himself; and Elizabeth Townsend's efforts to send a rescue party for her brother, Moses; and he offered a map (that my husband, Jerry, tweaked for this edition). Bancroft offered speculations about routes taken, which rivers were crossed, and mused that any trials at the cabin "were likely greatly exaggerated." Easy for him to write. When the railroad was built, it largely followed the route Stephens had taken the wagons.

A second document, *The California Trail: An Epic with Many Heroes* edited by George Stewart, offered a possible timeline, the separate group makeups and explanations related to Sutter's conscription for the war. *Forgotten Pioneers: Irish Leaders in Early California* by Thomas F. Prendergast, along with obituaries, the Sacramento Public Library's *Sutter's Fort Pioneer Guide*, and histories of early California towns such as Stockton, San Rafael, Sacramento, and Sunnyvale, and the histories of Irish immigrants to Canada, then Missouri and California helped me create this narrative of remarkable people. The book *Before the Gold Rush: The Sinclairs Of Rancho del Paso* by Cheryl Anne Stapp gave facts and insights about this early California couple who welcomed the horseback party.

A few discrepancies in the various accounts exist. The name of the Missouri priest (suggesting to Martin Murphy Sr. that they seek religious freedom and schools in Alta California) varies. One account of the Yuba site says Miller and family all arrived and "spent Christmas at Sutter's Fort," but other accounts tell of Miller starting out with his son in January, reaching help, and returning with food, but finding the women having left, then joining up with them much later. Still another says Miller went alone and then there are reports that all the women were at the cabin until March 1 of 1845 and were part of the rescue and crossing at the Bear and Feather Rivers.

Mary Sullivan Sherrebeck traveled with her three brothers, arriving as orphans from Montreal, their parents having died just
before departure. Mary does not show up at Sutter's nor as part
of the Murphy rescue party either. But she does marry Peter Sherrebeck, who worked for Sutter, so she must have arrived at Sutter's
Fort at some point. Peter was Danish and the two owned lots in
San Francisco, where he was a trader, Mary working at his side.
Her brother John for several years also lived with the Sherrebecks,
as John became a woodcutter and broker, supplying lumber for
building in San Francisco and shipbuilding. John built the first
house in that emerging city and was later involved in banking, investments, and managing his properties. We don't know any more
about Mary, but she became a symbol of strong women making
choices, doing what must be done while redefining themselves in
the West.

Sarah Armstrong Montgomery is listed as a participant on the
trip, but neither she nor Allen show up in the list of arrivals at Sutter's Fort in the spring of 1845 nor were they part of the Bear River/
Feather River arrival at the Hock Farm. Yet Sarah is said to have
learned to read and write while at Sutter's, "waiting for Allen to
return from fighting in the Bear Creek Rebellion of 1846," though
he did not participate in the Micheltorena skirmish of 1845. Allen,
a gunsmith, brought enough rifles, guns, and pistols and a good
supply of ammunition, planning to open a gunsmith shop in California. Allen was one of the Wagon Guards who hiked out with
Joe Foster, leaving Moses behind. Did Sarah hike out with him?
Did Joe and Allen even encounter the Wintering Women? No one
knows. As the epilogue states, he did get all his weapons returned.

Sarah hosted the first quilt gathering of twenty women at Sutter's Fort. In 1847, Allen headed to Hawaii and abandoned Sarah.
She divorced him and married Paul Green, who turned out to be
Paul Geddes, who had abandoned *his* wife and family in Pennsyl-
vania. Pregnant, Sarah had the marriage annulled and garnered
a large settlement from Green/Geddes for his betrayal. The sum

allowed her to purchase land and run a boardinghouse in Santa Clara. She became quite wealthy, eventually marrying a third time in 1854 to Joseph Wallis, an attorney, judge, and later senator. They had four children. Sarah was active in the suffrage movement, elected president of the California Women's Suffrage Association in 1870, and she and her husband worked to pass laws allowing women to become attorneys. She died in 1905, six years before California women received the vote.

Ellen Murphy—mentioned in two places as Mrs. Townsend but in Bancroft accounts is Ellen Murphy—was not the widow of Dr. Townsend's brother (name unknown), so my giving her that status is literary license fed by those earlier mentions of her possible widowhood. The daughter of Martin Murphy, Sr., she was part of the Horseback Party, where her brother John nearly drowned. That party arrived at the Sinclair Ranch in early December and at Sutter's before Christmas. In 1850, Ellen married Karl Weber and changed her first name to Helen. Karl, known by Mexican authorities as "Carlos," went by Charles in the new state of California. He and Ellen were married at Tuleberg, which they owned, and Charles changed its name to Stockton for Commodore Stockton, Charles's former commander. Staking prospectors heading into the gold fields, the Webers had a lucrative business, and Charles had been successful himself in finding gold at a creek he named Weber. Helen presided over a large hacienda, raising their three children and meeting French Canadians who wintered at French Camp on their property known as the "end of the Oregon Trail." Ellen/Helen was described as a "spirited beauty." The Novenas dated 1820 was a book that belonged to her mother that Ellen carried with her. Her brother John was known for his hunting skills, though I made one of them to be an Irish slinger.

Both John and Daniel struck gold in the Sierras, and the two operated a general store, which led to the township called Murphys.

Elizabeth "Beth" Townsend did suffer from an illness, perhaps asthma or residuals of malaria that induced the family to come west. The Townsends were friends of the Montgomerys back in Missouri. Beth did ride an Indian pony that proved to be the best trade Dr. John likely ever made, as the pony led the party safely across many rivers, including the American. Their arrival at the Sinclairs is as described. In November of 1848 Elizabeth gave birth to John Henry Townsend in San Francisco, where John's political dreams came to fruition by being named the Fourth American *Alcalde* or mayor. He served but a few months before moving to the Pueblo of San Jose. John was the first American doctor in California. Elizabeth acquired land in her own name (perhaps selling those tacks) in San Jose, which she left to various friends and to Moses in her will. Tacks were indeed valued in the West, but whether Beth brought them is unknown. Both she and John died in the 1850 cholera epidemic. Their son was found by neighbors playing beside his deceased parents. Moses Schallenberger took the boy as his and with his wife, raised the boy as his sister had raised him.

Mary Bulger (some documents read "Bolger") Murphy is known in this book as Maolisa as a way to help the reader keep straight the numerous Marys on this journey. Maolisa (Mary) was thirty-six at the time of departure. She traveled with her five children and her husband, Martin Murphy Jr., whom she'd married in Quebec in 1831. Three of their children had died before the trip began and Elizabeth Yuba was born at the Yuba Camp in either November or early December of 1844. They headed west seeking religious freedom and the chance to build Catholic schools to educate their children—which they did—the first school in Sacramento County being attributed to their efforts. They built a chapel on their hacienda. In association with the Society of Jesus, they began Santa Clara College, a boys' school, and Notre Dame de Namur, a girls' school. Mary/Maolisa presided over the family ranch purchased from Mariano Castro called Rancho Pastoria de las Borregos. The Murphys named it Bay View because they could see the water from their front porch. Maolisa was known for her generosity and her exceptional housekeeping and organizing skills. A room in the Sunnyvale Heritage Park Museum in Sunnyvale, California, is devoted to the Murphy family. Exhibits and docents preserve the Murphy family's rich history of community development and contributions through education, religion, law, and other important roles in the settlement. Martin Murphy Jr. had a home milled to his specifications in Bangor, Maine, then shipped the lumber around the horn in 1850. There being no sawmills, the home was pieced together with "wooden pegs and leather straps." Photos of the home and many of the Murphys, including Elizabeth Yuba Murphy Taaffe (named for her mother's sister), can be seen at www.heritageparkmuseum.org. Martin Murphy Jr.'s son BD was quite the charmer and did make the comment about the toothpick to Moses Schallenberger. Martin Jr. and Mary also held the largest private party in California in July of 1881, the Murphys' fiftieth wedding anniversary. An estimated 10,000 people attended.

The Murphy aunts—Margaret and Johanna—both married Irish countrymen in California—Fitzgeralds and Kells.

Mary (Ailbe) Murphy Miller was born in Wexford, Ireland, around 1815. She emigrated to Canada at the age of three and married James Miller September 1, 1834, in Lower Canada, Quebec. James, too, had been born in Ireland. They departed from Missouri and headed west with four children, their fifth born at Independence Rock on the Fourth of July, 1844. Six more children joined the family in California. The Millers were the first to acquire land in Marin County under the new provisions of land transfer following the skirmish the Murphys and others had gone to war over. As Ailbe's family grew, so did their holdings, the family eventually owning 8,600 acres near San Rafael. In 1849, James drove 150 head of his steer into the placer mines, as gold had been discovered, and slaughtering cattle at the site proved more lucrative than drying and hauling the beef to miners. He later had a manor house built, large and square with wide verandas, known as

Miller Hall. Given the prosperous life Mary/Ailbe had, if she had premonitions of things going wrong, she was heartily mistaken.

Little is known of Isabella Hitchcock Patterson except that she was born in Tennessee, the daughter of Elizabeth and Isaac (who was sixty-four at the time of their departure). She was the second wife of Andrew Patterson, whom she'd married Christmas Day in Missouri in 1828. She was thirty-two when he died, and she took her five children west with their grandfather. She is mentioned as being the one who ate boiled hides as they neared starvation at the Yuba River. She died in San Benito, California, in 1887.

Ann Jane Martin Murphy, married to James, was twenty-two when the family left Missouri. A son had died two years before departure, and they traveled with daughter Mary (Ide in this story) and she gave birth again in 1846 at Sutter's Fort. James became the first bank commissioner in California, a successful lumberman selling lumber for the first wharf in San Francisco. They were landowners near San Rafael and had large land holdings near Milpitas. Ann Jane's brother Dennis, the rescuer of Moses, struck gold after working a few years for Sutter as a lumberman. Ranching became his future. He bought land, built St. Dennis church and cemetery (where he is buried), and later sold the property to Leland Stanford of Stanford University fame.

His father, Patrick Martin Sr.—"Old Man Martin," who had remained with the Wintering Women at the Yuba—lived to enjoy California. He died in 1868.

Capt Stephens in his early years in South Carolina and Georgia was said to be "gangly and homely with a hawk nose." He migrated west and became a blacksmith for the Council Bluff Sub Agency serving Chippewa, Ottawa, and Potawatomie Indian tribes. He resigned that position in 1844 to take the lead of the wagon train. He was a respected leader. That he had a wife and child who died is part of my fiction. It's said, however, that after the arrival of wagons at Sutter's Fort in 1845, he became somewhat of a hermit, raising bees and chickens in the Bakersfield area. A story is told of his continued generosity when a family named Baker moved nearby and Capt brought hens for the grandmother that she might begin to raise a flock. It was a custom of the Appalachians to make such gifts to newcomers that they might know of both their welcome and offer a way for them to feed their families. Capt and the Baker grandson became friends, the boy likely drawn to the kindness and integrity of the man who led this Irish party to new lands.

A creek is named for Capt and a road in San Jose, but both are spelled Stevens. In 1994, Mount Stephens, north of Donner Pass, was named for the leader. I kept to his original spelling in this novel. The lake the travelers called "Stephens Lake" is known today as "Donner Lake," as the 1846–47 Donner party faced their challenges at that lake and summit. Some members used the cabin that Moses, Joe, and Allen had built. The tragic outcome of that journey compared to the Stephens party shows a remarkable contrast. The Murphys listened to experienced mountain men. They risked separating, shared horses (Dr. Townsend did bargain for that Indian pony that likely saved lives at various river crossings), rationed food, and demonstrated incredible fortitude and courage in bringing the wagons over the mountain as they did, then choosing to leave some behind along the Yuba. Their feats are overshadowed by the Donner Party disaster. It's my hope that this story might celebrate the honor of self-sacrifice, the wisdom of working together, and the power of persevering through community and faith.

Finally, Moses Schallenberger. His sister raised him as a baby, as their mother died at his birth. Born in Ohio, he moved to Missouri with the Townsends and was seventeen when his family headed west. He wrote *Overland in 1844* when in his fifties, sharing episodes on the journey, including his hunting skills, losing Allen's rifles, almost getting people killed over his halter dispute, and of course his guarding the wagons. He spent his winter feasting on foxes using Capt Stephens's traps. He wrote of his effort to summit, his terrible cramping, making snowshoes that hindered the trek, and his decision to turn back. After his rescue by Dennis Martin, he joined the other rescue team, saved Mr. Neil at the Bear River, and was there for the final crossing of the Feather. Until he had to manage the Townsend estate, he'd been in a business trading Mexican goods at Monterrey. He married Fannie Everitt, an Alabaman, in 1854 in San Francisco, who shared the task of raising his sister's child. They had four children of their own, including Margaret McNaught, who became a physician like her uncle Dr. John. Moses died at the age of eighty-three in San Jose, California.

There are uncertainties about the number of wagons the party left with, how many were taken over the mountains. One account said six wagons were left to the Wagon Guards, three summited and two remained at the base. What kind of cabin was built at the Yuba River, or if there were more than one, whether the men built them before they left or Mr. Martin and James Miller built them were also certain facts. The description of the Wagon Guard cabin was quite detailed in Moses Schallenberger's account. Four other men were a part of this journey but unnamed by me. For the descendants who may have heard stories from them, they are Edmund Bray, Vincent Calvin, John Flomboy, and Matthew Harbin. The Horseback Party did have a French-Canadian servant along, as well as a French ox driver, each with a horse and two pack animals. What became of the French-Canadians is unknown, but they were there for the rescue of John Murphy.

There is no mention of a dog named Chica on the train, but many parties brought dogs. I had this one travel with the horseback group around Lake Tahoe, which had less trouble and arrived earlier. This impish black-and-white Chica was named by Skip and Linda Paznokas, who were the winning bidders in a Bend First Presbyterian Fundraiser to name a character in one of my books. The real Chica is a highly trained dog who would easily have been a pal with Joker, the horse that Ellen Murphy rode. I thank the

Paznokas for their generous hearts in letting me create my Chica. Joker was the name of my sister's favorite horse.

I offer additional thanks to my publishing partners at Revell— too many to name all, but to Michele Misiak, Karen Steele, Cheryl Van Andel, and Erin Bartels—thank you. I would be lost without you! Thank you to my prayer team of Loris, Judy, Carol, Gabby, Susan, and Judy. A special thank-you to friend and colleague Leah Apineru, who makes my social media life easier; to Teresa Hansen, who manages my calendar; and to Paul Shumacher, who tends my website www.jkbooks.com. Thank you to my faithful readers whose emails and tweets and posts make the efforts worthwhile. Thank you as well to my agent of many years, Joyce Hart of Hartline Literary—I wouldn't be here without her. I'm especially grateful for the incredible support I receive from family and friends who allow me to separate myself for hours at a time to write these stories.

Special thanks, love, and gratitude go to my husband of forty-three years, Jerry, who despite significant pain works on the maps and reminds me that whatever I've added to a manuscript on a given day isn't "'the worst thing you've ever written.' It's part of your process." I hope he's correct and that this story of remarkable people who lived out the last line of Arthur Hugh Clough's poem "Say Not the Struggle Naught Availeth" resonates in your hearts. "But westward, look, the land is bright." And so it was and is.

With gratitude,
Jane Kirkpatrick

For more information about Jane and her books visit www.jk books.com and sign up for her monthly e-newsletter, Story Sparks.

Discussion Questions
for Book Groups

If her schedule allows, Jane is available for Skype book group visits or in person if she is in the area for research or other speaking engagements. Contact her at www.jkbooks.com to schedule.

1. Which characters on this journey resonated with your struggles? Mary Sullivan, haunted by choices and wanting to be herself, though it wasn't part of the usual woman's path? Sarah and her fear of abandonment? Ellen, hoping to put a hard past behind her to make a better choice in love? Maolisa Murphy and the challenge of keeping order in a chaotic world? Ailbe Miller and her premonitions and fears? Beth Townsend, seeking healing and finding it by standing up for herself? Isabella Patterson, who hoped to transform herself in a wilderness without her husband?

2. Where did each of these women draw their strength from?

3. How do you suppose the Wintering Women made sense of the decision the men made to go to battle rather than send the rescue party for them? Have you ever felt betrayed by a decision someone else made? What helped you or do you still struggle?

4. Moses Schallenberger demonstrated remarkable resilience. What helped him continue to hope for rescue? Do you think he harbored any ill will toward Joe Foster and Allen Montgomery? Why or why not?

5. Mary tells us that the word *family* comes from the Latin word *famalus*, meaning "servant." How did Mary act as a servant? Sarah? Beth? Were other travelers servants to each other? What role did family play in this unfolding story? Is family only bloodline or did others find a family within the trials they faced?

6. Decisions, forks in the road, which way to turn, are themes of this story. How does memory help us put poor choices aside so we can move forward?

7. Isabella came to find a new meaning for the words "fare thee well." Do you think of that phrase as a way of saying goodbye or as a hope for the future?

8. When Capt Stephens explores leadership, what qualities do you think he demonstrated himself? What role did leadership play in this effort to bring wagons into California and keep people alive?

9. The author hoped to convey the importance of giving shelter to each other and accepting it from others in a time of trial or hard decision-making. Did she make her case? Would you agree? Why or why not?

10. Moses remembers his mother saying, "Adversity can destroy or redefine." What do you think about this view of challenge and trial?

11. Tell a story of when you were strong. Are having courage and being strong the same? What do you think of the poet's words that "courage is a small voice saying 'I will try again tomorrow'"?

Jane Kirkpatrick is the *New York Times* and CBA bestselling and award-winning author of more than thirty books, with nearly two million copies sold, including *Everything She Didn't Say*, *All She Left Behind*, *A Light in the Wilderness*, *The Memory Weaver*, *This Road We Traveled*, and *A Sweetness to the Soul*, which won the prestigious Wrangler Award from the Western Heritage Center. Her works have won the WILLA Literary Award, the Carol Award for Historical Fiction, and the 2016 Will Rogers Medallion Award, among others. She speaks around the world about the power of story in our lives. Jane lives in Central Oregon with her husband, Jerry, and their cavalier King Charles spaniel. Learn more at www.jkbooks.com and sign up for her Story Sparks newsletter.

WEAVING THE STORIES OF OUR LIVES

Get to know Jane at

JKBooks.com

Sign up for the *Story Sparks* newsletter
Read the blogs
Learn about upcoming events

There is more than one way
TO TELL A STORY...

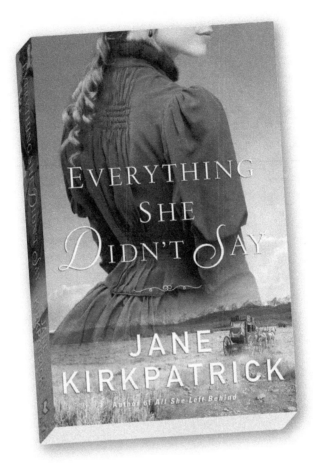

In Carrie Strahorn's life, there are two versions of everything: the one she'll share with others and the one she actually lives. As she follows her husband through the American West, her journey takes her through heartache, disappointment, and a life of unparalleled adventure.

ℝ Revell
a division of Baker Publishing Group
www.RevellBooks.com

Available wherever books and ebooks are sold. f

"Once again, Jane Kirkpatrick creates a bold and inspiring woman out of the dust of history. Jennie's triumph, in the skilled hands of one of the West's most beloved writers, leaves its mark on your heart."

— SANDRA DALLAS, *New York Times* bestselling author

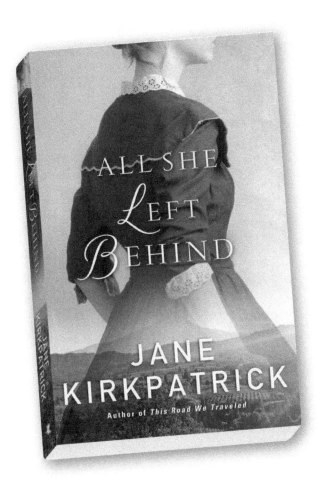

Revell
a division of Baker Publishing Group
www.RevellBooks.com

Available wherever books and ebooks are sold.

Jane Kirkpatrick
Inspires the Pioneer in All of Us...

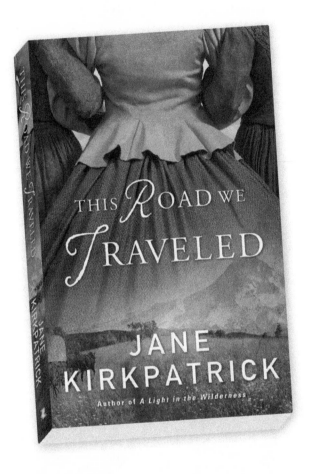

Three generations of the Brown women travel west together on the Oregon Trail, but each seeks something different. The challenges faced will form the character of one woman—and impact the future for many more.

Ɽ Revell
a division of Baker Publishing Group
www.RevellBooks.com

Available wherever books and ebooks are sold.

CPSIA information can be obtained
at www.ICGtesting.com
Printed in the USA
LVHW041829281019
635573LV00009B/311/P

9 780800 737061